"The Wall of the World does not separate the numena and their armies," said the elf. "It summons them."

"Summons them?" Zagorka said.

"Yes. Averru is a numen of war. He built this place to be the ultimate battlefield," Elionway said. His face was white. "They're preparing for a world war."

As the forces of Phage and Akroma clash, an eons-old force awakens, and Otaria trembles.

The Legions are preparing to march.

EXPERIENCE THE MAGIC

MAGIC
The Gathering®

ONSLAUGHT CYCLE · BOOK II

Legions™

J. Robert King

Wizards
OF THE COAST®

For Tim Ryan

LEGIONS

©2003 Wizards of the Coast, Inc.

Distributed in the United States by Holtzbrinck Publishing. Distributed in Canada by Fenn Ltd.

Distributed to the hobby, toy, and comic trade in the United States and Canada by regional distributors.

Distributed worldwide by Wizards of the Coast, Inc. and regional distributors.

Made in the U.S.A.

Cover art by Ron Spears
First Printing: January 2003
Library of Congress Catalog Card Number: 2002113211

9 8 7 6 5 4 3 2 1

US ISBN: 0-7869-2914-6
UK ISBN: 0-7869-2915-4
620-17851-001-EN

U.S., CANADA,
ASIA, PACIFIC, & LATIN AMERICA
Wizards of the Coast, Inc.
P.O. Box 707
Renton, WA 98057-0707
+1-800-324-6496

EUROPEAN HEADQUARTERS
Wizards of the Coast, Belgium
P.B. 2031
2600 Berchem
Belgium
+32-70-23-32-77

Visit our web site at www.wizards.com

CHAPTER 1

CLINGING TO THE WURM

Some folks hate life. What rubbish! They just don't know how to live.

Braids knew how to live. Her hair streamed in the smoke and fetor of battle. Her mouth, bloodied as if with scarlet lipstick, gaped in a long, glad cry. Her hands clenched in little white fists on the horns of the great wurm, and she rode.

Most folks who found themselves straddling a league-long wurm as it bucked across a battlefield—a wurm that tore holes in armies and reality alike—would consider this a bad spot. Not Braids. She whooped.

The enormous beast arched its rubbery neck high above Greenglades Forest. Its stupid little eyes studied the layers of canopy and seemed to glimpse movement below. The wurm jabbed down. Its head was as massive as a house, and it crashed through foliage as if it were a black meteor.

Braids clutched the wurm, laid her head back, and thought of the Cabal.

Ahead, translucent horns slashed leaves aside and dug out a green tunnel. Three crashes through three layers of growth, and the wurm plunged upon its prey. A brief shriek was the last word spoken by whatever it was. *Boom!* The teeth struck ground and dug through it. Braids pitched forward against the backs of the horns but held on.

The wurm's massive jaws came together, dragging away its prey and a good hunk of world as well. A sucking darkness opened, and wind howled in the hole. The deathwurm reared its ugly head again, dirt pattering across the leaves as it rose.

Braids clung on, thrilled to see the layers of canopy descend once again.

This was life. Braids was no poet, but she was mad, which was the next best thing. Madness told her that every creature rode the wurm of death until it threw her and ate her. Everyone was created in an instant, and the rest of life was simply holding on.

The creature reared up above the highest canopy. Its black muzzle broke into the beaming sunlight, and teeth splayed in gritty fury. It roared, and Braids roared too, her voice small but voracious.

Beyond the forest stretched a field strewn in dead. Smoke bled into the sky. Even now, Braids's shattered army fled before a thousand such wurms. They pounded the Nightmare Lands, ripping open more sucking pits. Few mortals would survive this day. None would survive this year. Phage had released these horrors upon the world, and soon there would be no world left.

Sinews coiled beneath the wurm's rumpled hide, gathering for another strike.

Braids clung on, laughing all the way "Ha Ha HA!"

A small squealing sound came, and the wurm suddenly deflated. Rubbery flesh sucked in upon itself and shrank. The league-long beast collapsed into a narrow line, sputtered once, and shot away toward the battlefield.

Braid's legs pinched together on nothing, and her hands clutched into empty fists. Instead of sitting on muscle, she sat on air. "Oh!" One hand whacked leaves as she tumbled down. She crashed onto a bough, the impact like a club blow on her back. The branch bent, its end dipping down to make her roll. Braids tumbled sideways, got a slap from retreating leaves, and fell through clear air. Her hands clawed for something to hold onto, but her knees found it first—another bough.

She hooked her legs around the branch and flipped over it, slowing her descent considerably. Fingers raked the branch and came away with bark under the nails. She couldn't hold on. Her legs swung loose, and she plunged again.

It was fifty feet to the next canopy and a hundred more from there, a killing drop—for anyone else. Braids turned her eyes inward and glimpsed dementia space. She willed a corner of it to open beneath her. Momentum carried her through the verge between worlds. Setting one foot on the ground in dementia space, she flashed back into reality. The step had shifted her course slightly horizontal. Gritting her jaw, she hurled herself into dementia space again and back out and again. What had begun as a headlong plunge turned into a swooping dive above the lowest layer of canopy.

Braids sang out as she flashed from world to world. The sound in either place was a furious rattle, like the rasp of a cicada. She ran madly through the air, just above a bough that grew wider and stronger as it neared the bole. Her feet spun down to tiptoe on the branch and touched down with real weight. Braids slowed her run but still crashed solidly against the tree bole. Her arms clutched it, and her fingers clung to the vines there. Between deep breaths, Braids laughed.

One benefit of madness was living simultaneously in two worlds.

Braids had escaped the wurm above and the ground below. No wonder she loved life. She was good at it.

Something struck her . . . something with the weight of a boulder but the tawny pelt of a great cat. It dropped from above, driving her head down onto her shoulders and ripping her hands loose from the vines. She pitched back, struck her head on the bough, and might have tumbled off except that four paws pinned her.

Braids stared up into the face of the beast. It obviously misunderstood matters. This cat thought it was the killer instead of the prey.

She disappeared from beneath the jaguar's belly and rolled into dementia space. The paws of the great cat slapped the bough where she had been. Meanwhile, the little woman scrabbled atop the beast's shoulders. One arm wrapped the creature's throat, and the other shoved sideways on its head. The beast fought wildly, knowing this was its last moment. Braids grinned at its ear and twisted harder. Soon there would come a satisfying crunch.

It came, but it was not the sound of a spine cracking. It was the sound of hitting ground. She had been so focused on killing the jaguar that she hadn't realized they were falling. The cat landed beneath her, and it clattered like a bag of bones. Braids smashed atop it. It had saved her from death but not from maiming.

She was laughing and crying when she went black.

* * * * *

The sun averted its eye from the corpse-strewn battlefield. By day, it was a horrible place. By night, it was unbearable. Elves lay spiked on dead crab folk. Aerial jellyfish settled gassily atop giant serpents. Dead and undead soldiers lay indistinguishable in the darkness. Three great armies had fought and died here, and the ground itself had been ripped open. Pits howled like hungry mouths, sucking air from the world.

It was no wonder every living thing fled the Nightmare Lands. This place would corrupt flesh, mind, and soul.

Thankfully, the two unmen had none of these. They were mere shadows standing in air, one tall and gaunt and the other short and stout. In daylight, they had hidden their gray forms behind a fly-covered centaur. Now that the sun had set, they stood in the open and spoke.

"Well," said the gaunt one, his voice like grating glass, "you've gotten us into quite a spot. Where do we go now?"

The short one shrugged and lifted empty hands. "Dunno."

"Look, there's Kamahl." He pointed a thin arm to where the sun had set. A single figure strode westward. "We could follow him to Krosan. Perhaps the secret we seek is hidden there, in the mysteries of flora and fauna—"

"Ughh . . . *bo-ring*."

A backhanded slap merely cracked off the outline of the fat one's face. "I don't know how you and I could be shadows of the same man. Look at you! Fat, short, stupid, a living puddle—"

"Look at you! You might as well be a stick."

"You've got none of the master's redeeming qualities. You even abandoned him—"

"You were right behind me!"

"I was just trying to bring you back."

"Why didn't you?"

"When the master got eaten, well, what was the point? And since you got us into this, how about you get us out? Where do we go next, Mr. Puddle?"

"Well, Mr. Stick, let's follow Phage," said the stout one. He gestured excitedly toward a dot on the southern horizon, where Phage strode. "The coliseum would be great! All the fights! All the food! All the women!"

Mr. Stick made a flatulent noise. "What do you need food for? You can't eat anything. What do you need women for? You've got nothing they're looking for."

"Who cares? I want to live!"

"We can't live! We're *un*men. Before we can live, we've got to be just plain men. We need a spell, and we won't find it in the coliseum."

"Don't tell me you want to go to a library."

"Why not?"

Mr. Puddle made his own rude noise.

"Shut up," said Mr. Stick.

"Ha! That's funny."

"What?"

"I'm a living portal, and I'm supposed to shut up."

"Shut up!"

"Ha ha ha ha."

"All right, we're not getting anywhere—"

"Ha ha, yeah, we're just standing here—"

"I mean all you want to do is have fun, and all I want to do is—"

"piss and moan—"

"—learn." Mr. Stick hissed. "Oh, you're worthless. Go ahead. Go to the Cabal. Let them turn you into a slave." He turned toward the dark east and started to march away.

"Where are you going?" asked his partner, capering along behind him.

"Eroshia. Why do you care?"

"Full of libraries, right?"

"Yeah. It is a center of magical learning."

"Ughhh," said Mr. Puddle, stopping in his tracks.

Over his shoulder, Mr. Stick replied, "Libraries . . . and everything else."

"Everything else. . . . ?"

"Parties . . . cockfights . . . bones games . . . women. . . ."

Dark feet pattered across the sand. "Why didn't you say so before?"

"If you're going to tag along, you'll have to shut up."

"Ha ha ha!"

"I mean it."

"All right."

In silence, Mr. Stick and Mr. Puddle strode east across the Nightmare Lands, heading for Eroshia.

* * * * *

Everything had changed. She was no longer howling in joy but in misery. Her fearless heart now knew only fear. As good as she had been at living, she was terrible at dying.

Braids woke up in the midst of crawling. Even with her mind absent, her body had known what to do. Her hands left red prints on the mossy sticks beneath her, and she glanced back to see a trammeled trail of blood. Never before had she felt such agony, such terror. What had she been crawling toward? Looking ahead, Braids saw a dark den beneath an arching root. Shelter. If she could only reach it, could only hole up away from the predators and soldiers, she could tend her wounds.

I am maimed, she realized. I am dying.

That thought changed her. The former woman, indomitable and irrepressible, was gone, and only this panicky animal remained. If not for the rag of mind that bore her name, she could not have believed that she once was Braids.

Fastening hands on a half-buried stone, she dragged herself forward. Her leg bones rattled like bamboo and dragged limply through the leaves. She would have to make splints and set them, and even then her legs might die. It they did, she would gnaw them off.

One leg snagged on a root and dragged her to an excruciating halt.

She couldn't even crawl—she who had bounded around the rim of the coliseum couldn't even worm her way across the ground.

Braids wept. Something in her had broken, and she would never be the same. Still, she had to survive.

Dementia space . . . if she couldn't crawl across real dirt, perhaps she could crawl across dementia space. Braids rolled her eyes back into her head, seeking the mad world. She needed only a corner of it to slip through, but where was it? Her mind searched its deep recesses. She had spent years in dementia space, had brought thousands of creatures into being out of it, but suddenly it was gone

Something howled in the canopy above. Something hungry.

Braids's eyes snapped open. All she had was this terrible moment. That hole in the ground was her only hope. She would use its roots for splints and her own braids to tie them up. There would be mushrooms and grubs to eat. She could live if only she could reach that dirty womb. Teeth in a grimace, Braids clawed her way forward. It was agony, but the yowls above kept her going.

At last, Braids clutched the root above the hole and hauled her limp legs in. She lowered herself to sit and scooted back out of the light. Beyond her den, the creature screamed again.

Braids stared watchfully out and trembled.

* * * * *

It didn't matter that the deathwurms had disappeared from behind them. It didn't matter that none of Ixidor's forces pursued. Once the coalition armies had begun to run away, they kept on running.

Stonebrow was not built for running. As tall as a two-story tower and twice its weight, the giant centaur was more a bulwark than a bull. He was meant to move slowly and relentlessly into the teeth of an entrenched foe, not gallop in fear away, but gallop he did. Massive hooves dug divots from the ground, and a fine froth worked across his shoulders. For what seemed an eternity, he had run—beyond the Nightmare Lands, beyond the desert, and into the rocky badlands beneath the Corian Escarpment—but still he pelted on.

Beside him galloped another ill-suited beast. Chester was a giant mule with strong shoulders and spindly legs. He could have plodded beneath a half ton of baggage, but just now he galloped beneath an old woman. Fear had made Chester a better beast, but the bumpy ride had made his owner a worse one.

"Enough!" Zagorka growled. Her old face looked craggy under its mask of dust, but her eyes beamed bright with exasperation. "I'm nearly split in half!"

"Next time . . . try sidesaddle," Stonebrow groaned, breathless.

Jamming her feet against the mule's flanks, Zagorka stood and hauled on the creature's lead. "Whoa, you stupid ass! Whoa!"

Stonebrow snorted. "She's right. We're safe enough."

The momentum that had driven them across leagues of wasteland and desert spent itself. Eight giant hooves thudded to stillness on the gravel, and eight knees locked up beneath heaving torsos. Even Zagorka slid down, high-stepping to stretch the bruised muscles in her backside.

Chester lifted his nose and watched the ungainly dance. He snorted eloquently.

Stonebrow laughed.

Zagorka glared, but her gray-black hair jutted in such sweaty spikes it made the centaur only laugh more. He got his comeuppance when dust turned his laugh into an earnest cough.

The old woman crossed her arms and scowled. "Well, look at us! Three sorry sacks. . . . Ditch our masters. . . . Run for our lives. . . . Three hunks of steaming dung. . . ."

Flinging a handful of foam from his pelt, Stonebrow nodded.

"What are we supposed to do?" Zagorka muttered. She dropped her head back and shouted, "What now?"

Her cry rolled out across the rocky wastes, past other such stragglers, to the great wall of the Corian Escarpment. The sound reverberated among those stony faces, as if they discussed the question then came bounding back: "What now. . . now . . . now . . . now . . . ?"

Chester began to stroll slowly forward. His hooves made the scree crackle as he went. Zagorka let her head slump and strode slowly after him. Stonebrow brought up the rear. In their flight, they had veered away from the main road, which passed the escarpment at its lowest point. Instead, they had arrived at a great wall of stone, remote and uncharted.

"There's no more coalition," Zagorka mused aloud. "No more army. The Cabal has lost thousands. . . ."

"So has Krosan," Stonebrow said. All hints of laughter were gone, and he ground his teeth. "I guess all we can do is head home."

"*Home*?" Zagorka replied. "I got no home, and if I did, it wouldn't be a swamp. I'd rather live in this blasted place." She looked ahead.

J. Robert King

The land before them was rising. The rugged bones of the world jutted brokenly through a thin skin of sand. Chester picked his way among a field of ragged rocks, each one larger than the last. It seemed as if they had been hurled out by some great explosion. Zagorka glanced back at the huge centaur, who glowed strangely with the sunset light. She said, "You don't belong in Krosan either."

The centaur's simian face creased. "What do you mean?"

Zagorka shrugged. "There's too much war in you. You're more a mountain beast than a forest one."

"I belong with my creator," Stonebrow rumbled.

A bitter smile spread across Zagorka face. "Your creator is finished. So's mine. Krosan, Cabal—they're in chaos."

Stonebrow didn't respond, only trudging irately up the hill. His hooves made rings of dust trail him in the air, as if he had walked all the way down from the sky. "Chaos is better than . . . this. . . ." He spread his arms to indicate the wasteland. His shadow, its blue arms uplifted, marched massively beside him as if to urge him up the hill. Three more paces, and he topped the rise. His hands dropped, and so too did his jaw.

Chester came to a halt. The mule's eyes glowed orange like fire.

Zagorka was the last to see it, and her eyes grew from crescents to gaping orbs.

Before them towered a city of gold. It clung to the side of a cliff that rose from a deep valley. A green river ran below the city, and the lowest buildings were overgrown with verdant vines and trees. As the metropolis climbed the cliff, its gleaming walls pulled free of foliage. Towers and battlements, turrets and bastions, amphitheaters and temples piled one atop the other. Mazelike streets rose up switchbacks and around spirals. Aerial bridges linked raised porticoes, and balconies jutted beneath arched windows. Across all of it, the sun laved golden light.

But no one walked the streets or ran the footpaths to the high altars above. . . .

"Is it real?" Zagorka wondered aloud.

Stonebrow nodded deeply.

Sunlight shifted, and shadows seeped up from cracks in the walls. The momentary glamour of gold faded, and the travelers saw those walls for what they were—simple stone. The blocks were large and regular, though their faces were pitted with age. Windows and doors had elongated with erosion, as had the serpentine paths among them. This place had endured millennia of wind and sand.

"An ancient place," murmured Stonebrow.

"Where are the people?"

"They must have vanished with the ages."

Zagorka blinked, considering. "Why would they leave a place like this?"

"Plague. Famine. Drought," Stonebrow said. "People leave their homes for all kinds of reasons." His eyes glinted darkly. "It might've even been war."

"Yes," Zagorka agreed. The shadows of the city deepened as the sun sank. The riddled walls floated in blue darkness. "The day is almost done. We need a place to camp. So will others."

Stonebrow gestured toward a stone archway beside a ford in the river. Across the ancient gate were carved savage runes. "I wonder how restful it will be."

"After what we've been through, it looks like a sanctuary," Zagorka set off again, trudging up over the ridge and starting down the scree valley.

Shaking his head, Stonebrow said, "One night. Then we head on."

"I may just stay forever," muttered the old woman, not looking back. Chester clomped behind her, resigned.

In the shattered wastelands behind them, many more refugees wandered. All of them would find the valley, the abandoned city, and their new sanctuary.

CHAPTER 2

THAT PENETRATING GAZE

Akroma sat on the topmost balcony of Locus Palace. It was not her palace but the master's, who had been gone for two months. Even so, Akroma and Locus belonged together. Both had been forged in beauty, as white as alabaster. Both had been marred by evil and reforged as composites. Akroma's upper body was that of an angel, though below the hips she was a jaguar. So too, Locus's white marble was shored up with sections of baser stone.

Master Ixidor would not have done it this way, but he was gone. So was the perfect beauty he had made. Akroma could only patch what was left, preserving it.

Her gaze lifted past the gray lake that surrounded Locus, past the tan ribbon of shoreline and up the long trunks of Greenglades Forest. It was a haven for fugitives. Every day, Ixidor's disciples flushed out more, and Akroma distributed justice. The dead bodies were hauled to the Nightmare Lands, where putty people flung them into the sucking pits. Soon all of Topos, from the Shadow Mountains to the oasis, would be cleansed of evil beings. Akroma pined for that day. In preparation for it, crab men quarried stones and rolled them toward the Nightmare Lands—plugs to seal the pits. Then the land would not howl night and day.

Still, it wouldn't be enough. Akroma could patch a broken world, could scour it clean of foes, but she could not truly heal it. Only he could do that, and he was gone.

Clasping her hands together, Akroma closed her eyes and prayed. "Return, O Creator. Return. I am not worthy to rule your world. . . ." The words floated away on the wind. She opened her eyes to a sky obliviously blue, to a world that did not ache for Ixidor as she did.

Something moved beneath the sky—an azure spark amid the boles of Greenglades. It was a disciple of Ixidor—a sentient point of light. It buzzed like a bee as it ascended through the leaves then shot arrow-straight toward the balcony where Akroma waited. It must have found another straggler from the invaders' armies.

Akroma's nostrils flared, and a bitter smile crossed her face. Here was something she could do. Absently, her hand dropped to the axe slung at her waist, and she lifted the dark, heavy thing. It was always cold, for its head was denser than stone and smoother than glass, and its metal haft bore gems that stole away heat. This axe—Soul Reaper—had been forged for the purpose of slaying her. Akroma had found it in the Nightmare Lands on the day after the battle. Since then, she had worn it at her side, a reminder of her own death.

Like a will-o'-the-wisp, the disciple whirred up to the balcony, vaulted over the rail, and impacted Akroma's forehead.

Suddenly, her mind swam with visions: A caravan of brightly painted wagons waited alongside the Nightmare Lands, with servants bearing trays of delectables; a deathwurm plunged down amid screaming nobles and ate and ate to the sound of wild laughter; the laughing one straddled the beast, which bucked across the landscape; the laughter ended only when a jaguar fell upon her—yes, it was a woman—and pinned her; terrible pain, then fear and hunger, the taste of worms and roaches, legs seeping blood past root splints tied with golden braids. . . .

Braids, Akroma told the disciple. *I know this one. A dementia summoner.*

The disciple showed more visions: a glimpse of Akroma through the canopy, the scent of fear like urine in cloth. . . .

Braids knows me as well, Akroma thought. She has hidden out these two months, but no longer.

The disciple brought forth scenes of crab men surrounding and killing other stragglers. . . .

No, I will do it myself. There are things that I could learn from this one, things about our foes.

This was a dismissal, and the disciple knew it. Sparking one final time through Akroma's brain, the creature tumbled down into her throat and fled from between her lips. It sped out over the balcony rail and back toward where the refugee hid.

Akroma's jaguar torso gathered to spring, and her claws gripped the smooth stone. She leaped, clearing the rail easily. Her white wings spread on the wind. Below, the palace pulled away, massive and silent. Akroma soared down in the wake of the disciple, feeling the air grow hotter and thicker as she went. The stone-headed axe glinted in her hands, and righteous fury glinted in her eye.

Braids was the quintessential foe. Her foul lips had belched out thousands of dementia horrors, troops that invaded Topos. She had even sold tickets to the event, turning injustice into entertainment. To find Braids alive and holed up within Greenglades was a miracle. Why hadn't she fled? Why hadn't she summoned monsters to guard her?

The answer was clear: Because she couldn't. Braids's wounds had prevented her from doing anything but surviving. She was ripe for the picking.

* * * * *

"I wonder where Braids is," the First mused quietly to himself as he peered out of his luxury box within the great coliseum. In this inner sanctum, he was utterly safe and wore no armor, but only silks.

"Braids would have come up with something more interesting than animal follies."

His comments ended as a hundred thousand souls shrieked in delight. The tiger cages had been opened, and the huge beasts rushed out to devour the prisoners. All were condemned murderers, so this public execution was an object lesson: This is what happens to those who kill outside the coliseum. The fans were cheering for the death of lawbreakers and of lawlessness itself.

"The fans seem to like it," Phage responded. She wasn't watching the match but sat on an iron chair in the corner, her eyes seeming to scratch at the black-painted walls.

"You think she's dead," ventured the First, turning to study her. In that dark corner, in her black silk suit, she seemed no more than a head and pair of hands. "That's why you're in a foul mood. . . ."

Phage still stared intently at nothing. "If she's dead, she's got nothing to worry about, and neither do we. If she's alive, she'll come back."

"Then what're you worried about?" The First crossed the room, passing a leather chair where Phage dared not sit. Her touch could rot anything that had ever lived, anything except the First. He sat down across from her, taking her hands in his own. His hands killed, and hers rotted, but when they touched each other, they felt an agonizing ecstacy.

Phage pulled away and stood, beginning to pace. "There's plenty to worry about. You yourself said it: Without Braids, the shows are falling flat."

"The stands sell out, and the local arenas are working too. They feed regional talent here and teach Otaria to come to the arena for entertainment. Soon people will come to solve conflicts, then for government. Our shows are slowly taking over the continent." The First slid up behind her and reached out to draw her into his arms.

Like a shadow, Phage slipped away. "Akroma won't rest. She's purging her lands of opposition and raising an army. She wants war."

The First intercepted her, no longer coy. He grabbed her arms and pulled her inward. His hands, so deadly with anyone else, were deft as he felt the contour of her side. "No more escaping. You can't hide behind Akroma. I made you what you are, and we are one." Lifting his other hand behind her head in an enervating grasp, he kissed her.

The pain felt like pleasure—overloading, overwhelming. It was the ferocious sizzle of red-hot iron dipped in ice water. The First held his lips to hers a moment longer than he could bear, and a wave of numb exhaustion moved through him. Then he broke away, took a step back, and caught himself against a low table.

The First panted. How many centuries had it been since he had touched a woman without killing her? Even then, his heart had not foundered like this. The First realized he might in fact love this woman, and unless she loved him in return, he was terribly vulnerable. "We're one, you and I," he said quietly. "There have never been two others like us. We're destined to join—"

"Yes," she said, though the tone of it was more like no. She retreated toward the windows and watched the tigers gorging. "But I won't risk what we've built. We can't allow Akroma to mass an army while we sit idly by."

"The coliseum is our army," the First said. "We have a hundred thousand souls."

"No, our army never returned from Topos." Phage glared at him, and the fire in her eyes was beautiful. "They camp at the Corian Escarpment, or hadn't you heard? Zagorka and hundreds of others."

The First shrugged. "What are hundreds to us?"

"The crack in the dam. If they defy us, thousands more will. I'm going to get them. I'll reckon with Zagorka and bring back our army." She stormed out.

The First might have stopped her, but it was so erotic to watch her go.

* * * * *

Akroma swooped down amid massive trees: They would have seemed giants had they not bordered so enormous a palace. The first canopy rose above her, and Akroma dived through a clear space in the second. The air beneath was hot and dark. She plunged through the final leaf layer, stroked twice, and lighted upon the spongy ground.

Ahead, the disciple waited. It circled a massive trees whose root ball had eroded on one side. Beneath an arched root was a dark alcove. A trail of trammeled forest and old blood led to the spot, and Akroma wondered why it had taken so long to find Braids. When she glanced toward the end of the trail, she saw the scattered skeleton of a jaguar. It would have seemed that the cat had dragged itself all that bleeding way . . . except that the undergrowth lay in the wrong direction.

Stepping lightly, Akroma approached the hole. She sniffed, smelling the worry-reek of the place. Braids had fallen far indeed, she who once had been fearless. What had happened to her that she would live like a wounded badger?

"Come," said Akroma softly, not to Braids but to the disciple. It wove among the trees and rushed to touch Akroma's forehead. *Find out what she's doing here, why she can't leave, what's reduced her to this.* Akroma spoke again, this time to Braids, "You can't escape." With the words went the disciple. It flew from her lips and beneath the raised root and struck. A strangled cry came and the sound of thrashing. A moment later, the blue spark emerged. The disciple arrived and melted into Akroma's head, conveying the mind of Braids.

It was a piteous ruin, a city sunk in a swamp. Every chamber of thought was inundated with murk and filth. Every idea not tacked down floated brokenly through the streets. Braids's brain was a shambles. It had been so for a long while, and she had lived happily within its wreck, but when the flood waters had come, she had climbed to the roofs of her mind and waited for rescue.

What were these waters? If Akroma understood that, she would understand everything about Braids.

Tell her if she comes out into the light, I'll spare her life. Tell her if she remains in the darkness, I'll kill her.

The disciple sped from the angel's lips, crossed to the hole beneath the tree, and entered. It flashed blue, and Akroma glimpsed the eerie face of Braids before the cave went dark. This time, there was no thrashing, no yelp of struggle, but only soft sobbing.

"Come out, Braids," Akroma said, meaning to comfort even as she commanded. "Come out, and we'll speak."

From the hole came a shuddering sound and a gentle thud. Another followed, the footfalls of club feet. A pitiful creature shambled forward, and with merciless eyes Akroma studied her.

Braids's head ducked into the light, and she could not be called Braids anymore. Some hair had been pulled out by the roots, some worn away by friction, some cut by sharp rocks. Braids's scalp showed through in numerous places. Scars crisscrossed her skin, and a misshapen gray mound showed where Braids's skull must have cracked and healed wrongly. She staggered up the slope, and her emaciated shoulders came into view. Breaths pulsed in her chest, and walking was a labor.

Akroma saw why.

Braids's legs were festering and crooked within their root-splits. The hair that bound the wood had turned brown. She had improperly set the bones, but at least she had avoided gangrene. Braids stumped the rest of the way out of the hole and stood before Akroma.

The angel stared. "If you were so wounded, why didn't you simply kill yourself?"

In a voice that was quiet and strangely clear, Braids said, "I didn't want to die. I wanted to live."

Now Akroma knew what the flood waters were: fear. Fear of death, fear of discovery, fear of everything. Once, Braids had had great power, and power destroys fear. When that power was removed, though, the whole ramshackle labyrinth of her mind sank. She abandoned it all to the rising waters and climbed on the roofs. Fear prevented retreat into dementia space, for Braids had become an animal. She hoped only to survive.

Animals were easy enough to train.

Akroma padded across the distance to Braids and, without hesitation, wrapped the woman in her angel arms. "I was broken, as you are. Master Ixidor healed me. I will tell you of him, and he will heal you too."

"Yes," Braids said quietly, "heal me."

"And you will tell me of the one you once called 'master.' "

"Yes." The uses of fear were obvious and easy.

Embracing Braids, lifting her, Akroma took wing. "Ixidor has a Vision to take this broken world and remake it in beauty. He will take you from the state of ugliness to a state of transcendence, and you will love him as I do."

"I will love him as you do. . . ."

CHAPTER 3

ARGUMENTATION

Zagorka smiled into the morning. This might have been paradise. From tea in an ancient cup, steam rose, golden in the sunlight. It curled beside an ivy-covered wall, slid through the petrified beams that jutted above her balcony, and fled up along the cliff face. Every facet of the escarpment stood in stark relief, and above it arced a deeply blue sky. Mornings and evenings made the city shine, but all through the sizzling day, the cliff sheltered the walls and streets. This might have been paradise, and it certainly was home.

Sanctum, they called it, since all of them had sought sanctuary.

All of them. The very night that Zagorka, Chester, and Stonebrow had arrived to camp out, sixty-some others did as well. Most were former slaves of the Cabal—dwarfs in plenty, humans, and goblins among them too. After the ravages of the coliseum and the Nightmare Lands, the various species were nearly indistinguishable. Other refugees had come from Krosan—elves, mantis-folk, and centaurs, all modified for war. Each group had staked a claim in the city, as if planning to stay. They did, and more came the next day, and more over the next weeks, until there were nearly five hundred. Stonebrow had left, intent on returning to Krosan, but nearly everyone else stayed.

Just as many of the wilder folk—serpents, dryads, rhinos, and gigantipithicus apes—took to the scrub forests within the valley and the plains beyond.

It would seem nearly impossible for these disparate folk to live together, but in fact they had much in common. All had survived an horrific war, refused to return to their supposed homelands, and squatted on this ancient city of rock. At first, they had needed no leadership, for their lot was the same. Inevitably, though, squabbles broke out over this and that, and Zagorka naturally gravitated toward them. She knew how to wrangle mules, and wrangling people wasn't much different. Soon, she was the ad hoc leader, the acknowledged Mother of Sanctum, who kept her many children from beating each other's heads in. They had become a family, a diverse but happy commune living in a city left to them by the ancients. There was room for all, work enough to keep everyone sane, and leisure enough to keep everyone glad.

And there was tea. Zagorka lifted the cup. The last person who had drunk from this cup had been dead for thousands of years. She drew the steam into her lungs and let it permeate her body. The scent of it was almost better than the taste, though the taste was quite good. It helped to have elves in the city, for they had known what wild plants to pluck for tea. It helped also to have humans, who knew how to germinate the grains they had scavenged from supply wagons— oats, barley, rye, hops, wheat, corn, and even tobacco—and cultivate the plants that the elves had found. In three months, they had taken their first harvest off the bottom lands beside the river, just before their stores ran out. Their bellies were full and their coffers empty—a perfect state for true happiness.

A shout rang out below; most everything in this city was either above or below. Zagorka stood from the centaur-fashioned chair where she had sat, put a hand on the stone edge of her balcony, and looked down.

An elf stood on one plat of black soil, shaking his head slowly and pointing downward. On an adjacent garden stood a dwarf,

whose hands were spread as he bellowed, "Of COURSE . . . food
. . . TREE-hugging . . . strangle VINE! The REST . . . STARVE . . .
plant something to EAT!"

Zagorka could catch no more, but she'd dealt with this argument
before.

"Za-GOR-kaaa!" shouted dwarf and elf in unison.

On the street below, Chester heckled her impatiently.

"I'm coming, I'm coming."

Zagorka set down the teacup and sauntered into her apartment. It
was spare, though it had a straw bed, a cheery fire, and a few extra
cloaks, scavenged from the army's supply train. If anyone in the
colony wanted to wear anything but military issue, they would need
to start spinning and looming. Zagorka descended a narrow set of
mud-brick stairs to a street that wound along the belly of the cliff.

Chester waited there, just outside his own apartment next door.
The giant mule had chosen a nice cube with a good view and had
lugged a few hundred pounds of river reeds up to make a nest. He
never fouled his quarters, taking himself out like a seven-hundred-
pound dog. Whenever the folk of Sanctum heard those hooves clomping along the street, they made way, expecting either a desperate
mule or a visit from Governor "Mother" Zagorka.

"Well, big boy, off we go."

Chester bowed his front legs, letting the old woman amble up
onto his shoulders. She grasped his mane and clucked twice. The
mule rose and trotted down the street. Folk before them parted and
stood beside the walls. Others emerged from their apartments to
smile and wave at their rulers. This was the human district, and
Zagorka was especially popular among her people.

"Go get 'em, Chester!"

"Give them a kick for us!"

"Be braaaaaaay-ve!"

Actually, Chester was the one with the fan club.

In mock fury, Zagorka sneered, "Shut up!"

It was the signal they had waited for, and those along the roadway cheered and waved their hats. There wasn't much entertainment in Sanctum.

Zagorka grumbled beneath her breath. She struck the mule's rump, a little too sharply for a love pat, and he quickened his stride down the lane. The avenue descended around an echoing turn and broadened between two-story stone structures. Wide steps led downward, and Chester took them two at a bound. By the time he rushed out onto the flat lands beneath the city, Chester was at full gallop. Zagorka clung on for dear life.

Between the silly clamor of the mule and the frantic face of the governor, this arrival was anything but grand. Ahead, the dwarf and elf turned red faces from their shouting match, stared for a moment, and broke into laughter. Zagorka's disarming arrival did as much as anything to defuse difficult situations, but she still had to pretend affront.

"What're you laughing at!" she shouted indignantly as she pulled her mule to a halt. Hooves sent dust from the streets out across the black fields and over the wide, green river. "Drag me off my balcony with your bellowing 'Oh, help! Oh, help! We're having trouble! Oh, we're too stupid to figure things out! Oh, help!'"

Laughter died to smirks then scowls. The dwarf spoke for both of them. "Mind who you're calling stupid, Guvner."

"Well, if you're not too stupid to solve your own problems, what are you then? Too stubborn? Too perverse?"

"It's a difference of philosophy," the elf said unfolding one slender hand beneath his chin. He was middle-aged, perhaps half a millennium, and he had the cynical air of his generation. Beneath graying brows twinkled playful eyes, but his slender lips smirked. He folded his arms over his chest. "Which is better, Guv-ner," he said in mockery of the dwarf, "to live joyously or merely to live?"

"What?" barked Zagorka, sliding down from Chester and ambling toward the men.

"Don't listen to this talking leaf," the dwarf snarled. He too was middle-aged at two hundred, and his beard was a gray forest around his rocky face. Soil made his hands black to the wrists. "Here's the problem—he's taking a plot that should be planted with grain and is planting tobacco. You can't eat tobacco!"

"You can't smoke grain," replied the elf. "He would have us live in a colony without the simplest pleasures—tobacco . . . and *tea*," he added significantly.

The dwarf shuddered with fury. "He'd have us starve!"

"Governor, don't you want to enjoy a pipe after a meal?"

"Don't you want to enjoy a meal at all?"

Zagorka shook her head and spat, summarily ending the argument. "You two . . . you two . . ."

"Don't you say the word stupid!" the dwarf growled.

"No, blind is what I'd say. Blind! The answer is right in front of you," Zagorka said. She strode up to the two plots of land, both churned by crude hoes. She held one hand out toward the dwarf's garden. "You want this land for food."

"Right," the dwarf said.

Zagorka held out her other hand, gesturing to the elf's land. "You want this land for pleasure."

"Right," the elf replied.

"Grains here, and tobacco here, food here and pleasure there."

The elf and dwarf chorused, "Right! So?"

"Well, has either of you even thought about beer?"

"What?"

"Beer! Beer! Something that is both food and pleasure. Has anyone thought of raising grains for making beer?"

In shame, the dwarf stared at his shuffling boots, but the elf's smirk had turned into a genuine smile.

"Well, get to it. Each of you donate a third of your plot for hops and barley, and you'll work that center piece together. I suppose you don't even know each other's names. How do you work together if you don't even know each other's names?"

The dwarf sullenly extended his filthy hand and said, "Brunk."

"Elionoway," the elf replied absently, shaking the hand.

"Fine. Glad to bring sight to the blind. Now get to work. I'll be personally inspecting the beer from your crop. Until then, 'scuse me. My schedule's packed." She turned and walked back toward Chester, who seemed to wear a secret smile.

Elionoway followed. The mockery was gone from his voice. "That was well done."

"I aim to please."

"So do I," Elionoway replied. "If, by chance, the illustrious governor should need the talents of an elf scribe, I would be happy to provide."

Zagorka let out a brief laugh. "Yeah, sure. We've got lots of reading material here."

Elionoway gestured toward the nearby stone arch, at the river ford. "Actually, there are inscriptions all over these stones. Those runes there, for example, read 'Battlefield of the Numena'."

"I like the name Sanctum better," Zagorka said, climbing onto Chester's back. "If you find anything interesting, let me know. Otherwise . . ." she glanced surreptitiously around, "what do you want in trade for a pound of tobacco?"

* * * * *

General Stonebrow strode through Krosan, through hell. Those who hadn't known the forest before might not have realized how tormented it was.

The giant centaur walked along a great tangle of boughs a mile thick and braided out of limbs so broad they might have been trees themselves. Some would see this enormous skein as verdancy. Stonebrow saw it as blight. The braid lay within the bed of a onetime river. It had clogged the ancient flow so that the lakes downstream had become but mud pits. Instead of a crystalline river, the flood was a wide, miasmatic swamp, water only inches deep above ruined ground. Every tree within a league had died and every animal in the trees perished as well.

"How long before the Cabal moves in?" Stonebrow snorted. He marched stolidly through the slough, his hooves sucking muck with each step. Swarms of mosquitoes feasted on his face and hands, despite the wrappings over them. Stonebrow felt like a mummy, and not just because of the cerements. He felt dead.

Kamahl was not coming out.

Three months ago, the giant centaur had begun a vigil beyond the thicket, waiting for Kamahl to emerge. He did not, but only sat. Vigils for living creatures become interminable. After the first month, Stonebrow had gone to seek his tribe. It took another month to find the village, buried under a hundred feet of foliage. No one remained. The able-bodied had fled, and the weak and sickly had been entombed beneath boughs. Stonebrow had mourned them and his vanished home.

Now he returned to the Gorgon Mount. Kamahl had had three months to emerge, and it was time to roust him.

Rising from the dead swamp, Stonebrow ascended a tumbled hillside of branches. He shook the clinging wraps from his hands and face, letting them fall where they would rot. A swipe of fingers across his cheek left red trails where mosquitos had been. Stonebrow reached to his waist and unslung the axe. Once, he would never have wielded a blade against the woodlands, but they were no longer his home. He chopped through a gray wall of wood and climbed toward the swollen mount. His hooves at last clambered atop the Gorgon thicket itself.

The hedge was a mile thick in a great ring, its thorns large enough to transfix a giant. Stonebrow leaped bough to bough, ever on the verge of skidding one way or another and falling on the impaling spikes. At last, he reached the inner curve of the great hedge and ascended onto the Gorgon Mount.

No sane creature remained long on this great tumor. It warped wood and mind, both, but Kamahl had remained. He would be mad now, assuredly. The only question was whether the Mount had made him so. . . .

Ahead lay the ziggurat. Once, four great trees had stood entwined on that spot and reached to the sky, but now, all four had grown grotesque. The ziggurat lay sideways like a huge dreadlock, and Kamahl sat at its base.

Stonebrow strode toward the still figure.

How had the man eaten? What had he drunk? As he neared, the great centaur saw.

Kamahl was thin, his muscles like grainy wood. He had sunk his fingers into the soil, and the green magic that glowed gently up his forearms told where his nourishment had come. He was communing with the heart of the wood—as corrupt as that heart was. Stonebrow had once worshiped man and forest both, but they sickened him now.

Clomping to a stop, Stonebrow stood before his onetime master. His mud-crusted legs did not bow. "Well, Kamahl, when're you going to stand again?"

The man did not respond. He did not even blink. Only the imperturbable rise and fall of his chest told that he lived at all. At last, as though the words began some league distant and had taken all that time to arrive, Kamahl said, "I've stood enough for any man. I—"

"Get up!" Stonebrow growled.

"—stood all I could stand." Kamahl had not ceased speaking, as if the words that stretched across that vast space could not stop. "I walked across a continent, once, twice, three times in search of Jeska. I held her for just a moment, and she was gone."

"There's more in the world than Jeska," rumbled Stonebrow, "more than you, Kamahl. Akroma's building a nation, sending those damned blue bugs of hers to convert the neighboring tribes. She'll soon have a priesthood and a new army."

Kamahl answered, but his words again were delayed: "Not in my world."

"And your precious sister is busy too. She's sent out wagons to the villages to get them lined up in the coliseum system. They're all going to have arenas! Akroma's converting half the continent, and Phage is converting the other half. They won't share Otaria, these two. They're building up for war. This isn't over, you know."

He did not seem to know. He stared toward Stonebrow as if the centaur stood on a distant mountaintop.

"We're going to be caught in the middle—Krosan is, not that there is anything left to defend. The native species are dead, Kamahl, and the perversions created by you and the Mirari sword are rampant. We lost tens of thousands in the Nightmare Lands and a thousand more to the Corian Escarpment."

"It is for me," Kamahl replied quietly.

Stonebrow's face darkened. "Now I get it. I used to think there were two evil empires on Otaria. I figured Krosan was just a victim. Now I see there are three evil empires. Topos and the Cabal fight over the continent, and Krosan withdraws into itself. We're coconspirators with them."

Kamahl blinked as if thinking. "Dig your hands into the soil, Stonebrow. Feel the heart of Krosan. Abide. You will know the truth."

"I know the truth. I know that you've made a mess and won't clean it up. You're not Kamahl anymore, so somebody else will have to be Kamahl. I'll have to clean up your mess." The giant centaur turned and walked away, his mud-crusted hooves cutting into the jumbled coils of wood that had become the ground. He had almost reached the thicket when Kamahl called out to him.

"Where are you going?"

"I'm going to my new home: Sanctum. Zagorka was right. I don't belong here anymore. In Sanctum, there are others like me—people trying to figure out what to do when the gods are gone. We'll stand before the three evil empires." Stonebrow crested the thicket.

"Go then," came the voice of Kamahl, puny with distance. "Go, son of Krosan, with her blessing."

CHAPTER 4

WINNING HER OVER

*F*orgive me, Daughter," Akroma said gently as she paced before the chair.

Braids sat quietly there, listening and watching. Three putty people worked around her, strapping down wrists and knees. Their gray skin was smooth and cold like clay, but in the center of each one's forehead, a blue disciple twinkled.

More disciples spun in an hypnotic circle around Akroma. Her jaguar claws clicked on the marble floor of the cell—not a prison cell but the chamber of a new initiate.

"The straps aren't a sign of mistrust. You believe in Ixidor. That's enough. Your belief is young yet, not wholehearted, and there are corners of your mind you haven't surrendered—"

"I wish to, Mistress," Braids said, seeming on the verge of tears. "It's so hard to surrender everything—"

"It's enough for us, for now. The straps are only to help you through the pain."

"I understand."

Akroma turned and knelt, her hand fondly cupping Braids's jaw. "You do, don't you? You know you've been broken. All of us have been broken, as was Ixidor. The death of Nivea destroyed his spirit, the desert destroyed his mind, the turtle destroyed his flesh, and only then did he come into his true power. In brokenness we partake in the creative strength of our master."

Braids nodded, her eyes wide with hope or fear.

"I lost my legs battling your former mistress, but Ixidor gave me new legs—the legs of a jaguar. You lost your legs battling a jaguar, and now look at them." The angel studied the twisted, agonized limbs. "This is what happens when we try to heal ourselves. We end up maimed, crippled. Only with the creative power of our master, Ixidor, can we be made new."

"I want to be made new."

Akroma gently stroked a red welt across Braids's thigh, beneath which the bone had set at an angle. "This will have to be rebroken."

"I know."

"Believe in our master, and he'll help you. He'll recreated you in beauty. Scream if you must, for there's no shame in passion. Perhaps the pain of the first break will be great enough that you'll be asleep for the rest. I pray to Ixidor that it might be so."

Braids could only tremble.

"Before that, though," Akroma said, gathering disciples on her fingertip, "I want to learn more. I've told you more about our glorious Master. Now you'll tell me more about the inglorious First." She lifted her finger, the tip of it scintillating with blue disciples.

"Oh, Mistress, the pain is so great. Can't it wait until my legs are set again?"

Akroma's eyes were gentle as she said, "No." Her finger touched Braids's forehead, and disciples burrowed in like hungry chiggers.

* * * * *

Chester trudged to the heights of Sanctum. The path was scarcely wider than one of his giant hooves, with a wall of rock to his left and a sheer drop to his right. Far below, the city gleamed in the late sun. Chester rumbled irritably. Though the old woman and the scrawny elf were a light load, Chester resented the sheer folly of the trip.

"The runes below are scant compared to the ones you'll see up here," Elionoway said, clutching a slender pipe of bone in his teeth. He himself had fashioned the white object and had raised the tobacco that smoldered in its narrow bowl. "But even the runes below are enough to place this city back twenty millennia."

Zagorka, who sat ahead of him on the mule's back, turned a dubious eye his way. "You're saying these buildings've stood here for twenty thousand years?"

Elionoway shrugged. "The rain doesn't touch them, nor the wind. The city is hidden from eyes that don't seek it. The river begins at a desert spring and sinks away again into the sand, so who would find it?"

The old woman nodded. "What kind of folks would've settled here?"

"Folks who wanted to control the 'Wall of the World,' as they called it. Whoever holds Sanctum holds the center of Otaria." He blinked at her, "Besides, *we* settled here."

"I mean what kind of folks would've built a city like this. Every door's double tall and so thin I scrape my knuckles. The walls are foot-thick rock. Gates let you shut off one level at a time . . . the place feels like a fortress."

"And here's the lookout." Elionoway gestured ahead.

Chester had reached the top of the escarpment, and the sudden panorama was startling. Above stretched a cloudless dome of sky, and beneath a bald dome of rock. Unlike the rugged stone of the cliffs, this prominence had been polished by the ages. It was utterly smooth in its gradual curve, marked only by a footpath toward the center of the peak, where megaliths stood. The great wedges of rock formed a huge circle, like a crown on the head of the mountain.

"How'd you find this place?" Zagorka asked, openmouthed.

Elionoway smiled. "Elves don't like to sit." He slid off the haunch of the mule and walked lightly alongside. Despite Chester's size, Elionoway's strides made him faster. He hurried along with eager steps. "I found a path and followed it upward. There's no stair, no road. This wasn't a place for the masses. Only priests ascended here. This is a high, holy place. Here, they evoked their numena."

Zagorka dug her heels into Chester's sides, urging him along. "What's a numena?"

"Lore says that a numen is a spiritual creature—a force of stone or sea, growth or decay. They are living mana. Mortals once served them and gained great power. The numena, it's said, threw down the Primevals of old and established the first great mortal empires. If these folk served the numena, they must have lived here twenty thousand years ago."

Zagorka struggled to keep up with Elionoway's words as Chester cantered to the stone ring. Each rock towered five times the height of a man, wedges of red granite that seemed like sanguine teeth. Taken together, the stone circle looked like a mouth gaping to bite the sky. Long blue shadows stretched from each stone and dragged across the escarpment. Chester passed through those shadows, and Zagorka felt a sudden chill. They entered the great ring and saw, all across the inner faces of stone, savage strokes—a thousand petraglyphs.

Zagorka slid down from Chester's back. She turned in slow circles, studying the angular runes. The characters were the height of a hand and marched in long rows across the stones. At the edges of the megaliths, the glyphs were cut off. "There's a lot missing."

Elionoway nodded, his eyes shining with the figures. "But what remains will take awhile to parse out."

"How can you know any of it? How can you know a language that is twenty thousand years old?"

"That's just twenty generations of elves," Elionoway said. He turned slowly, the smoke from his pipe wrapping his shoulders. "Not that this is a dialect of Elvish. In fact, these runic symbols belong to a family of languages spoken by elf foes—the first human empires. For obvious reasons, my people learned these languages well."

"What've you figured out so far?"

Elionoway lifted his first finger and wore a look of pleasure. "Look at the top of the monoliths, beginning in the east and continuing through the southern arc to the west. See the word on each stone? At first, I thought they were the names of the stones, but read together, they form a sentence. 'Return, numena, return, that what once was will forever be. . . .'"

"Thrilling," Zagorka said flatly.

The pleasure drained for Elionoway's face. "You think I'm wasting my time."

The old woman pursed her lips. "It's your time."

"Don't you feel it, though?"

"Feel what?"

"The power of this place. It's like a whisper, the brush of invisible wings. Don't you feel it tugging at your blood, the way the Glimmer Moon once tugged?"

Zagorka released a long hiss. "I'm old, but I ain't that old."

The elf's gaze turned to inward spaces. He seemed a specter standing there, illuminated by the dying light. "You're not old. Your whole species is young. You don't need to forget the past because you never lived it. You've never seen a Phyrexian, never watched an ornithopter fly. The world has changed ten times over, but for you, now is all that is. Not for me. I feel the power of this place. The numena were here, and something remains of them."

His words hung on the air, and Zagorka listened to their echo. Then came the call of a ram's horn—the warning alarm for Sanctum.

"Yeah, yeah," she griped. Zagorka snapped her fingers, and Chester knelt. She scrambled onto his back. "Let's see who's trying to plant beans in the wrong patch."

Crossing his arms, the elf watched her go. In moments, Elionoway was left alone among a crowd of glyphs.

* * * * *

She was still screaming, poor girl, as Akroma strode out of the initiate cell. The hallway trembled with her pain. It was a tragic sound, hard to bear, but if ever Braids would walk again, her legs had to be rebroken and reset. Soon, the agony would be done, and Braids would be remade. The screams ceased as Akroma stalked away, and she hoped the girl had fainted. Into the silence came a rending crack and a fresh howl. The putty people were doing their work, awful work, but at least they could smooth over their ear holes so as not to hear.

Akroma meanwhile resumed her search for Ixidor. She vaulted up a set of stairs, her jaguar legs sure on the curving stones. Blue disciples trailed her. They did not know what she had planned, for she had not invited them into her mind. The stair opened to a flying buttress, and Akroma climbed it to a broad tower.

The sound of rushing water came ahead, and Akroma descended a final stair to a hall half-flooded and gushing from the windows. The water poured from a room in the center of the tower. Akroma knew it well, for here Ixidor had vanished. She waded through the current, leaving wet handprints on the wall as she passed. Reaching the doorway, she stood and peered within.

A man stood there—not a man, but the silhouette of one, an unman.

He was a living portal, shaped in the outline of Ixidor. The master had created six such unmen as bodyguards. If ever he was in jeopardy, he would leap through one of the living portals and reappear in another part of Locus. After the other five unmen followed him through, the one that had been used would close forever. This particular unman had not closed, though.

Akroma wanted to know why, and at last she had a way to find out.

She breasted the cold flood, fighting the current until she reached the living portal. Above her head streamed the blue disciples. They seemed to tremble with hope. Akroma reached up to them, stirring her finger through the swarm until one disciple settled on the tip of it. She brought it down and touched it to her brow.

The azure being twinkled in her mind, and she said to it, *You will join with this unman. Bring the other half of the portal into this room, shutting off the flood. You will empower the unman to think and will and want. You will remain with him and be a shadow man and will be called Umbra.*

Drawing her finger away from her brow, Akroma slowly pressed the creature into the cold flood. The moment her fingertip touched the unman's forehead, the disciple and the unman joined. The waters stopped gushing, and a silvery outline of the creature appeared, standing in space behind it.

As the waters drained away, Akroma spoke softly, "Welcome, Umbra."

The second silhouette lifted his blank face. He took a step, pivoted, and saw his other outline, standing still. He looked back to Akroma.

"Yes, that's your other self, the stationary half that will remain forever in this room in Locus. The part of you that moves is the part that had been with our master, Ixidor. That part is free now. Tell me where Ixidor has gone."

Umbra stood mutely, his hands trembling.

"You can speak. I know you can. Simply draw air through your figure and shape it with the plane of the portal. You're like a reed in a woodwind. Now, speak."

Umbra averted his head, gathering his thoughts. With a voice like quartz cracking, he said, "Master Ixidor . . . was chased . . . by a great black beast—"

"A deathwurm. Yes, I know."

"It found us in his chambers. . . . We fled through the first unman . . . and into the Nivea garden. It found us there, too. . . . We went to the unfinished gallery. It—"

"Found you, yes, I know, and you went to the bunker beneath the lake, where it found you again," Akroma prompted eagerly. "What happened next?"

"The master leaped through me into this room. . . . I waited for the other two unmen. . . . They never came."

"The other two?" She counted on her fingers the number of portals that Ixidor had used, and two remained. Anger creased her temples. "Yes, the other two. When did you last see them?"

"While the master slept, the two of them spoke. . . . They said they did not want to die, as the other three had. . . . To close forever. . . . They said I could come with them, and we three would escape and learn how to live."

Akroma's eyes blazed. "What did you say?"

"I said, 'Better that I die than that he die.' " Umbra gestured downward, as if to the bed where Ixidor had lain.

The angel's stony heart grew soft. As waters receded around them, Akroma tried to pat his back. Her fingers went right through, jutting from the unman's other half, across the room. She withdrew her hand and said, "You were loyal to the last."

"Yes," he replied quietly, "but only too loyal. . . . The wurm came and the others fled. I awakened Ixidor for his escape, but when he leaped through me I did not close behind him. I waited for the others, as he had instructed. The wurm jabbed its head through—a horrible, dark, presence, stretching me—and it swallowed him."

"Swallowed!" Akroma echoed in dismay. Then quietly she repeated. "Swallowed. . . ." She blinked. "Was he whole? Was he alive?"

"Yes. It swallowed him whole and alive."

A small smile curled her lip, though it made her seem only the more grave. "Then he's still alive. He's inside the wurm, wherever it is."

"I'll go find it," Umbra said.

Akroma shook her head. "No, I'll find the wurm that swallowed our master. You'll find the other two unmen. Find them and bring them to me."

Already, Umbra's voice was solidifying, no longer like cracking quartz. "What will you do to them?"

"I'll devise a fitting fate for those theocides. . . ."

* * * * *

It took nearly an hour to ride Chester from the high, holy place down to the city's main gate. All the while, the idiot with the ram's horn blew it. By the time that Zagorka reached the gate, the ford was crowded with most of the settlement's thousand souls. Farmers, shopkeepers, weavers, street musicians, miners, both blacksmiths, the glass blower, and even a couple mercenary brothers who had appointed themselves the "muscle" of Governor Mother Zagorka.

These last two crowded toward her, their shoulders arched absurdly forward and their jaws jutting angrily.

"Jus' say d' woid," began Bret, the older of the two. His brother Jaimes finished the thought, "An' we'll take 'er out."

"Thanks, boys. Nice to know." Zagorka didn't even slow Chester, but rode him at a gallop right through the crowd. Bret and Jaimes fell back, shoving the other spectators behind them. The mob parted. Zagorka reined up in the midst of them and bellowed, "Unless there's a ten-headed monster knocking at our gate, you're all in for it!"

"There is," came the quiet reply, and a woman garbed in black silks stepped from the midst of the crowd.

Zagorka gaped. To hide her dread, she spat. "Phage. I figured you'd stop by sooner or later. I'd hoped for later."

"Well, here I am."

"I s'pose you've come for your army."

"I have."

Zagorka barked a laugh. "Well, army, what did you tell her?"

The group all talked at once: "Not on your life," "Go back to the swamp," "Forget it," and some less civil refusals.

Zagorka shrugged. "You heard 'em."

"Yes," Phage replied. "More than once."

"Well, then, what're you still doing here?" Zagorka asked pointedly.

Phage's eyes twinkled darkly. "I was under the impression this was a free colony."

"It is."

"Then I want to join."

Zagorka scowled. "Well, now . . . none of us here's from an enemy camp—"

"Neither am I," Phage replied levelly. "If you remember, we were allies in the Nightmare War." Her piercing eyes drifted across the crowd, poised to impale. "Does anyone here consider me an enemy?"

Moments before, the crowd had talked over each other, but this time, they were silent except for Bret: "Jus' say d' woid."

Zagorka snorted. Bret and Jaimes had no hope of "taking her out." Zagorka's hackles rose. She was in a spot and knew it. "Look, we're all refugees here, working together. If you want to stay, you'll have to join the commune—you know, swear off every other loyalty."

"All right," Phage said, "I swear."

The old woman gaped. "You mean you break from the Cabal?"

"Yeah."

"And from the First?"

"He can go to hell."

Zagorka was speechless. What could she say? Everyone looked at her, and the wind whistled as if amazed. "Well, I guess you're in." She added quickly, "But behave yourself, Missy. One wrong step, and I'll say 'd' woid,' and my muscle here'll—"

"Take 'er out," Jaimes said, cracking his knuckles.

CHAPTER 5

THE CORRUPTION OF INNOCENTS

Braids knelt weeping in her cell. At least she could kneel. Twice broken, Braids's legs had fused crooked for three months then straight for a month more. They still bore casts above and below each knee, but she could kneel and did so, praying. Braids clasped scarred hands on the mean mattress. Tears left red streaks on her cheeks, as taut and white as drum skins.

"Thank you, Dear Master, for sparing my life. Thank you for re-creating me."

Disciples listened. They tended Braids, circling her head in a prickly halo. Better that than have them burrow through her brain. Just now, they allowed her time for prayer and thanksgiving. Braids *was* thankful to Ixidor for sparing her life, just as she was thankful to the jaguar. Both were predators, one a flesh eater and the other a soul eater, and prey always worships that which consumes it. Any creature broken by a greater power can worship or die. Braids worshiped.

"Build me up, Great One, and I will serve you. Search me and know my heart."

Still, what lover gives all to her beloved? There must be some private thoughts, or the two beings melt into one, and consummation becomes onanism. Braids had given herself to Ixidor but still guarded a few secrets.

The disciples buzzed irritably, as if they could hear her thoughts.

Braids blurted, "Master, I hear your call, and I obey—" It was too late. One disciple jagged down to strike her. It seemed only a mild blue spark until it touched her flesh. Then that spark became a shooting star. It pierced her brow and roared down toward her brain.

Braids retreated inward to battle the disciple. Her mind was a great labyrinth in stone and iron. She had built this immense fortress, block by block, to imprison the thousands of dementia beasts she had caught. Many were dead now, slain by the flood waters of fear or by disciples who ran afoul of them. The cells of her mind were heaped with bones.

The disciples actually cared nothing for monsters, living or dead. They were after memories—gold and keepsakes locked in dark vaults. Already, they had pillaged many such banks, dragging out every last coin of thought about the Cabal, the First, Phage, and dementia summoning. What chamber would this disciple ravage?

Braids clambered up a mental stair and came out on a parapet. Above her, the star-creature streaked across the cranial hemisphere. It headed for an inviolate chamber of mind. Braids would have to reach it first.

She took wing. This was her mind, and in it she could fly. Braids soared above spear-topped ramparts, rankling walls, and rooftops. She matched the disciple's course and speed and outflew it.

She knew the memories it sought. A sanctuary dominated the center of Braids's mind. It had begun as a chapel and grown with cloisters and steeples, transepts and clerestories into a cathedral. It was the center of her devotion to the First. Until now, the disciples had left it alone, seeking tactical knowledge instead of worship. No longer.

Braids dived, tucking her wings to her sides and plunging down on the glorious structure. She sang. The sound of her voice struck the stone walls and turned them to iron. Tones rattled the stained glass until it transformed into steel. The slates of the roof amalgamated with the vault within, turning the great nave into a mountain. The sprawling edifice sealed as solid as a bunker.

Would it be enough? Would the disciple pierce it still? Braids spread her wings and rose to see.

The blue being roared in, shifting its course toward a neglected antechamber. If it penetrated there, it would burrow through to the sanctuary.

Braids dived headlong, shed her wings, turned to pure thought, and plunged through the antechamber's roof. Within, she found a dark chamber cluttered with dusty memories—a chair with a broken leg, a lamp that no longer gave light, an out-of-tune harp, a suit of armor pierced at heart and head and gut. Each item bore a memory. Braids inhaled the whole room into herself. She became the antechamber and hunkered there, waiting for impact.

The disciple crashed into her. Its weight rocked her mind. Its heat boiled her will. Sparks leaped from the creature and scraped like a boring tool inward.

Braids could only wait, resist, endure. Meanwhile, memories tumbled through her, agonizing like broken bones. They were almost as lethal as the disciple. . . .

* * * * *

Being Governor Mother of Sanctum was, for the most part, a thankless job, but there were some moments of joy. This was one of them.

Zagorka stood in the midst of a happy throng. They had gathered on a stone portico before one of the largest buildings in town. A human joiner had fashioned its beautiful double doors from wood supplied by dwarf sawyers. Across those great doors stretched a slender ribbon in red, product of elf looms that had come with a Krosan family. In place of a podium, the speaker used a wooden chair built by a centaur. The speaker was none other than the doughty dwarf Brunk, who had been so embarrassed about forgetting hops and barley.

"And though I ain't much for speechifying," he said, despite the fact that he'd been speaking for a quarter hour already, "it was that day when our own Guvner Mother come whooping her ass—er, I mean riding Chester to my aid, that the thought of this pub come into my pate. So, thankee, Guvner, for pointing out a city ain't a city without a pub and a citizen ain't a citizen without a beer."

As the crowd applauded, Zagorka bowed happily.

"And while I been planting and growing and harvesting and brewing, there've been others shaking the roof and coopering the barrels and tuns, joining tables and this here chair, chandling the tapers and—ha!—look at Clive over there! He nearly blew his brains out making all the snifters and such. Anyways, all of you here got the special invite cause you're the ones who made this place, and so you should be the ones what would first come in and enjoy it."

"Let's get to the beer," shouted the Governor Mother.

The group cheered while Brunk fiddled in the pocket of his barman's vest for a small pair of snips. Finding them, he cried out, "The Gilded Mage—" he turned and snipped the ribbon—"is officially open!" As the red halves fluttered down to the ground, the crowd shouted again and pressed forward.

Zagorka wasn't shy. Tea had been fine for six months, but it was time for something better. She strode up to one door, turned the knob, and pulled it open. In she walked with an eager crowd at her back. They flooded into a beautiful space.

The building was one great room with new whitewash over ancient walls. They rose to a hammer-beam ceiling in black, above a clerestory of square windows meant to bleed off smoke. Two great chandeliers hung from the beams, but their tapers were not lit in the midday glow. Beneath them was a main floor divided into numerous seating levels, all of which led down to a long, polished bar. The tables throughout the room were stout and round, the chairs inviting, and in the midst of each cluster were decks of cards and piles of dice. Shelves near the bar held a gleaming assortment of glassware and also jacks of leather and steins of pewter, the last imported from Eroshia. The pride of Brunk himself, the great tuns of beer, waited in their cooling niches.

As other citizens flowed around her, Zagorka lifted her hands in benediction. "This here's a blessed place! We all pitched in and made Sanctum in miniature!"

The citizens—friends, all of them, from all corners of Otaria— rushed to the bar. Brunk had to waddle frantically to catch up. He rounded the bar, stooped underneath the trapdoor, snatched up a few steins, and started pouring. The clamorous laughter was music to Zagorka's old ears.

Sanctum was no longer a collective. At last, it was a community.

The sounds of celebration suddenly ended, as if a hand had just gripped all their throats. Zagorka turned to see the reason.

Phage stood there in the midst of the room. She did not touch any of the tables or other furnishings, and she wore her steel-soled shoes.

Zagorka gaped at her and said, "What'er you doing here, Phage?"

The woman looked serenely back at her and cocked her head. "I'm here for the grand opening."

"Oh, no, yer not!" Brunk trundled out from behind the bar. "This here's a private party, only for the folks who contributed to the making of this place."

Phage opened her palm upward in a shrug. "A hundred decks of cards and five hundred dice seems a contribution."

In the stunned silence that followed, Zagorka strode over to the nearest table. "Your hands would rot cards." She opened one set and spread it out. Each one gleamed silvery.

"Mica," Phage said. "They're foil-covered." She smiled. "I wanted to be able to play. The dice are stone. I ground them down myself, drilled the pips, painted them. Lots of work. Of course, the mica cards are rare—each deck's worth a few hundred gold."

She had done it again. Phage had entered among them by outdoing them. This time, though, Zagorka wasn't angry. She was impressed. Shuffling the deck, she said, "I s'pose a pub's not a pub if there're no games. Come over here. I'd like to know how cocky you'll be after I hand you your ass."

Phage approached, a smile on her face and a metal stool in her grip. "As long as you don't hand me your ass. I don't need a thousand-pound mule."

The Governor Mother laughed, and the rest of the crowd too. At last, they were a community.

* * * * *

Braids could bear no more. As the disciple bored into her mind, memories overwhelmed her:

"My new fighter's doing well, don't you think?" Braids spoke the words while spitting bile from her mouth. She so worshiped the First that she couldn't enter his presence without vomiting. He kept cuspidors around his private chambers for such obeisance.

"Yes," the First said. He didn't even turn to greet Braids, but only stared out the window. In black leather, he seemed not so much a man but an avatar of darkness. The First watched Phage in the pits of Aphetto. She was fighting. "She is splendid."

How cruel he was to use that word about Braids's rival.

"Remember how useless she had been before I found her—nearly dead, terrified, oozing? I made her something."

"You made her something. Then I made her everything."

Braids had to steady herself against a black-marble table. She was trembling, and for all the wrong reasons. "Why, Master? Why did you choose her—?" She stopped before saying, "—over me?"

The First was angry all the same. It was not Braids's place to question him. He turned toward her, eyes like candle flames in his stony face. "Take it as a sign of my love that I do not kill you for asking."

Only the First could so casually speak the words love and kill in the same sentence. Braids vomited again into the cuspidor.

The First turned back toward the Pits. "Though I needn't answer your question, I will. I did not choose Phage. Another power did. The same power that chose me. I tried to kill her. I took her into my arms to destroy her, but another power intervened, and all the killing hate I poured into her strengthened her."

He took a deep breath and crossed his arms over his chest. Though he continued to gaze out the window, he seemed to see another scene. "My mother had tried to do the same to me. When I was yet in the womb, she hated me and wished to be rid of me. She poured upon me every magical poison she could, that I would be stillborn. Each poison only made me stronger. By the time I was born, my soul was full of darkness. The woman who had hated me in utero fell in love with me at birth. I had been chosen, and I was the apple of her eye— a poisoned apple. When I came of age, I killed her."

The First returned from his reverie and watched Phage fight. "She and I are the same, chosen by the same power. In all the world, I can touch only her, and she can touch only me." The crowd beyond cheered violently, and the First himself smiled, clapping. "You can't even be in the same room without vomiting."

"Oh, Master," Braid pleaded, "it's not revulsion. It's desire."

"I know, Daughter." That word was the cruelest of all.

Braids turned away, taking the cuspidor with her. She knew how to be cruel as well. "If you killed your mother, and you and Phage are the same, someday she'll kill you . . . Father." As she fled, Braids glanced back.

She had never before seen the First's face look so white.

A blue and terrible light shattered the vision. It smashed Braids's final defense. She escaped the antechamber while the blue radiance ransacked it, snatching up every memory. It wouldn't stop with this one chamber. It would rob the whole cathedral. Soon Akroma would know everything.

Flinging her wings wide, Braids launched into the cranial sky. Three strokes, and she pierced through, out of her mind and into her initiate's cell.

She knelt again by the bed, hands clasped and elbows digging into sackcloth sheets. Bitter tears rolled down her cheeks, and she stammered out, "Thank you, Master, for breaking and remaking me. Break me more!"

The blue spark tumbled from her lips, stealing her very thoughts.

Braids turned to the bucket Akroma had provided and poured her belly into it.

* * * * *

General Stonebrow stood in the rocky ford, his hooves steaming in the cool water and his eyes roving over Sanctum. The city glowed brightly with morning, as golden as on the day he had left her. Now, though, folk moved along the streets, faces peered out of eroded windows, and voices laughed and spoke. There must have been a thousand refugees in those walls.

"A strange city," Stonebrow murmured, "built by gods but abandoned to mortals."

He could empathize. The god who had made him had abandoned him. Kamahl and Krosan were sliding together into damnation, but Stonebrow would not go with them. Sanctum would be his new home, and here he would stand with other mortals against Krosan and Topos and the Cabal.

The great arch ahead of Stonebrow seemed an enormous zero.

He ground his teeth and strode toward that giant cipher. The runes that arced across it seemed somehow even more savage than when he had last seen them—deeper, more angular, with a violent slant. Whatever they said, it wasn't Welcome to Sanctum. Stonebrow strode into the shadow of the arch and through it, expecting at any time to be accosted. Only on the far side did he see a guard leaning in a wooden chair, his back to the arch as he whittled a stick down to nothing.

"I'm General Stonebrow of Krosan, once second to Commander Kamahl," announced the centaur. "Now I'm a free agent."

"Hi," replied the guard with a little wave, his whittling knife still clutched in his hand. "I'm Gabo." He blinked beneath a haystack of hair and carved off a few more curls of wood.

"I wish to join the colony."

"Sure," said Gabo. " 'Course, you'll have to work. See, like I'm doing."

Stonebrow pursed his lips. "You're working. . . ."

"Sure." Gabo paused to squint at the centaur. "You could be a guard too, but you'd better bring a bigger chair."

Patting the axe at his waist, Stonebrow said, "I'd also bring a bigger blade."

Gabo looked back to his stick. "Hard to whittle with an axe, and we ain't got much use for generals. You could farm or weave baskets or haul stuff like our asses, but I think guarding's not so bad."

"I think your guarding is not so good," muttered Stonebrow as he marched on.

"See ya, Stony. . . ."

Stonebrow growled and continued on. The road rose slowly across wide fields of black soil with bounteous crops waving in them. Bent backs showed here and there among the stalks, and in a few places, harvested grains lay bundled. Beyond the fields, old folk sat on the rocks and separated heads from stems, placing the food in baskets woven from the same sort of stems. Among the rocks, grapevines stretched across trestles of wood and wire. An elf worked with a team of dwarfs to build a stone pit for stomping them. Ahead along the road, crude wagons and travois trailed behind dumb beasts and others not so dumb, conveying food into the city.

Stonebrow felt his expression soften. Perhaps Sanctum was relaxed, but it was not lax. The folk here worked together and reaped a common reward. It seemed impossible without a ruler to drive them or a power to inspire them. These were disparate folk who had, months before, made war. Now they lived in peace and worked to revive an ancient city. As the general made his way up the sloping street, he realized the gate was not so much an empty zero but a great, encompassing circle.

Entering the city proper, Stonebrow encountered more folk—humans, avens, goblins, dwarfs, elves—some busy with work and others busy with pleasure. No one gawked at him, though a few nodded or said greetings. The centaurs knew him, of course, but they only tilted their heads his direction, as if to say, "I'm glad you finally made it back."

Ahead, the noise grew. A crowd had gathered at the head of the hill just beyond a public well. The water had not drawn them, though, for their backs were turned away from the bucket and winch. Voices rose in debate. Occasional shouts of joy and groans of despair rang out simultaneously. What was this?

Stonebrow neared the back of the crowd, and as he crested the rise, he could see over the heads of all the rest.

A group of perhaps a hundred souls, a tenth of the whole city, stood in a wide circle. At the center crouched a ragged-looking man and a trembling aven, warily watching each other. In the crowd, gold and silver glinted from hand to hand to pocket, and those same hands rose to cup shouting mouths:

"Come on, Bret! Give it to him."

"Don't back down, Delda!"

"He'll fold like an aven!"

"He *is* an aven!"

Blood sports, here in Sanctum? Stonebrow's hopes for a free colony began to crumble. Moments later, the erosion of hope became a landslide.

He spotted, on a balcony nearby, none other than Phage.

Stonebrow glared at her and muttered, "Phage!" He shook his head in disbelief. The arms of the Cabal had grown long, indeed.

"Stonebrow!" Zagorka called, rising from a seat just beside Phage. "I'm glad you're back!"

He snorted. "What are you doing, sitting next to that woman! I can't believe you allow this cruel spectacle!"

"Cruel?" Zagorka asked. "Cruel to what, the dice?"

"What?"

Phage spoke up. "Our friend is confused. He saw a crowd around two sweating combatants, saw bets changing hands, heard catcalls, saw me—and assumed this was a fight."

"It's not?"

"No. This is a bones game. They throw dice, not fists. The game will decide who owns a lean-to between their houses."

Stonebrow blinked and looked to Zagorka. "Uh, well, I still can't believe you're allowing this."

The old woman shrugged. "Phage suggested a death match. I suggested they share the lean-to. This was their solution, and as you can see, it's a popular one."

"And profitable," Phage put in. "The colony gets a tenth of all bets. Sanctum at last'll have money in its coffers. More such disputes and we'll have a treasury."

Stonebrow had always felt tongue-tied in the presence of Phage but never so much as now. "Well . . . it's such a . . . it's the smell of it. It smells like the Cabal!"

Phage laughed, a chilling sound from her cold lips. "I've sworn off the Cabal."

"Oh, you don't believe her, do you, Zagorka? You know what she's doing? She's taking the colony from you, not with an army but with a pair of dice."

Zagorka glanced at the woman beside her. "There's a seduction going on here, yes, and she may think she's taking the colony away from me, but in the end, we'll see who's seducing whom." She let out a great huff. "Now, if you don't mind, General, I've two gold on Bret. . . ."

CHAPTER 6

STEPPING THROUGH DOORS

On the Stubble Field—the renamed Nightmare Lands—stood Akroma. Her face was cold and serene. Her wings spread white beneath blue heavens. Though her angel-half waited with calm resolve, her jaguar-half panted with fear.

Nearby, a platoon of putty people gathered beside a great stone stopper that sealed a sucking pit. Today, the pit would be reopened.

"Get to work," Akroma said darkly.

The putty people stooped to the stone, hands of clay moving down edges of rock. They set their tacky fingers in place, took a grip, and began to haul upward. The stone did not budge. They pulled on it again, and a hiss of air began along one edge. The stopper rose more smoothly then, and as the crack widened, the hiss became a whistle, and a shriek.

The pit was calling to Akroma. Its voice was the voice of death. She smiled, for she sought Death and its prisoner, Ixidor. The death-wurm was nowhere else in Topos, so it must have escaped to the sucking pits. If it was there, Akroma would find it, find Ixidor, and bring him back to life.

Still, she was reluctant. Her jaguar-half felt mortal fear.

The putty people lifted, their backs straightening and the stone stopper pulling free of the hole. It moaned. Gingerly, the workers maneuvered the stone toward one side. A worker's heel slipped on the edge of the pit, and the man threw his arms out to grab hold. The wind yanked him down. His puttylike head hit the stopper and stuck, and he dangled there a moment, limbs flailing. Gray flesh peeled free, and he was gone. The rest of the putty people shifted the stopper onto the rumpled ground.

Akroma stood, staring at the pit. It was unutterably black, and she sensed within it the dark intelligence that she must wrestle.

"The deathwurm."

Tucking her wings, the angel hurled herself headlong into the pit. Reluctantly, her jaguar-half followed.

*   *   *   *   *

Umbra felt as if he had checked every room of Locus, but he couldn't have. The place was enormous, and he was but one man.

No, he was not even that. He was nothing, and the creatures he sought were even less than he.

Umbra strode down a stone corridor. He grasped knob after knob and flung back doors to reveal rooms furnished with fantasies of mind. Some were appointed in crimson paper, and others were bright with windows into impossible views. More still had the amorphous contours of anatomy. All of them smelled stale, though, long unoccupied. None of them held the other unmen.

They had to be somewhere. Each unman was an open portal that led someplace in the palace, and so the anchor halves of them would be in one room or another. They would be hard to see, mere outlines standing still, but tell tale signs would lie at their feet. Perhaps there would be blades of grass broken off by the unmen's walking feet, or puddles from rain that had lashed through them. Perhaps there would be insects or birds.

Another empty room. Umbra slammed the pearl-handled door and softly cursed. He was the ghost of Topos—doomed to wander the palace, half seen in his restless rounds, slamming door and uttering blasphemies. Umbra descended a twisting stair to find himself once again in the grand entry. The shadow man's frantic pace slowed. He trudged to a boot box near the front doors and sat down to think.

Why would they leave? What purpose did unmen have except to save the master? If they betrayed that purpose, their lives were simply meaningless.

Suddenly inspired, Umbra stood and flung open the boot box's stone lid. He staggered back, staring into a dark eternity. It was as if one of the sucking pits of the Nightmare Lands—that is, the Stubble Fields—were within the palace itself, except that this pit didn't draw air inward. It was simply black and bottomless. Ixidor had created many such spaces in his palace, larger on the inside than on the outside. It was anyone's guess why.

The rogue unmen would not be in there. The master would not have created a portal into such a place. Umbra closed the cover and resumed his search. He took a little-used stairway up to a secret fourth floor, hidden behind a grand frieze. Umbra had searched this floor once already and found nothing, but he did not know where else to look.

Voices came down the dark corridor. Umbra stalked toward them. Someone was in the third room on the right. Treading lightly, Umbra reached the door and listened. There were not just voices but street sounds—metal wheels rolling across cobbles, horses whickering in the distance, water draining down half-clogged grates. Umbra set his hand on the knob and slowly turned. The door swung in, revealing a dark library, bookshelves along every wall and ancient spines cramming them. On smooth-topped tables glowed yellow lamps, and on one wall stood a white-marble fireplace, its warm hearth inviting readers who never came. The eternal flames seemed smoky, but a closer inspection showed that the gray vapor came from the center of the room, through a manlike shape. It was not smoke but fog.

There, on the watery carpet, stood one of the two rogue unmen.

A hound in the corner awoke, lifted its head, sniffed, and trotted straight for Umbra. He lunged to close the door, but the dog bolted right thorough him. He heard its yelp as it appeared in the room where his anchor self remained. It was trapped there behind another closed door.

The dog had gotten in through the other unman.

Umbra stole into the room, creeping across thick carpets toward the gray outline. After months of fruitless search, he was eager. He threw himself through.

The library vanished, and a crowded street at night appeared. Tumbling across slick cobbles, the shadow man rolled to a halt just in front of the two rogues he sought.

* * * * *

Akroma dived into the roaring vortex. The sucking pit had the same diameter as a deathwurm's mouth and was even ringed by its tooth marks. She plunged through.

The blackness beneath stung like ice water, tricking away heat and vitality. Unlike water, though, it did not buoy Akroma. She dropped headlong. Spreading her wings, Akroma caught the winds of chaos and soared out through it.

Formless energy pressed up all around her. It ached for a unifying structure, and Akroma was unifying enough. Power condensed on her flesh, forming a second skin. She stroked her wings, and the stuff peeled away. It retained her form for a moment before dissolving. More energy accreted upon her shoulders and arms, thickening quickly. She ran her nails through the stuff to strip it. Would it make another one of her, given time, or would it simply suffocate her? Shivering, Akroma threw off the membranes.

She glanced up through the swirling energy, hoping to see the hole through which she had entered. It was not there. Akroma banked and tried to climb. She craned her neck and searched the maelstrom above, but there was no sign of escape. Her heart thundered. Did it matter? If she would find her master, she must plunge deep into the storm of energy. Only after she had caught the wurm and torn it apart would she need to worry about escape.

On outstretched wings, Akroma soared. She sought wurm spore—a darker patch amid the blackness, a sinewy coil among fanciful twists of energy. Colors blazed into being and faded again. In places, energy accumulated around some stray idea, forming a dog, a chair, a rock, a boot—then eroded. Everywhere she looked, chaos boiled like stew. She wouldn't see a deathwurm even if it swam by in front of her.

Closing her eyes, Akroma flew by feel. Perhaps she could sense the wurm through changes in pressure. It was no use. The wing nerves that could read every nuance of normal winds were overloaded by this pummeling. She could not feel the wurm, could not see it, and her ears rang with the roar of sucking winds.

The roar. The hole. Escape!

The mouth of the pit was the only continuous noise in this tintinnabulation. She banked right and followed the sound back to the surface, back to life. It felt like cowardice to stroke toward that sound.

Above her, the hole glimmered—a small circle dim in the wash of power. Akroma yearned toward it. If she were a coward, Ixidor had made her so.

Just before she shot out through the hole, she saw it—a black head and glinting teeth. They vaulted up out of the darkness. . . . A bright hole above and a dark hole below, but which would she chose? Akroma set her jaw, gathered her wings, and soared through. . . .

* * * * *

Umbra rolled twice more then got snagged on the broken bar of a sewage grate. Yanking his outline loose, the shadow man scampered up onto the pavement, just out of the way of the two walking unmen. He melted into the shadows of an ivy-covered wall and waited for his quarry to pass.

They strolled on in the misty night and spoke to each other in soft but avid voices. The fog was thick, but their forms were occasionally outlined by enchanted street lights. This city, wherever it was, was rife with magic.

Umbra slipped out behind the unmen and furtively followed. He had found them, the two traitors who had abandoned their master to death only to preserve their own lives. Umbra was disgusted and wished he could spit. Akroma would do the spitting for them both when he hauled these rebels in. Now was the easy part. He needed merely to leap over them, forcing them through his own form, and they would appear in the once-flooded room in Locus. Then Umbra would take them to Akroma and . . .

How could I lead them anywhere? he thought. I would close forever. Once these unmen pass through me, I'll be gone.

Of course Umbra was willing to make the sacrifice, but what would keep the unmen from running away again? Akroma wouldn't be there to detain them, and Umbra's death would be for naught.

Death was too strong a word. Umbra would merely close, that's all. Close and vanish. There would be no pain, only the cessation of being. . . . Umbra renewed his pace, walking on cat feet to catch up.

Down a broad set of stairs sauntered a weary old professor. He crossed right in front of Umbra, who had to leap aside to avoid over-running him. Rolling to recover, Umbra cantered up behind the unmen and matched them stride for stride.

Each had Ixidor's outline, though one was tall and spindly and the other short and stout. Umbra tuned his portal membrane to their voices and could hear even the soft whispers very clearly. The tall one was speaking.

"—don't know what you were thinking to climb in there with her."

"I expect you don't. Ain't you ever looked at a girl?"

"Girls, no. Women, yes—"

"Well, that gentlewoman was all woman all right. You saw, beneath the steam and bubbles! You saw!"

"The point is, you're a living hole. What would a woman want with a living hole?"

"It don't matter what she wants with me but what I want with her."

"Eeek, man! You've got desires in organs you don't even have."

"What about you, always on about reading books? You got neither eyes nor brain."

"Still, I can read, but how you intend to, well, experience carnal knowledge when you don't even have any carne!"

"Who said anything about caramels?"

"Idiot!"

"I wasn't after nothing but a little peep."

"You can peep without climbing into the tub with her! Didn't it occur to you what would happen when a living hole climbs into a tub full of water?"

"It weren't full for long!"

"Of water or woman. Your peep ended quickly then, didn't it? And you certainly lived up to your name, Mr. Puddle."

"And you too, Mr. Stick."

"How did I do anything to live up to that damned name?"

"You've got a stick stuck up your—"

"I felt like a stick the way those noble hounds laid in on me!"

"Oh, them dogs didn't hurt nothing!"

"We're just lucky none of them barreled through us."

"One barreled through me."

"Oh! You lout! What will happen when that dog is found in the room where your anchor is? It wouldn't take a genius to realize you must be standing right there. They could find us any moment."

"Well, why didn't you just say so?" Mr. Puddle let out a whistle. "Here, boy! Here, boy!"

"That's not going to work," Mr. Stick groused.

Umbra silently agreed since the dog was inside him now. Suddenly the beast leaped through him and, yelping, dashed down the street.

"There, y'see. Problem solved."

"You're incorrigible, Mr. Puddle."

"Thanks loads, Mr. Stick."

"That wasn't a compliment."

"Well, then, piss off."

"Piss off, yourself. You're the reason we haven't found a flesh spell."

"You are. There ain't gonna be a spell like that in a library. You gotta sneak into a wizard's place."

"How? They're all warded against portal magic. We're portals."

"Easy. We just get invited."

Mr. Stick seemed to consider. "You've an imbecile's idea of wizardry, but at base you're right. If we got invited to a wizard's party, we could slip off and find something useful. We'll start by attending lesser affairs and building up a reputation."

"You make crashing a party sound dull."

"Hold! What's that!"

"What!"

Umbra froze in his tracks, fearful they had heard him.

"Do you see it? Right there, over your shoulder, the line in the air?"

Umbra trembled, taking a step backward.

"I see it! A clothesline!"

"Precisely, Mr. Puddle. A noble's clothesline. We simply shimmy up that brick wall and make off with the clothes, like a strong wind."

"Now you're talking!"

"We get some masks—society masks—dress up, and crash a party, pretending to be someone else."

"Happy day!"

"Come, friend Puddle, let us climb."

"Yes, let's."

Umbra withdrew. Once they clothed themselves, they would be easier to follow. Besides, Umbra wouldn't mind crashing a party or two. . . .

* * * * *

Akroma hurled herself into the circle of death.

The wurm's teeth gaped, a steel trap filled with deep blackness. This creature was the death of Ixidor, and it might be the death of Akroma too. It didn't matter. Without the creator, life was meaningless.

Tucking her wings, Akroma plunged through the wide-spread jaws. Sepulchral folds of flesh encompassed her and dragged her down into utter blackness. She reached her hands forward, parting the throat. Her fingers sank in and hurled her deeper.

"Master! Ixidor! I'm coming for you!"

She grasped more of the rubbery flesh, but it dissolved. Her feet lashed out for a hold, but the wurm's muscles shredded. Soon, instead of a sinewy tube, she descended through tattered flesh then through the boiling belly of chaos.

The deathwurm had been just another phantasm. It had never been real, only a projection of her mind.

Akroma spread her wings, pivoting toward the roar above. This was a place of phantasms. She would never find a true deathwurm here.

Tattered and weary, Akroma climbed. Tumbling energies tore plumes from her wings, traced their logic, and turned them momentarily into birds. The cooing creatures dissolved back into the forces that had formed them. Chaos was meant for creators, not creatures. Ixidor could have dipped his finger in this stuff and painted out a whole world, but Akroma was just part of the painting.

Fixing her eyes on the circle of light, Akroma stroked once more and hurled herself out. She arced above the gray ground, felt the yanking hand of the world, and fell on her face.

Winds clawed her, trying to hurl her back into the pit, but she held on. "Close it!" Akroma shouted to the putty people. "Close the sucking hole!"

CHAPTER 7

SWALLOWING SOULS

The coliseum was full to overflowing, but it felt empty. Phage had been gone for two months, working to establish a Cabal arena at Sanctum. Zagorka and the slave army had been gone for eight months. They could refuse to return to the Cabal but could not keep the Cabal from coming to them. Braids—who knew had happened to Braids?—apparently was gone for good.

"My trinity," the First muttered, "Phage, Braids, Zagorka . . ." He clenched black-gloved hands that could kill with a touch. His shoulders flexed, his back and stomach. . . . The First had a powerful physique and an even more powerful metaphysique, but without those three women, he felt weak, abandoned.

He turned away from the balcony window, not even remaining to see the kill, and retreated into his chambers. Past black-painted walls and looming mirrors he went, among woolen tapestries and seats done in leather. As palatial as this luxury suite seemed, it was in fact only half of the First's domain. Beneath it were secret chambers kept from all the world, even Phage.

Lifting aside a tapestry, the First slid his hand along the wall until he felt a seam. Gentle pressure separated the panels, revealing a spiral stair down into darkness. He needed no light. Descending, he let the chill of stone seep into his fiery blood.

His trinity was gone but not his god.

Down a long corridor lay a room all in black, with a single mat of reeds laid upon the floor. The First stepped over the mat and walked to the center of the far wall. It was cold metal, polished to glimmer even in the darkness. He removed his gloves, spread his hands on the cold metal, and spoke quietly—words not of magic but of devotion.

"Great ruler of my heart, I beg audience."

The wall before the First began to shift. A slender line of gold ran from ceiling to floor—a seam opening. The warm light broadened, as if morning sun poured between the metal doors. The First took a step back, drawing his hands away, then a second step. The radiance grew, bringing with it a ringing rumble. Something massive had been leaning against the doors—stacks of gold coins. They toppled. In a crashing wave, the fortune flung the doors wide and spilled across the chamber floor. By the time the tide of wealth reached the First, he lay prostrate on the mat, and the coins flowed all around him. Their metal voices chattered to silence, and the First spoke reverently.

"Great Kuberr, your servant lies before you. I have done your bidding. For you, I slew my own family, I created the Cabal, I devised the pits and the coliseum. Now I remake every city and village in Otaria in your image, through your power. Soon, there will be no law except the arena, no government except the Cabal, no god except Kuberr. All this I have done for you."

The First lay panting before his lord. For centuries they had built their empire, and all the while Kuberr had grown in strength. At first, he had appeared only in dreams, but now he manifested sun-bright in this great horde of gold and in every bet laid in the coliseum. Soon he would work within every wager throughout Otaria.

"You taught me the currency of hearts, that greed buys all souls. So, in greed, I come to you. All that you have given me I have given back to you. Now I ask for one thing that will be mine forever." The

First paused, and in an intense whisper, he said, "I want Phage. Bring her to me. Buy her soul and give her as a gift to your greatest servant. Grant me this one boon, great Kuberr."

In the heart of that blinding radiance, the pile of coins shifted. They rang, and their metal murmurs joined into the voice of an ancient power. *She will be yours, Virot of the Maglans.*

The First's heart quickened in thanksgiving. "You are great, Kuberr. Your light shines on the obverse of my soul, but the reverse is cast in shadow. I must ask: Will she betray me?"

There came no answer from the gilded lord.

"You have blessed her, have made her your servant as you made me also, but when you made me, you called me to sacrifice my family. Will you call her to do the same? Will you ask her to slay me?"

At first, only silence replied, then the shifting riches spoke again: *I have greater plans for her. Here is what you shall do: When she arrives, you will take her as you wish and make her wish it too. She will be yours as long as you want her.*

"She will be mine," the First repeated, avaricious. His gray cheek creased in an all-too-brief grin. Once again, the light of Kuberr shone bright on the face of the deal, but darkness lurked on the other side. "You have not told me whether you will send her against me, to kill me. . . ."

I have not. In this matter, you must remain as all mortals— guessing.

The First lifted his face, staring into the radiance. "Then you *will* command her to kill me."

Only remain faithful to me, Virot. Otherwise, your death is assured.

Bowing his head in acceptance, the First said, "For centuries I have served faithfully and will still, forever."

Yes, you will.

With that, the gold was moving again. It scuttled like roaches, one atop another, in shimmering swarms toward the shrine. Coins pattered across the First's back, rushed over his arms, and clambered toward their beaming divinity. In moments, the floor was cleared, and a great heap of gold sorted itself into neat piles. The First could only lie there and watch, awed by the spectacle. The chamber that held the gold seem endless, filled with infinite wealth. As the last coin rolled back into place, the massive doors swung silently to. A world of wealth diminished to a single golden hairline and that to nothing at all.

The First remained there on his face in the darkness.

Phage would return, and when she did, he would take her as he wanted and make her want it too. She would be his as long as he wished—Kuberr had promised it, and before she could turn on him, she would be dead.

How to do it? The First would meet her with roses, yes, but not real roses that would rot in her hands. Steel roses. He would sharpen their petals so that after he captured her heart, he could cut it out of her body.

* * * * *

Stonebrow stood sentry at the great stone gate of Sanctum. He did not lean against the archway and certainly did not whittle. Still, he felt a failure.

He had sworn to fix the mess Kamahl had made but now was just part of it.

Yes, Stonebrow defended his community—that was a start for any hero—and Sanctum was a place worth defending. Communal farms stretched along the Deepwash River and bore bounteous crops. Refugees came day by day to inhabit the stone houses, to refit the millwheel and restock the granary. Trade had even begun with cities as far away as Eroshia. The people of the world flocked to Sanctum for a new start, and they lived together in a strange, cooperative peace. Sanctum might have been enough to fix the mess made by Kamahl—except that Phage was here.

"Phage . . ." Stonebrow gritted his teeth. He lifted a slab of limestone the size of his palm and hurled it across the ford. The rock bounded from coruscating waves once, twice, thrice . . . The fury of the throw carried it toward the rocky shore beyond. Nine times and ten. . . . It struck the far bank, clattering against other slabs the centaur had thrown there. He picked up a new stone.

The problem with a free society was that it was free to everyone, including Phage. She had arrived seeking sanctuary and was not turned away. Like every other refugee, she was asked to contribute according to her talents. Her talents were games, and the colony was in dire need of entertainment. The people had, of course, embraced her games, but in doing so, they had embraced the Cabal. It was an inevitable corruption.

Even as Stonebrow guarded the gates against armies, a single woman conquered Sanctum from within.

"Curse her," Stonebrow hissed under his breath.

"Curse whom?" asked a woman behind him. *The* woman.

Stonebrow's hackles rose, but he managed not to startle. It was just like Phage to sneak up on a gate guard. "Curse you." He should have whirled, brained her with this rock, and kept pounding until she was dead. Then the river would carry her corruption away. . . .

"You won't, though," she said, walking around before him and staring at the stone in his hand.

Stonebrow scowled. "A mind reader too?"

"Not really," Phage said with a gentle shrug. "It's just that my brother created you, and you want to be like him. Kamahl wished to kill me—as you do—but he couldn't." Her finger lightly ran along the jagged lightning emblem on her belly. "You couldn't, either."

Stonebrow dropped the rock, and it shattered by his forehoof. "Well," he began, but when he stared down into those big, intense eyes, he couldn't remember what he was going to say. "Well . . . maybe I *don't* want to be like him. Maybe I left Krosan to do the things Kamahl wouldn't do."

She nodded, her short black hair bristling above her pretty face. "Maybe I left the First for the same reason."

"I know what you've been up to," Stonebrow said, snorting.

Phage crossed her arms over her chest. "What have I been up to?"

"You and your games are changing this place. You're making it into a colony of the Cabal."

"These aren't blood sports, Stonebrow. No one has gotten hurt. People look forward to the games after long days of farming or weaving or smithing. Besides, the games are more than entertainment. They decide quarrels." Her face was as guileless and beguiling as a child's. "Don't you see? I've left the Cabal. I'm trying to build Sanctum, just like everyone else. I want it to stand against the Cabal, and against Topos and Krosan. I want Sanctum to thrive, just as you do."

Stonebrow stared at the river, churning ahead of him. "Don't get preachy. Don't act like you're doing anything great for Sanctum."

"Well, don't act like you are, either," Phage said, looking down for the first time. "Fine. Don't believe me. It doesn't matter. I don't need your help."

"Is that why you came down here? For my help?"

Phage turned away. "There are stronger backs and more open minds. Forget it."

"It's forgotten," he spat.

She kept walking, but her voice carried easily to him. "Keep guarding your rocks, Stonebrow, but every once in a while, look to the heights. That's where I'll be, with a team of workers, building a new Sanctum."

Stonebrow shook his massive head and kicked the shattered stone into the water. With a series of wet plops, it sank. Yeah, what could Phage build for Sanctum?

Still, he couldn't resist sneaking a peek up toward the cliff top. What if she did build something there, something grand?

J. Robert King

* * * * *

Umbra crouched beside a potted plant and watched in amazement as his comrades made their way among the party guests.

Lord Sash (Mr. Stick after his ascension into clothing) looked outlandish in black-buckled boots, red trousers, a gray tunic, and his signature yellow sash from shoulder to hip. He also wore a carnival mask in white ceramic beneath a wide-brimmed hat hung with a head-curtain. The clothes were the right length for him but draped limply on his frame, which was, after all, flat. Duke Waistcoat (Mr. Puddle) looked no better in riding boots, green knickers, a dark blue waistcoat, and a cap to which a dog-faced mask had been attached. It was the only other mask they had been able to find, and now he was stuck with it.

They had worn these costumes to four parties over the past month. The first, they had crashed. Their absurd clothes and doltish manners convinced everyone that they were paid entertainers. Lord Sash and Duke Waistcoat protested, telling of their vast holdings and their wartime valor, all in hopes of establishing legitimacy. The guests only laughed and congratulated them on being "very funny, indeed." At the end of the evening, the host even paid them three gold apiece. Sash and Waistcoat garnered more "invitations," and they attended each party. Waistcoat was in heaven, surrounded by edibles, potables, and pinchables, but Sash was frustrated. He didn't like being the butt of any joke and especially not a joke so public that he could not sneak away into private places. He was trapped in high halls such as this one, with gentry on either elbow and perils everywhere.

"—a stable of, eh, well, twenty-five thoroughbreds," Duke Waist-coat boasted, seeming to polish his nails on his chest, though he wore white gloves.

"Oh, Duke Waistcoat, you *do* lead a high life!" said the dowager— sweet, old, and pillow-faced. A twinkle came to her eye. "I imagine you and Lord Sash have a whole army of debutantes after you."

"An army of deputes!" Waistcoat gasped in alarm, squatting as if to avoid notice. He hissed across the room. "Sash! They're on to us!"

The dowager laughed, a sound like the call of an exotic bird. "You *are* a delight! Not deputes, but debutantes—girls! Young girls."

"Ha ha," Waistcoat said. " 'Course! Ha! Yeah, the girls go for us—well, for me, mainly. When it comes to girls, Sash is all thumbs, but I'm all fingers."

Sash approached, hooked his partner's arm, and dragged him abruptly away. "Forgive us, Lady Stelling, but I must have a word with my partner."

"By all means," the dowager said, chuckling as the lean lord half-carried his portly friend along to the deserts table.

In a low voice, Sash said, "Listen to me. I'm done with these parties. We only mingle and hobnob with not a magic tome in sight, and your carousing is getting more and more dangerous. Drop it!" Sash finished, slapping the hand that had just lifted a puff pastry.

Waistcoat looked up with the wounded mask of a dog and said, "They look so tasty."

"You don't even have a tongue! If someone sees you pick up a thing like that, you'll have to eat it, and that'll leave more clues back at the palace."

A new voice intruded, "Lovely loaf you have there, Waistcoat!" It was the mustachioed host, Governor Dereg, his eyes staring in astonishment at the two-foot-long pumpernickel clutched in Waistcoat's hand.

Caught and trembling, Waistcoat did what his partner had recommended. He tilted his dog mask up just enough that he could ram the whole loaf where his mouth would be. The bread vanished into him, and as Waistcoat lowered the mask, he produced a small belch. "Almighty good bread, Guvner."

"Astonishing!" the man said, irritation turning to amazement. "Whatever else could you eat?"

"What've you got?" Waistcoat shot back, pleased he had discovered a new way to be entertaining. He looked toward Sash as if expecting a "good boy."

Sash didn't see, too busy slapping his ceramic forehead.

"Everyone, gather round!" called Dereg gladly. "Our entert—ahem, *guest* Duke Waistcoat is going to demonstrate how he can swallow large food items in one gulp."

The guests buzzed excitedly as they made their way over, eager to see the new spectacle. Dereg waved them in with both hands. They settled around him, and he turned to the wide-spread desert table. A likely fruitcake waited there, as heavy as a brick. Dereg hefted the desert and waggled it aloft.

"Don't be cruel," objected Lady Stelling. "He'll choke."

"I'll lay you two to one odds he won't."

"I'm in for ten gold!" she said, and a few of the other guests anted up as well.

During the hubbub, Sash nudged Waistcoat and said, "Pretend to choke."

Governor Dereg said, "All right, all right! The betting is final." He handed over the fruitcake. "Show the good folks, Duke Waistcoat."

Waistcoat took the proffered fruitcake, seemed to sniff it with his dog nose, and rammed the thing home. He made a regurgitation sound and tried to haul the fruitcake back out, but it slipped from his grip and was gone.

The crowd broke into amazed applause, and even those who had lost gold surrendered it eagerly.

"Utterly remarkable."

"I've never seen the like!"

"No one else in the world eats that way."

"Sash does," Waistcoat blurted, and when a black-buckled boot crashed down on his foot, he added quickly. "I mean, *Lord* Sash does."

"You know this trick as well, Lord Sash?" asked the governor in amazement.

Lord Sash waved away the comment. "No, really. I'm trying to cut down."

The room filled with laughter, and a number of cakes and pies were proffered. "Please, Lord Sash, you must show us."

"Come on, Sash!" Waistcoat said.

The tall man only stood there, shaking with fury or confusion.

Wanting to move things along, Waistcoat grabbed a pie in one hand and the nose of Sash's mask in the other. He hurled the pie, lifted the mask, and watched with satisfaction as food, tin, and all vanished through Sash's head. The mask flapped back down, and the delighted cheers of the crowd helped cover the clangor of the tin hitting a stone floor back in Topos.

Buoyed by the cheers, Waistcoat said, "Oh, it's not just food! We can eat anything."

"Anything!"

Waistcoat serenely nodded while Sash vigorously shook his head.

Governor Dereg had a wild gleam in his eye. "Come now, Lord Sash, we cannot bet again on the talents of Duke Waistcoat, but if you would eat something—a large, inedible something—I would think this the finest party in all of Eroshia!"

The other guests cheered, looking to Lord Sash.

He seemed to rally. No longer trembling, he spread a gloved hand on his chest and said, "As you no doubt have gathered, my friend the duke and I are dabblers in magic, by which we perform these astonishing feats. Still, for us to continually hone our entertainments, we need more spellcraft." He turned toward Governor Dereg, and the eye holes of his mask seemed to smolder. "If you were willing to provide me a book of spells—no slim volume, but a real trove, out of your library, I will swallow that potted plant there." He pointed to a two-foot-tall evergreen in a marble base.

The crowd oohed.

Umbra discreetly slid away to find new cover.

The governor smiled an incomprehensible smile. He shrugged. "I am no magician. It would be worth it." He lifted a hand and snapped.

A servant set his tray of drinks on a nearby table and ran off to the governor's library. He was not gone long, and when he returned, he carried a wide, fat book. Magic glowed in the inscription on its cover.

With an eloquent gesture, Governor Dereg indicated the book. "What do you think? Will it suit? Will you eat my bush?"

Lord Sash directed the young man to lay the book on a nearby harpsichord. Sash placed his hand on it, as if sensing the spells within. Drumming his fingers, he said, "I'll do it."

Those three words inspired a hundred more as folks marveled at this strange trick.

While the rest of the guests worked out odds and percentages, Waistcoat sidled up beside his partner. "Sure changed your colors, eh, *Mr. Stick?*"

"What are you on about, *Mr. Puddle?*"

The duke crossed arms over his chest and spouted, "Only that when everybody's looking to me, you try to ruin it, but when they're looking to you, well then it's all fine and dandy, ain't it?"

"Idiot! Don't you see what I've done? I've gotten—"

"All the attention, all the glory. Well, now you're in my territory, and we'll see who comes out on top!"

"Dolt."

"Moron."

The wagers were made, and all eyes turned once again upon Lord Sash.

Duke Waistcoat slouched sullenly away.

As if to rub it in, Lord Sash held out his hand in carnival fashion and said, "Behold, the wonders of conspicuous consumption! This mouth of mine, whenever it opens, conveys volumes beyond the ken of mortal men. Now I turn my ravenous gaze upon this bush, intending to teach it where it lies in the hierarchy of being!" Lowering his hand to the top of the shrub, he wrapped his fingers around it and yanked. The whole plant, root ball and all, lifted out of the marble urn that held it. Lord Sash hoisted it high, a rain of black grit falling down beneath the thing. "As I said once already, I'll say again: Behold!"

Tilting his head back, Lord Sash lifted his mask and rammed the bush down. It slid easily through, the mask settling in place as the last needles flipped in.

Applause rang out along with shouts of joy.

Lord Sash bowed deeply, his hands forming dual flourishes to either side.

The ovation ended abruptly as a woman screamed, "He's eating the harpsichord!" Everyone spun about to see Lord Waistcoat crouching at the narrow end of the instrument, having already swallowed a third of it.

"My harpsichord!"

"My spell book!"

Just then, Waistcoat swallowed the part of the instrument with the book on it. His mouth seemed to stretch from forehead to navel.

"Back off, you fiend!" shouted Lord Sash and Governor Dereg in unison. Both bolted to grab him, but his clothes tore away in their hands.

Duke Waistcoat was revealed in his true form—a flat gray shadow enveloping a harpsichord. The keyboard vanished entirely, and the portly unman turned, raising his hands in victory.

Dead silence answered.

"Guards!" shouted Governor Dereg.

"Run!" shouted Lord Sash.

Clothed and naked, the two unmen ran for the front door. A pair of red-suited guards appeared before them, barring the way. Waistcoat and Sash didn't even slow, running right into the men. One grabbed Sash's arm, but the shirt simply tore from him. The other tried to straight-arm Waistcoat and ended up falling through him. The two unmen pelted out into nighttime streets.

"Idiot!"

"Moron!"

"He's the governor! We'll be hunted throughout Eroshia! Worse, you lost the spell book that was our only hope!"

"I did not! It's in here, on top of the harpsichord!"

"In where?"

As if to demonstrate, a red-coated guard bolted, yelping, out of Waistcoat and fell to his face on the dark cobbles. Waistcoat jumped over him and kept on going.

"It's in there," Sash said, realization dawning on him. "You genius!"

"Oh, pshaw."

"Keep running. Up here, I'll ditch the rest of these clothes, and we can head out of Eroshia for good."

"I like life, Mr. Stick."

"You and I both, Mr. Puddle."

Unseen, a third shadow followed.

CHAPTER 8

REVELATION

Akroma knelt, her jaguar breast resting on the stone floor and her angel wings folding to her shoulders. She reached to comfort her beloved initiate.

In a welter of sweat and torments, Braids lay on her straw pallet. She had been strapped to the frame lest she tear her own flesh or fling herself through the window. Day and night the disciples worked her over, dutifully rooting up the demons within and dragging them away. The evil spirits did every harm they could, and poor Braids was driven nearly mad. Even now, the disciples streamed in a blue cascade into her mind while Braids bucked and cursed.

"There, there, sweet daughter," Akroma soothed, stroking her knotted brow. "I'm here. It hurts, I know, but you'll survive, and you'll be purified, freed, redeemed."

Braids's rolling eyes turned to fix on the glorious face before her. "Akroma . . . Mother . . . please! No more!" From her lips, disciples flew like specks of spittle. They bore with them hunks of memory— the horrors that plagued this child.

Braids exhaled the disciples, and Akroma inhaled them.

"I know your pain," Akroma said as dark visions flitted through her mind—skinless ogres, scaffolds above lava, bursting bellies, a man with chains for arms, bodies turning to dust. . . . None of it had strategic value. "I know. When we're done, you'll be cleansed, and I'll know how to protect you and all of Otaria."

Braids's hands struggled against her shackles, and she managed to grasp one elbow of the angel. "Mother . . . please . . . make them stop! Make them stop!"

Akroma didn't hear. In her mind, a new memory bloomed. It unfolded with all the elaborate beauty of a rose.

Braids wept, not strapped to a bed but on her face and on the floor. The cold stone drank her tears, and the dank air of the slave cells prickled her skin.

The First towered in the doorway, looking down on his weeping servant. He had the studying eyes of a murderer, staring at his victim after the stroke but before death. "It's not as bad as that."

Braids shuddered, struggling to calm her voice. "Isn't it? Isn't it bad for a master to be made a slave?"

"Phage will be good to you. She won't harm you."

"She was my slave. You gave her to me. . . . Now you give me to her?"

The man's response had the slow certainty of a guillotine blade: "Yes."

Braids shook her head, rubbing her face on the stone. "What did I do? How did I displease you?"

"You didn't."

"I was your girl—"

"You still are—"

"No, I'm Phage's girl now. Why did you choose her instead of me?"

The First walked slowly into the cell, as if each step were a decision. He sat down on the edge of her bed and whispered, "I'll tell you something that no one in the world knows but me—and now you."

Braids quieted her sobs and even her breath. She sat back on her heels and clutched her hands together as if in prayer. The posture helped keep down her gorge. "Tell me."

"The god Kuberr chose me before birth. I was born a maculate child. He raised me up to serve him, and when time came to fullness, he called me to slay my family and inherit his blessing of power. Kuberr chose me, and he chose Phage as well."

Braids stared, uncomprehending.

"When you brought me the sister of Kamahl, I wished only to destroy her. I wrapped her in a killing embrace and poured on her all the hatred in me. I've killed giants with that hatred, but I couldn't kill Jeska. The hand of Kuberr lay upon her. He shunted that hatred into her soul and spared her flesh. He made her into Phage, for he has great plans for her. She was given as a slave to you to be trained, according to the will of Kuberr, and now, according to his will, you'll be her slave."

Braids was panting again, trying to understand it all. "Then you have not done this? This is not your choice?"

"I'm the servant of Kuberr. His choice is my choice."

"But your heart isn't with Phage. . . ."

He didn't reply, and the sudden silence was deafening. "I've learned to see in her what Kuberr sees. Don't weep, Daughter. She's the only woman—the only creature—in all the world whom I can touch. Of course my heart is with her." As if to demonstrate, he reached a hand toward her cheek to wipe away her tears.

Braids lunged away, trying in vain to reach her water bucket. Stones that had drunk tears now bore a worse flood.

The First stood, staring pitiably at her. "How can you love a creature that so repulses you? It's better this way. You'll be her slave, and you'll be away from me." Braids clutched the bucket and heaved nothing. Even the emptiness in her was desperate to pour forth. She felt a fool, crouching there and pining for a man whose presence sickened her, whose touch would kill her. Hearts know nothing of foolishness, though, only of desire.

"Don't fear for me, Daughter," he said to the weeping dementia summoner. *"I know Phage is my rival, my foe. Of course she'll try to kill me, as I killed my own family, but I'll kill her first."* The First turned and left.

He was the real fool. All the pieces lay there before him, and yet he couldn't see. Why would Kuberr create the First and Phage, who could touch only each other in all the world? He did it so they would touch each other, so they would come together and conceive. And why would an ancient and disembodied power wish his two avatars to conceive a child? So that Kuberr himself might be born of the union and walk Otaria again.

The First was the fool. He was in mortal peril and now immortal peril. This time, though, Braids would not tell him so. . . .

Akroma trembled, the memory bitter in her mouth. What horrors Braids had endured! She had calmed, and her sweat was cold now. Akroma said, "That memory had poisoned you deeply. The strain is gone from your face. It can hurt you no longer. I've taken the horror of it into me, and it doesn't hurt me. It helps me very much."

"Mother . . ." Braids said weakly, "I'm cold."

Akroma leaned toward the foot of the bed and drew up the heavy blankets folded there. "I'll take care of you. You've shown me your true foe and his deepest weakness. He'll never harm you again."

A smile that contained as much misery as joy spread across the woman's face. "Thank you, Mother."

* * * * *

Phage wore metal gloves and metal shoes as she rode up the great conveyor, careful not to touch the thick rope lest it rot to nothing. She would have been happy to climb the switchback path to the summit of Sanctum, but as the designer of this lift, she felt required to use it. Clinging to the cord that suspended a basket in which she stood, Phage gazed at the marvel she had created.

Two great wooden wheels ran the device, one anchored within the central square of Sanctum and the other poised atop the escarpment. Each was twenty feet in diameter and lay on its side. Across the grooved tread of each wheel ran a thick rope that had taken a month to weave from the hemp crop and another month to stretch. Stout spokes radiated at an angle above and below the treads, making sure the rope could not slip its groove and providing the winch operator with handholds. It took a strong centaur on each wheel to work the winch, and brawny assistants to lift stone counterweights into the empty baskets.

The construction seemed a great extravagance, but Phage had used only a small portion of the municipal coffers to pay for materials and labor. After all, if it were not for her, there would be no municipal coffers. She had promised the folk of Sanctum that the lift would pay for itself within a month. A small tax on every bet at the summit had already done the trick.

Yes, the whole point of the lift was to provide easy access to the stone ring, where Phage had established a local arena. The high, holy place was still high but not holy. Its rune-covered rocks rang with odds and bets, shouts of exultation and groans of agony. Dice here, cards there, knives for mumblety-peg, a circle for wrestling, a ring for pugilism—so far, the many games used for entertainment and conflict resolution had not yet progressed beyond a fist in the face, but true blood sports were only a few months away. Then there would be more regulations, more guards, laws and law enforcers. Soon Sanctum would sue the Cabal to allow their arena into the continental network.

The arena and lift had operated for a month and already rendered dividends. At full volume, the lift could bear fifty citizens per minute to the top—or the whole colony in half an hour. The arena itself could accommodate more than twice the fifteen hundred who called Sanctum home, and there was plenty of room on the dome of stone for more amusements. Every day, new folk came to Sanctum, drawn by freedom and fun. Enthralled, they became thralls of the Cabal.

Phage's basket swayed as she rode up the final few feet to the lip of the cliff. There, none other than General Stonebrow marched around the wheel, working it like a capstan. He had come to Sanctum suspecting her, but he couldn't resist her eyes. Stonebrow was so like Kamahl, and in all the wrong ways. Phage had convinced him that he must oversee the contraption, lest a weaker creature let hundreds of folk fall to their deaths. Grumbling still, Stonebrow conceded. His conversion was an impressive case study for the work Phage had done here.

She lifted her steel-booted foot, stepped out of the basket, and strode up the wooden platform. An ebullient shout came from ahead. Phage allowed herself a small smile as she climbed the ramp. The First would be pleased. Without a single soldier, she had captured the most strategic city in the coming war with Topos. Whoever held Sanctum held the escarpment, and whoever held the escarpment controlled the heart of Otaria.

When Phage topped the ramp, passing a shoulder of stone, she realized the shouts ahead were not joyful. She looked toward the summit. Perhaps eight hundred people stood among the stones, not one of them bent at gaming and all of them yelling at the creature in their midst.

Akroma.

No ghost of a smile remained on Phage's face. She broke into a full-out run.

Everyone knew Phage's corrupting touch, and the crowd parted to let her through. Still, they cheered their hometown girl.

"Here she is!"

"Phage'll put her in her place."

"Let's see who rules who."

Zagorka stepped from the crowd and strode alongside Phage. "She's threatening war. She says unless we surrender Sanctum to her, she'll bring an army to take it."

Gritting her teeth, Phage nodded. Akroma knew the value of this rock as well. "Thank you. I'll handle this."

As Zagorka backed away, both women realized that their roles had reversed. From this moment on, the colony belonged more to Phage than Zagorka. The arrival of a real foe had only sped up the Cabal's domination of Sanctum.

Akroma was a real foe. The angel's alabaster eyes stared soullessly down at Phage. Wings like those of a giant eagle arched menacingly to either side, while below, the jaguar body gathered to spring. In utter arrogance, the woman wore at her waist Soul Reaper, the axe forged to kill her. If Akroma dared approach close enough, Phage would take the axe in hand and put it to its purpose.

Phage strode within striking distance of the woman, set one foot just before the other, and crossed her arms over her chest. "Nice legs, Akroma. I'm trying to remember how you lost your real ones."

"Don't try to claim credit," hissed Akroma. "Your brother did this!"

"That's right, my brother . . . but I could undo it. Just try me. You'll be stumping around on a cat skeleton. You'll not get new ones, now that Ixidor is food for wurms."

The angel's eyes narrowed, and she seemed barely able to contain her fury. "Since when does this colony belong to the Cabal?"

Phage wanted to say, "since you landed" but instead replied, "I'm a citizen of Sanctum, as are all of us here. This is a free colony, and we free people can speak for Sanctum."

The crowd around gave her a great cheer.

"Besides, the Cabal is an ally to Sanctum. Any threat against this colony will be responded to by it and its allies."

As folk applauded, another voice boomed from the edge of the circle. "Krosan, too, is allied to Sanctum, and we will fight for her freedom." General Stonebrow nodded to Zagorka and said, "I came as soon as I heard."

Akroma stared first at the giant centaur then at Phage. "There have been no reports of these alliances—"

"This is a different sort of war, Akroma," Phage said flatly, "not one of swords but words. This is a war you can't win."

Akroma replied with cold certainty. "Don't presume to teach me about this quiet war. I've been waging it. Ixidor's disciples have gone throughout Otaria and spoken the truth in the minds of the people. Pilgrims have been flooding into Topos, believers armed and ready to fight. While you've gathered cards and dice, I've gathered an army." Her words ended in an eerie hush, as if the people of Sanctum could see the hordes of Topos ready to descend.

Phage spread her arms to indicate the fearful folk around her. "Here we are, Akroma. The people of Sanctum. Let's hear your ultimatum, and let's see who quakes."

The angel's lips drew into a razor line. "I've said it before but I'll repeat it in front of these . . . *allies*. Sanctum must declare itself a colony of Topos or face my armies."

The crowd burst into a storm of shouts. Phage stood unmoving and silent in their midst, waiting for the uproar to cease. Folk spent their anger and one by one hushed to hear what she had to say.

When at last all were silent, Phage said, "This is a society of free people. Over half the citizens of Sanctum are here today. A unanimous vote of this quorum will decide our actions. Those who favor subjecting the colony to the rule of Topos, say aye!"

The only sound that answered was the wan echo of her own voice among the stones.

"Those opposed, say nay!"

Every voice shouted in response, a vote that became a cheer.

Akroma listened without comment. When the sound died to nothing, she said simply, "So Sanctum has spoken, but you'll wish you'd been surer of your alliances before deciding."

Phage shook her head. "The Cabal stands with Sanctum. Go back to your dreamlands."

Stalking forward on jaguar legs, Akroma drew very near to Phage. The axe was almost in reach. One more inch, and this angel would be sent to heaven.

Akroma said, "I have two words that will change your mind." She whispered, "Virot Maglan."

Those two words—the true name of the First—had power on their own, but with them came also a swarm of blue disciples. They shot from Akroma's lips and dived into Phage's ears. The creatures plunged through her tympanic membranes, into the cochleas, through the auditory ganglia, and into the brain. They arrived like bombs, their concussions tearing apart her mind with thought-shrapnel.

Memories exploded, the horrible memories of Braids—

Braids felt a fool, crouching there and pining for Virot Maglan—a man whose presence sickened her and whose touch would kill her. Still, she knew what he did not: Virot and Phage were to conceive a child—Kuberr himself, born to walk Otaria in the flesh.

Virot lingered at the door to Braids's cell. He thought he knew what plagued her, but he knew only the half of it. "Don't fear for me, Daughter," he said to the weeping dementia summoner. "I know Phage is my rival, my foe. Of course she'll try to kill me, as I killed my own family, but I'll kill her first."

Reeling, Phage clutched her head. Her knees collapsed beneath her, and she fell before Akroma. She trembled, unable to believe what she suddenly knew, but certain it was true. . . .

She suddenly knew . . .

* * * * *

Akroma stepped back as her mortal enemy fell to her knees. The axe remained at her waist. She had never allowed herself to forget it, had been baiting Phage to grasp it. Now it was too late for Phage. "I did not touch her. I merely spoke two words, and this is, as she said, a war of words." She studied the trembling, helpless woman, but then spoke to Zagorka. "Your alliance with the Cabal is at an end. You may not know it yet, but soon you will."

Raising her eyes toward Stonebrow, Akroma continued, "You'll find that this centaur does not speak for Kamahl. Kamahl doesn't speak at all these days. . . . My disciples fly far afield.

"So, instead of a colony with two great empires behind it, you're but fifteen hundred hopeless souls in the way of an army. Sanctum has spoken, and so have I. Be ready for war."

With that, her great wings stroked the air, leveling those who stood nearest. She rose above the fangy monoliths and shot into the sky above Sanctum. Those who had tried to shout her down watched in silence as she soared above them.

* * * * *

What could Zagorka say? No aspect of mule-skinning could have prepared her for this. She watched in dumbfounded amazement as Akroma dwindled to a white dot. Phage struggled to her feet. In reflex, Zagorka reached out to her then drew her hand back.

Phage's eyes were wild, and they focused on no one. "I have to go. I have to return to the coliseum." She turned, staggering toward the switchback descent.

"Wait," Zagorka called. "What about the war? What about the Cabal standing with us?"

Phage did not respond, only straggling away.

"I think you have your answer," Stonebrow rumbled quietly. "We should never have believed her."

Zagorka turned to him. In a trembling whisper, she asked, "What about you? Should we have believed you? Does Krosan stand with us?"

The giant centaur flushed, and his teeth ground together. "It wasn't a lie, but a bluff. Krosan stands with no one. Kamahl has given up on us."

"Damn it," said Zagorka, shaking her head bitterly. "You're all the same. Pick a fight and leave me to fight it."

"No," Stonebrow said. "I left Krosan because I'm not like Kamahl—because I wanted to undo the wrongs he had done. I didn't know how to do that until today when I saw Kamahl's axe hanging on Akroma's belt. Now I know what to do. I'll go to Topos and take the axe and kill her."

Zagorka shook her head in disbelief. "Nobody can kill Akroma; nobody but a god."

Stonebrow said. "There are no gods, just us. We have to be our own gods."

CHAPTER 9

SHADOWS NEW AND OLD

Sash and Waistcoat, no longer lord and duke, sat in a hidden grove a league from the main road. They were not out of danger.

The living shadows had had quite a time evading the hounds. Sash had smelled strongly of old pie, and Waistcoat had had the wire-and-chestnut odor of a harpsichord. Remembering advice about evading hounds, Waistcoat had led them into a river. The water flooded into them both. By the time they made their way out the other side, the pie had been washed well away, but the harpsichord had hung half out of Waistcoat, waterlogged and out of tune. It had taken a good hour to drain the thing and wrestle it back through, especially since Waistcoat had insisted on plinking out the birthday tune.

At least the spell book seemed unharmed, though it smoldered ominously and smelled of fish. Later that afternoon, Sash got mired in a mud field and Waistcoat got him out by disgorging brackish water on him. Stick had been stuck and Puddle puddled.

It had been a watery and weary journey, two months dispossessed of body and country. The unmen would surely have been caught already if the hounds hadn't been marginally stupider than they. Only marginally. In two months, Sash and Waistcoat hadn't even escaped the lands of Governor Dereg. Hound patrols still combed the countryside.

Thus, they sat in a dark camp. Nothing is more miserable than a dark camp, even for those who have no bodies to warm and no eyes to fill. Light is life for living things, and it is even more so for shadows.

"C'mon, Sash. What could it hurt?"

"What could it *hurt? What* could it *hurt?* We might be captured, imprisoned, made magical slaves, forced to do abominable things . . ."

"Abdominal things is all we do—"

"Freely, though! We have done abominations in utter freedom. It's better to be miserable and craven by your own designs rather than due to the will of another."

"Really?"

"Of course."

Waistcoat knew he came from the fleshy side of Ixidor, that he was carnal desire without higher mind (at least that was how Sash constantly explained it). Still, the flesh can be crafty. "How 'bout we have a look at that magic book?" He reached into his chest and drew the thing out.

"At last a worthwhile suggestion," said Sash, reaching for the tome. It still smoked a bit, and heat peeled in ribbons from its cover. Sash sat down on a fallen tree, crossed his legs, propped the book on his outline, and opened it. "Oh, you monstrous man! You know I can't read without light!"

"How 'bout a fire?"

Heaving a sigh, Sash said, "What do you propose we light one with? Our insides are all wet and there's no flint for leagues."

"A fire spell! They put them up front in them books. Wizards need fire first off for smoking stuff and lighting brassieres—"

"Braziers! And I already told you, I can't read a spell without light! How can I read a fire spell when I need a fire spell to read one?"

"Wizards! You'd've thought they'd've thought of that and made the words of the fire spell glow in the dark! Morons. I bet they shower with the curtain on the outside."

"Wait! Look here! Letters glowing in the dark. It's a fire spell!"

"They ain't so stupid after all! They thought up what I did."

"Not a sign of much intelligence. All I need do is say these words over a pile of combustibles. Quick, Waistcoat, grab some combustibles."

"I'll just get some wood."

"Dolt," hissed Sash to himself. "First a fire spell, then a flesh spell . . ."

"Here's the wood," Waistcoat said, dumping a pile in the middle of the clearing.

"All right, good." Sash leaned forward on the log, the spell book on his lap. He ran the words once more through his head, extended his hand over the pile, and spoke the incantation. "*Kuel baebee nelsin onda belchen baebee onda sib, stobcol inme sib!*" The arcane incantation rolled out with a strange rhythm, ritualized words that wizards had used for years. Magic mounted in Sash's empty form. Red energy flared and discharged.

Waistcoat let out a shriek of glee.

Nothing happened. The jumbled pile of wood sat dark and silent.

"I don't understand," said Sash. "It says simply, 'Say these words over combustibles—' "

"Your arse is on fire!"

"What!" Sash shouted, leaping up.

It was not his arse, but the fallen tree where his arse had sat. The two unmen bounded away. The whole trunk, a hundred feet of it, had burst into flame.

"Nice," said Waistcoat.

"Powerful," said Sash. "With power like this, I'm sure I can devise a way to give us bodies."

"I want in," said a third voice.

The unmen whirled toward the sound. The fire cast their dim shadows on thick foliage, but a third shadow stood there.

Sash crossed his arms over his chest. "I had the feeling we were being followed."

"It don't look like a hound."

"I'm one of you—the third unman. I've been following you for months, watching what you're doing, learning. I had no wish to join your previous escapades, but now—yes, now, I want in."

Sash clutched the spell book protectively against his chest, accidentally pressing it through so that it disappeared and dropped to the floor within. "You want to join us, do you? You let us take all the risks in getting this spell book, in running from hounds—"

"In lighting our arses—"

"In lighting our—Oh, would you shut up, Puddle!"

"Waistcoat!"

"And now you want to join us? Why should we let you?"

The other unman moved from among the leaf shadows. "We want the same thing. We want to be real people, not shadows. We want to be like our creator, flesh and blood. Isn't that reason enough to work together?"

"Nope, it ain't," sneered Waistcoat. He turned toward Sash. "Right?"

"You mistake us, unman. Altruism is the highest form of humanity, and we're still struggling to gain the lowest form. You had your chance back in the bunker under the lake."

"I'll give you another reason," the unman said, stepping nearer, as if attempting to snare them. "Akroma sent me. She considers you traitors—theocides—and wants me to bring you back so that she can torture and destroy you. If you don't let me in, I'll tell her right where you are. She can leap through me and be on top of you two in minutes."

Sash and Waistcoat weren't sure what to say to that.

"That's the bad half. The good half is that I don't want to bring her to you or take you to her. I want what you want. We'll seek it together. Once we have real bodies, we'll need a place to go with them. I know of a place, a refuge from all this madness. It's called Sanctum—"

Waistcoat barked a laugh. "Yeah, right! There's a town named Scrotum."

"Sanctum, you idiot!" snapped Sash. He stared appraisingly at the third unman. "What is your name?"

"Umbra."

Nodding, Sash said, "I'm Sash, this is Puddle—"

"Waistcoat."

"I know."

"Do you know anything about magic, Umbra?" Sash asked.

"No," he replied, "but I know what hounds sound like. The fire drew them."

"I tried to tell him!" said Sash.

"*You* lit it!" replied Waistcoat.

"Let's go. You might want to give the spell book back to your partner, since he can set it on the harpsichord—off the floor and away from mud."

Sash stooped, feeling around within his feet, and grasping the tome. "Good thinking." He handing the spell book to Waistcoat, who stashed it, and both started out after Umbra. "Any ideas for escaping dogs?"

"Yes," Umbra replied. "Cats. There's a farm over the ridge, with a barn full of cats."

Sash said, "How will that help?"

"We each get ten or so in us, and when the dogs close in, we bring a few out. Which would a hound rather chase, cats or shadows?"

"Brilliant!" said Sash. "That's the sort of strategic planning we've lacked!"

"Don't praise me too much," Umbra said. "First, let's see how the plan works. Off to the barn for Operation Cat."

* * * * *

Zagorka stood near the crowded arena of Sanctum. It seemed the whole city was here, gorging itself on games like a condemned man eating his last meal.

It had been a month since Phage's departure, but if anything, Sanctum was a more raucous place. Despite Zagorka's attempts to raise a militia, she found only fifty volunteers. The other citizens acted as if resistence was futile. Akroma would come, and that would be it. Who could stand against her fanatical army on that terrible day? Why not live now so that death would come without regrets?

Zagorka had regrets. She wished she had stood up to Phage, had kept her from turning this refuge into a den of desperation. Zagorka should have confronted Akroma too. That would have worked better than false alliances that crumpled like paper.

A loser crushed his betting slip and let it drop free. It bore the indentations of his fingers as it fluttered in the afternoon breeze. A blizzard of such scraps filled the air and fell thick on the ancient stone circle.

"I know it's hard to concentrate on glyphs while a good dice game is going on, but I don't think you're even listening, Zagorka."

The old woman blinked. "Sorry, Elionoway. What did you say?"

Drawing a long pipe from his lips, Elionoway turned the bone stem to point over the heads of the throng. He indicated the monoliths all around them. "They fit together. These stones that encircle the holy place—they were once a single slab. The writing on them was done before they were cut apart. By reading each level across, we find the meaning of the whole. Some of the figures are severed or weathered mostly away, but I can make out much of it. It begins there, in the east, and follows the course of the sun. The southern stones mark its winter passage, and their shadows mark the summer passage."

"I don't follow," Zagorka said blearily.

"Follow this," Elionoway said, blowing a ring of smoke that encircled them both. "You know the first line: 'Return, numena, return, that what once was will forever be.' Here is the next line: 'Unto you we call, Great Conqueror Averru, that the wall you built will stand forever between your brothers.' And below it: 'Unto you we call, Lord of Streams Lowallyn, that your rivers will run forever to this valley.' And on the fourth line: "Unto you we call, Grasping Hand Kuberr, that you will hold all in safety forever.' "

"Forever and ever," Zagorka echoed. "What's it mean? What's it matter?"

"These are ancient prophecies, twenty millennia old. These names—I know these names. The myths of our people speak of three great sorcerers who ruled for a thousand years—three brothers who built the empires of old. They wrestled the world from the Primevals."

"The Primevals?"

"The dragon rulers before the age of humans."

Zagorka pursed her lips. She had much on her mind, not the least of which was the need to transform these gamblers into warriors. "Again, what's your point?"

The elf gave her a look that mixed condescension with envy. "Your race is so young." He pointed again with his pipe, just above the gamblers. "The fifth line, there, reads: 'When again the mortals worship in the high holy place and in the depths where the water goes, then the numena shall return.' "

"Spooky."

Elionoway laughed. "You have no concept how fortunate you are to have me."

"I get it, Elionoway. I just don't believe it. We're not bringing back these three dead brothers. Look around you. Who's worshiping? Not a one. They're screaming for jackpots, thanks to Phage. Do the farmers by the river worship? No, they plant—and bicker. We're all just trying to survive here and maybe have a little fun. We got real enough enemies to worry about."

Instead of answering, Elionoway merely crooked his finger, beckoning her to follow. The elf stepped lightly across the stony headlands, as if he were delighted with himself. His pipe sent out merry blue smoke that curved around him, seeming to tap his shoulder before wandering away.

Zagorka followed the man. Her head buzzed with dire warnings and the cries of bones shooters. It was a maddening din. Perhaps this was the worst part of leadership, deciding which voices to heed and which to ignore.

Elionoway reached the wooden walkway that led to the takeoff point for the great winch. In the absence of Stonebrow, a gigantipithicus ape had taken up duties there. He trudged in a steady circle while his associate, a doughty dwarf, hoisted stones into their cradles for counterweights. Elionoway lifted his hand, "No stones for the next two cradles."

The dwarf sniffed and nodded.

Elionoway waited for the next basket to swing into position. He stepped in and held onto the rope.

Behind him, Zagorka boarded the lift somewhat less gracefully. Her shadow dropped away from her across the red stone, and the cliff vanished. Below opened a panorama that never failed to take her breath away—ancient Sanctum now a thriving city. Smoke wended up from the stacks of stone buildings, farmers worked the bountiful fields beside the river, and a steady stream of carts crossed at the ford. This is what she worked to protect.

"Don't look down, Zagorka," called Elionoway. "Look back!"

She did and saw the brow of the cliff, covered with deep-cut runes. "So, what do those runes say?"

"I don't know. They weren't there yesterday."

Zagorka's blood turned cold. "Are you sure?"

"I'm positive. I've begun to catalog the runes, and those have never been there before."

The old woman felt weak. "All right, Elionoway. You keep right on cataloging and translating. It's your official work now." She gazed at those jagged, warlike characters. "I want to know where they're coming from. I want to know what they mean."

CAPTIVATION

Phage had gone alone to Sanctum, and she returned alone—but her mind was crowded. The disciples of Ixidor had filled her head with terrible things. Her own thoughts battled those of Akroma, Braids, and the First. Their colors clashed, combined, and aligned in new conjunctions. Phage stared at the collage of them, and the truth was inescapable.

She and the First were equals, chosen by Kuberr to be his avatars. Nevermore would Phage be a slave to him, nor his daughter, nor his creation. She was no longer his. That much was liberating.

The enslavement came next: Phage was destined to conceive a body for Kuberr to inhabit. The First didn't realize this, though he was to be the father. Braids only guessed at it, but to Phage it seemed a certainty. She was willing, for Kuberr had saved her. She would let him be conceived within her and would bear him, yes, would raise him and all the while wear steel gloves. Perhaps someone could devise a metal mechanism by which she might even nurse her suckling god.

The third revelation was the worst: a death pact. Kuberr had demanded that Virot Maglan sacrifice his family. What if Kuberr asked Phage to sacrifice her lover? Was she a black widow and Virot her consort, wishing union but fearing to be eaten? Whether or not Phage would kill him, he would kill her.

From liberation to slavery to destruction . . .

As a child in the Pardic Mountains, Jeska had once seen a wildflower and thought it was like truth—rising from rocky ground and opening in beauty. Now she knew that truth was a pack of wild dogs, voracious and relentless. Truth harried Phage all down the escarpment, across the swampland bridges, and onto Coliseum Island.

The First knew she was coming. Eager guards bowed before her and threw rose petals in her path. Blossoms that touched her turned black and dissolved in ash, but still it was a beautiful gesture. The First thought he was seducing her. In truth, Kuberr was drawing together his two darkling souls.

Phage crossed Coliseum Island with its clutter of tents and stalls, hawkers and odds men, fans and gladiators. All were amalgamated into a smooth wrapping on the present she was meant to open. She walked untouched in the shoving throng, climbed past tote-boards pale with chalk where lives were marked and rubbed out, walked amid banners proclaiming which noble houses were "in court" watching the blood sports, and came to the rear entrance of the First's luxury box.

A young boy waited there, a child Phage had never seen. He was pallid, his bones as fragile as a bird's beneath tufts of black hair. His suit was impeccably tailored, though, and he greeted her with a smile that showed no teeth. "Hello, my darling," the child said, and extended to her a rose.

"Who are you?" Phage asked.

"I am Virot Maglan, when a boy," he replied. The lines sounded rehearsed. "I wanted to gaze on my beloved with boy's eyes." He extended to her a single red rose, its blossom profuse and its thorns gleaming.

Phage eyed the thing. "I cannot take it. It would be destroyed."

"My love for you will endure," the boy replied, handing the bloom to her with such confidence that she took it.

The flower did not wilt. It was steel, painted with nonorganic pigments to seem a living rose.

Yes, his love endures, thought Phage, but its thorns are nails and its petals are blades. Aloud she said, "Thank you, Virot."

He bowed his head gently and gestured toward the obsidian doors. "My older self waits within. He has remade his suite in your image." His hand did not even touch the doors, but they swung open.

"Thank you, my young love. You were very handsome as a child." But the poison already ran in your veins. Phage walked between the doors of black glass and into the dark receiving room beyond.

Virot *had* been busy. The room had always had an ominous aspect, with floors and walls of polished black marble and a ceiling painted so dark that its seemed the night sky. Only floating bulbs, like planets in their wandering paths, gave light to the space, but now the room was even more spare. Gone were the tapestries and rugs, the clustered furnishings, the mirrors. In all that skiagraphic space, only one item remained—a statuette in white stone, set in the middle of the floor.

Phage approached, staring down at the figurine—a female gladiator exulting above a fallen foe. Phage stooped to lift the statuette. The gladiator was she. The sculptor had captured her every muscle and contour, only just hidden beneath the silken bodysuit she wore, and had rendered her foe in the grips of instantaneous rot. Phage studied the object a moment more before setting it down again in the center of the floor.

She walked on, her steel soles clanking on the marble. Annoyed, Phage flipped them off her feet. She was more deadly that way, and silent.

A curtain hung in the next doorway, and when Phage touched the cloth to draw it aside, it dissolved. Rot swept like fire through the fabric until it was gone. Phage stepped into the next chamber.

It too had been prepared for her. The floor and walls were done in gneiss of deepest indigo. This chamber was half the size of the last, and at its center stood a hip-high statue in white marble. Phage stooped to examine every detail. Again, the figure depicted Phage, standing in victory over another foe. This time her clothes were tattered and hung revealingly from her muscular form. With hands on her hips, she cast her eyes sternly downward on the vanquished. A man lay prostrate before her as if in worship, and Phage knew immediately who this was.

"Brother."

She stood, gazing past the figure toward the next door. It too was hung with a curtain. She strode to it and pulled it back, not even waiting for it to rot away.

The next chamber, smallest of all, had floor, walls, and ceiling of red granite. The veins ran so fat through the stone that they seemed the vessels around a great heart. The room was absolutely dominated by a life-sized statue, again in white marble, again depicting Phage. This time, though, she was resplendently nude. How the sculptor could have known the shape of the rib there above her waist, how he could have discovered the beauty mark just below her hip, or learned how her thigh muscles folded into her pelvis . . . He had rendered her perfectly, with the attention of a worshipful eye. She stood in the attitude of domination, victor over a foe laid low. Phage, though, had never fought a battle naked.

She looked down one sculpted leg to see the man who lay there, prostrate before her. He was nude as well, his flesh apparently rendered in ivory. Slender at the waist but strong at the shoulder, with every muscle standing in relief across his figure, the man lay in utter subjugation. Though his flesh bore many scars, not a single one rotted.

Quietly, to herself, Phage said, "How have I laid him low, then?"

"A wound to the heart," said the man.

Phage startled. He was not a sculpture but a living man. "Who are you?"

"You wound me again," replied the man, lifting his head. "I am your lover. I am Virot."

"What are you doing?"

"I have wanted you from the moment I first saw you. I have tried everything to win you to me. Now, I will try even this, to lie naked and shaved, a newborn creature in worship."

This was the First, the most powerful man in Otaria—Phage's onetime master, Father, owner. He now lay in submission before her. All the arguments that had crowded her along the path had fallen to silence.

"I will do whatever you command," Virot said.

"Stand up," Phage replied levelly.

Virot stood, not the ruler of the Cabal but only a man.

Phage was no longer the slayer of thousands but only a woman.

They were two bodies sharing a common spirit, and soon sharing all.

Phage drew off her silken clothing and let it fall on the heart-red floor. She stepped to him and wrapped him in her arms, and the touch of flesh to flesh was excruciating ecstasy.

* * * * *

General Stonebrow crouched in the last scrubby cover at the verge of the Nightmare Lands. The place brought back horrible memories.

Here, he had fought among tens of thousands, had watched the massacre that followed, had fled the dead and dying while death-wurms ate them all. This was a place of shame. Stonebrow had never run from battle before and certainly not from fallen comrades, but that day, he had done both. In the rout, he had even left behind the single weapon that could slay their greatest foe—the axe of Kamahl.

All these wrongs would soon be righted. Stonebrow would recover Soul Reaper and slay Akroma. That one stroke would avenge the armies of the coalition and destroy the warlike empire she had built.

Stonebrow stared out at the Nightmare Lands and wished for battle.

Unfortunately, this was not battle but stealth, and the giant centaur was ill-equipped for stealth. He had spent a careful month secretly advancing on Topos. Day and night, blue-white disciples streamed overhead, and new converts in pilgrim bands streamed back below. By the sheer number of tracks, Stonebrow guessed that Akroma had gained a whole legion. By the way those tracks disregarded trails and headed straight for Topos, he guessed it was a legion of fanatics.

Akroma had not been lying about her army. It was large and devoted.

Hoping to infiltrate the force and get near enough to snatch the axe, Stonebrow had even tried to join a band of pilgrims. They sat around a campfire, and he happened in as if on the same quest. Very quickly, though, they found him out. He knew nothing of the Vision of Ixidor, of preserving the Glorious City, of battling the corrupted mob. Stonebrow was not simply an infidel but an infidel spy. They attacked him, and in defending himself, Stonebrow slew one of them. Unwilling to kill more, he bolted from those fanatics and galloped for a day before circling back.

Surely, they had reported him to Akroma. Even if she didn't know where Stonebrow was, she knew he was coming. The moment he ventured from the verge of the scrub forest and out onto the Nightmare Lands, he would be seen. There was no cover here, only thousands of stone circles that plugged the sucking pits.

He needn't survive his quest—just as long as Akroma didn't survive it either.

Stonebrow stepped from the thicket where he had hid and marched across a weedy transition zone. Just ahead, true ground gave way to false. There, the sands of the desert had transformed under the touch of Ixidor's insanity. The ground looked like gray leather. Stonebrow set one hoof on it, and the memories of that awful day flooded into him. He had not intended to break into a canter, let alone a gallop, but he did. It was fine, for it would bear him farther in before they stopped him, would raise greater alarm and therefore bring Akroma all the more quickly.

Charging, Stonebrow swerved to avoid the great stone stoppers. Soon they were too thick around him. He bounded onto one, feeling the stone tremble with his weight. Leaping off, he dashed along a narrow lane of ground.

Ahead, putty people rose. They formed a long line with their hands linked, as if they hoped to catch him.

Snorting, Stonebrow barreled toward them. They would splatter like mud when he hit. Hooves cut crescent wounds in the world, and Stonebrow smashed into the gray crowd.

Dull and dumb, the claylike warriors went to pieces and fell. They didn't slow Stonebrow a whit, and he trampled them. He pounded on, his teeth clenched tightly. Hoofbeats resounded among the stones, growing louder with each second. This was no echo, but the sound of a pursuit. Stonebrow looked back and saw a dozen more giant centaurs charging after him. They had his own face, his own body.

Putty people fought by taking on the likeness and power of their foes, mimics deadly in their mimicry.

Stonebrow glanced ahead and saw his chance—a large stone circle sunk deep in a wide pit. His pursuers were but a length behind him when he leaped for that stone. He brought all four hooves down together like a great cat pouncing on prey and felt the plug sink. Bounding away, he shoved the stone deeper.

The first of the pursuers landed, driving the plug on through. A terrible roar followed, and torrential winds. The false centaurs bolted into the sucking mouth of that pit and were gone forever.

Grinning a battle grin, Stonebrow galloped past the last stone circle and into the Greenglades Forest beyond. He had had no hope of getting this far and began to wonder if he might reach the palace itself.

A scabrous thing lunged out from behind one of the great trees. Crablike pinchers clawed Stonebrow, cutting a shallow line down his pelt. The giant centaur escaped by sheer speed. Two more crab men lunged at him, one seizing his mane and the other his wrist. They clung on, dragged by his momentum. A third dropped from a tree limb on his back.

Swinging his elbow, Stonebrow cracked the mouthparts of one crab man and hurled the beast off his wrist. He reached over his shoulder to grab the creature on his back, all the while bulling through underbrush. His hand was knocked away, though, by a fourth and a fifth assailant. Already, they equaled his weight, and when more clambered down vines like army ants swarming a kill, Stonebrow went to his elbows.

"Summon . . . your . . . mistress!" he shouted, panting beneath the horrible weight. It seemed they would suffocate him. "I demand . . . to see . . . Akroma!" All this would be for naught if these creatures tore him apart before Akroma arrived. "I bear news . . . for Akroma . . . dire news!" It wasn't working. These beasts were too stupid.

Stonebrow's legs weren't working either. The pile crushed him to his belly. It swayed atop him and shuddered with each new body added.

"Summon . . . Akroma!"

Already, no one could hear but he.

* * * * *

She lay there beside him, their bodies drinking in the coolness of the floor. After so blazing a union, the smooth marble was a comfort.

Virot had been astonishing, passionate, seductive, and tender. Phage had been the same. It was as if together, they made up for the ragged emptiness in each one separately. Now, they were separate. They could little have endured more contact, flesh to flesh.

Phage was changed. She was no longer ragged and empty. Something germinated in her. Already she could feel it—the distillation of her power and Virot's power in a single cell. It would grow in her, be born from her, and become the greatest creature to walk Otaria. Fondly, Phage put her hand on her belly, and she turned her head toward Virot.

He seemed not filled but emptied, spent. His job was done. So it was for any male in procreation, and Phage understood why the black widow ate her mate. Otherwise, that empty shell would simply go to waste.

"What are you looking at, my love?" he asked groggily.

She answered with a single word. "You."

* * * * *

Stonebrow had known the moment Akroma arrived because the chitinous pile shifted off of him. He breathed more easily as the load lightened and decided to look wounded so that he could draw her in. It would take just one quick glance and a quicker lunge to get that axe. The pile was nearly gone. A moment, and he would be ready.

"I know why you've come," Akroma said flatly. "You want this."

Stonebrow cracked his eye, seeing that she patted the head of Soul Reaper. Its handle glimmered with blue motes of power.

Gingerly, the angel lifted the axe from the band that held it to her. She extended it, handle first, toward the giant centaur. "Take it, then. Do with it what you came to do."

It seemed a dream. Still, Stonebrow had to try. Though he yet lay on his belly, one hand was free, and with it, he could kill this tormenting tyrant. His hand lashed out, fastened on the glowing hilt of the axe, and swung it to slay Akroma.

Stonebrow's arm froze. Something had entered his hand. It jagged up the nerves of his arm, into his shoulder, up his neck, and gushed through his brain like blue fire. From there, it rushed through his whole being.

"Let him up," Akroma commanded. The last crab man climbed off.

Stonebrow, aching from his wounds but energized by the blue spirits, stood. There was something he had wished to do with this axe . . .

"Move aside. Let him approach."

The crab men scuttled out of the way, waiting near the great trees of the forest.

Nothing lay between Stonebrow and Akroma. He strode up to stand before her.

"What are you going to do?"

Stonebrow lifted the axe, studied its scintillating head, and extended it toward Akroma, handle first. "Return it to you, my lady."

"I thought so," she said. She took the weapon and slipped it into her belt. "Do you know the Vision of Ixidor?"

"A world recreated in beauty, with ugliness purged forever."

"Yes. Do you wish to preserve the Glorious City?"

"Locus must be defended at all cost."

"Who are the corrupted mob?"

"The Cabal, the rabble of Sanctum, and the monsters of Krosan— these and all who threaten the creator's world."

"Very good. Come with me."

THE CAT'S IN THE BAG

*U*mbra's cat trick worked, throwing off the hounds that first night. For the next month, though, the problem was throwing off the cats.

As it turned out, cats liked unmen: living shadows on the wind, there and not there, tantalizing! A cat that leaped at those lines, which curved and flitted through the air, suddenly found itself in a secret room of a secret palace. What delights! Like fleas to mongrels, cats had converged on the unmen.

Umbra was host to two families of tabbies. Sash was full of half a dozen black short-hairs. Waistcoat, by virtue of the fact that his soggy bread had attracted the mice of Topos, had become a cat hostel, with nearly thirty of every color and configuration.

Cats played ceaselessly around their shadowy feet, appearing and disappearing on the dusty roads where they walked. Felines occasionally left to hunt nearby fields and returned bearing hares, stoats, mice, rats, and the occasional skunk—some still kicking. The unmen began a frantic high-step to keep the hunters from hauling their prey inside. Inevitably the cats succeeded. The whole pride within would play with the poor creature until it died then battle each other over the carcass. The host unman thus spent hours emitting screeches, howls, hisses, and purrs.

Still, these noises were preferable to the nighttime operas that yowled from one unman to the others, accompanied by the leaping of avid forms. Already most of the females were pregnant, and in another month the cat infestation could well blossom into a pandemic.

"So go the traumas of life . . . for unmen," Sash said eloquently.

The three walked wearily up a stone bridge that led to a little town on the plains. There was no way around the burgh except by fording the river, a practice they had rejected after having drowned three cats doing so. The stench of their decay had lasted for two weeks. No, the unmen had to go straight through town, but with luck, they would get beyond earshot before the sun set and the opera began.

Sash extrapolated: "Isn't it insult enough to spend one's life as a mere disturbance of air, a strange sound, an odd odor—?"

"Sounds like you're a living fart," Waistcoat said.

"That's what we are," Umbra said bitterly. "Bad air. Spirits without bodies."

"Oh, we've got bodies, all right, and in plenty—cat bodies. Just shake a leg and out falls a bagful," Sash complained. As if to demonstrate, he kicked. A black cat whirled through the air, flipped over once, tried to get its feet beneath it, and dropped back into the uplifted leg.

The three unmen strolled on in quiet frustration.

To either side, small shops loomed over the road. The setting sun reached its golden fingers between them, enticing the travelers westward, though it would then leave them benighted outside the village. It would be another dark camp, another night of cat song and feline fornication.

Umbra growled. "I've reconsidered my plan."

"About the cats, you mean?" Waistcoat blustered. "It's a damn sight late!"

"No, I mean about how we get our bodies. We'll never learn enough magic from this book to make bodies for ourselves. A soulshift is a powerful spell. We need a powerful advocate."

Sash and Waistcoat shook their heads, and Sash said, "Just whom do you propose?"

"Well, I've been thinking: If you turned yourselves in to Akroma—"

"Ah, ha! Just as we thought!" Sash cried.

"All this time, you say we're heading to Scrotum—"

"Sanctum."

"—but really you're taking us to Topos! You're still working for that old witch."

"Quiet!" Umbra glanced around irritably. Anyone could have overheard their bickering. "We'll be discovered!"

"Are you? Are you working for Akroma?"

"Of course not! I'm one of you. I can't believe you would suspect me, after all we've been through!"

"All *we've*—! All *we've*—!" Waistcoat roared.

"Hush!"

"What have you done," Sash asked, "except guide us toward trouble?"

"Look, I think if we go to Akroma and apologize and say we've learned our lesson, she'll forgive us. Then she can give us bodies."

Sash laughed brashly. "Yeah. She'll welcome *you* home, good and faithful servant, and thanks for rounding up those traitors. *You'll* get a body, and we'll get obliterated."

"That's not what I want!"

"Hey, how about we go right away to Topos?" Sash said sarcastically.

"Yeah!" Waistcoat sneered and added, "What?"

"I know a short cut, right here, though this fellow!" Sash leaped for Umbra's outline.

The shadow man skipped away, two tabbies tumbling out of his toes. "Hey! Look out! That's murder! You know I'd close forever!"

"Hey, yeah!" Waistcoat said, catching on. "A short cut!" He too leaped for the shadow man. A great lump of sleeping cats dropped out of him and landed atop the others spilled by Umbra. All the cats assumed they were under attack and lashed out with wicked claws and hisses.

"Murder, he says!" Sash laughed. "And what would it be to turn us over to Akroma? Justice?" He swung a roundhouse, trying to hurl his fist through his comrade.

Umbra leaped to avoid the blow, but one of his feet accidentally scooped up a biting ball of cats. The beasts rolled into him, encountered the tabby toms that had already marked every corner of the unman, and started an all-out war.

Fate intervened in the person of the village lawman, who happened to be an ogre.

"What in blazes!" the beast slurred, exploding from a pair of double-doors that were scarred from such abrupt appearances. It plodded out onto the dusty street, its nail-studded club over one shoulder and its remaining eye bulging with suspicion. It took a deep whiff, air filling its shirtless chest, and stepped out into the road. "Lil? Is that you?" When no answer came, it muttered, "First I hear what sounds like a cathouse afire, then I smell me something like a lion in heat." It took another sniff. "Lil?"

The unmen had devised a strategy for times such as these—lying down and blending with the shadows. Luckily, there were plenty of shadows in the trammeled road at sundown. Unluckily, there were plenty of cats to crawl out and give them away.

"Meow," quipped the first, a spotted kitten that stretched luxuriously before adding, "meow."

The ogre squinted at this creature in the dust, awash in man-shaped shadows where no men were. Something seemed queer about that cat. The ogre scratched its trousers, which seemed a great gunny sack held up by a spiky belt. It blinked twice, looked around, and whispered, "Lil?"

The kitten replied, "Hiss, hiss, spit, yowl, spit!" not to the ogre, but to the pile of other cats that suddenly emerged beneath it.

"Poor kitty," the ogre cooed, "givin' birth right here in the dirt, and to all them grown-up cats. Reminds me of me own mum." It reached down to pick up the young thing. Only an ogre or a dog-lover would reach into a cat fight. This creature was both.

"Hiss, spit, spit YEOWWWL!" the kitten explained. To demonstrate, it tore open every vein in the ogre's arm. The other cats helped.

The ogre tried to curse, managed only "Ig ig ig ig ig!" and hurled away the furry furies.

They flew across the street, tails calmly whirling as they brought their legs beneath them. More cats boiled up from the shadows.

Fearful it would lose a leg, the ogre brought its club down. The cats scattered. The club struck empty ground, encountered no resistance, ripped right out of the ogre's hand, and vanished as if down a hole. It goggled after its missing club and said, "Well, now."

The law keeper reached to its spiky belt, yanking the thing off in one quick gesture. The belt was attached to the monster's pants, which pulled away as well. The strange fabric unfurled, proving itself to be a voluminous gunny sack. It could easily snag all the unmen.

"Beware the pants!" Sash wailed.

He, Umbra, and Waistcoat might have thought to flee, but a pantsless ogre is an arresting sight. Next thing they knew, those pants swept out overhead and descended on them. The wooden stakes rammed into the ground in a wide circle around the unmen. Clearly, these were magic trousers. They closed with the surety of a fist.

"A dementia trap!" Sash said.

Umbra snorted. "A little late, professor."

"We can't escape a demented trap!" Waistcoat said. He was right. The unmen could have escaped any other enclosure, sliding through a seam or under a door, but not a dementia trap. "How're we gonna get outta this one, Mr. Smarty?"

"Shut up," advised Sash.

"Meow," added something inside him.

Umbra whispered, "Waistcoat, pull out the spell book and give it to Sash. There has to be a spell in there that we can use."

Even as Waistcoat rummaged through himself, a disembodied ogre voice came through the bag, asking, "Lil?"

* * * * *

"How're we gonna get out of this one, Mr. Smarty?" asked Zagorka, standing on her balcony in Sanctum.

Elionoway stood beside her, his elf frame as narrow and rigid as an old stump. Bluish smoke rolled from the pipe clenched in his teeth. "Don't know."

They stared above the red rooftops of the city, out across the Deepwash River, to the rocky hills beyond. There, Akroma's army encamped—three thousand troops. They outnumbered the citizens two to one, these brainwashed automata. Akroma had taken her most fanatical followers and fashioned them into warriors and priests. They had come to lay siege to Sanctum.

Zagorka loosed a long whistle of irritation. "Fortify, I said. A wall, a ditch, I said. Make weapons—arrows, spears . . . Even a pile of rocks'd be nice just about now. Nope. Instead, we read ancient scribbles on stone, we gamble like there's no tomorrow. Well, I guess we hit the jackpot! There *is* no tomorrow!"

Elionoway seemed to consider, smoke dragging from his nose like a silver mustache. "I think you just hit the jackpot."

"What're you talking 'bout?" demanded the old woman, rounding on him. At last, she had had enough. "Death's the jackpot?"

The elf smiled inexplicably. "There's a bit of poetry for another day. No. I mean you can't out-wall, out-ditch, out-arm, out-fight a crew like that. If they draw you into a conventional war, you've lost already."

Zagorka sighed heavily. "What choice've we got?"

"Have you learned nothing from Phage? She conquered this place with a pair of dice."

"Conquered paradise with a pair of dice."

Elionoway tapped the pipe on the rail. "You're full of poetry today. Don't spend it all on me. You have another admirer." He pointed to the pathway above the ford, where a blue-robed priest strode at the head of a heavily armed contingent. "You want backup?"

"Ah!" Zagorka bellowed. "In peacetime it's, 'yeah, yeah, Zagorka, whatever.' When there's a spear point to talk to, everybody's backing *me* up. Course, I want backup. My sage, a couple dozen giant centaurs, and my doughty ass."

"A sage, now, am I?"

"No, Chester's the sage."

The elf only smiled the more as he followed Zagorka through her apartments, down the stairs, and out onto the street. There, Chester and a fearful crowd waited. The mule knelt, letting his mistress climb on. For his part, Elionoway chose to walk. The procession picked up muscle along the way—Bret, Jaimes, gigantipithicus apes, ogres, and giant centaurs—all of whom had been spoiling for a real fight.

Today, they might have one.

Zagorka rode Chester down the switchback high street of Sanctum, out along the abundant fields of the river lowlands, and toward the arched gate beside the ford. She had meant to affect a martial air, but not with this motley parade around her. They laughed—sang!—as if she were their deliverer. She felt more like a sacrifice.

Chester clottered to a stop in the literal shadow of the arch. He snorted and pawed the ground. The rest of the Sanctum contingent came to a halt around him. Their cheerful songs quieted and died altogether in the face of the approaching contingent.

At the head rode a slender albino garbed in white robes and riding a pale horse. His head had been shaved bald, and between his pink eyes rested a blue spark like a third eye. A priest. In attenuated hands, he bore a thin sword that twinkled with magic. All around the priest of Ixidor were warriors. Some were thick-carapaced crab men. Others were humans or elves, armed and armored. All looked deadly serious. The contingent descended the sloping trail and without hesitation entered the ford. Plumes of foam shot up prettily before the horse's hooves.

Zagorka felt like surrendering.

"Draw him in to your battle," advised Elionoway beside her.

The albino reined up before her. His skin was so pellucid that every blue vein stood out, seeming a tree tattoo across his face. His pink irises looked like puckered gouges. Aback his icy steed, he sat and studied Zagorka, showing neither disdain nor compassion. "It has been given to me, Aioue, to deliver to you an ultimatum: Surrender Sanctum to the rule of Topos or suffer siege."

Blinking, Zagorka shook her head. "I don't get it."

The priest at first could devise no response. The blue disciple twinkled brightly on his pallid brow. "It has been given to me, Aioue, to deliver—"

"We don't get it. Ultimatums, I mean. You can't give us an ultimatum if we don't get ultimatums. You'd might as well preach to ants."

Beside her, Elionoway stifled a smile by puffing on a newly lit pipe.

"What . . . *do* you . . . get?"

"Bets."

"Bets?"

Zagorka nodded. "Games of chance. Cards. Dice. That's what we get."

Anger kindled in those pink eyes, cinching like sphincters in his face. "An ultimatum cannot take the form of a wager."

"Anything can," Zagorka said glibly. "How about this? We roll dice, you and I. If your score is high, you take the city. If mine is high, you go away. If they are even, you stay and lay siege—on one condition."

"What condition?"

"That you send your army, one platoon at a time, for R&R in the city. Course, they gotta swear to make no war." She pulled a pair of dice from her pocket and rolled them enticingly in one hand. The human soldiers behind the priest looked eagerly at them.

"These terms are unacceptable," Aioue said. "There is no percent chance that we will go away."

Zagorka's lips pursed. "Sure. Let's get these odds even. You roll high, and you take the city without a fight. We both roll the same, and you lay siege, like you planned. I roll high, and you lay siege, but give your troops R&R." She glanced toward the hungry eyes of the soldiers. "What've you to lose?"

Under his breath, Elionoway said, "Your principles, your will, your sanity."

After conferring with the disciple on his brow, Aioue said, "This is my ultimatum made into a wager. I will do it."

"Here," Zagorka said, tossing one of the dice to the pale priest. "Twenty sides, no weights. Check it over."

He did.

Zagorka said, "Roll 'em if you got 'em."

Aioue lifted the die to the blue spot in his forehead. He brought his hands together, shook the die, and tossed it toward the rocky ground. It bounced amid stones, shimmering a dull blue, and came to rest with a nineteen uppermost. The crowd pressed to see the number but apparently missed the darting blue spark that leaped up to return to Aioue's brow. He said placidly, "Roll higher than a nineteen."

Quietly, Elionoway murmured, "He cheated."

"I know," she whispered through her smile. "Clears my conscience."

She rolled. Her die leaped among the stones and rolled to a stop, the number twenty on top.

A great cheer rose from the people of Sanctum, and the soldiers with Aioue seemed at least amused.

Aioue stared at Zagorka. "This changes nothing. You'll still fall to us. The platoons will begin their day trips tomorrow, swearing nonaggression, but while they are outside the city, they will continue the siege. One way or another, our people will soon swarm your colony."

"I don't doubt it." Zagorka bowed to Aioue. "On behalf of me and my people, welcome to Sanctum."

Aioue made no reply, but his white horse snorted as he turned it about. Through the tossing waves they went, back across the river ford, with the contingent of warriors around him.

Zagorka and Elionoway stood waving like a pair of friendly farmers. The elf muttered, "I didn't know you knew magic."

"It's not magic."

"But the disciple rolled for him and got only a nineteen."

"That's 'cause his die only went to nineteen."

"You said it had twenty sides."

"Twenty sides, but nineteen numbers. There're two sixes. As to my die, well, it's got twenty sides but just one number."

"Twenty."

"Exactly."

Elionoway puffed philosophically on his pipe. "You're a clever leader, Zagorka. With a pair of dice, you've forestalled an invasion, but there's another."

The old woman visibly slumped. "Another? What now?"

In answer, Elionoway merely pivoted, his arm indicating the cliff face.

It was covered with new, deep glyphs. The words seemed visibly to shift and multiply. Growling, Zagorka ducked her head and walked toward Chester. "Looks like we're in for a war of words."

Following, Elionoway could only smile.

CHAPTER 12

ASSASSINS

The time had come. Virot had gotten what he wanted out of his black widow, and now he would kill her before she killed him. Today, Phage would die.

The First strode purposefully from his quarters into the public halls of the coliseum. Though fans crowded the way, he did not slow or pause. Folk instinctively parted before him, pressing against the walls. The innermost row recoiled against the next, and they against the next, so that it seemed everyone in the corridor wilted, slain by his mere presence.

He would not slay them today. Only Phage.

For two months, they had been together, he and she. Their passion grew hotter every day. Soon it would burn straight through to Phage's heart, and she would turn on him. It was inevitable, unless he struck first.

"My sweet. My darling," the First said through gritted teeth. Behind his back, within the long black folds of his cloak, he clutched a dagger. Its pommel was wrapped in leather from his mother. The hand guard bore bone inlays from his siblings. The First himself had forged the serpentine blade, as black as night, by annealing steel and magic. It never dulled and never rusted as long as it fed on souls.

When he struck Phage, she would die, and her soul would be

within the weapon forever. He would never have to let her go. She would join the rest of his family.

The First descended a wide stair, only then glimpsing the yellow cloaks of the hand servants that followed. They had come dutifully, their own arms twisted behind their backs and their own sleeves concealing blades. Their daggers could not capture Phage's soul and so would not strike her unless the First were imperiled.

The steady beat of the First's boots was belied by the thready beat of his heart. He had killed tens of thousands before. This single slip of a girl should have been no different, but she was. He loved her. Love and power were irreconcilable. He who loved most had the least power, and he who loved least had the most. Until now, the First had had all power, but Phage made him powerless.

That was why she must die—and why he could barely imagine slaying her.

The First didn't have to imagine. He had simply to bring this dagger down into her heart. It was merely a matter of muscles—his triceps contracting and her cardium splitting. Then their love would be gone, and the First would rule again.

His reverie broke, and he found himself standing outside of Phage's quarters. Unlike his chambers, high and lifted up, Phage's rooms lay in the bowels of the coliseum. Deep and windowless, the chambers were done up in silk and iron—things that would not rot. The appointments were fine, yes, but the place still felt and smelt like a slave pen—dark, mildewy, and cold.

"Why do I wait?" the First asked himself. Quietly, he prayed to his master: "Lord Kuberr, protect your servant."

The First lifted his hand, and the obsidian door swung soundlessly inward. It was magically locked to all but Phage, but no door in the coliseum was locked to the First. He stepped across the threshold. His hand servants followed in a golden flock. Despite the sepulchral darkness of the antechamber, the First moved with confidence. He had been through this space countless times.

The air was different today—warm and scented with jasmine. She was in the bath.

All the better.

The First walked stealthily through the next chamber, down the hall, and to the arch where the fragrant steam rose. He tightened his hold on the dagger and gazed through the mist.

Phage indeed lay in her bath—a deep, wide basin carved from black marble. It was full to her neck, the surface of the water thick with steam. She might have been asleep, lying so still—or perhaps dead.

The First fantasized it was so, and his heart leaped from both relief and fear. He stepped beneath the arch and approached the side of the tub. She did not stir. It would be so simple. Do it swiftly. The hand that held the dagger shifted from his back to his side. He drew a deep breath of that lovely air and prepared the simple muscular contraction that would return him to power.

She shifted, raising her chin and opening her eyes. Though her gaze immediately fell on him, standing there, she did not startle. Not even a ripple of fear crossed her placid face. "Hello, Virot."

"Hello, Phage," he replied.

She lifted her arms from the water and stretched, logy and slow. Once those arms went down again, her heart would be undefended. He would strike then. She yawned and said, "I didn't hear you come in."

"I . . ." he began, unsure what to say and hoping merely to strike instead. She folded her hands behind her head, too ready to grab a dagger. "I have something for you."

She blinked, her focus shifting past him to the yellow-cloaked figures that had come with him. "I have something for you as well."

"You do?" the First blurted, withdrawing the dagger deeper into his sleeve. "What is it?"

Phage rose from the water. It ran from her body like a silk robe falling to the floor. Her skin gleamed, as white as porcelain. She was magnificent, standing there in the pool. Its waves lapped at midthigh, and its steam whirled about her. The First could not keep his gaze

115

from roving across her figure, but when he raised his eyes, he saw that she stared fixedly back. With a graceful gesture, she ran one finger across her belly and said simply, "This."

The First almost dropped the knife. Why would she offer herself this way, with the hand servants waiting just beyond? Surely she knew what he intended. She meant to seduce him into the bath, take the knife, and slay him. He was most vulnerable now. "I have pressing duties—"

"Not that," she said, her eyes remaining level as she gestured again. "This."

He looked down at her hand and saw only the deep scar that her brother had struck there, but she didn't mean that.

"I'm pregnant. I bear your child," she said simply. "Your daughter, your son—the one who will carry on for you."

The First trembled, clamping down on a welter of emotion. What a regrettable creature, this child, this fearsome beast. No child can carry on unless the father is destroyed, but the First felt also tenderness and hope. He who had slain his own family might regain a family in this one, and even if he did not, would it be so terrible to die, to be released of centuries of struggle and torment? Was this child a destroyer or a deliverer? The last emotion Virot felt was terrible curiosity: What angle would send his dagger through both hearts at once?

Phage still stood there, dripping and beautiful. She had been studying his face. To most folk, the visage of the First was an impenetrable mask, but Phage had learned its lines and folds. She often could feel his emotion as if they were her own.

"What did you have for me?"

The First's blood ran cold. The passions in him froze. Phage must have known what he brought, but she pretended ignorance to save herself and her child.

"You said you had something for me?"

"Yes," the First demurred, "but it seems no longer suitable."

"I'd like to see it."

"Lie back down," he said coldly, nodding over his shoulder. "They're hand servants, but they have eyes too."

She sat. The water closed over her, rising to her collarbones. Water would not stop the knife, and lying there she could not dodge. Phage watched him, her fingers knitted together across her stomach.

"I brought you this," he said, drawing the dagger from his sleeve and holding it levelly above her. The black blade seemed almost a viper poised above her throat.

Phage was pale beneath that dagger. "It looks powerful."

The First nodded. "It is. It holds the flesh and bone of my family and the souls of hundreds of others."

The purple light glimmered in her eyes. "And it's mine?"

"No," he said then added. "Not now, while you're wet. The blade's poisoned."

She stood suddenly, stepping from the tub. The First staggered back from her as Phage slid on a robe of silk. "Then, give it to me now."

He withdrew again, holding the knife back. "No. It was for fighting in the coliseum. You can't fight in your condition."

"I can," she said calmly, approaching him with her palm level, "and I will. Give me the knife."

He could strike now. The silk would not stop a blade like this, but she was wary, even advancing. If he made any move to attack, she would spring, the blade would not strike true, he would have to stab her twice or thrice, and the hand servants would fall in fury on her. That was not what he wanted. To pierce her once and to the heart was the poetic kill. He retreated once more.

"I want it. Did you bring it for me or not?" Phage asked.

He thrust the dagger toward her belly, turning it at the last so that the handle jutted there for her to grab.

She took it. Her hand was swift and sure, and she ripped the weapon from his grip. The blade rose above her shoulder, and its wicked tongue pointed down toward the First's heart. "I like the way this feels. I've never fought with a weapon, but this one suits me."

The First watched her, preparing to dive away should she ram the blade at him. She had never before needed a weapon; her touch would kill anyone except the First. Now she needed a weapon because she wished to kill him.

Her hand dived like a falcon, and the First hurled himself backward. The blade came nowhere near him—a practice swing—but to every side, hand servants surged forward, their own daggers out. Still, none closed with the deadly lady.

Phage ignored them, smiling as she stared at the weapon. "I love it, Virot. Thanks for giving it to me. I'll keep it with me always. Our child will be safer for it."

The First could only nod numbly, stumbling to his feet.

"Set up some duels for me, so I can try out my new toy."

His eyes narrowed. "Yes. I'll do that. I'll set up some duels."

* * * * *

"Look at us!" Sash shouted, pacing the cell. "Pathetic! We began life cast in the very image of a god, living in an infinite palace in paradise. Things were going great until I listened to you!" He jabbed a finger at Waistcoat, who lay on a bed of iron slats.

"Yeah, right," responded the unman, unmoving lest his figure fold and he fall through. "Things were going great. We were dying off like flies. We're only alive 'cause I thought up a plan."

"Yes! Your plan! One little rebellion—"

"One very significant rebellion," Umbra put in miserably. He sat beside a door that had been sealed with lead. Though all of them had tried, none could squeeze beneath it.

"Yes. One monumental rebellion. Because of you, our master is dead, that mad witch Akroma is running things, and we've been on a long, horrible decline. From palaces to noble houses, from noble houses to barns, from barns to ditches, from ditches to the pits," Sash finished angrily. His words were belied by contented purring from within.

Umbra shook his head. "I've said it before. We could all be done. If each of us just steps through one of the others, no one will die, and we'll all be back in Topos."

"Nobody'll die?" Waistcoat shot back. "Nobody but the two of us. No dice! We made our decision, and we ride it out!"

An uneasy silence settled over the three. Sash had paced himself out and sat down on a bench, sliding through to end in a heap on the floor.

"Who's the puddle now?"

"Shut up!" Sash growled. "Or I'll shut you up with a sleep spell!"

"If you were a real mage, you'd've learned more than a sleep spell by now."

"That's it! Boogala boogala—"

"Stop. No spells. We need everyone awake if we're going to get out of this." Umbra said pensively. "I just wonder what they have in store for us. We'll be fighters, sure, but how? We have no bodies."

Waistcoat said, "Maybe they'll figure that out and let us loose."

"No," Umbra answered. "The Cabal is crafty. They'll do something with us. Maybe they'll fill us with tigers and press us between two sheets of metal so the cats can't get out. They lower the metal sheets into the coliseum, open them up, and out come tigers."

"Ingenious!" said Sash, warming to the discussion.

Umbra glanced his way. "Of course, we'd be lucky if it was tigers. They'd be more likely to fill us with ogres or goblins."

Sash snorted. "Ogres."

From his bed, Waistcoat said, "Goblins aren't bad." He reached to scratch and fell through the slats.

"As long as they're not infectious or lice-ridden, but I'm sure the Cabal screens for that kind of stuff," Umbra said offhandedly. "Unless, of course, the goblins are undead. Then there'll be maggots wriggling inside us day and night, fly swarms, and that putrid stench. Still, it's better than being full of banshees, screaming at all hours. There are worse things, but I guess I shouldn't talk like this. You fellows seem upset."

"Upset? Upset!" echoed Sash, who shook so that he made a sound like sheet metal. "Of course we're upset! It's about time you shut up!"

"What worse things?" asked Waistcoat.

"Well, all these slave quarters have offal holes, and all of them lead down to a deep cistern, and when you got all these monsters eating each other day and night, they must be producing some pretty noxious effluvia, if you know what I mean—"

Sash growled, "We know what you mean! Get to the point!"

"Well, somebody has to empty that cesspit, and what easier way than sinking one of us to the bottom and letting it all flood in? Then they just drag us out, horizontal, haul us somewhere, turn us over, and let the stuff pour out. That's probably what they'll do with us— make us into the cesspit crew of Otaria, working day and night as living portals for offal."

Waistcoat leaped up before his partner and cried, "Oh, Sash! Let's jump through him now, you and me! We'll take our chances with Akroma. I just don't want to be a living outhouse!"

Slapping his empty face, Sash shouted, "Get! Hold! Of! Your! Self!"

"Back!" bellowed a voice through the door. The command was punctuated by metal shattering under enormous weight. The lead seal around the door broke, and the force that broke it shoved the door into the cell. Metal jags chattered and shrieked as they ground across the stone floor. The massive ogre that had captured them blocked the exit.

The unmen scrambled back. All thought of escape fled.

"Stay back, or I'll twist you into knots," the ogre growled.

Umbra and Sash retreated. Waistcoat shouted, "I'm not an outhouse! I'm a human being!"

"Shut up," the ogre replied. It bowed its head, flipped its hand in a small flourish, and said, "Our master."

Into the cell stepped a creature who lived in the deepest night-mares of the unmen: the Cabal First. They knew this man from the mind of their creator. Though Ixidor had never seen the First per-sonally, he knew him to be the puppet master who had pulled Phage's strings. In Ixidor's mind—and therefore in the minds of his unmen—there could be no greater evil, no more terrible avatar of death than the First.

"Our . . . our . . . master . . . !" Waistcoat said breathlessly.

The black-clad man did not respond. His face seemed chiseled of stone—a thing incomprehensible. A black flame burned in his eyes. He strode purposefully to the three unmen, reached out with hands as quick as a scorpion's stinger, and grasped them.

The unmen screamed. They shuddered and convulsed like hearts laid bare beneath the knife, but they did not die. Still, the First held onto them. His teeth gritted behind taut lips that soon seemed to be smiling. At last, he hurled the three pathetic creatures to the floor and turned.

"They are cowards, of course, and mewling weak—" he was talk-ing to the ogre, not to the unmen "—but if I couldn't kill them, she couldn't either. I'll devise magical membranes to hold them, all that you'll need to train these new assassins. You will teach them to fight—and to hate."

The ogre responded only by bowing deeply to its master.

"Oh, and wash these things out—whatever it takes. They smell like they're full of cat."

* * * * *

What a fool I am! Instead of killing her, I gave her the one weapon with which she could kill me . . . and I gave her a child. She thinks if she is pregnant that I will not kill her. How wrong she is. I have no use for a son who will grow up to overthrow me. I'll kill them both, mother and son, and soon.

Great Kuberr, you gave me the strength to slay my family once. Give me the strength to slay them again.

I am the First, and I shall be the Last.

* * * * *

In one simple action, I gave Virot and Kuberr what they wanted. Virot wanted a sexual conquest, and Kuberr wanted a body. Now I bear a god within me, and Virot doesn't even glimpse the nature of our child.

He fears me. He knows I could destroy him. Does it matter that Virot plans my death? Kuberr wouldn't allow it, not until he is born. For the time being, I am invincible. No one can slay me—not Virot . . . not even Akroma. . . .

I will have to pay her a visit. . . .

Praise be to you, Master Kuberr, my god . . . my son.

CHAPTER 13

OUT OF THEIR ELEMENTS

It was absurd, this dress—lacy and white like a doily. Akroma shuddered to wear it. Slender straps crossed her shoulders, shoulders that had slain deathwurms. The plunging back line revealed not a slinky spine but massive muscles and the roots of her huge wings. The petticoats and frills below kept getting snagged in her anxious claws. Akroma was completely out of her element, but the new ministry of diplomacy said this dress was necessary—and that this party was as well.

"Welcome to Topos, King Ruhtra and Queen Nagrom of Ulbion," Akroma said, bowing slightly at the waist. The little monarchs were only half her height, with white hair and black skin. Even in bowing, Akroma did not reach their level. She seemed instead to loom over them. A gentle nudge from Minister Lindolth reminded her to smile. Akroma tried, but it was really just a baring of teeth. "Please avail yourselves of all that Topos has to offer."

Minister Lindolth nodded, more to encourage Akroma than to agree with her. Lindolth was a short, round man, a trusty convert to the faith of Ixidor, and an expert in international relations. Tonight's party for the unallied rulers of Otaria had been his brainchild, and he had planned it to the last detail.

Beside the ruddy man stood Priest Aioue, as tall, lean, and

white as a birch sapling. His pink eyes fixed on the king and queen. "Please remove your shoes. This palace is holy ground, sacred to Ixidor."

King Ruhtra laughed once, realized it was no joke, and spluttered. He slipped off his shoes, and his queen did likewise. Aioue stooped to lift them and bore them to a white stone box beside the front door. He tipped the lid and dropped the shoes within.

As Ruhtra and Nagrom made their barefooted way toward the crowded banquet hall, Akroma whispered in a voice like the hiss of a jaguar, "How will my eating with these . . . puffed up dolts . . . save Topos?"

Minister Lindolth wore an ingratiating smile. "Mistress, forgive me. You're not just eating with them. You're befriending them. It'll save Topos by providing allies and armies."

"Our armies should be sufficient. We should have taken Sanctum, impressed its citizens, and marched on the coliseum."

"The situation is complex," Lindolth continued, his smile not slipping a mite. "Before we could even lift a sword, Sanctum was waging a war of words. . . ."

"Corruption fills that vale," said Aioue. His weird pink eyes seemed to see the distant battlefield. "It destroys the morale of our troops. They've lost the will to fight, to do anything but gamble. Only two months into the siege, and already our folk are too divided to follow orders, let alone mount an attack. Every day they grow weaker."

Akroma's brow knitted in fury. "This is your failing, Aioue. If you had kept their faith strong, they would be ready for war."

The priest did not flinch. "Actually, their faith is stronger than ever. They have even converted many of the citizens of Sanctum. This is a colony of artists and free thinkers, and they see our master as the embodiment of all they believe. The laws of Ixidor have become the laws of the colony, and some of your warriors and priests have defected to join the folk of Sanctum in order to convert and lead them. In fact, you might say the siege of Sanctum has won you their souls but not their bodies."

"Bodies are important too," interjected Lindolth as he took her arm, guiding her toward the banquet hall. Only now did his placating smile harden. "It'd be terrible if the faith of Ixidor lived on but his lands were conquered and parsed out among the nations."

"Jackals," Akroma snarled, her fists clenching and unclenching.

Lindolth changed his tack. "Not yet, they aren't. They could be guard dogs. Give them table scraps, teach them to sit still with a treat balanced on their noses, and they'll work for you instead of against you. This is how to save Topos."

Akroma visibly trembled within the dress. "If Ixidor were here—"

"He's not, though," Lindolth said intensely, staring into Akroma's eyes, "and that leaves us mortals to protect and preserve the things he made. He'll come again, but until he does, you need to learn the ways of mortals and work within them, or all that the master made will be destroyed."

Panting, the angel-beast chewed on those words.

"Do it for Ixidor."

She nodded. "For him, I'll do anything." Akroma straightened her back and steeled her expression. Her lips spread in a grimace that slowly became a smile. Shaking the stiffness from her arms, she grasped the skirts of her dress and walked toward the banquet hall. She had utterly transformed by the time she passed beneath the high-arched double-doors.

A few of her guests shied back as she arrived. They stood nervously among long tables draped in white linen.

"In the name of Ixidor, master of this palace and creator of this land, I welcome all of you. It's a night for feasting and music—a night long overdue. We've been your neighbors these three long years, and yet only now do we get the chance to be neighborly. Strike the harp, blow the reed, bang the drum—players, let us have music! Steward, let us have drinks!"

Already, the guests looked more at home. When a happy gavotte began on the musician's dais, some even started to mingle and smile. More delights were in store.

The tall doors to the kitchen swung wide, and a huge face showed itself there. A centaur bowed to fit beneath the high ceiling. His coat shone like spun gold, brushed and coifed. He stalked slowly into the room, wearing across his back a contraption that turned him into a giant drink cart. Barrels of ale hung along one side, with jacks available for drinkers to fill their own. On his other side, jeroboams of wine hung from leather thongs, with long-stemmed glasses dangling nearby. Trays fanned out before his chest, offering a wide assortment of elegant snacks.

The guests laughed to see so powerful a creature made into so ingenious a servant.

Akroma joined their laughter.

They converged on the giant centaur, surrounded him, and set to feeding. In moments, their lips were red with wine and their throats filled with flesh.

* * * * *

Stonebrow stood there as they drank from his gushing sides and ate from his pounding heart. What else could he do? This was the will of Akroma and, for now, the will of Akroma was the will of Ixidor.

Stonebrow believed. It was not blind belief now—not as it was in the beginning. When she had caught him in the Greenglades Forest two months before, Stonebrow had had the unreasoning, all-enveloping belief of new conversion—of hostile conversion. He had wanted none of it, but the disciples had plied his mind and shot it full of belief. At that time, there was no questioning, no resistance, but only prostrate obedience and worship.

Now, though, the disciples were gone from his mind, and Akroma had ceased her vicious probes. She had learned all she wished to know of Krosan and its helpless leader and had seen too that the seeds of faith so violently thrust in Stonebrow's mind had borne true fruit.

Stonebrow believed in the Vision of Ixidor: that the world, with all its ugliness and suffering, could be transformed by art and law into Beauty. Ugliness and suffering were evil, and by eliminating them, true believers in Ixidor could recreate the world. They could enter paradise.

Stonebrow was a true believer, and Akroma trusted him. She thought that devotion to Ixidor was devotion to her, but it was not. For all her desire to preserve the Vision of Ixidor, everything she did destroyed it. Perhaps that was why Stonebrow believed, because he and Ixidor were allies against Akroma and her corrupt regime.

A ball of cream cheese tipped from its tray and rolled down one of Stonebrow's fore hooves. He shifted, feeling the white trail of goop on his fur, but did not move to wipe it off. His job was merely to stand. Other attendants would retrieve the cheese and do the cleaning.

"Ixidor," he muttered beneath his breath. "Give me the strength to wait."

His eyes fixed on Akroma. She hardly seemed herself, wearing a smile that would convince only those who didn't know her. Always before, small talk was too small for her. Not now. Her ministers had convinced her that Ixidor was in the details, and she mingled with the same fury she once reserved for war. Her breastplate was a bodice, and her shield a small fan. The only blade she bore was her tongue, though it was deadly enough. Stonebrow was almost saddened to look at her, working so hard to live up to her master's call but failing so completely.

"Show her your truth, Master," Stonebrow prayed for his enemy. "Show her, so that when she dies by the axe, she might return to you."

The only blade she bore was her tongue. . . .

Once the course of drinks and appetizers was done, Stonebrow would shuck this contraption, go to her chambers, and take the axe. Better that she die rather than continue to pollute the minds of the world against Ixidor. Better she die, and her falsehoods with her, than that the truth of Ixidor perish.

It was ironic: Stonebrow had set out to clean up the mess made by Kamahl, but now was cleaning up the mess made by Akroma. Either way, he was fulfilling the Vision of Ixidor. "It will not be long now, great master. She will return to you."

*　*　*　*　*

Elionoway walked nimbly along the narrow trail. His bare feet found easy purchase between the stone face to his left and the sheer drop to his right. He held aloft a lantern, for the sun slept beneath the world. Below them, Sanctum glowed like a bed of coals, the city and the besieging army separated only by the slender Deepwash. Above came the clamor of gamers among the standing stones. Elionoway and Zagorka walked the cliffs between.

The elf's free hand ran along the deeply carved wall. "These petraglyphs are still relatively new," he said, "only as deep as my fingers. The ones ahead, though, are the oldest I have found."

"Good," Zagorka replied breathlessly. Though she was four hundred forty years his junior, she was old for a human. She had twice his girth and half his balance, so this passage was a true test. "What do . . . the glyphs say?"

Leaping nimbly across a narrow crevice, the elf said, "Same as the others—warnings of the war of the numena. This spot here says, 'Brothers ever rival brothers, and when one rises, so the others, until they gather, full-fledged and formed, to crack the sky and storm the Wall of the World.' The name the ancients gave the Corian Escarpment is the 'Wall of the World.' "

Zagorka stepped across the crevice, clinging on desperately. "You think . . . this is talking about a war?"

"The numena were rival brothers, each striving to best the others in sorcerous power. They rose together. The success of one spurred on the achievements of the others. In time, they had snatched up all the land, and even the sky and water, so that they could gain no more except by stealing from each other." Elionoway rounded a small curve, and his voice began to echo. He stood in a large cave mouth, his lantern reaching tepidly back into the yawning throat. "That story comes from other texts. They also mention the war. That's what this business about cracking the sky and storming the Wall of the World is. War." He nodded into the cave. "We're here."

Wiping her sweaty brow, Zagorka stared into the darkness. "How'd you . . . find this place?"

Elionoway pointed toward the runes, which circled the corner and delved into the cave, growing bigger and deeper as they went. "I followed the glyphs."

She scowled. "It's pretty dark."

"I'll be able to see if there are any animals," Elionoway said. "So stay close."

"Mind if I hold your hand?"

"I'd be flattered."

"Cradle robber."

Like two children lost in the woods, they walked side-by-side into the cave. Elionoway kept Zagorka between him and the wall, and his lantern splashed eerily across the characters.

"This says, 'And how shall the numena rule if they have no mortals to serve them? Thus when they rise they bring us with them too, whether from muck or sand or rock, we rise to serve.' "

"Not very comforting, here in the dark," Zagorka groused.

"I take this bit to mean that when the numena come, they each bring a new nation into being, a nation of servants."

"When they *come*?" Zagorka said. "Ain't we talking about rulers dead twenty thousand years ago?"

The elf paused, his eyes tracing out the lines in the wall. "Yes, and no. Yes, the numena fell twenty millennia ago, but the prophecies say they'll come again—when we worship in the 'high, holy place,' they'll return and bring their people and make war again at the Wall of the World."

"Nonsense," replied Zagorka, clearing her throat.

Elionoway lifted his eyebrows and walked on. The passage suddenly opened into a great, round chamber. As far as the light reached, walls, ceiling, and floor were covered with great glyphs. These were the largest of any in Sanctum, deep enough and tall enough to hide a person in their folds. Stranger still, they were in the shape of people, crude pictograms. The images were of warriors with swords or spears, bows, clubs, shields—staffs spitting fire and globes spitting lightning. The chamber was crowded with them.

"What do these say?" Zagorka asked with quiet reverence.

"They don't say anything anymore. They used to, though."

"What do you mean?"

"These used to be words, written in glyphs the size of my hand. I deciphered a few, which spoke of the 'Nation of Servants,' but I paid little heed. Now, the runes have grown and joined, reconfiguring themselves into this pictographic army."

"An army." The steam of her breath lingered in the air.

"They are coming back, Zagorka."

"The numena, or the people depicted here?"

"Both," he replied. "These aren't just depictions. These are the people themselves. Look at that warrior there." He nodded toward the nearest of the petraglphs, a man with a rectangular body and a triangular head. His eyes were a pair of conjoined ovals. The irises were holes bored deeply into the stone. "Look at his eyes. Stare a moment and tell me you don't sense that he is staring back."

"Don't be a fool—"

"No, Zagorka. You're the fool if you don't see this," said Elionoway with sudden intensity. "Look."

She did, her eyes locking with those two deep, black holes. She could stand it only a moment. "Get me out of here."

"Yes," Elionoway said. "Yes, I will."

* * * * *

Akroma stared levelly at King Ruhtra, her eyes intent, but her smile welcoming. "Then I can count on you for support in the coming war?"

The old man lifted a finger, his breath sloshing with wine. "If war comes, yes, you can count on me. Our armada will keep all the eastern ports open to you for supply and transport."

The angel-beast was pleased but not satisfied. She walked with him slowly across the thick red carpet of the banquet hall. "Thank you, sire, but I need more than just open ports. I need an ally on the high seas. One willing to fight."

"I see," the old man said, nodding his white-haired head. The chandelier reflected little yellow lights on his bald pate. "Of course, if we were attacked, we would defend ourselves."

"It's not enough," Akroma said, all friendliness gone. "I seek honest allies, not folk whose loyalties shift with the tide."

Ruhtra looked wounded. He reached out, grabbed Akroma's white hands in his dark ones, and said, "I pledge to you my support, my aid, my alliance. Your foes will be our foes, and your friends ours."

Akroma did not just bow to the little man this time. Instead, she knelt on her jaguar belly. "I am deeply grateful for the friendship of our nations."

The man smiled, a beatific expression, and patted her hand. "Well, I must go gather the queen."

As if on cue, a high wail came from the entry hall, "My shoes! What have you done?"

"Please, excuse me," the angel and the king said in unison. Side by side they rushed to the entry hall.

Dignitaries lingered there, murmuring in consternation. A red-faced Lindolth and a white-faced Aioue stood with them. All gaped at the stone box by the door.

"What's the matter?" Akroma asked.

A number of voices rose in explanation: "They won't give us our shoes." "They don't know where they are." "I saw him put them in the box, but now, there's nothing." "I wonder why Ixidor wants our shoes."

A day before, Akroma would have struck the man dead for such flippancy, but the laughter that answered helped defuse an ugly situation. Akroma strode through the midst of them, directly to Lindolth and Aioue. "Well, what of it?"

"They're right," said Minister Lindolth, his voice trembling. "They're gone."

She hissed quietly to him, "An evening's work undone by a shoe thief."

"No one took them, Mistress," he said. "They're just . . . gone."

"What do you mean? Get out of the way!" She pushed past them to peer down into the boot box. Nothing was there—neither shoes, nor sides, nor bottom to the box. The space was utterly black and seemingly infinite. "You threw their shoes down a bottomless pit?"

"It's worse than that," Priest Aioue said wanly. "Take a deep breath and tell me what you smell."

She shot him a murderous glare but breathed in anyway. She knew the smell immediately—the pungent scent of a deathwurm's flesh. It wasn't a putrid odor, but the kind that came from the living beasts.

"It's down there," Aioue said. "Hiding in that space."

Akroma nodded. "The deathwurm is down there, and so is our lord, Ixidor."

CHAPTER 14

BATTLING DARKNESS

*B*acklit by a huge torch, Phage stood at the rim of the coliseum. In her black silk gladiatorial garb, she seemed a sliver of night. The crowd roared to see the infamous Phage, undefeated in combat, builder of the coliseum, lover of the First. It had been nearly two years since anyone had seen her in battle. Tonight, a hundred thousand souls would.

Only one soul mattered. Phage rubbed the red jag across her belly. Beneath it lay her child, three months along. The fetal creature was the reason she had agreed to fight—a stalling tactic to keep the First from striking the child directly. He hoped that his monsters could do away with Phage and her child, that he could publically mourn them even as he privately exulted. She knew his murderous intent and would dance at the end of those strings but not die. Kuberr would see to that.

"Protect us, Kuberr," Phage prayed, lifting her hand to wave to the rabid throng. She descended the stairs, heading for the battle floor. *When the child is born, everything will be different.* She wasn't sure if the voice in her head was her own or Kuberr's, but it comforted her. Her feet quickened on the stair. She vaulted over the final rail, dropping down catlike on the sands. Rising, she drew the wicked-bladed dagger from her belt.

The crowd erupted.

Phage endured the storm of sound and peered across the coliseum. What horrors had the First arranged? It didn't matter. Kuberr would protect her. With his strength and the inspiration of her child, she would fight as never before.

The ovation died suddenly as the far doors swung wide. They revealed a black rectangle of space, a glimpse into the slave pens. As if the very air of that foul place coagulated, three shadows stepped from the darkness—shadows without anyone casting them. They strode, side by side and determined, toward Phage.

She studied them a moment more and stalked across the sands. Her flesh could not eat away mere shadows, but if these shadows moved, surely they had souls. Surely this dagger could steal them.

Gritting her teeth, Phage broke into a run. It was good to fight again. For the first time, she would be fighting for something rather than for nothing.

* * * * *

Behind Akroma, kings and queens argued about stolen shoes. Stolen shoes! They stood beside a god's coffin—an infinite boot box that held a ravenous deathwurm—but all these cretins cared about were shoes.

"Quiet!" Akroma shouted, not even turning to address them.

The royals ceased their bickering if only to glare at their host.

Ignoring them, Akroma grabbed the bodice of her white dress and yanked. Lace tore, and satin separated. The two halves fell away, straps dropping from powerful shoulders. Out of that riven dress stepped a warrior.

Her allies watched her transform from a genteel woman to an angel-beast. They stared on a creature who was bare not just in body, but also in soul. Whatever they had thought of her previously, they saw her true self now.

"My axe," Akroma called out, holding her right hand high. Lifting her left, she said, "My lightning lance, my breastplate!" While varlets scurried up the stairs to fetch the items, Akroma turned to dismiss her guests.

Sight of her nude flesh brought gasps of displeasure from the queens and avid shock from the kings.

"Forgive my departure. Battle calls. Your shoes were swallowed by the same beast that swallowed my master—a beast I go to slay."

Shock turned to admiration. One duchess asked, "What beast lives in a boot box?"

"In this one: a deathwurm."

The crowd recoiled. Among them came varlets with equipment.

Queen Nagrom asked, "Are we safe?"

"Only as allies are we safe," Akroma replied, letting her servants strap the breastplate in place. One young man handed her the lightning lance—a long jagged rod that glowed with waiting power. "I won't be gone long. Minister Lindolth and Priest Aioue will look after things in my stead." She glanced at them, dubiously. "Even above them, I trust my loyal servant, Stonebrow. Defer to them in all things."

A servant rushed up and bowed low before her, touching his forehead to the ground. "Forgive me, Mistress, but your axe is gone from your room. The door was forced, the lock broken, and the axe gone."

Akroma's eyes narrowed. Soul Reaper had been forged to slay her, and now it was in hostile hands. Who had taken it? One of the guests? A spy? It didn't matter. Whoever had taken it could not reach her while she was within the boot box. If she emerged from it, she would have Ixidor with her, and he would protect her. "You are forgiven," she replied benevolently. To her guests, she said, "Do not fear. Lindolth, Aioue, and Stonebrow will find the thief. Soon the axe will be in their hands, and until then, they will double the guard. All of you are safe. I can waste no more time with arrangements. Farewell, allies. I must go." Akroma turned to face the wide stone box and the reeking darkness.

She tucked her wings, clasped her hands as if in prayer, and dived headfirst into the box. There was a tight moment as her plumes scraped past the walls of the thing, then she plunged into dark infinity.

This was not chaos, as beneath the Stubble Fields, but an infinite, air-filled space. Why the master had made such a place, she did not know, but indeed the wurm was here.

It coiled up toward her through the darkness, its rubbery flesh sending off a stink. Piggy eyes fixed on her, and translucent teeth opened in a hungry grin. The monster soared upward with incredible speed. Its mouth gaped to swallow her whole.

"I am coming, Ixidor. I am coming."

* * * * *

"She's coming!" Waistcoat howled. The three unmen stood in the midst of the coliseum, waiting as their terrible foe approached. "Phage is coming right for me!" He tried to dodge behind Sash.

Sash kicked sand at him. "Get away from me, moron!" The granules sparked as they struck the magical membranes that bound the unmen. "You're the one who wanted to be in the middle."

"Both of you, stop fighting and start fighting!" Umbra immediately recognized the idiocy of that comment, but there was no time to laugh.

Phage arrived. The infamous gladiator had lost none of her speed or finesse. Flipping head over feet, the woman hurled herself at Waistcoat. She clutched her crooked dagger in her teeth, ready to draw it out and stab.

"Waah!" said Waistcoat as he flung himself sideways. He was too slow.

Phage rammed her curvy dagger into Waistcoat's head. The black-bladed weapon sank through and dragged Phage in after it. Hand, arm, shoulder, head, body—she vanished into Waistcoat like a girl down a well. Suddenly, Phage was gone, and the shouts of the crowd fell to silence. Amplification magic let everyone hear the words that followed.

"Ach! Get her out! I got a woman in me! A rotting woman!" Waistcoat wailed. He raced around the sands as if a swarm of bees chased him. "She's doing something! She's doing something bad! Get her out! Ow ow ow ow ow!"

Umbra watched his comrade bellow and snort.

Sash laughed. "Sure, I'll get her out. Just let me jump through!"

"No! No! Get away! Ah, she's in me. I don't feel so good."

Crowd noise mounded up again, this time built on laughter. Folks began throwing their food on the sands, shouting obscenities, pantomiming the flapping antics of Waistcoat.

Sash whispered to Umbra, "You think she'll hurt him?"

Umbra shrugged. "No. Maybe if this is absurd enough, the First will let us go."

"Or kill us."

"Or that."

"Oh, what's seeping out of my feet? Oh, she's doing something! Ach, get her out!"

* * * * *

A moment too late, Phage realized her foe was a living hole. She plunged through him, the knife cleaving the shadow's head. What lay on the other side? The portal man swallowed her from fist to feet, and the roar of the coliseum diminished. She vaulted into a long, low chamber filled with ogres.

They had not expected her: They hunched around a harpsichord, plinking tunes with their filthy claws.

Phage, still flying, introduced herself by landing, dagger-first, on the throat of the nearest ogre.

"Huh?" it said.

The blade ripped out its voice, and the pommel tore out its soul. Her feet landed on the thing's chest and rotted out two deep wells. Like a woman sinking in mud, Phage ran. Her feet sucked with each step up the collapsing monster. She hurdled its face, giant eyes glazed in death, and flung herself to attack the next ogre.

It was quicker than its cohort. A huge claw grasped Phage and squeezed. The monster smiled as flesh pulped in its grip. The flesh, though, was its own—rancid, gray-green tissues. The ogre howled, its hand reduced to white sticks.

Phage tumbled free and landed on the stone floor.

At least twenty more ogres converged.

She turned, spotted the standing shadow of the man, and dived.

With a dull roar, the ogres lunged, piling atop her. The weight was immense until her skin ate a soft spot. Phage tried to lever the monsters off of her or to crawl from beneath them, but she could only rot deeper into the pile. More beasts landed. Phage was buried alive in ogres. There was only one way out, to dig up through the suffocating heap and hope her breath lasted long enough.

Scooping gobbets of slimy flesh with her fingers, she swam through dying bodies.

* * * * *

Akroma dived toward the teeth of the deathwurm. Foul breath blasted up from its gullet and plumed over her. She raked her lightning lance out, bared her teeth in a shriek of fury, and hurled the weapon.

It thundered down into the beast's rubbery muzzle, sparked on a nostril, and jabbed within. The lance disappeared, and the puny eyes of the wurm lit. Charges arced through the creature's brain. It roared, its mouth snapping spastically.

Akroma tried to dive aside, but the jaws were too quick. Translucent fangs cut into one of her forelegs. The other leg came down on the beast's black gums, dug its claws in, and shoved off. She pulled free. Angel wings spread, gripped the darkness, and hurled Akroma away from the beast. Another pulse carried her over rushing convolutions of flesh.

The leviathan shuddered, floating in space. The lance sent surges of agony through it, but even that peerless light could not survive long in a brain so utterly dark. Its final charges flared in the eyes and mouth of the beast, and it was gone.

Akroma banked low across the tail of the monster. She had no weapons, but during the Nightmare War, she had slain deathwurms by turning their teeth against themselves. Plunging, Akroma grasped the tail of the creature and clung on. Her claws sank through folds of flesh, stinging the beast.

A league away, the massive head rose and arched, neck spreading like the hood of a cobra. It saw her, a stinging fly on its tail, and curled back on itself.

Akroma dug her claws in deeper. She wanted the wurm to be infuriated, wanted to wait for the final possible moment. Beneath her, dark muscles slid and tightened.

The monster trembled. It curved into a huge loop, the head crossing miles in seconds. Jaws gaped, and the throat sucked a cyclone of air.

Still, Akroma waited. If she leaped away a moment too soon, the wurm would not bite its own tail. If she leaped too late, it would swallow her whole. Jaguar legs gathered to spring, and eagle wings folded to fly.

The deathwurm's head eclipsed all else, its teeth a deadly horizon. Akroma leaped . . . too late.

* * * * *

Waistcoat hadn't ceased his shouting, but now everyone in the coliseum saw that he had good reason. Out of his running figure gushed a river of gray goo. Phage was grinding his innards, turning them to a tide of decay. The poor unman had taken to running backward so the paste could emerge freely, but still he ran in circles. The membrane enchantment laid on him kept him there in the center of the arena.

"So much for his ogres," Umbra said laconically to Sash. "The lesson is to release your monsters before she arrives."

"Lesson learned," replied Sash.

Umbra took a few strides away on the sand and crouched in readiness. "Here she comes."

Phage fought her way out of the gray ooze and emerged, mantled in the stuff. Moments later, it had boiled away, leaving her clean. She had lost her wicked-looking dagger, but her hands were lethal by themselves. Shaking her head, she turned toward Umbra and Sash and broke into a run.

"Ready?" called Umbra.

Sash flung his arms wide. "Ready!"

"Release the beasts!" Umbra cried.

His membrane spell flickered. Out of him stepped a single strange creature—an Argoshian. The man's flesh was pocked with a thousand of eyes. Even on the soles of his feet, eyes squinted closed to keep the sand out. He took two steps and launched himself into the air. A spell of levitation grasped him and lofted him above the coming melee. He would hover there, seeing all and directing the assault.

It would come from Sash's beasts. His membrane sparked, and acrid whiffs of smoke emerged. Through them charged dementia creatures—living nightmares. First came a huge millipede with daggers for arms and a scorpion tail. It chittered as the Argoshian sent it to one side of the battlefield. Next emerged five creatures that looked like wingless wasps. Their abdomens pulsed eagerly, trailing venom across the sand. Then were enormous maggots, white and pustulous, and rank after rank of dog men, scythers, and crocodilians. They flooded out, embodiments of every neurotic fear. A whole army of them gathered under the all-seeing Argoshian.

Umbra felt sudden sympathy for Phage. Why did the First hate her so much?

In moments, it wouldn't matter. She would be dead.

* * * * *

It was absurd, this battalion of mortal fears. Phage had long since put such fears behind her, and her god Kuberr told her what to do. She ran straight for them and ducked low, hands scrabbling across the sand.

The giant millipede pivoted and coiled toward her. Mouth parts clicked eagerly, and the head lunged.

Phage leaped just above the snapping mouth. She caught a foothold between scaly antennae and ran up the millipede's armored back. In her hands, she clutched fistfuls of sand. Her first step had rotted the brain, and the centipede began to undulate. She timed her steps with the agony of the beast and the will of her master. Just ahead, the scorpion tail rose and fell. Phage leaped on it and was hurled high by its next spasm. She flew above the battle, and her hands flung the sand.

The Argoshian's all-seeing eyes would see nothing for the next few moments.

Phage grasped the floating man's leg. She climbed him, rotting him, emptying eyes with horrible gushes. Beneath her grip, the all-seeing beast was dying. It struggled to break free but couldn't. Blinded, the Argoshian plunged from the sky. Phage rode him down. The joy of the crowd followed them all the way. They struck sand amid beasts in disarray.

The monsters turned on each other or fled outright.

Phage fought all those she could—a dog man here, a scyther there, but her foes were in a rout. Each kill redoubled the roar of the crowd until the clamor was deafening. At last, when she threw aside a dead wasp creature and bounded forward to engage the next foe, she found only empty sand. Or almost empty. Three shadowy forms lay on their faces in surrender.

Smiling, Phage lifted her arms triumphantly. The stands erupted, and within her, the infant Kuberr kicked.

* * * * *

Akroma hurled herself aside, but the deathwurm's jaws closed. Its teeth sank through its own flesh, cutting skin, muscle, bone, and nerve but also trapping Akroma.

She fought against the gory flood. She wanted to stay near the teeth so that when the jaws opened again, she could fly free. The wurm's severed tail lolled crushingly against her. Akroma scrabbled forward, but in the darkness she couldn't see the teeth. She set her claws and drove ahead. Where was the tongue? Had she been swallowed already? Perhaps she had fought her way into the severed end of the monster and needed to turn around. Which way?

The wurm had swallowed its tail. It had become a great circle with no beginning and no end. Death was all, and there was no escape.

* * * * *

Stonebrow strode down a corridor of Locus, Soul Reaper gripped in his hand. This very night, in the name of Ixidor, he would find the false prophet and slay her. He headed toward the banquet hall. He would kill Akroma before all the delegates, that they would know for certain she did not represent the truth of Ixidor.

Stonebrow entered the narthex to find it overflowing with folk, rumbling about the strange goings on. Stomping into their midst, Stonebrow said, "What is this? Where is Akroma?" He had not even hidden the axe he had taken from her room, and his intention seemed unmistakable . . . until Minister Lindolth intervened.

"You are too late, Stonebrow!" he said. "You could have stopped her, for she trusted you, her right-hand man. She would have listened to you, but instead she flung herself into that dark pit."

Scowling, the centaur waded through the crowd to stare at the stone-lidded box. "Dark pit?"

"The deathwurm of Ixidor is down there," Priest Aioue said with utter certainty. His pink eyes seemed to cloud over. "There is no hope for Sister Akroma. She fell to pride, believing she could best the wurm that bested our creator." The albino looked up. "Only you, Stonebrow, could have stopped her. It is too bad you arrived so late."

"Yes," the centaur said quietly, his fingers rolling the hilt of the axe, "too bad."

Minister Lindolth said sadly, "At least you have recovered her axe! She knew you would. She named you her successor."

"Her successor?" Stonebrow said.

Lindolth replied, "Yes. All here heard. She esteemed you above even us."

"Even us," the priest echoed with strange satisfaction.

Shaking his head, Stonebrow said, "I cannot take her place."

"No," Lindolth said. "No one could, but you can lead in her absence. Don't worry, I'll be at your right hand—"

"And I at your left," said Aioue.

"We will be your wings, to lift you as your mistress once was lifted." Lindolth turned toward the nobles. "Assure them, Stonebrow, that every alliance forged tonight will be only strengthened by the departure of our sister, that Topos is in capable hands until she returns, if ever. Tell them you will rule." As if impatient with his reluctant candidate, the minister clapped Stonebrow's flank and said, "Kings and queens, dukes and duchesses, grand folk all, I introduce to you the new ruler of Topos, sovereign Stonebrow."

There was applause among the crowd. Folk who earlier had drunk from his sides and eaten from his heart now bowed politely before the centaur. Their bright faces and conniving eyes surrounded him. A new piece had appeared on the political game board, and all the players eyed it eagerly, hoping to take it.

CHAPTER 15

TO KILL THE KILLER

On the docks of Coliseum Island, brightly painted caravans waited. Their red and gold paint reflected on the brown-black water. The barges alongside them sank just perceptibly as sacks of grain were loaded atop building materials, weapons, and other supplies. Soon, the caravans themselves would perch on the rest of the cargo. Each barge was bound for a different dock, where the caravans would be offloaded and piled full of materials. There, the overland route began, with wagon trains rolling to the far corners of Otaria. These simple provisions would enlarge the arenas begun in towns and villages throughout the continent.

Lowly though it might seem, this fleet was nothing less than an invasion army.

The First watched sullenly as dockworkers checked the trim of the barges. Each craft needed only a foot of gunwhale above waterline to navigate the dredged channels. There was little current in the swamp, and few waves. The First's mana engineers had done their job well, turning a wide wetland into a vast bayou. It grew every year, reaching farther throughout Otaria. The spreading swamp had become an image of the Cabal itself, growing through erosion.

A hand grasped the First's shoulder. He startled, stepping forward and turning, elbow raised to smash the face of his attacker. He still had the reflexes of a gladiator.

Phage bounded back and stood there, hands on her hips. Though she was four months along, she still had the beautiful figure of a young woman. "A little jumpy, aren't we?" she asked. "Who else could touch you and live?"

Yes, who else? She was lover and assassin, both. "I'm sorry. My mind is elsewhere."

Phage approached again, a crooked smile on her lovely face. "What've you got to worry about? Today, you send out boats and caravans. In a month, they'll reach their destinations. In six months, your local arenas will be the established judiciaries of the land. You're just a year away from controlling all of Otaria."

"Not Topos. Not her allied states," the First replied grimly, turning away to stare out across the waters. Gray trees twisted their roots down to probe the muck. "As long as Akroma lives . . ."

"Then I'll kill her," Phage said, as though the suggestion were a minor thing.

It would be a sweet thing for Phage and Akroma to battle to the death. Whoever won, the First would be happy. "Don't be a fool. In your condition?"

"What's my condition?" Phage asked, wrapping her arms around his waist and easily lifting him from the ground.

The corruptive power of her touch sparked ecstacy across the First's flesh. "Put me down!"

"Even four months pregnant, I can defeat any gladiator you throw at me." She set him down but kept him in her withering embrace. "I can defeat even you."

You think so, but I am the First and the Last. Your grave will be overgrown by millennial oaks before I die. "I suppose you could, but are you a match for Akroma? She'd have killed you in the coliseum if not for your brother."

That lit a fire in her. "My brother," she spat. "What's become of him? He's a toadstool. What's become of me? I'm a servant of Kuberr, lover of the First, terror of the coliseum . . . of course I'm a match for Akroma." She growled into his ear, a sound that was half-purr. "Mention my brother again, and you'll die in my arms."

She should be slain for such treason, but who was sufficient to the task? Perhaps Akroma. "I die in your arms every time we're together."

"Then let's be together again, before I leave." She wrapped herself around him.

It felt as if the First were buried in hot coals. He wanted to burn away to nothing in that embrace. It would be such sweet release to stop fighting her, to give Phage the victory. His flesh ached for hers—that was the worst of it—and for the sake of flesh, he could willingly surrender all.

"Yes," he said, tingling with enervation. "Once more before you go." *Once more before you and the baby die.*

"I'm not sure I can wait," she said, gesturing toward the yellow-robed hand servants. "They could form a circle around us. . . ."

"No," the First replied, marching up the wharf, back toward the coliseum. "We're not dogs."

Phage took his hand and strode beside him toward the coliseum— a temple to battle. Beneath the stones of that temple, a great battle would soon rage. . . .

* * * * *

It was utterly dark in his chambers, but the touch of flesh to flesh seemed to send sparks and flames out to light the shadows. Virot climbed atop her and pinned her. Phage wrestled free and drove him to the ground. Neither would submit for long, and for all its panting desire, this was more war than love.

Phage knew what he wanted: to loom above and do whatever he wished, and what he wished was to kill her. For four months, her lover had not brought her flowers but weapons, had sent her no troubadours but gladiators. All had failed, so he would send her off to die at the hand of Akroma.

Too bad Virot wouldn't get what he wanted—not here in the wrestling dark, nor in Topos, far north.

Yes, Phage would travel there in secrecy, would penetrate the palace and assassinate its ruler, but she would not do it for the First. She would do it for herself and for her child. Once Akroma was dead, Topos would belong to Phage.

Virot could not best her. He pulled back, standing nearby in the dark. Unsatisfied. He would remain so as long as he opposed her. "What do you want me to do, beg?"

Phage smiled. "It would be a start."

She knew he hated her. The line between love and hate was slim, and his love was as perilous as his hate. Phage would survive them both.

"I should have you killed," Virot said even as he went to his knees.

"You've already chosen," she replied, standing above him.

The First of the Cabal knelt before her and began to beg.

*　*　*　*　*

Waistcoat had come up with a game: cockroach derby. The creatures were native to the cell, emerging from three separate nests in the crevices of the wall. Waistcoat had chosen a champion from each nest—the fastest creatures. Catching them, he rubbed them on variously colored mold on the walls—making one red, another yellow, and a third green. He kept his champions in the stopped-up bowl of the latrine, letting them out only to race.

Sash considered the game vile. Umbra said it was better than sitting and staring at the walls. He had even arranged with a guard to bring a hunk of bread each day, that the roaches might race for it.

Today's match drew near. Waistcoat timed it for shift change, so that all the yelling wouldn't bring an ogre running. He knelt beside the latrine and saw the three runners sleeping in their separate sections. He prodded them with a gentle fingertip. "Wake up. It's almost time to run for bread!"

"Run for bread," Sash said bitterly. "Hah! How pathetic. Not only do we race cockroaches, but we also feed them food we can't eat. These roaches are better men than we are."

"Yes," agreed Waistcoat. "Expecially Bluey! Old Bluey sure can run!"

Umbra sat across the room, his hand idling on today's bread chunk. "Runners, take your marks!"

Pinching them with the edges of his paper-thin frame, Waistcoat excitedly lifted the three creatures. They dangled in the air and kicked their little black legs.

"Go!"

Waistcoat dropped them right before his feet. They landed, gathered their wits, and scuttled across the cell. Though they could just as easily have run for their nests, the three creatures always chose bread over freedom. Across the stone floor they went, straight for the hunk at the far wall.

"Better men than we are . . ." Umbra muttered. He turned the statement over in his head. "Nah. They run for bread instead of freedom. They aren't better, just the same—captives of desire."

Sash shook his head. "What desire? We don't need food, drink, sleep, women—"

"Phage's shadow was hot," Waistcoat said, focusing on the race. "Go, Bluey! Go!"

"No carnal desires of any kind," Sash said.

"That's not true. We want all those things but don't have bodies to enjoy any of them. That's our greatest desire: bodies. To be real. That's the hunk of bread that keeps us running back into one cell or another."

"Bluey wins by an antenna!" Waistcoat cried as the three racers set in on the hunk of bread. He ambled across the floor, gingerly scooped up the bread and the three runners, and deposited them all in the latrine. "Nice derby, boys."

"I'm telling you two," Umbra said, "the First knows what we want, and he keeps us captive with it."

A voice from beyond the door spoke: "I'll agree with half of what you said. I do indeed know what you want."

Umbra scrambled away from the wall and withdrew to the far side of the cell. Sash stood beside him, arms crossed. Waistcoat sat down on the latrine, as if his transparent body could block sight of the roaches.

The First's voice came again: "Crack the seal. Let me in!"

An ogre guard crashed against the door, and it boomed as if it were a great tympanum. The second strike broke the lead seal, and the third sent the door screeching inward. The ogre's figure eclipsed any chance of escape, and behind him entered the First.

Clad neck to toe in black, with a head the color and shape of a limestone block, the First fixed his glassy eyes on the unmen. "I know what you want, yes, and with that knowledge I will not enslave you, but set you free." The First gazed at each unman in turn.

Waistcoat nervously shifted on the latrine, hoping to hide his pets but accidentally slipping within.

The First went on. "You want bodies. . . . I can give them to you."

Umbra bowed his head. "You can do it? A soul-shift?"

"Yes. I will give you preliminary bodies, which you will use to perform a small task."

"Here we go," Sash said sourly.

"Remember the woman you fought a month ago? Phage?"

"She has a great shadow," Waistcoat said.

"She is going to Topos to kill Akroma."

Sash and Waistcoat shuddered.

"Kill Akroma!" Umbra tried to calm his voice. "You think she can?"

"If Phage doesn't kill that witch, you must," the First said.

Umbra replied, "But, how . . . how could we do such a thing?"

"You'll be more powerful in your bodies, and you can figure it out along the way," the First replied.

"Let me get this straight. You want us to travel north with Phage to kill Akroma?" Umbra asked.

"Yes."

Waistcoat said, "So if Phage kills her singlehanded, we won't have to do a thing?"

"Actually, no," the First said. "If Phage succeeds at killing Akroma, you must kill Phage."

The three unmen gaped. Umbra spoke for them all. "You want us to travel to Topos and kill an angel-beast or a demon-girl?"

"Or both. Don't be disrespectful of Phage. She bears my son."

Sash snorted. "Oh, we'll be perfectly respectful right up to the time we kill her."

Umbra was working through the logic of it all. "How will you know if they are dead?"

"Because you will bring me their heads. Both heads, and you will trade your provisional bodies for your permanent ones. If you don't return, or return with one head or no heads, you will never have your permanent bodies."

"You see what he's doing?" whispered Umbra. "Run for the bread, boys. . . ."

"If you agree to this plan, you'll have bodies and walk freely from this place. You can even pretend to accompany Phage then flee in the night. You'll have to avoid Cabal guards, of course, but you would have the physical forms that you long for. Consider these provisional bodies my gift to you, simply for humoring me, but I think you'll want to continue the mission and receive the handsome, chiseled, youthful forms I have prepared for you."

Sash nodded slowly. "Oh, I get it. These first bodies will be old and diseased—"

"No, you'll have superhuman strength, speed, stealth, endurance, and battle abilities. Why would I send you out in weak forms? You may not be handsome, may be downright ugly, but you'll be strong and capable."

Umbra said, "I feel like this is a trap, but we just don't see it yet."

The First's icy demeanor became a little hot. "This cell is a trap. These empty forms—these are traps. I'm offering you the very thing you want, and you're not men enough to take it?"

"Give us a moment," Umbra said, walking to where Waistcoat sat awkwardly on the latrine. Sash approached too, and the three unmen huddled together, speaking in whispers.

"Why not?" Waistcoat asked. "It's everything we want. We get bodies, we get out of this pit, we don't have to be packed full of ogres and nightmares anymore. Oh, to really eat something!"

Sash hissed, "We're about to get bodies, and all you can think of is food!"

"Well, what'll you do with your body?" Waistcoat asked.

Leaning closer to the others, Sash said, "I'll run off and study painting, or work in a library, or learn more magic. What about you, Umbra? What will you do?"

Umbra sighed and wished he had lungs to make it worthwhile. "Just having a body—any healthy body—will be enough. For a while, I'll just sit and be real."

"Oooh! I like that!" Waistcoat said. "Except while I'm sitting, I'll be eating and drinking and smoking and whatever else people do with their bodies."

"It sounds like we're in agreement," Umbra said.

"It's better than sitting in a hole."

Waistcoat laughed. "Three holes sitting in a hole." Their huddle broke, and they turned outward to face their master.

"We've decided to take you up on the offer," Umbra said. "We'll take these provisional bodies—if they're healthy and strong

"They will be—"

"—and we'll go with Phage out of the coliseum. If we bring her head and Akroma's to you, we'll get to trade our starter bodies for better ones—pinnacles of beauty, health, strength, and grace."

"Well put," the First said, stepping toward them. "Let us begin."

The First grasped all three unmen in a shocking grip. They jittered and struggled, trying to break free, but his hold was implacable. His tongue twisted around words that were older than the continents, syllables that delved back to the birth of the first creature. He named the breath of life, and it emerged from his mouth in a rushing wind that struck the unmen. Their outlines rattled then folded up entirely. The First crumpled them in his fist and clung tight.

His other hand reached down into the latrine, three fingers separating above the roaches that ate there. Power jagged from his fingertips, danced along every scale on the bugs' back, and stabbed within.

The roaches grew. At first thumb sized, then fist sized, then head sized, the black bugs swelled until they were half the height of the First. They no longer fit in the latrine and spilled out on the floor.

Clenching his other hand, the First wrung the unmen's souls out of their tangled bodies. In three pulses of light, they rushed through his shoulders and into his other arm. Lightning leaped from his index finger into the first bug, from his middle finger into the second, and from his ring finger into the third. A trio of pops resounded, smoke rolled to the ceiling, and the First stepped back to admire his handiwork.

"What've you done?" wailed Umbra, his voice hissing and shrill.

"Just what we agreed," the First replied nonchalantly. "I gave you provisional bodies."

"You made us into roaches! Giant roaches!" cried Sash.

"Indeed."

"This isn't what we wanted," Waistcoat said. "Who would want to lay a giant roach?"

"Another giant roach," the First replied, and the three bugs quivered. "You have superhuman strength, speed, endurance, battle abilities, and protections. These are fine first bodies, and if you want human ones, you'll complete your mission."

Two of the unmen were left speechless.

Waistcoat squealed.

"Oh, shut up!" hissed Sash. "At least you got to be Bluey!"

CHAPTER 16

EMISSARIES

Stonebrow occupied an uncertain throne. Never before had Topos had a throne. The rule of Ixidor had been absolute and needed no ceremony, and the rule of Akroma had been unquestioned. Stonebrow, though, needed a throne, and Minister Lindolth and Priest Aioue—the architects of his reign—made sure he had one.

Topos had become a place of politicians.

Akroma had not been gone half an hour before Lindolth and Aioue realized they needed a grand figurehead. In Stonebrow they had found one. They had made him grander still in raiment and throne.

It was a centaur throne, made not for sitting but for standing. To Stonebrow, it seemed a sort of stable, though his promoters insisted it was a lofty niche. It resided atop twelve generous steps, covered with red silk that made his hooves slip whenever he ascended. On three sides of the throne rose elaborate oak carvings gilded in gold, and across the front draped a banner emblazoned with the motto of the new administration: TOPOS FOR ALL. Perhaps the most significant aspect of the throne were the booths to either side, one for Minister Lindolth, chief political liaison, and one for Priest Aioue, chief spiritual liaison. They stood slightly lower than their figurehead and by use of built-in speaking tubes could quietly command the new ruler.

Except that Stonebrow had his own mind. He put up with all this stately idiocy only so that he could rescue Topos from the Akroman heresy and make the Vision of Ixidor come true.

Throngs assembled. Once news had gone out that Akroma had vanished and a new, benevolent centaur had been installed, the people of Topos and all the neighboring lands had come to see Stonebrow. They had discovered a ruler who was patient and wise and daily heard petitions. Pilgrims had become supplicants. Today, two hundred such folk waited to plead their cases before him.

Currently, the elders of a small band of refugee elves stood before Stonebrow. They had come from Krosan, where their ancient homelands had been desolated and half their population destroyed. They came to Topos seeking a new home in Greenglades. Their leader was a wizened woman who had live two thousand years but who had the eyes of a child. In the tongue of Krosan centaurs, she was imploring Stonebrow, ". . . that you of all people know the ruin of Krosan and the plight of her people. You also know that a forest is lost without elves to tend it. What we propose would aid Greenglades as much as it aids us."

Stonebrow stared at her, thinking. This was a difficult decision. He understood the terrors these folk faced, but to invite into the heart of Topos a people who were not part of Ixidor's original vision could ruin all.

Whispers came frantically from both sides.

Lindolth: "Don't take them. You'll destroy hope for alliance with Krosan."

Aioue: "They'd dilute the Vision of Ixidor."

The men continued, trying to pull the strings of their political puppet.

Stonebrow was no puppet. "Wise woman," Stonebrow said to the elf, addressing her in her own language, "you and your people wish to become stewards of Greenglades, but do you know what that means? It is not simply an ecology you would be overseeing, but a theology. I must know that you will not only care for every plant and beast but also that you will faithfully keep the Vision of the one who created it." He leaned forward, his voice dropping but still audible to all those in the audience hall. "Do you believe in Ixidor?"

The old woman lowered her head. "We do not."

"Are you willing to learn of him? Are you willing to embrace him?"

Without looking up, she said, "We are not."

"Then go from this place and seek a home somewhere else. Or return here when your hearts are open, not just to the beauty of creation but to the glory of the creator."

Though the woman and her contingent of elves turned dejectedly away, the crowd seemed impressed by the wisdom of this centaur. In their separate booths, minister and priest said, "Well done. You put it back on her," and "You remained true to Ixidor."

The fact was that Stonebrow had hoped the wise woman would embrace belief, that she and her people would inhabit the forest and become emissaries to elves everywhere. This had not gone Stonebrow's way at all.

Pages directed the next supplicant forward, a man dressed in workman's leathers. Wide scroll cases hung by his hip. He smiled, teeth crowded between bristly whiskers, drew out one of the scrolls, and unrolled it. "Your Majesty," he said, bowing.

"Call me only General," the centaur rumbled.

"General," corrected the man, bowing again. "I am Borsoom, an engineer of stone structures. Anyone who has visited the great coliseum has seen my handiwork. I have a proposal to bring such a great work here to Topos and to greatly improve the beauty of the land—and that's what Ixidor wanted—beauty." He pointed to the scroll, a map of the region, with a lake that did not currently exist. His finger came to rest on a wide wedge that crossed Purity River. "A dam at this site would create a second lake atop the Stubble Fields, a waste space now. It would be idyllic, in keeping with your all-important

Vision." Brawny and brainy, this engineer grinned at his plan. He even had the audacity to say, "I could bring to Topos the same glory I brought to the Cabal."

Whispers flew in gnat swarms from the mouths of minister and priest, but Stonebrow only waved them away. He needed no advice to know how to deal with this one. "If Ixidor had wished a dam on his river, he would have built one himself. The Nightmare Lands— and let's officially abandon the term 'Stubble Fields'—are the sacred site of the battle that saved Topos, the battle in which Ixidor died. It is not a wasteland but hallowed ground. Please go from here, take your tools and ideas, and never return."

That judgment brought cheers and applause from the audience, and kudos from Stonebrow's advisors. The man withdrew, anger written on his face.

A small woman in initiates' garb approached. Her head was shaved bald and covered with old scars. She walked to the base of the stairs and instead of standing to address the centaur lay on her face.

The display silenced the crowd, and all strained to hear.

"Daughter," Stonebrow said gently, "what is your petition? What may I do for you?"

"It is what I may do for you, Sovereign," the woman said, not daring to lift her face. "I was a pupil of our lost lady, and she made much use of me, but since she vanished two months ago, I have had no use except to pray for her return."

"And you have prayed?"

"Every waking moment. I pray even now, with every breath, but I would do more. I would serve you in Ixidor's name."

Stonebrow strode out of his throne, his giant heart fluttering. Regally, he descended the silken steps until he stood just above the woman. Crouching, he reached for her head and gently lifted her face. "I would see your face, Daughter."

She lifted her head, and her face shucked its shadows.

Stonebrow gazed into a much-scarred mask with deeply sad eyes, and deeper devotion. "Braids!" he whispered.

"Let me serve," she said. "I wish only to serve."

Drawing her up, he embraced her to his chest, a child in the arms of her father. "Look at her, all of you. She pleases Ixidor. She comes not to receive but to give, but she will receive tenfold."

Braids nestled against him and trembled like a child.

"I will keep you with me," he said quietly. "I will show you the true Vision of Ixidor."

* * * * *

Each rooster bled, but the blood only fed their rage. They strutted, puffing their breast feathers and spreading their clipped wings. Eyes gleamed like glass beads. Talons lifted to tear more flesh away. The cock with the purple comb lunged, nipping the neck of its rival and yanking feathers from its leg. The other fowl shrieked and flapped away.

It couldn't go far. Human legs hemmed it in, and bloodthirsty shouts shook the air. For the roosters this was a fight to the death, but for the humans it was merely an afternoon's entertainment.

The purple-combed bird came at a run, its claws hurling little jets of brown dust behind it. Wings wide and beak gaping, it was a monster. It seemed almost to shake the ground. The other cock dived low and used its wing as a shield to cover its dodge. The purple-crested rooster only wheeled and followed, knowing its foe could not escape.

But it did escape. An avenue had opened through those human legs, leading away from the dust circle and toward the center of the main street. The frightened fowl ran full-out, past the rolling wheels of a brightly painted wagon and into a cool alley.

The cock's deliverance had come in the form of a carnival caravan. It had shaken the ground, made the humans turn, and covered the escape.

The caravan rattled to a halt. Its horse team stomped and snorted. Behind it, a wagon loaded with lumber stopped as well. A tan veil of dust rolled up from the wheels, momentarily obscuring the figure that leaped down from the buckboard. From that dust curtain he emerged like a man on a stage.

"Hello, Lordsburg! It's been a dusty road to your fair metropolis, and I've paid for it in my tail bone, but here I am!"

The people of Lordsburg—which was hardly a village, let alone a metropolis—only stared at this strange man.

Slight, blond haired, and handsome in the way of predators, he wore a bright yellow suit with tails. The inside was royal blue. He carried a cane of silver but did not lean on it, instead twirling it idly in his fingers. "Isn't anyone going to ask who I am?"

"Who are you?" one of the yokels blurted.

"I'm your dream come true. My name is Ringer."

"Ringer what?"

"Just Ringer, like just Yawgmoth—Ha ha! That's a little joke."

"What are you doing here?"

He jabbed his silver cane at the speaker. "Glad you asked, friend. I've come to give you an upgrade. I saw what you've had to settle for, entertainment-wise. Cockfighting. Shameful. You deserve better."

A gaunt farmer, whose voice box looked like a second chin, said, "We happen to like cockfights."

"Yes. Exciting! Interesting! But when was the last time you saw a cockfight in the coliseum? You're part of the coliseum circuit. You ought to have real coliseum entertainment. Why, just looking at this crowd, I can see there are five, maybe ten great gladiators standing among you."

The group chuckled at the flattery, but they moved closer to Ringer. Others who walked the dusty porches of the shops came down to listen.

Ringer began throwing open panels of his caravan. Each section folded out into a brightly painted backdrop, so that piece by piece the conveyance transformed into a broad, open-air stage. From the interior of the caravan, two sturdy-looking dwarfs emerged, their muscled arms crossed over their chests. While making his preparations, Ringer explained, "We don't need senseless violence—fowl tearing each other apart. That's not the coliseum ethic. We need real fights, resolving real conflicts. That way, not only do we get rousing entertainment, but we make our communities better."

"Uh, what?"

Ringer raised an eloquent eyebrow. "Oh, I'm sure Lordsburg has a few conflicts—those little things that cause strife. For instance: I notice you have lots of goats: Has anyone witnessed any impropriety regarding goats?"

"Im-pro-pr—?"

"Do any of the villagers prefer the company of goats to the company of women?"

Dead silence met him.

"Yes, I know. It is a terrible blight, and nobody wants to talk of it." Dramatically, he reached into his vest pocket and drew forth a gold piece. "This coin says one of you has witnessed such an encounter."

Ten hands went up in the crowd.

Ringer smiled graciously and leaned forward, selecting a certain young man—whip thin, with a harelip and cavernous nostrils. "I saw your hand first, and here is your gold piece. What is your name?"

"Clem."

"A sturdy name, Clem," Ringer said, bringing the gawky man up from the crowd and turning him around to face the other villagers. Putting his arm in a friendly way around Clem's shoulder, Ringer said, "If it's not too traumatic, we'd like to hear what you observed."

"It weren't dramatic, but just funny, really. See, I was coming back from the crick, going to put up my pole in the shed, when I seen it was kind of shuddering."

"Shuddering," echoed Ringer, a tremble in his voice.

"And I seen that my goat Maisy weren't tied up where I left her. So, I creep up to the doors to peek inside, and I got a eyeful."

"Of what, Clem?"

"Of Maisy and Delbut Tule."

The crowd released a sound that mixed disapproval with glee. Overtopping that noise came the cry of a portly man, "That's a lie!" Whom could be none other than Delbut Tule scrambled forward. "He's lying because he owes me for that goat and never paid. I was in the shed looking for a knife to cut her loose, and she just wandered in!"

"Come on up here, Delbut!" Ringer called, motioning. "And you folk thought there was no conflict in Lordsburg. Here, we have one man accused of inappropriate animal 'husbandry,' and another accused of defaulting on his debts."

"I didn't do it, I tell you," Delbut raged, face red. "I just want my property back."

"He means he wants his wife back—"

Delbut launched himself at his scrawny accuser, and the crowd erupted in shouts for a fight. Delbut would have caught Clem around the throat except that the two dwarfs leaped in, one grabbing either leg and bringing him down. The roars of the crowd devolved into shouts of "Ring-er! Ring-er! Ring-er!"

Though the yellow-clad showman pretended to aver, his smile told how much he enjoyed the attention. "It is a sort of cock fight after all, isn't it? All this while, you've lived with these two men at each other's throats, and only now do we bring it out in the court of public entertainment to sort things through. You should all get on your knees and bless the First of the Cabal for sending out arena hosts such as me. We will bring you the fruits of a duelist culture. Speaking of duelists, how many of you would like to see these two men battle to resolve this issue once and for all?"

The villagers shouting exultantly.

"A trial by conflict! Excellent. One of these men will be exonerated and the other damned. You can both get out of this if one of you admits he is lying. Clem, were you lying?"

"No, sir."

"Delbut?"

"Of course not! This is absurd."

"They want to fight, folks."

A great cheer rose, and the crowd waved wagers in the air.

"Yes, of course. Let's do this the Cabal way. My assistants are trained bookies and will assure all bets—for a ten percent commission, of course. The victor will receive half the Cabal's take and can remain for other challengers." He watched eagerly as the two dwarfs trundled through the crowd. Only Delbut and Clem looked less than excited. "This crude little street fight is but a foretaste of the glories that await Lordsburg. I have here, on this sliding panel, a depiction of the arena I will be building on the outskirts of your town." He gestured lovingly toward the painting, which showed a low circle of benches around a sand pit, with a "host's tower" to one side. "A community center that will entertain you, unite you, and give you a safe means for solving problems. Lordsburg will be part of the coliseum circuit. Your best and brightest might one day fight before the First himself."

The dwarfs returned, fists clenched around the money they had collected. They deposited it in a lock box in the caravan.

"Very good!" said Ringer. "Now, everybody get where you can see. Combatants, you must stay within the circle that Stumps is scribing there with his heel. Otherwise, this is a bare hands, bare feet competition to first blood."

"Make it to knock out!" someone shouted.

Ringer looked to the two combatants, who trembled, white-faced. "What do you think?"

Clem spat, "Why don't we fight till Delbut wets himself. That'll be about half a second."

"To knock out!" shouted Delbut, swinging a right hook. It caught Clem's jaw and spun the narrow man away.

Clem fell in the dust, his lip bleeding and one of his teeth loose. He spat blood and scrambled up, ramming his shoulder into Delbut's stomach and driving him onto his back.

The crowd roared.

The men fought, and the blood only fed their rage.

* * * * *

As dusk seeped up from the corners of the throne room, the petitioners dwindled. Stonebrow heard one more plea, and the rest of the crowd was dismissed by Minister Lindolth and Priest Aioue. They too took their leave, going to steaming suppers waiting in their quarters. Only the general and his guards remained.

"Stand outside," he ordered them.

The guards withdrew through the doors and shut them.

Stonebrow sighed. Rarely did he have time alone. Just now, all he wished to do was breathe. The air was warm and redolent with the scent of the masses—the smell of a herd. He was their shepherd, and a shepherd must always watch for wolves.

Lindolth and Aioue were wolves in the fold, and Stonebrow was vigilant against them. Even now, his eyes flicked to the doors and the windows, hardly certain his "advisors" were truly gone. Day by day, he struggled to tame them, and in time they would be more like herd dogs than wolves.

The real dangers were the predators Stonebrow couldn't see. They hid just beyond the hills and breathed just beneath the aural threshold. He would find them out now.

"Disciples," he whispered, "come. Report."

A nearby curl of gilded oak glinted blue as if with a speck of moonlight. That speck, though, lifted free of the frieze and soared toward a nearby window. It slipped through the glazing and sped out into a starry night to call the other disciples. The speck shone in the spangled heavens, flashing a summons.

It would take time for the disciples to gather. Many labored at the far reaches of Otaria. They flew as fast as shooting stars, but still it would take them minutes to converge. In the intervening time, Stonebrow breathed.

At last, he had reached a position where he might do great good. He could clean up the mess left by Kamahl, could even undo the evils of Akroma and avert a war with Phage. He had ascended to the throne of Ixidor, the throne of a god, and he would cleanse the land and the people of evil.

The disciples arrived in a furious blue firestorm. Like windblown sand, they struck the glass and tapped along it until they found cracks. Disciples poured through and streamed toward Stonebrow. They impacted his forehead in a merciless torrent.

He saw things. He saw the faith of Ixidor in the upraised hands of avens. He saw human believers abducting prostitutes from the dark cells of Aphetto. He saw parades of elf pilgrims venturing from the ruination of Krosan toward the glories of Topos. These things made him glad.

Other things made him sad. In Sanctum, the once-faithful soldiers of Ixidor turned their faces down from him and cupped their hands around dice. In Cabal City, a duelist had decked himself out in the semblance of Ixidor and mocked him as he fought. Worst, though, in the Pardic Mountains, Ixidoran faith had turned warlike, and those who refused to convert were slain.

Stonebrow wished to right these wrongs, but he hadn't a moment to think. More images flooded him—nations gearing for war, voices hoarse with praise, men hanged for their sins. . . . The terrors of a wide continent flooded into his narrow mind. It was maddening. Stonebrow bellowed, but the disciples would not stop. They sluiced through him, bearing the petitions of a multitude. It was as if every voice in Otaria pleaded or praised, cursed or laughed, converted or recanted, and all of them did so in his shouting mind.

This was what it was to sit in the seat of a god.

CHAPTER 17

VIGNETTES

So," Phage said wearily, "you three are the finest spies the First could find?" She glanced down at the dog-sized cockroaches that scuttled along the road beside her.

"The best he could find, yes," said the one who called himself Sash. "The better ones are so good that no one can find them."

Phage allowed herself a smile. She knew these "assistants" were assassins. Still, they were funny and clever, the most amusing companions she had had in years. Beneath their black shells, their hearts were not black at all. Phage stared ahead to where the Corian Escarpment rose. "What are your specialties?"

"I'm good at scuttling," said the one called Waistcoat.

Sash put in, "He means covert movement. My own specialty is intelligence."

"I'm also good-looking," Waistcoat added.

Phage laughed. "And what about you, Umbra?"

"I'm a handler. I keep these two in line."

"I don't buy it," Phage replied. "I think you're an assassin."

Umbra didn't flinch, black-barbed legs continuing their ceaseless movement. "Why do you say that?"

"This is a mission to kill Akroma. Wouldn't the First naturally send an assassin?"

Umbra still rushed along in silence.

"And assassins never tell their true job."

"I told you, I'm the handler for these two."

"You just confirmed it," Phage said placidly. She glanced askance at the other two. "So Waistcoat will sneak up on me, Sash will learn all that I know, and Umbra will kill me."

"No! No!" they chorused, and Umbra said, "We're on *your* side."

"I mean, if I were Akroma."

"Oh, yes." Umbra said.

Not the best spies, giving away their roles, their mission, their dispositions. No, these weren't killers at heart, but it didn't take a heart to kill.

"What's your plan for getting past the siege of Sanctum?" asked Sash.

"I thought you specialized in intelligence," Phage said. "The siege of Sanctum is a joke. The army sent to capture the town has been captured by it. The camp has become a new district. We'll walk right through it."

* * * * *

Stonebrow, Priest Aioue, and Initiate Braids packed for a trip to besieged Sanctum. It had become an international joke. Instead of gaining a colony, Topos had lost an army. It was time to end the siege, to regain the folk lost to the seduction of Sanctum, and to seek alliance with this crucial settlement.

Stonebrow shouldered his own pack. Though he was a sovereign, he was still a proud centaur. His eyes roved across the wagon train and the great tent where he, Aioue, and Braids would stay, and he said a blessing on the soul of Ixidor.

Stonebrow was setting things right. In two months, he had already rectified much of Akroma's heresy. In two months more, he would bring Ixidor's Vision into reality.

* * * * *

Zagorka was sitting on her balcony, feet propped on the stone rail, when a loud knock came at the door. She swung her legs down, discovered they had fallen asleep, and ambled stiffly into her apartments. The rooms smelled of her, clean and earthy, with lots of wool and stone. The place was truly hers now, but she wondered how much longer it would be.

The knock came again, metallic as if made with brass knuckles.

"Threats everywhere," she grumbled to herself. "I'm coming!"

Descending stone stairs to the street level, Zagorka opened the door and had to catch her breath.

There before her were a set of brass knuckles clutched in a black fist. More ominous still was the wan face behind those knuckles, and the piercing eyes that gazed at her. "Hello, Zagorka."

"Hello, Phage."

Phage lowered her fist, slipped off the brass knuckles, and slid them into a breast pocket. "Didn't want to rot your door."

"Appreciate it," Zagorka said, only then noticing the three huge cockroaches that stood around the woman. "These yours?"

"Friends of mine, yes," Phage said. "Cleaner than most people think. Funnier too. They'll behave—that is, if we're invited in."

Zagorka stared at her onetime boss, the woman who had transformed Sanctum in the image of the Cabal then abandoned it to the armies of Topos. "I'm still mad at you. You saw Akroma's army. It would've been nice to have some help with 'em."

"You seem to've done all right," Phage said.

Zagorka arched her eyebrow. "You said you'd sworn off the Cabal, but then you set up a Cabal arena, and last you backed out on us. Where do you stand, Phage?"

"Right here, Zagorka."

"That's not good enough."

Phage hitched her smile. "If you have to know, I'm heading to Topos to kill Akroma. That'd be in both our interests."

"You're not staying here?"

"A night, maybe a week, but then we have to get on," Phage said. "I've got just four months to do this and get back to the coliseum."

"What's the rush?"

Phage gestured down across her belly. "You can't see it yet, but I'm pregnant."

Something broke in Zagorka. Her own child, born sixty years before, already lay in his grave, and every day she remembered him. When she had given birth, her heart had migrated out of her body to hang halfway between herself and her son. It had never returned.

"Come in," Zagorka said. "Come in. How far along are you?"

Phage smiled, stepping up onto the threshold. She wore steel-soled shoes so that she wouldn't rot whatever wood she stepped on. "Five months, by my best reckoning."

Behind her, the roaches edged forward, their antennae licking at the door stoop.

Zagorka shot them a narrow look. "You're sure they won't eat things and, well—pass things?"

Before Phage could reply, one of the roaches did, its voice a controlled shriek. "I assure you, madam, we're quite civilized as regards eliminations. We do eat, just as you do—at a table, with plates and flatware."

"Sorry," Zagorka said. "I didn't realize."

"For a colony that prides itself on tolerance, Sanctum is certainly prejudiced against roaches," the creature said.

Phage laughed, an unusual sound. "The gate guard chased them with a stick."

Another of the black bugs chimed in. "One whack, and we chased him."

"Have you thought of names?" Zagorka asked, changing the subject as the group reached the top of the stairs and entered the main room.

Phage sighed. "No time yet. I should, though, shouldn't I?"

"I wish my mother had spent more time thinking about names," Zagorka said. Both women laughed. "How long do you think you'll stay?"

"I thought, perhaps, a couple days, though I'm a little more weary than I had expected."

"Make it two weeks. You need to take it slow. I have an extra room I'm not using. I want to know who the father is. I want to know everything . . ." Zagorka led Phage out onto the stone balcony. Phage seated herself on the stone rail, and Zagorka poked her head back in. "You boys settle in. We've got some talking to do."

The three roaches meanwhile scuttled up into seats, stretching their legs out before them. "Don't mind us. We like stories."

"You're a strange bunch of roaches," Zagorka said.

"Yes, we are."

* * * * *

Akroma battled through the never-ending gullet of the beast. The dark was absolute, filled with groping organelles. She wished for her axe, for the lightning lance. Her wings had become shields, and they smoldered with gastric juice.

Ahead, something glowed—a creature embedded in the wall of the gut. It was a dwarf, still alive. His extremities had been absorbed, but his torso and body remained within the digestive envelope. The dwarf stared out at Akroma. His bleary eyes no longer hoped for rescue. Surely he had watched multitudes pass this way, had cried out to the first hundred, and had witnessed their own slow, torturous absorption.

Still, Akroma questioned him, as she had all the others. "Where is Ixidor? Where is Nivea?"

The dwarf's eyes rolled whitely in his head. His voice rattled with phlegm. "Gone . . . gone . . ."

"But where? They must be here."

He strained as the membranes thickened around him. "Everyone is here. Everyone dies, but the wurm never dies."

Akroma gnashed her teeth and strode on. Her feet slipped on the slick gut.

"Everyone!" he called out behind her.

She tried to set her claws in the gut wall but foundered. A glance showed that her claws were gone, dissolved to pale nubs. The pads had grown tender, years of thick calluses worn through. Soon, the juices would eat into living flesh.

"Everyone!"

Akroma flexed her wings, driving herself with small surges. Her heart trembled in panic. What if she didn't find Ixidor? What would it be like to have her wings fuse to the wall? To hang there in slow agony while all the rest was eaten away?

She could not think such things. She could only plunge from one soul light to the next and hope that Ixidor still shone.

* * * * *

Phage and her cockroach friends crouched behind a great boulder on the edge of the Corian badlands. They were but a day's hike north of Sanctum, and already they had run into trouble.

"It's a contingent from Topos," Phage said, studying the tents and guards on the desert below. The sun raked across the camp, hurling giant shadows behind every creature. Soon it would be dark. "A royal contingent. Do you see those white-tower banners? That's the emblem of Akroma. She must be inside the large central tent."

Beside her, Umbra lifted segmented antennae to taste the air. "Doesn't smell like her. She smells like hate."

Phage looked quizzical. "What does hate smell like?"

"Lightning. She's paranoid, vengeful." The roach paused, its ink-drop eyes shifting to glance at her. "Um, well, that's what I heard."

Phage liked these bugs more and more. "What else have you heard?"

Umbra glanced back out at the camp. "Well, ah, they say Akroma doesn't travel like this. She doesn't sleep in tents. She flies, attacks, and returns to her nest."

The creature had a point. "Would Akroma sleep in a tent if she were on a diplomatic mission?"

"Chckkch Chckkch," laughed Waistcoat. The other two roaches joined in. "Akroma diplomatic? Chckkch Chckkch."

Phage had to laugh as well. "Then who is down there under her banner, with guards all around and state ceremony?"

"I'll see," Waistcoat suggested. He dashed away from the stone, onto the desert.

"Wait," Phage said, but it was too late.

The bug tore straight across the wastes, his black form easily visible on the sun-dappled sand.

A guard on the perimeter spotted him and shouted. The man drew his sword and ran toward Waistcoat.

"I thought you said he was an expert in covert movement," Phage growled.

"I didn't say that. He did," replied Sash. "He's also an expert in lying."

Waistcoat's black legs flew, bearing him on a collision course with the guard.

Sword raised, the man judged the moment and brought the steel down in a penetrating jab. All it penetrated, though, was packed sand.

Waistcoat jigged aside and shot for the big tent. He slid beneath its wall, disappearing from view.

Someone within bellowed, and someone else screamed. Waistcoat was heard to add "Chckkch Chckckch." A huge fist hit the tent side, knuckles standing in brief relief. Something crashed over, and a large volume of liquid spilled.

Shouting, the guards converged on the tent, their steel drawn. They shoved through the flap only to get tripped by a giant roach pelting out. Most of the warriors fell to the side, but one had a brief and bouncy ride on Waistcoat's back before he tumbled to the ground. The men rolled over and stood just in time to be bowled down by a huge figure that rushed from the tent.

"General Stonebrow?" Phage wondered aloud as the centaur galloped in pursuit of the darting roach. "What's he doing working for Akroma?" In the dusty wake of the general ran the arms men and a priest whose face was as white as paper. "A splendid diversion. You two go join Waistcoat. Keep them running in circles on the far side of the camp. I need to get a look at Stonebrow's plans."

The roaches warily watched their comrade dart through a gauntlet of steel, one sword even clanging off his back. "What if they catch us?"

"What kind of spies are you?" Phage hissed. "Get going."

Umbra was the first to move, not running out across the sand but drawing back his coverlets, spreading iridescent wings, and rattling his way skyward. Sash followed, his wings making a metallic buzz.

Phage took a moment to stare in wonder at those crazy bugs as they drifted through the air. They looked like machines, their plates sharp against the sky. In mere moments, Sash and Umbra had crossed the wastes and dived down to strafe Stonebrow's head.

The centaur instinctively swatted at them and roared, bedeviled. Arms men turned and ran toward him, swords upraised.

Seeing her moment, Phage stole quickly out along the sand. She kept to the deepening shadows and moved rapidly toward the tent. She rushed to the small indentation where Waistcoat had entered and pulled herself through.

Inside was a silken space in disarray. An overturned table had crushed a wine barrel, and it gushed red across the ground. Plates lay shattered on the floor, and the food they had carried was scattered nearby. Stonebrow must have been eating his supper when Waistcoat barged through—a typical roach scenario. No wonder Stonebrow and his albino friend pursued with such fury. Phage made a visual search of the wreckage, saw no orders or battle plans, and strode on through a curtain into the next chamber—a shrine to Ixidor.

She stopped cold. She had emerged behind an altar of blue shells and stones, and in front of it knelt a woman in prayer. The woman wore a simple cloak of homespun over shoulders bowed with guilt. Her head was shaved in penitence, and her hands trembled with the depth of her devotion. Final prayers mumbled from her lips, and she sat up, looking square into the eyes of Phage.

It was Braids. Somehow Akroma had captured her and brainwashed her to worship Ixidor. Her eyes were glazed and her cheeks tear-stained. She opened her mouth to scream.

Phage shoved the altar over. It toppled, heavy shells crashing on Braids's skull and knocking her to the ground. She managed only a moan before she collapsed. Phage walked around the fallen mess, sized up her prey, and ripped down the silken curtain between the rooms. She hoisted the altar and used a conch shell to roll the unconscious woman onto the curtain. A few quick knots turned the silk into a sack, and Phage dragged her old friend through the tent and out the front flap.

The roaches were doing their jobs admirably, and the sun had set, leaving the camp darkened. Phage dragged the bag through trammeled patches and down a swale. They wouldn't find her track until morning, and by then it would be too late.

"Don't worry, sweet sister. I'll take you away from this cult. I have friends, buggy little friends. They'll take you back to your home, to the First. He wants to kill me, but he'll want to save you. He'll return you to what you were."

Phage dragged the silken sack toward the badlands. Her underlings would meet her there, and she would give them their new assignment—to carry Braids back to the coliseum. Freed of comrades and assassins, both, she would continue alone to Topos.

Phage smiled. She'd be sad to see the roaches go.

* * * * *

"You want us to do what?" asked Waistcoat, still panting after his narrow escape. He had lost a leg to Stonebrow's hoof, but somehow he could run even faster with just five.

Phage stared down at the three bugs, her figure a dark blot against the starry sky. "I don't *want* you to do anything. I'm *telling* you to take Braids to the First."

Umbra groomed sand out of his antennae. "Our mission to Topos takes precedence. The First himself assigned us."

"You'll have time to catch up. Take Braids to the coliseum then fly straight for Topos," Phage said.

Waistcoat groused, "Have mercy! I've got just five legs!"

"I'll yank off the rest right here unless you take Braids," Phage said flatly. "You can complete both missions or complete no missions. It's up to you."

Sash said, "She puts a fine point on it."

Phage averred. "Yes, I'll kill you if you fail me, and the First will kill you if you fail him—trapped between one death and another. A sticky spot." She paused to consider. "Let's put it this way: Who would you rather help, me or the First?"

"You," announced Umbra, to the surprise of the other two roaches. They shot him worried looks, but Umbra responded, "I specialize in wrangling these two. We'll get Braids back and return with our heads on our thoraxes and meet you in Topos."

In the darkness, Phage smiled. "You do that."

CHAPTER 18

TO SET THE CAPTIVES FREE

Stonebrow, Aioue, and the royal guard strode angrily among his siege troops. The camp outside of Sanctum was in chaos. It was more than Stonebrow could take.

He'd had a rough few days. Two nights ago, he had fought off giant roaches while someone desecrated the shrine of Ixidor and abducted Braids. A long day of march followed while he chewed on those losses. Now, another day had dawned to reveal this!

"Weak-willed licentious imbeciles," Stonebrow growled through gritted teeth.

No one stood guard in the camp. The only soldiers out and about were hunched above dice games in the path. Everyone else still lay asleep in their tents, rising only to run to the ridge and relieve themselves. They had had half a year to dig latrines, but still they urinated off a hillside.

Ixidor had elevated these people with divine vision, but Zagorka had debased them with puerile pursuits. Truth was powerless against pleasure.

Stonebrow had dreamed of marching to the center of his army and delivering a speech that would stir their hearts to devotion. In the glare of the morning sun, though, that dream had faded to nothing. The army had been captured by degrees. It made no sense to rail at them, but to go to Sanctum and negotiate their release.

Stonebrow felt sick. Ever since the giant roaches had attacked, nothing had been right. He himself was beginning to doubt Ixidor. It was easy to believe in him in Topos, where his creations were everywhere and nothing existed that was beyond his reach, but here, in the Corian badlands beneath the escarpment, other creators had greater power. In the shadow of that ancient cliff, Ixidor's truth seemed small and limited—beautiful but unnecessary.

The Vision was blurring, and Stonebrow feared it might go utterly dark.

Feared or hoped . . .

Stomping deliberately through a bones game, Stonebrow drove the dice into the ground. He snarled to his contingent, "Let's get to this city we have supposedly captured."

*   *   *   *   *

"Be calm, fair creature," the First said quietly to the young antelope he had caught. He leaned forward in the small boat, set the oars in the water, and stroked once more. "Your time is done. Death will be swift."

The antelope dangled over the stern, above black waters. It no longer struggled, only hanging in its net. Its fore hooves occasionally dipped into the liquid, trailing droplets. Though the swamp was utterly still around the boat, death lurked beneath the waters and waited for its chance.

The boat nosed among cypress roots and slid through curtains of old-man's beard. Despite the stealth of the craft, the First's mere approach silenced the creatures in the trees. They sensed his presence, lethal and angry, and kept their distance. He only hoped that the creatures beneath the water couldn't sense him. Would the young animal be enticement enough?

It bleated plaintively.

"There, there," soothed the First. "You die not just for pleasure, though that would be reason enough. You die to serve the Cabal. To serve me."

The First needed this excursion. He had to work some things through. Murder had been growing in him like an infected boil, swelling every day. He had come out to lance the boil and bleed away some of his fury. Killing a few animals would help, but it would not get rid of the infection. Only one thing would do that: the death of Phage.

For so long, the First had lived without a heart. Phage came, and she became his heart—an organ that weakened him, would kill him. He would never be well again until he had cut her out of his chest and hurled her into the fire. Perhaps the roaches had already done it. That thought made him glad.

Something stirred beneath the surface, and the First watched eagerly. "It won't be long now, sweet creature," he purred, stowing the oars and waiting. The wake of the boat stilled, rippling out beneath twisted roots. "Now, if only you could speak—but a word. A single word, and we will have our prey."

The antelope complied, bleating once.

The glassy surface shattered, and from the black depths erupted a great green creature. A huge muzzle broke through and opened. Swamp waters poured past triangular teeth and into a cavernous throat. The mouth of the monster yawned around the struggling antelope. Then teeth snapped closed, not touching the creature but severing the pole that held the net and nearly swamping the stern of the craft.

The First held on, watching delightedly.

The behemoth splashed its jaws on the black water, shoved downward, and vanished.

"Remarkable."

The First dived. His leather-garbed figure was sleek and small after the scaly monster, and he sliced into the water with the smallest splash. Black currents dragged him down after the beast.

Light failed in the gritty water. The First's hands cupped the flood, and a kick drove him onto the creature's back. He latched on, jamming his hands beneath the thing's scales so that flesh touched flesh.

The behemoth hissed at the shocking touch, huge bubbles belching up from its teeth. A kicking antelope went with them, drifting toward the surface. The monster thrashed, trying to shake off its attacker, but the First held on.

He had known this would be a ride. It would take longer for his deadly touch to kill a creature this size, but a longer kill was a better kill.

It thrust toward the surface, webbed claws hurling water downward. The monster broke through and took another breath, and the First did likewise. It plunged again, twisted, drove its back up against a snarl of roots, to no avail. Already, its spine was dying. When it lost use of its hind legs and tail, the First could climbed higher to kill arms and lungs and finally the brain of the thing. It would be a long day full of killing, and the First would feel much better after it all.

He would raise the beast again, an undead behemoth for his growing army.

* * * * *

Stonebrow's anger stoked only hotter as he strode up the abandoned streets of Sanctum. The few residents about were old or dull or both, but at least they could point, and all of them pointed to the top of the escarpment.

"*Everyone* is up there?" Stonebrow asked a toothless old man sitting on a bench.

" 'Cept me," came the laconic reply.

"Why?"

"Some buzz."

J. Robert King

Stonebrow shook his head, shielding his eyes with one hand. The fastest way to the top was the lift he used to run. Something niggled at his mind—how he had been coopted by Phage then by Akroma. "I can't ride that lift."

The old man cocked his head toward Aioue. "Your white friend can. You'll have to climb like a goat, I 'spect."

"Climb like a goat," Stonebrow said through gritted teeth. "Climb like a goat."

Angrily, he took the man's advice, galloping up the stone road. Aioue and the royal guard shouted, but their words were drowned out by his thundering hooves. Switchback after switchback led him up the steep face of the cliff, up ancient thoroughfares and through new settlements.

Soon, Stonebrow had risen above the highest rooftops and ran along trails at the brow of the cliff. Deep-scarred runes covered the stone wall. When last Stonebrow had been here, this rock face was clear. Now not a bare patch remained.

Was the whole world going insane?

Stonebrow reached the plateau. A froth had built on his shoulders, and he shook, flinging foam down on the rocks. Winded, he climbed steadily toward the circle of stones.

Around and among the megaliths stood a crowd—perhaps two-thousand men, women, and children. They were hushed. Only the occasional murmur broke the silence. All stared toward the center of the ring. To one side sat Zagorka aback Chester, her old neck craned for a better view.

Stonebrow headed rapidly toward her but kept his hoofbeats light. The red stone beneath him crackled, and soon the horizons were lost, as if this mountaintop floated alone in the sky. He sidled up next to Zagorka. "Some new game?" he asked in a whisper that seemed to carry for miles.

"Yep," she replied, not looking toward him. "It just ain't *our* game."

Turning toward the center of the circle, Stonebrow at last saw what everyone else stared at.

A man stood there, not a flesh and blood creature, but something like hot glass—solid but amorphous, translucent and weird. It was taller than any man or elf Stonebrow had ever seen, and slender, with rodlike limbs. Each of its extremities ended in a rounded point, and heat rose in waves from its shoulders.

"It's still hot," Stonebrow murmured. "They stood it up while it was hot?"

At last, Zagorka glanced toward him. "What are you talking about? Oh, hi, Stonebrow."

He didn't return her greeting, focusing on the red figure. "I'm talking about the statue."

"It isn't a statue," Zagorka said, again staring. "Look. It moves."

A frisson made the fur on Stonebrow's back stand on end. He saw it now. The figure's head, shaped like a glass bead, pivoted slowly about on its stiff neck. Eyes that were no more than oval bumps on that smooth face gazed out with strange intensity. No one stood within twenty feet of the creature, and the space around it widened as its gaze swept the crowd.

"Where did it come from?" Stonebrow asked quietly.

"The glyphs," Zagorka replied. She nodded toward the nearest monolith. "They've been shifting, forming figures."

On a pillar not twenty yards away, a similar stick-man was carved, poised as if to step from the stone. "You think it came out of the stone?"

The old woman shrugged. "I don't know what to think. None of us saw where it came from."

Someone shouted, "Get back!"

"You don't know what it'll do!"

"Clive, you idiot!" This final comment came from a woman near the glyph-man. She had just lost a tugging match with a man, presumably the idiot.

Clive ventured into the no-man's-land around the amorphous figure. Jaunty, he thrust his thumbs in the pockets of his tattered vest and flashed a gap-toothed smile back at the crowd. More people shouted warnings to him, but Clive seemed only encouraged. He studied the slowly moving figure, rubbed the sparse beard on his chin, and stepped forward, hand extended.

The throng gasped.

Clive said, "Welcome to Sanctum."

The moment his hand touched the glyph-man, skin seared and adhered. Clive shrieked, trying to pull free. A visible burn line advanced up his arm, turning it black. The line crossed his shoulder and marched up his neck.

Clive slumped, held aloft only by the flaming flesh of his hand. The rest of his body cooked on the bone. At last, his hand gave way, and Clive fell into a pile of meat. Even it was rendered to oil that flashed away and was gone.

"Clive!" the woman screamed. She staggered into the clear space and fell to her knees beside the grease spot. Wailing piteously, she reached in to grab bits of charred bone. "Clive! Oh, Clive!" There was very little left of him. Soot-blackened hands groped, by chance finding a stone. She gripped it and hurled it, shrieking, "Damn you! Take me too!"

It sailed through the air and struck the glyph-man's side. The rock shattered, spraying jagged shrapnel on everyone around.

The woman got her wish. She folded up on the black spot and lay there, unmoving. Perhaps twenty more fell too. Others nearby stampeded away, trampling those that fell.

As the last shards dropped and rolled, Stonebrow bellowed, "Hold your ground! Don't panic!" The words worked, and the crowd steadied.

The glyph-man didn't advance and made no hostile move.

"Thank you," Zagorka said breathlessly. "You saved dozens of lives."

"I'll save more," Stonebrow said, watching a brave few in the crowd edge close enough to drag the wounded away. "My army can be your army—"

"*Your* army? Since when is it your army?"

"Akroma has been gone for nearly three months. I have been ruling Topos in her stead."

Zagorka smiled raggedly. "So, you actually did it. You killed Akroma."

Stonebrow blinked. "To all intents and purposes . . . ."

"And now you're in charge." She grinned. "Congratulations."

"Thank you. My offer is genuine—my army will be your army—"

"It already is."

Stonebrow didn't take the bait. "We will fight for you . . . if you ally with Topos and break all ties to the Cabal."

"Ally with Topos?" Zagorka laughed. "Look, I know you're the honcho over there now, but you're starting to sound like another sword-swinging dictator."

The giant centaur narrowed his eyes. "I believe in Ixidor, if that's what you mean."

"Ixidor. Wow." Zagorka looked rueful. "Look, Stonebrow, a lot's happened since you left. It's all taught me that Sanctum stands alone. We're not allying with nobody—Cabal or Topos."

"You need military might now more than ever."

"No offense, but have you looked at your army lately?"

Stonebrow snorted defensively. "I'll take care of that. I'll whip them into shape, leave them here to become the security force for Sanctum. Either that, or I'll take them back with me and leave you alone to fight—whatever these things are. It's your choice, Zagorka."

The old woman sighed. "We've been abandoned before. Allies've only ever hurt us. Sanctum stands alone."

Stonebrow shook his head, staring at the glyph-man, who just then was staring back at him. "Not for long, I fear." He turned and began to walk away.

"Aren't you going to stay to see what happens?"

He shook his head and cantered on toward the cliff path. "I have my own nation to rule." It looked as if he would be making his rousing speech after all. Surely when his troops heard of the horror coming into being above Sanctum, they would return to the truth, to the Vision of Ixidor.

* * * * *

Ahead in the tunnel of black acid, there shone a brilliant light.

Akroma quickened her pace, running now on the bone-ends of her dissolving legs. How long she had survived in the belly of this beast, this timeless place of agony, she did not know, but she had seen hundreds of abscesses. Only this one shone like a trapped star.

It had to be Ixidor.

Akroma hurled herself on, using half-eaten wings to shove against the ceiling of the passage. With each surge, the light intensified. Squeezing through a foul sphincter, Akroma plunged into a wide spot in the deathwurm's endless gut.

The muscles here had distended, as if incapable of moving along a creature too large to swallow. On the far side of the space, imbedded in a dripping wall of gray flesh, there hung a bright vision.

Not Ixidor, but Nivea. The woman's face was the perfection on which Akroma's had been based. Smooth skin, large eyes, full lips, a long mane of hair, a slender and young body, strong arms and legs, fingers and toes. She was whole and pristine, encased in a sac of transparent fluids. She shone.

Where was Ixidor?

Standing on bone ends, Akroma searched the darkness. There was no sign of the master. Still, Akroma could save Nivea, fly to Topos, and there recover for another mission to save her master. Spiderlike, Akroma ambled on her stumps to the beaming bolus. Her hands ripped at the membrane that held the lady. That face—it was as if she were freeing herself from captivity. . . .

Something latched onto Akroma's waist and yanked. The thing shrieked, but its arm was weak. Akroma took a step back to strike away the foul creature. Her blow stopped short.

It was Ixidor.

He was emaciated, his skin raw from digestive juices, but otherwise was whole and certainly alive. His right arm was gone, of course, for he had sacrificed it long ago to create Akroma. His mouth and eyes gaped, and he screamed. "No! Akroma! No!"

Filled with joy and terror, Akroma collapsed at the feet of her lord. "Master! I've come to free you."

"Don't touch her!" Ixidor cried. Juices flung from his jutting beard. "Never touch her!"

Akroma didn't know what to say. "We can't just leave her here. We have to take her with us."

"No!" he shouted. "Never. She can't leave, and I won't."

What could Akroma say? "Are you real, Master? Are you sane?"

A feverish light shone in the creator's eye. "I'm real, yes," he gestured to the bag of waters, "but she is only a ghost. Don't you understand? This is the deathwurm of Nivea. This bolus is attached to the gut wall beside its heart. It holds her soul. She'll never live again, but her spirit lingers here. If you cut open this sac, she'll be gone forever, and the wurm will die. You mustn't, my child. I could not bear it."

Akroma shook her head. "You can't stay here! You'll be eaten alive."

"No," Ixidor said. "The wurm wants me here to complete it, and I want to be here. Only foes, such as you . . ." he let the words trail away as he saw her ruined figure—wings and legs, skin burned by acid, all in tatters. "You've done so much, sweet Akroma, but you can't free her. You can't free me."

Never before had the angel wept, but now she wept, and her tears mixed with the acids that ate away her legs.

Ixidor's mad tone had softened, and he cupped her chin in his hand. "I will not leave you desolate, my darling. I will not send you back in ruin."

Here was the greatness of the man: Even in the heart of a monster, standing beside the ghost of his beloved, emaciated and without hope of ever seeing the sun again, Ixidor was a creator. With his only hand, he reached out to the gut wall of the monster, dug strong fingers into it, and ripped away a long ribbon of black flesh. It wriggled spastically in his hand, dying even as he held it. With a simple flick of his wrist, he folded the flap of muscle and sent his will into it. Blue sparks scintillated from his fingers, straightening the sinews. Black meat flattened and transformed, attenuating. He carried the stuff to Akroma, who still knelt beside the shining bolus. With the decorum of a king mantling a champion, Ixidor laid the metamorphosing flesh on her back. It fused with her ravaged wings, renewing them. Suddenly, they were white and bright and huge again.

Ixidor staggered back, dizzy. That one act of grace had spent him. "I can do no more. . . . Go. . . . Now. . . ."

"I won't leave you!"

"Do not disobey!" the man said. "Go. . . . Burst through just there, before the wurm heals."

Rising on her bone ends, Akroma wept. "I'll return for you!"

"Go!"

She leaped into the air, her wings spreading in the chamber. She could stroke but once. It would be enough; her new wings held the strength of a god. They hurled her into the severed wall, and her head split the membranes. Tucking her wings, she blasted through. Her upper body jutted from the outer skin of the beast, but the wurm's muscles constricted, squeezing as if to pinch her in half. Gritting her teeth, she spread her wings to widen the wound. The opening dilated, and she shot free.

Akroma spread her wings in the airy void and hurtled away from the wurm. Another stroke, and the beast was only a black circle beneath her. She flew. Thanks to the creator, she flew. How long she had spent in the gullet of the beast, she could not know, nor how long she would fly these darkling winds, but even as her wings carried her higher, toward that minuscule boot box somewhere above, her heart remained with Ixidor below.

CHAPTER 19

EMERGING

Stonebrow was gone. A month ago he had marched out, taking the troops of Topos with him. Since then, many other staunch residents of Sanctum had fled as well. Who could blame them? The city was haunted.

The high, holy place burgeoned with Glyphs, fifty or sixty of the angular men who seemed to be made of molten glass. Every day, more emerged from the megaliths themselves—carvings becoming statues becoming creatures. They moved very slowly when first they emerged, but in time they grew in speed and fluidity. Most of them congregated above, where no one lived.

But today, one Glyph had descended.

Zagorka and Elionoway marched side by side, their faces set. Occasionally, they would glance at the brow of the cliff, where morning sunlight gleamed in hundreds of rubious figures. The runes in the deep caves had already transformed into Glyphs, and now all those along the brow of the hill were emerging. The rock was pregnant with a red army. Soon, Gylphs would outnumber citizens. Zagorka had given strict orders for all folk to avoid these glass men, but today she would break her own rule.

"But, Governor, I'm telling you, I won't be able to understand him!" Elionoway insisted. His long legs struggled to keep pace with the angry woman, and his pipe belched smoke like a little dynamo. "I understand this language when written, but the pronunciation—"

"You're our only hope," Zagorka interrupted.

Elionoway nodded stiffly. With shaking fingers, he drew a battered parchment from his pocket and began flipping through it, trying words on his tongue.

At the head of the road roamed the Glyph who had slain twenty-three citizens on that first awful day. It moved at a laborious pace, but still, many settlers rushed for the ford, taking their every possession and not looking back. Others stayed but barred themselves behind doors. Only Zagorka and Elionoway walked the streets, and they were on their way to meet the red-stone man.

Elionoway's trembling finger traced the words. "The . . . ah . . . curve indicates inflection: The deeper the curve, the greater the, ah, emphasis. . . ."

"What about writing everything?" Zagorka asked.

The elf's eyes were ringed with fear. "How's he supposed to write back? He'd burn the paper, melt the quill, boil the ink!"

Zagorka whistled ominously. "He could burn the words into stone."

"Is that supposed to be funny?"

"No."

The parchment trembled in Elionoway's hand, and he stared toward the ford and the fleeing people. "We could go too, Zagorka. It only makes sense."

"Go where? Topos? Krosan? Aphetto? There's nowhere for people like us."

"What about Eroshia?"

The old woman snorted, flicking her finger toward the paper. "Mind your letters. Sanctum's our home. If we lose it . . . we'll never be home again."

Side by side, they topped the road, entering a plaza where the Glyph walked. With deliberate steps, it approached the fountain in the center of the space.

It was a stunning sculpture, the edges done in red granite and the base lined in one smooth sheet of obsidian. Once, magic had made it run, but now it was a basin of dust. It had hosted neighborhood bones games, but otherwise was unused. For each step that the creature took toward it, Zagorka and Elionoway took ten. They came up alongside the Glyph and strode out ahead. It studied the fountain with eyes like glass globes. Though its face was inscrutable, Zagorka could have sworn the thing looked sad.

Standing alongside the fountain, Zagorka took a deep breath and visibly steadied herself. "Tell it we . . . welcome it . . . to Sanctum."

Elionoway folded back parchment pages until he found a blank sheet then sweated over the characters.

While he wrote, the Glyph came to stand before the fountain. It looked down, arms at its sides.

Careful not to touch the red figure, Elionoway positioned the page before him. The elf removed his pipe so that he could pronounce the words with slow clarity.

The Glyph glanced only a moment at the parchment, its attention shifting to Elionoway's hand—to the long-stemmed pipe of bone he held. Slowly, ruby-colored fingers clamped onto the stem and lifted it. The smoldering bowl of the pipe rose before the Glyph's face, and blue smoke rose in a fragrant circle around it. The pipe did not burst in flames, as had the man on that first day. The Glyph lowered the pipe, giving it back. It spoke in a voice like bubbling lava.

Elionoway listened, his face growing pale. "It wants to know . . . if I'm one of them."

"Tell it you're one of us."

Scribbling again, Elionoway worked out the runes and presented them.

The Glyph pivoted its translucent head toward Zagorka and spoke.

"It wants to know who we are," Elionoway said in a trembling voice, "and what Sanctum is."

"Tell him we're the people who live here, that Sanctum's our home."

Elionoway performed the translation, and the Glyph turned a querulous look on him. Its response was an angry gurgle. "It says we're wrong. It says its people live here." He swallowed. "This is their home."

* * * * *

Akroma had spent an age in that airy darkness. Thrice on her ascent through the boot box, she had passed the eternal wurm. Each time she had thought she had left it below but eventually had found it again above.

At last, the tiny rectangle of light appeared. Akroma's strength was almost spent, but the wings of her god stroked still. She climbed. With each surge of her plumes, the light grew, seeming almost a heart that pulsed and enlarged. The rectangle above widened to receive her. Akroma stroked once more, folded her wings, and vaulted up into the space.

Head, shoulders, and arms shot through to the narthex of her palace. A stout iron rod had been welded to prop open the door of the box, and Akroma desperately grabbed it. She pulled herself through. Her wings unfolded as if emerging from a chrysalis. Groaning through clenched teeth, Akroma fell on her back, wings splayed. She must have seemed a new-formed moth, legs weepy and soft, body panting. Still, she had survived.

That thought pierced her like an arrow. Since when had it mattered that she survived? Her creator was dead eternally, and yet she lived?

Akroma rolled over, legs stubs aching on the stone floor. She had to find someone, anyone. Had she been gone so long? Who ruled Topos now?

"I have returned," she said through a phlegm-charged throat. When no response came, she said louder, "I have returned!"

Someone pounced on her back. Akroma tried to spin to throw off her attacker, but viselike hands fastened on her neck. The rotting touch was unmistakable. Akroma had escaped one death only to fall to another.

"I have returned as well," said Phage.

* * * * *

Zagorka tried not to flinch, though the sheer towering presence of the Glyph was terrifying. "Ask him if his people built this city."

Elionoway worked that question through in his mind and pronounced it image by image. He translated the reply.

"He says they did, and not just the city, but the whole escarpment. It was a defensive wall to separate the numen of the north from the numen of the south."

"Ask him why they left, and where they've been for twenty thousand years."

Elionoway translated: "He says that when the numena were slain, these servants—what we call *Glyphs*—lived on in the elements that spawned them. They slept in the rocks for twenty millennia, to emerge only now."

"Why now?" Zagorka asked. With admiration, she watched the elf's face as he worked it all out.

"Because the numena will need their servants," replied Elionoway simply. "Remember the prophecy from the cave? Each numen brings with it a new nation and a new army to fight a very old war. This man here is a commander of the Glyph army."

Zagorka absently chewed her lip. "Tell him our names and ask him his name. Ask him who he serves."

Elionoway held up a staying hand as he pounded out his pipe and stuffed the bowl again. He lit the thing, and immediately began his questions.

Legions

The answers bubbled out of the crimson creature, and he gradually went to his knees beside the fountain.

Elionoway said. "This is Commander Gattac—a word that means war—and he serves Numen Averru."

"Why is he bowing?" Zagorka asked urgently. "What does he want from us? Will his people go elsewhere once they emerge? Will they swear to harm none of us? Tell him we want some answers!"

"One moment," Elionoway snapped sternly, "and I can answer for him on some of those things—stuff I've read, stuff you would know if you had listened to me. Of course they won't leave; this is the city they built, the city they have been waiting to return to for twenty centuries. What do they want from us? Nothing. We are nothing to them, not even impediments. They don't even have to toss us from their homes. They could burn their way straight through us. We are ghosts to them. As to why he is bowing—"

Without waiting for translation, Commander Gattac began to speak.

"He's calling on the power of Averru. He want the numen to reawaken the Pool of Worship, whatever that is, so that his servants might better call him forth." Elionoway added, "The Pool of Worship appears in other runes, a deep well of molten stone that is a kind of shrine for the Glyphs. There are prophecies saying that when the servants of Averru awaken the pool and return to their temple, the numen himself will return. I don't know where it is but—"

"Right in front of you." Zagorka said, gesturing toward the fountain.

The prayers of Commander Gattac had brought forth power. The obsidian bottom of the fountain had begun to melt, stone turning liquid all along a network of cracks. Air bubbles shoved up between the pieces and popped loudly. Soon, the only solid bits tumbled in liquid jets. As it boiled, the stone clarified. Zagorka could see deep into the pool, though she could not see the bottom.

Commander Gattac seemed satisfied.

Feeling numb from awe and terror, Zagorka asked. "What'll happen, then? What'll happen when Averru returns to his city, his temple?"

Elionoway's voice shook as he translated the question and the answer. "I made a mistranslation earlier. I said the Corian Escarpment had been built by the Glyphs to separate the numen of the north from the numen of the south. Their word for separate is like our word *cleave*—its common use is 'to cut apart' but it also can mean 'to hold together.' The Wall of the World does not separate the numena and their armies—it summons them."

"Summons them?" Zagorka said.

"Yes. Averru is a numen of war. He built this place to be the ultimate battlefield. He even called it the Battlefield of the Numena," Elionoway said. His face was as white as the bone pipe. "They're preparing for a world war."

Zagorka reeled, steadying herself on the granite edge of the fountain.

Commander Gattac was finished with the interview. He stepped over the granite rail and dropped easily into the molten glass. His figure sank into the well until he was infinitesimal then disappeared entirely.

*   *   *   *   *

Stonebrow brooded alone in his throne. He was lost. He had thought that his return to Topos would be a return to faith, but no.

The Vision of Ixidor, as beautiful as it was, was a lie—so many mortal dreams floating in the air. Perhaps Ixidor could create a real paradise out of sand, but his followers had created a falsehood—a beautiful, empowering falsehood that swept the continent. No one—not Aioue, not Akroma, and certainly not Stonebrow—could make it true. How many people had the Vision of Ixidor killed, and how many more lives would it claim when it led to war?

Stonebrow was furious. He had failed utterly. He could not eradicate the evils left by Kamahl or Ixidor. The only evils he could eradicate were his own.

He reached down to the axe at his belt—Soul Reaper—and he drew it. Its edge glinted, razor-sharp. The stony head was cold and black. He wouldn't even have to swing it, only drag it slowly, and his pelt would separate, the vessels beneath would sever, and it all would be done.

"I have returned!" cried a woman in the narthex beyond. Her shout reverberated down the stone walls and echoed around Stonebrow.

He knew that voice. "Akroma," he snarled. It could be no other, the embodiment of Ixidor's failure. A single stroke could wipe her from the world. Stonebrow's heart pounded with sudden glee, and he tightened his hold on the axe. Perhaps he *could* undo the evil that Ixidor had created.

"I have returned!"

Stonebrow smiled viciously. He took a silent step forward, then another, emerging from his throne. He descended the silken runner that led down the stairs and across his audience chamber, toward the narthex. The axe in his hand trembled. It had been forged for this day, to kill Akroma. It ached to reap her soul.

Stonebrow crossed beneath the final vault of his throne room and out the double doors. He came to a stop on the white-marble floor.

Akroma lay there. She must have dragged herself out of the boot box and across the floor, for she had left a bloody trail. Her wings flapped but could not lift her.

Stonebrow saw why. A small dark figure straddled the angel. Fierce little hands clutched Akroma's neck, and the porcelain skin was cracking and blackening beneath their touch. It was Phage. She did what Stonebrow had meant to do.

He almost laughed. Here was the evil of Kamahl strangling the evil of Ixidor. He could kill them both, and his quest would be done. Two strokes, and he would have cleansed Otaria of the stain of the gods.

Stonebrow strode forward. The desperate flapping of Akroma's wings covered the sound of his tread. Neither woman would hear.

He loomed up above them and lifted the axe. It hummed in his fingers, eager to bite into flesh. Down it came, with the force of his giant arm behind it.

Phage saw the shadow, and she glanced up.

Before that moment, he was going to strike Akroma, but centaur instinct is to attack head on. He turned the blow, and it sailed toward Phage's breast.

She flung up her arms, and the blade bounced downward, deflected from heart to belly. The axe cut into her, severing skin and muscle before it stopped as if on a rock. Phage flew off Akroma, carried on the blade that should have split her in half. She hurtled across the room and crashed down by a wall. Blood formed a gray curtain from the cut down across her belly, and she struggled to catch her breath.

Stonebrow followed through, the blood-tipped axe riding up over his shoulder. He stared at her, his mouth and eyes hanging open in fury. "You live! How?" He charged toward her and swung again.

Phage lunged aside but was too slow. The axe struck her abdomen, and it clanged without penetrating. Gritting his teeth Stonebrow leaned on the blade, but it would bite no deeper. He roared.

Phage smiled into the face of his fury. "You can't kill me, Stonebrow, for I bear a god inside me. I am pregnant."

He gaped at her, the axe blade pinning her to the wall. What had become of him? He had set out to end evil and now was poised to murder a pregnant woman and a wounded angel.

"No . . . You can't be. . . ."

"It doesn't show, but it is true. I am pregnant."

Stonebrow vomited.

Like a wounded moth, Akroma fluttered sideways across the floor, away from woman and centaur both. She lay there gasping. The black handprints were still visible on her throat.

"Finish her, Stonebrow. . . . Finish her."

He wiped his mouth and stared at the fouled floor. He had always thought death was messy, but compared to life, it was clean.

Topos guards came clattering up the hallway and slid to a stop, staring at the strange tableau. They looked to Stonebrow, standing between the two wounded woman. "What is your order, General?"

"Stand down," he growled.

Akroma shouted, "Kill her!"

The guards made no move.

With an inarticulate roar, Stonebrow charged across the room toward Akroma. Soul Reaper flew high in his hands. He stomped up above her, the blade trembling in the air. "Shut up! Shut up! Or I'll kill you! Both of you—the pregnant woman and the maimed angel. Yes, that's what I've become!"

"Forget this nonsense," Akroma snarled. "Kill Phage. . . ."

Stonebrow responded only with an animal shriek.

Akroma bared her teeth, and there was rot between them. "Then give me the axe, *my* axe, and I will do it."

Stonebrow lowered the blade, and sweat rolled down his simian face. "Go ahead, Akroma. You finish this. You and Phage can kill each other, but you'll do it with your bare hands. This isn't your axe. It's Kamahl's." He shoved the hilt of his axe in the leather belt at his waist and stalked toward the door. "I'm done."

Before he could reach the door, Phage scrambled to her feet and fled out ahead of him.

"Guards!" shouted Akroma. "Guards! After her!"

"Stand down," Stonebrow snarled to the guards, "or I will kill you myself." They did more than stand down, retreating down the hall. Stonebrow shouted. "I still rule Topos!"

The angel's face was torn with torments. "What are you going to do with that rule, Stonebrow? You have the axe, but you won't use it?"

"It wasn't made for me, but for Kamahl," Stonebrow said. "I'll take it to him."

"I'll come kill you both!"

"I look forward to it," Stonebrow growled, and he was gone.

CHAPTER 20

SHUCKING THEIR SKINS

F or a scrawny, hairless little thing, Braids sure is heavy," groused Waistcoat, scuttling along beneath the silken sack. The wooden suspension bridge pulsed with his every step. "How come the bug with a missing leg has to carry her?"

Sash made a hissing sound with his spiracles. "You need the exercise, you fat dung beetle. By the way, you're missing just half a leg." A new nub budded from Waistcoat's side, grown since they had left Phage. In another month, it would be complete.

Sash went on, "Besides, I have to keep up the sleep spell, or she'll bolt."

The morning after the abduction, Braids had done just that, heading for Topos. The three roaches had run amok, looking for her among the boulders, and they would have lost her if not for their excellent sense of smell. From then on, Braids had remained in the sack and asleep, except for stops thrice a day to feed her and let her relieve herself. It had been an aggravating month, but at last it was nearly done. The three roaches neared Coliseum Island.

"What about you, Umbra? Couldn't you lend a leg?"

"I'm busy, Waistcoat."

"Busy? Busy doing what? Waddling?"

"Busy figuring out how we're going to survive," Umbra replied. He glanced ahead to where the suspension bridge ended on Coliseum

Island: the First's lair. "Let's hope he's glad to see Braids. He'll be mad about Phage."

"He's always mad," Waistcoat complained.

"We have to convince him he needs us," Umbra said, thinking aloud. "Sash, you still have your fire spell?"

"You want me to burn the First?"

"No, but be ready to burn something, to show how deadly we are," Umbra replied. "I'm hoping we can finagle better bodies—something less obvious to Phage."

"What kind of bodies do you think he'd give us this time?" sneered Sash. "Maggots? Leeches?"

"Turds?" Waistcoat added.

"Turds don't have bodies, you idiot," Sash hissed.

"Quiet, both of you! We're near the checkpoint."

At the base of the bridge stood a Cabal guard—a gigantipithicus whose sloping brow showed the scars of magical surgery. His eyes were simian but intelligent. A black vest covered the creature's enormous chest, and he wore the trousers of Cabal livery. He held up a long-fingered hand and said, "Halt."

The bugs halted a bit too close to those grasping feet.

"You got hot stuff in that bag?"

The roaches buzzed among each other.

Umbra said, "If by 'hot' you mean 'stolen' or 'contraband' the answer is no."

"Open it."

Umbra rolled his eyes. "We're on a mission for the First. We've brought him something."

"Better be heads, or you can't pass. Strict orders."

The three insects exchanged the pheromones of fear.

"Sure. Heads," Umbra said. "We'll give you a peek, but then we have to get moving. Waistcoat, unship that bag and show this fine creature one of the heads."

"*One* of the heads?" the ape objected, "I have orders—"

"So do we. Our orders are to show these heads only to the First. We're trying to work with you here, letting you glimpse one of the heads, but if you cause trouble, no dice. Do you think a bridge guard has precedence over top-level spies?"

Waistcoat let the silk bag roll off his back. He prodded it to find Braids's head and work it toward the mouth of the sack. He untied the knot and slipped the bag open. Seeing the pale and apparently dead face of Braids in the gap, Waistcoat directed the guard's attention inward. "See?"

The ape scowled and peered through the circle of fabric. "Well, looks pretty good. Which one is this? Phage or Akroma?"

"Phage."

"Akroma."

"Phage," Umbra snarled, slapping Sash on the wing. "You can't even see the face."

"Seems an awful big bag for just two heads," the ape said.

"Oh, Akroma's got a big fat head. Really big. Like a boulder," said Waistcoat.

Wheels turned in the mind of the ape. "I'm going to have to see the other head."

Umbra stared steadily at his comrades. "All right. He wants us to open the bag or he won't let us through. So, we'll have to open the bag. All the way. Remove every restraint. Understand? Sash should go first then Waistcoat. Let's be careful to do this just like the last time, that first morning. Understand?"

"Of course," said Sash slyly.

"Huh?" said Waistcoat. The bag lurched so furiously that he lost hold. It fell open, and out rushed Braids. She shot right past the three roaches and the stunned ape and bolted for the coliseum.

"Quick, grab her!" cried Umbra even as he clamped onto one of the ape's legs.

Sash simultaneously leaped onto the creature's back, bowling him over on his face.

Waistcoat bolted, but the primate had stepped on two of his legs, and they yanked off at the shell. On one side, Waistcoat had only the half-grown leg, and so instead of moving forward, he only spun in circles, kicking sand and telling himself, "Go! Go! Go!"

The other two roaches did, tearing out after Braids. She darted ahead, dodging among trinket sellers. "If she gets away, we'll be truly dead!" hissed Umbra as he ran. "Try your sleep spell again."

"Right!" Sash said. At a full-out run, he bent his antennae toward the fleeing woman and pronounced the spell: "*Kuel baebee nelsin onda belchen baebee onda sib, stobcol inme sib!*"

A fruit seller's cart burst into spectacular flames.

"Wrong spell!"

"I know, I know!"

The gigantipithicus pursued, oblivious to the fact that he had picked up a passenger. With three and a half legs, Waistcoat clung on for dear life. He had accidently spun himself onto the back of the prostrate ape and held tight as the thing rose. Now, the ground was ten feet below him and speeding by at a nauseous pace. Waistcoat wished he could jump, but he didn't want to die like a bug . . . let alone *as* one.

Ahead, the bald woman and the two roaches had stirred up the crowd, and they were running too. Those at the head of the throng shouted, "Braids! Braids! Wait!"

She ran obliquely toward the coliseum, funneled by the lanes.

"Look out, fan-boy!" Sash shouted as a young man stumbled across his back.

The fan-boy grabbed on and yelled, "Yaa-hoo! Free cockroach rides!"

Umbra didn't slow to wait for his comrade. His hearts pounded in terror. This was the end, and he knew it. They'd never catch Braids, but the First would catch them.

The throng became a living tide, and it swept Braids, Umbra, Sash, the fan-boy, the ape, and a hitchhiking Waistcoat through one of the great archways of the coliseum. The roar of the crowd trebled within that stone tube.

"At last, we've got her!" Umbra shouted over his shoulder.

"Yee-haw!"

"I'm not a horse!" Sash said.

"Come back here, you filthy roaches!"

"Ugh . . . ugh . . . ugh . . . ugh. . . ."

At the head of the throng, Braids shouted to the gate guards: "Throw open the gates, in the name of Braids!"

The guards squinted, seemed to make out who she was, and quickly hurled up the bars on the doors.

Umbra called, "Close the gates, in the name of . . ."

". . . a giant roach," yelled Waistcoat.

The massive doors swung out onto the arena sands. Braids ran through without slowing. Behind her scuttled Umbra, a frothing Sash and rider, and the ape with his own passenger.

Already, the sands were crowded with a reenactment of the aven civil war. Tall bird warriors in white armor turned to see the flood of spectators. Their polearms went slack in their hands, and they gaped at the spectacle.

"Seize them!" shouted the gigantipithicus. As if to demonstrate, he swept his huge hands like hooks through the crowd, only inches from swiping the abdomen of Sash. The ape lunged, at last grasping flesh. He hauled it up but found a wriggling fan-boy. Tossing him aside in the stampede, the ape growled, "Seize the woman and the roaches!"

Avens turned. They were orderly warriors with slender figures, birdlike faces and feathered flesh. In a moment, they formed a precise phalanx and charged the mob.

The stands erupted. Bookies shouted odds on the mob, and coin and ticket darted after each other like schools of predatory fish.

Avens buried their horn-bladed polearms in the guts of the first civilians, dropped the fouled weapons, and drew their swords. The civilians who were armed fought back, but the rest scattered. After getting a shallow slice across his belly, the gigantipithicus went into a rage. He snatched up avens and broke them over his knee like a boy breaking sticks.

Waistcoat dropped off his back and on three and a half legs darted toward his comrades. Roaches shrieked and dodged through the melee.

"Well, we delivered her!" Sash said.

"Let's get scarce!" Waistcoat agreed.

"And be roaches forever?" asked Umbra.

"Stop!" The voice was imperious, magically amplified to fill the great coliseum.

The fight faltered then stopped altogether, and sand settled back down around the rioters.

"What is this?" the First shouted. He stood in the stands above, his arms outstretched and his eyes blazing. Below him, like living flames, his yellow-robed hand servants descended to the sand. They glided rapidly toward the rioters—his hands literally reaching out to take hold of them.

No one moved except Sash, who scuttled to Braids's side and grasped her heel. She fought to get free, but Umbra and Waistcoat ambled up to hold her other leg.

"What is this!" the First repeated. His booming voice made the crowd fall to its knees. The roaches wished they had knees to fall to. "You there—roaches. Answer me!"

Umbra said, "At the behest of your beloved Phage, we brought you this offering. This woman." The hand servants swarmed, their yellow robes flaring, and they grasped the three roaches and the woman. Umbra blurted, "Phage thought you would be pleased to see your daughter Braids."

The First swooned. He lowered his arms and stood there a moment, seeming to fight for air, then he strode down the steps toward the sands below.

"The First is coming," someone muttered fearfully, going prostrate.

More followed. The living gladiators lay down among the dead—all except the roaches and Braids, who were held up by the First's own hands.

He was coming, his boots kicking sand before him.

"Well, bugs or no," Waistcoat said, "it was nice to know you chaps."

"Me too, but shut up," Sash replied.

"We're not dead yet," Umbra muttered, "and, yes, shut up."

The First walked among the prostrate bodies until he towered over the roaches and their captive. The man stared at Braids. His face, usually as dispassionate as a block of granite, showed relief, regret, and self-reproach. Phage had been right. He was utterly grateful.

"Oh, Braids, my daughter, where have you been?" he said softly.

"I'm not your daughter," she spat angrily. "I serve only Ixidor."

The words seemed to cut like blades. "What has Akroma done to you?"

"Saved me!"

He shook his head. "No. That's what I will do to you. I will save you, my daughter. I will return you to what you were."

"I would rather die!" Braids cried, trying to wrench free of the hand servants.

"Hold her," the First said firmly. His eyes shifted toward the three roaches. "As for you—you have failed me. I gave you bodies. I can take them away."

The roaches squirmed to escape, but the hands that held them clenched tighter.

The First strode up to them, and his face was once again stony. He reached for Waistcoat. The fingertips of both hands plunged between the plates on the roach's back. The contact of flesh to flesh enervated the bug, but the First wasn't finished. He grabbed hold of the carapace, lifted the giant roach from the ground, and ripped him in half. From the two hunks of shell, white innards fell.

The First turned to Sash and rammed his foot down. Heel and sole went right through the creature's back and his belly and smashed into the ground below. Wearing Sash like a grotesque slipper, the First grasped hold of Umbra's head and twisted until it came off in his hands.

Kicking away the three roach corpses, the First straightened his robes. The fury of the kill washed from his face, and he gazed tenderly on Braids. To his servants, he said, "Take her to secure quarters in the slave pen and keep her locked there until I can begin her healing."

The hand servants wrestled the struggling woman away.

The First stared at the ground, covered with prostrate forms. "Get up. Get out of here. Never interrupt my games again."

Folk glanced up, trying to gauge whether he would attack. One by one, they rose and hurried away across the sands.

Among them moved three shadows, gray outlines in the air. They slunk away, hoping the First did not notice. He had ripped away their bodies but had left their empty souls.

The First walked up among them, though, and muttered. "Bring their heads, or you will be really and truly dead."

*   *   *   *   *

So, this was how it would be.

Akroma had sacrificed everything. She had descended into death to pluck her master out, had found him, and could have borne him away, but he had chosen instead to remain. He had rejected his living vision and clung instead to his dead one.

Ixidor had abandoned the world, his Vision, and Akroma too. He had refused to rise from death, but had granted her wings to do so. Now Akroma would have to be her own master, her own vision.

"Gently," she instructed.

Her servants, timid human followers of Ixidor, trembled as they slowly screwed the metal leg onto her stub. Already, a surgeon had wired into the bone the four mechanical joints that would hold the new-forged limbs. The legs were long cones of steel that would pierce like lance tips. With them in place, Akroma would be able to stand again, to walk, to fight. Then she would fly to the ends of Otaria that all might see her, the living vision, and believe.

She had become the Vision of Ixidor.

No longer would she direct worshipers to a dead god in the belly of the beast but only to her own glorious figure. No longer would she send disciples to bring the nations to Topos. It was time for her massive armies to march out and conquer a continent, and later a world.

The lancelike leg clicked into place. It was solid beneath her. Three more, and she would be complete. Otaria would behold the Vision of Ixidor, and fear.

CHAPTER 21

POSSESSION

 wenty hands dragged Braids through the coliseum. Their grip was implacable. These were his hands—twenty hands on ten bodies on one mind.

The First held her, as once he had—as he would forever.

Braids had been his child. Even the glories of Ixidor could not wash away the truth of that. The First had transformed her from a street rat to a ruler of the coliseum. He had taught her dementia summoning, had made her powerful and infamous. He would make her that way again.

She didn't want it. Braids lashed out. Her fingernails sank into the arms of the servants, and blood traced her cuticles.

They didn't let go but only looked down at her with long-suffering love. The First spoke through their eyes, saying that he would never give up on her, not again.

"Braids! Braids! Braids!" shouted the crowd, hailing the return of the coliseum's bloodiest, most twisted fighter.

She felt sick. She had become a new person. Braids had gazed on the face of glory and let its brilliance purge her of evil and bloodlust. Once she had been full of monstrosity, but Ixidor had emptied her and cleansed her. Once she had ruled in hell, but now she was a servant of heaven.

"Braids! Braids! Braids!"

If she didn't escape, the First would have his way with her, and her mind would once again become a zoo for monsters.

She knelt with her face to the floor. Tears washed the stone, and vomit lurked nearby. Beyond it stood the First. Oh, how she ached for him, and yet he loved another. He loved Phage.

Where was Phage? Had he consummated with her yet? Had she born him the child they were destined to bear? Had he killed her? Braids's blood turned to ice as she remembered the tales of Kuberr, the dark god that ruled the Cabal.

She tightened her grip, and her fingers were red. "Ixidor, my Vision, protect me. Keep my eyes on your brilliance."

Cold darkness enveloped her. They had passed from the sunlit coliseum floor into the stony passages within. The vault overhead channeled the crowd noise, amplifying it and shaking Braids. That voracious sound bore her down and down, into the bowels of the coliseum. There the Cabal would digest her and render her into offal.

*   *   *   *   *

Axe riding at his waist, Stonebrow marched against a tide of refugees. They wended their miserable way among the rocks of the Corian badlands and carried everything they owned on their bent backs. A year before, they had fled the Nightmare War and sought sanctuary. Now, their Sanctum was spewing them forth.

"Where are you going?" the giant centaur rumbled to no one and everyone.

A dwarf looked up at him, a creature who barely rose above Stonebrow's canons. Red-faced, the old man said simply, "Eroshia."

Eroshia? Stonebrow turned his head as the ragged dwarf strode past. "What's in Eroshia?"

"Freedom," was the simple reply, and the dwarf marched on toward the east.

Freedom. As Stonebrow continued southwest toward Sanctum, the word reverberated in his mind. Where was freedom on Otaria?

Every town and village had an arena, suckers on the all-grasping tentacles of the Cabal. Day by day, the folk in those towns gave up freedom for entertainment and rough justice. The First ruled their basest impulses, but Akroma ruled their highest impulses. Every village and town also contained believers in Ixidor, ardent in prose-lytizing. Temples and colleges taught his Vision, an equal tyranny. Between Akroma and the First, they had enslaved Otaria, and where was freedom?

"These hooves," Stonebrow muttered to himself. Here was free-dom, to chose a jagged path that has no reason but one's own.

On his long journey from Locus, Stonebrow had had much time to think. He had ascended the throne of Topos, hoping to right the grievous wrongs of the world, but every gain in power was a loss in virtue. By the time Stonebrow had reached that exalted place, ruling Topos and commanding a legion of disciples, he had become craven. He had tried to kill a pregnant woman and a maimed angel.

For all their power, the gods were slaves of fate. Only mortals were free.

In freedom, Stonebrow walked away from the throne of Topos. Akroma was welcome to it. The only way to right the wrongs of the world was one jagging step at a time.

The day was dying when Stonebrow crested the hill above the Deepwash River. He stared across it to the wondrous city of Sanc-tum, nestled against the rearing cliff. The sun inched downward, and its light caressed the buildings. On the streets and balconies glowed what seemed to be giant rubies. Oh, it was a beautiful place, even bleeding refugees as it did this night. Dark streams of creatures flowed up the hill past Stonebrow.

"Why do you leave?" he asked.

A bone-white elf woman glanced a moment at him, blinked once placidly, and said, "The army of Glyphs."

Stonebrow watched the elf woman as she disappeared over the hill. Turning, he descended toward the river ford, the looming stone arch, and its wicked runes.

His hooves splashed into the cool river, and Stonebrow knelt to drink and quickly wash. He was dusty and weary, but his heart pounded. An army of Glyphs. Looking to the rock walls, he could see red figures glimmering everywhere, ready to emerge. If they all came forth, they would overrun the city.

What new tyranny had arrived on this continent of tyrants?

Dripping, Stonebrow rose from the flood and strode up beneath the cold stone gate. The road ahead was filled with people, carts, and animals, but the farmlands to either side lay fallow. Neither grain nor tobacco grew, and perhaps it was just as well. What would these ruby men eat but rocks? What would they smoke but brimstone?

Stonebrow followed the road from the verdant fields into the foothills of the lower city. The way led to a stone-paved plaza where four avenues converged. There, the refugees were more tightly packed, and they shuffled through like cattle in stock gates.

In their midst stood a Glyph—almost Stonebrow's own height, but as lean as an elf. His every feature was angular, his flesh transparent and red. The figure did not move with the refugees but stood above them, shouting. He spoke with an alien voice, like boiling water, but his words were in the common tongue:

"—shall run from the coming terrors. Hear, then, O people of Sanctum, for doom is upon you. You dwell where numena will march. Their heels will grind you into the rock. You live in sepulchers and will die in them. The numena will make war on this place and bring it to naught. Flee, then, to escape the war that comes, but know that wherever you flee, it comes behind you. When they have climbed all across this wall and thrown each other down, one after the others, then the numena will unite and come to rule you. They will rule everything between the seas."

Stonebrow solemnly breasted the waves of refugees until he reached the empty circle around the Glyph. "What is your name?"

The folk around Stonebrow looked astonished by his question, but the rubious figure turned to face him. Eyes like glass beads fixed on Stonebrow, and the man burbled, "Judgment."

Drawing his lips into a tight frown, Stonebrow said, "Judgment is not a name."

The red man craned his neck. "It is a word. I am the word Judgment."

"You are a word?"

"Each of us is a word. I am Judgment, and I pronounce judgment."

A quick glance up the road showed other Glyphs moving among the populace, and people struggling to stay out of reach. "What are their names? Molestation, Intrusion, Sanctimony?"

"No. They are Purgation, Purification, and Execution."

"They are killing the citizens?" Stonebrow growled, hand on his axe.

"Only those who are impure and refuse to leave. The battlefield must be ready for the numena."

"What about those who refuse to leave but *are* pure?" Stonebrow asked.

"They are guests, of course—witnesses of the coming of the numena."

Crossing arms over his chest, Stonebrow jutted his chin toward the Glyph. "Well, Judgment, make your call. What am I? Impure refugee, or guest of the numena?"

The thing lifted its bead-shaped head as if taken aback. "You are, of course, a guest, General Stonebrow."

A chill rushed down the giant centaur's spine, and his hackles prickled. He drew the axe from his belt. "How did you know my name?"

"I am a word from the prophecies of the final battle. So are you."

"I didn't crawl out of a rock." Stonebrow snorted. "I'm no Glyph."

"No, but there is a rune for you. The ancient prophecies say, 'And shall come the mortal called Face of Stone to do battle on that day.' The rune that is you will be glad to know you have arrived."

Stonebrow felt dizzy. It was all too much. He had come here freely, on his own jagging path, but every step of his hooves had been foretold. He was meant to remain, to do battle with numena? All he could think to say was, "Who else was . . . foretold?"

"Oh, many. They are written in the Book of Death. They will come to witness."

"Zagorka? Elionoway?"

"Yes. His name means 'Seer of Ages,'—and 'the Seer of Ages will warn them, but none will listen to dead words, only living.' And Zagorka's name means 'She Disputes,' and the prophecy says, 'before the thrones of air and rock and water, She Disputes.' "

Stonebrow's face split in a grin, and he began to laugh. "For a moment, you had me. I nearly believed." He laughed again. "Ancient prophecies that speak of Zagorka?" A guffaw burst from his lips. "No. Seduce others with your warnings. I don't believe. You're invaders, pure and simple, and no amount of goat entrails will make it otherwise." The axe trembled, and the centaur's eyes gleamed, looking for an invitation to strike.

The ruby man did not provide one. "This too was spoken. 'Like the Wall of the World, he cannot see the runes written on his own Face of Stone.'"

Stonebrow made a flatulent noise and waved away the man's comment. "Excuse me. I need to go see Seer of Ages and She Disputes." Through the dark tide of refugees he went. Despite his laughter, his heart was heavy.

Who was in greater jeopardy, the masses that fled Sanctum or the guests destined to remain?

* * * * *

Deep within the coliseum, Braids lay in a dark cell. Leather straps held her supine, and iron bands fastened her wrists and ankles to the table. A metal halo had been screwed into her skull to keep her from thrashing. Even her mouth was held open with the fork retractor that Braids had devised for feeding Phage. The implement had been designed to keep food off of Phage's corrupting lips, but it was equally effective in keeping prayers off Braids's lips.

Even her prayers were restrained—even her thoughts.

The dementia summoner sitting beside Braids dipped his fingers into oil. It would facilitate the galvanic transfer skin-to-skin. He gazed at Braids, his narrow face ravaged by the horrors he had seen. In overlarge black eyes, nightmares swam, as if the sockets were fish bowls filled with drowning maggots. Yellow droplets hung on his fingertips, and he lowered them to Braids's forehead.

"Remember the true Ixidor. Remember the true man."

*He was young and lean, handsome in a severe way. From a robe of sky blue jutted strong arms—*Braids had never conceived of him with both arms, and she almost broke from the vision then, except for the insistent hissing—*which carried bars of lead. He lay them beside the iron stove. With one foot pumping the bellows, he opened the small door and peered in to see a ceramic ewer filled with molten metal. He inserted two thin rods into the rings at the ends of the ewer and drew it from the flames. Turning, he set it briefly on a brick platform and added a golden pigment. It spread quickly through the gray metal, transforming it. He then poured the molten metal into a waiting form.*

"He was a creator then too. He made lead seem gold. Creator, or counterfeiter."

Braids tried to close her mouth on the involuntary moan, but the fork prevented it. Ixidor was not a deceiver. The world he made was real, not an illusion.

He rooted his feet in the sands of the pit and drew to himself the power of water. The very sweat droplets that dotted his skin rose and evaporated, transforming into blue motes of energy. His mind gave them form, projecting a reality upon the world. The sparks whirled out along his hand, streamed across the sands, and struck the aven warriors who battled there. Running all along their figures, those azure points of light joined in a new matrix and imposed their facade upon the truth.

"He was an illusionist. His illusions only grew exponentially. No matter how compelling they seemed, they were still lies."

Braids wanted to say "No," but could say nothing. Ixidor had taught her that beauty was never an illusion, that the primal state of everything in the multiverse was beauty, that by moving toward beauty an artist did not create illusion but stripped away the illusion of ugliness. The evils of her past were lies, and the beauty of her present was truth. All this, she knew, or wanted to know.

The avens transformed. The mean angles of their bodies smoothed; the short plumes became long feathers; hawkish faces took on the aspect of angels. Where once had stood a tattered phalanx of avens, now flew a choir of archangels.

Across from Ixidor, the gigantipithicus who had come to battle him fell to his knees. The crowd roared, and the death bell tolled for the poor dumb beast. Angels dissolved to avens.

"Not always is the most beautiful thing the truest thing. Ixidor has led you down a maze of veils, along a perfumed path, but all the while you walked unknowing amid horrors. His is an inward vision, seen with the eyes closed. Open your eyes, Braids, and see the truth."

She hated this summoner. He raged through her mind, marring all that was beautiful in it. Why did the Cabal always destroy, always debase and demean?

"I want you to know what I am doing. I want you to understand what is happening to you." He shifted his fingers from her brow to the side of her head, above the temporal lobes, and slid his other hand to the occipital lobe.

Determined to stop him, Braids withdrew into her own mind. It was no longer a labyrinth of iron and stone, ugliness and paranoia. Ixidor had remade her mind in beauty and truth. The walls were whitest plaster, the rooms open and generous. In place of dungeons, she had art galleries, and to one of these she fled. It was the deepest place in her psyche, a gallery of paintings that Ixidor had given her.

They were beautiful, every one: sunlight stabbed down through a darkly romantic landscape to illumine grazing flocks; a woman in white floated ecstatically above a churning sea; a perfectly proportioned colonnade in Locus curved in upon itself; an icon of the one-armed creator depicted him with eyes like worlds. . . . These were her favorite paintings.

Among these images, he came—not Ixidor, but this hateful summoner. In his hand, he carried a jag of metal. He lifted it and slashed the portrait of Ixidor, cutting oil and canvas. One stroke divided the master's face in two. Another ripped open the creator's throat. Canvas drooped to reveal darkness beyond.

Braids lunged at the man, but he ran before her, slashing every painting in its frame. The fabric separated, showing more of the darkness.

Braids slowed and stopped, staring. These were not picture frames but window frames. These paintings were blinds, shutting out sight of what lay beyond. Ixidor had not torn down the labyrinth of stone and iron; he had only plastered over its rough edges and whitewashed it all. Trembling, Braids reached to one torn canvas and pulled back the edges, ripping it farther. She peered through a window and into the void.

As her eyes adjusted, she saw that beyond the glass the emptiness squirmed. It was a boiling mass of monsters: dementia creatures. She had placed them there in her mind, had caged them, ready for use. The light of Ixidor had not removed the horrors from Braids, but had only hidden them from view.

"You see? The truth is ugly. Beauty is the illusion."

Braids trembled, cold sweat drenching her. Tears flooded her eyes, and she tried to blink them away before she would drown.

* * * * *

"Hello, Zagorka," Stonebrow said heavily. He stood in a street that swarmed with departing folk and spoke through the old woman's second-story window.

"Good to see you, Stonebrow," she said gravely. "I take it you're among us 'pure ones'."

He nodded thoughtfully. "I take it."

Elionoway appeared in the window behind her, and he nodded to the centaur.

Zagorka said, "Let's move to a bigger place. Something big enough for a giant centaur. How about the Gilded Mage? It's got double doors and a stone floor with a groin vault below. It'll hold you and hold us all."

"I'm surprised these red things didn't close it."

"Oh, the bastards wanted to, but we told them we had to eat or we'd die. Might as well have a time while we watch the end of the world."

CHAPTER 22

GAMES OF THE DAMNED

I hate this!" Waistcoat complained. He and his comrades trudged through South Pass. Rock walls rose to either side into a dusky sky. Behind them, ten leagues away, lay the swamps of the coliseum. Just ahead was Deepwash Valley. "Look at us! Just look at us!"

"Look at you?" Sash snapped. "What's there to see?" In the shadows of twilight, the three unmen were invisible. "You're not even a ghost. You're not even a stain!"

"That's my point. It was better being a roach."

Umbra nodded. "Waistcoat's right. It was better to have bodies, even bug bodies."

Sash snorted. "Who wants to be a bug? Besides, when you've got a body, you can be killed."

"That's because you're alive," Umbra said. "You can eat and drink, grab onto things, fight and hope—"

"And love," Waistcoat said wistfully. "Some of them swamp roaches were cute."

"I wish I could vomit," Sash said.

"I could throw up a harpsichord."

"So, we're agreed then," Umbra said solemnly.

"Yes," Waistcoat replied. "We all want to puke."

"No . . . well, yes and no. Yes we all want to puke, and to puke we need bodies, and to get bodies we need to kill, and that's what I'm asking. Are we all agreed that we'll go through with this? That we will kill Phage and Akroma?"

Sash laughed harshly. "You make it sound so easy. Sure, let's kill the two most powerful fighters on Otaria. While we're at it, let's make ourselves kings of the world. Ha ha!"

Umbra threw his head back, staring at the dark skies. Though sunlight died in the heavens, the stars refused to shine. "All right, but say we had the chance, say we happened on a scene where they've both just about killed each other and we could finish them off. Do we do it?"

"I kind of liked Phage," Waistcoat said. "She was like a sister."

Sash blustered, "Are you out of your mind? She insulted us, abused us, bossed us around, and the touch of her skin turned everything to rot."

"Just like a sister," Waistcoat said.

"Oh, she deserves to die," Sash snarled, "and Akroma too."

"The question isn't whether they deserve to die. Nobody deserves to die," Umbra said. "The question is whether we deserve to live."

The trail widened ahead of them, and they stared down into a dark valley. The Deepwash River snaked like a black beast along the base of the cleft. Throngs forded that river and climbed the far slope of the valley, heading toward the rocky badlands. Where were they headed? Topos? They were leaving Sanctum, which glowed like a jewel on the near side of the river. Firelight shone from ancient walls, and crimson figures moved along the streets. Atop it all, the circle of standing stones gleamed like a diadem.

Sash murmured, "I certainly want to live."

"I do too," added Waistcoat.

Umbra nodded. "I want to live, but that means Phage and Akroma have to die."

The other two were silent for a time, then Sash said, "It's three lives in the balance against two. Mathematics dictates what we should do."

"It's not just that," Waistcoat said. "It's our lives against theirs."

Sash headed down a footpath that led toward the streets of Sanctum. "Enough. We'll never get the chance to kill either of them, and even if we had the chance, how would we do it?"

Umbra followed. "I've come up with an idea."

A gentle breeze mourned in their outlines.

Waistcoat said, "If you think you'll pump me full of acid, forget it."

"No, it's much simpler," Umbra replied. "We act friendly toward our victim—we pretend we're working for her, whichever one we meet. While one of us talks to her, distracting, a second one moves up to stand alongside her, and the third lies down behind her. The first of us shoves the woman backward, and she starts to fall through the third. The second then loops his head over hers and throws himself back. The edges of our portals are razor sharp, and if our victim's neck gets caught between two of us when we slide apart, she'll be beheaded."

The unmen shuddered. Sash said, "We make ourselves into living guillotines?"

"Yes."

"It'll be damned hard to catch just her neck," Sash said.

"It doesn't matter. As long as the cut happens below the eyes but above the pelvis, the wound will be lethal."

Waistcoat sounded despondent. "This is what we have to do to live?"

"Yes," Umbra said. "Twice."

* * * * *

Phage had thought she was dead ten times over. It had been a hellish month, her ninth month—when every woman wishes to be delivered. There had been no deliverance for Phage.

Bleeding from her twice-cut belly, she had swum across the gray lake below Locus and hid in the Greenglades Forest. At one point, a band of Ixidorans on pilgrimage found her blood trail and pursued her. She had to slay one to escape, and she stole his knife, which she used to gather food. Across the Nightmare Lands she went. In time she reached the edge of Topos, the desert beyond, and at last the Corian badlands.

Phage spent the next week alone among the stones. She dug beneath them to root out packrat nests and stab the creatures into chunks. By opening her mouth wide and extending her tongue as far as possible, she could get most of the meat inside without turning it rancid. For days, only their blood quenched her thirst. Water was difficult to find. Once she attacked a traveler only to take his waterskin. The leather rotted in her grip, but she did drink most of the liquid. By day, she cleaned the wounds in her belly, debreeding them. By night, she packed the cuts with sand and walked until she dropped.

All the while, she thought only of the child within her. The god-foetus had gown. She felt the weight of him in her abdomen, pressing against her pelvis, but still he did not show. Her stomach had not swollen, and she realized now that it never would. The child was ingrown. What kind of monstrosity would it be? She couldn't deliver a normal child here in the wilderness and certainly not a god. She had to reach Sanctum.

"Sanctum," she breathed raggedly, standing atop the final rill of the badlands.

Before her, the city glowed like a bed of embers under the starless night. It was beautiful. She ached to be there, lying on a stone bed in the apartments of Zagorka. If anyone would know how to deliver child and mother, it would be Zagorka. Phage's hand drifted down to the sand-crusted wound, and she patted it. "Not much farther."

But what were these folk doing, pouring out of the glorious city? Where could they be going? Why would they leave sanctuary?

J. Robert King

"More room for me," Phage muttered. She walked. The bones of her hips felt different, lose, as though the baby had broken them. She wanted to lie down in a room somewhere, with water on the fire and conversation nearby. The child would come, and someone had to be there to hold it. Phage had already planned to find gauntlets and a breastplate and cover them with silk. It would take the work of a smith to devise a funnel by which she might nurse. All this would be worked out in the next days.

Among the final stones she walked, toward the black river that would deliver her to sanctuary.

* * * * *

Umbra, Sash, and Waistcoat followed a narrow path along the escarpment and down into Sanctum. They arrived behind the wall of a fountain plaza.

"What's that red light?" Sash wondered, stretching to peer over the wall.

"What's that strange smell?" Waistcoat asked.

"Brimstone," Umbra said.

The red-granite fountain no longer hosted bones games. It held a bubbling pool of lava, steam hissing up from it and stone-cicles hanging like black fingers from the rail. Stranger still, creatures surrounded the fountain—translucent men whose bodies had the same red hue as the lava.

"New neighbors," Waistcoat said.

Sash sniffed. "They look serious."

"They are," Umbra said. "Look there." More of the red men went house to house, ripping open doors and driving out the inhabitants. Some folk fought—and died—but many stumbled away empty-handed or clutched what little they could carry. "Marshal law. These things are taking over. Maybe we should find some other place to stay—"

"Puddle, you idiot!" Sash hissed as Waistcoat's leg disappeared over the top of the wall. Sash turned to his other partner. "Well, we could abandon him—"

"Let's go." Umbra was already halfway up, feet scrabbling on stone.

As he climbed, Sash growled, "I'm surrounded by vacuous morons."

The three unmen dropped down in front of the wall and cursed in unison—surrounded.

Red creatures stood in a semicircle before them, shouting in voices like the roil of a hot spring. Though the words made no sense, the inflection was clear.

"We surrender!" Waistcoat cried, hands thrust into the air.

Shaking their heads, Sash and Umbra did the same.

The red folk turned, searching the shadows but looking right past the unmen.

"They can't even see I have my hands up!" Waistcoat groused.

"They can't see us at all," Umbra said.

"Shut up and run!"

Drawn by their voices, the creatures advanced, closing ranks.

Umbra darted to the right and turned sideways. He slid like a piece of paper between two of the glowing creatures. Sash did likewise to the left. Both felt heat coming off the strange men. Waistcoat meanwhile ran up the middle, right into the face of a red invader. All three unmen scrabbled out the other side of the plaza. They pelted up the next street, dodging among the glowing folk.

"Nice maneuver, Umbra," said Sash as they ran. "I can't believe we fit through."

"Me neither, but how did you get through, Waistcoat? I thought that one fellow had you."

"Actually, *I* had *him*," Waistcoat replied. He maintained a full-out run even as a disoriented red man stumbled out of him.

The creature tried to catch its balance but crashed onto the road and broke in half at the hip. The two parts struggled to find each other. A scintillating light ran along the edges of the break, fusing the halves back together. No sooner was the crimson man complete than it stood up, scanning the road.

"I think they see heat," Umbra said, "and we give off none."

"Still, we'd do well to get out of sight." Sash peered around for a hiding place. Before every door stood red sentries. All were dark except one large stone building ahead. "They left the Gilded Mage?"

Waistcoat said, "They can't be all bad."

Umbra said, "Let's slip in and hide among the shadows and hear what we can hear."

"And drink what we can drink," Waistcoat added.

"Idiot," Sash observed. "Hush!"

The living shadows slowed to a stealthy walk. On wafer-thin feet, they stalked closer to the two-story building.

The Gilded Mage was the first of many pubs in the freebooter colony and the most popular, specializing in potables rather than smokables. Its two-foot-thick stone walls had become famous for chilling the tuns of Brunk's beer. With broad inner spaces, high ceilings, a clerestory to carry away smoke and bluster, and wide views on the valley below, it was a favorite haunt of the artistic set—about fifty percent of the colony. Even after Phage had established the stone circle as the center for dice gaming, this hall had remained the house for cards.

On a wide portico before the double doors, two crimson men stood guard. They seemed statues carved of ruby, unmoving as the flat fools climbed onto the porch.

Waistcoat went to tiptoes, the equivalent of walking on a razor, and paid for it a moment later when both feet slipped into a seam between the stones. He sank to his waist. "Psst!"

Sash cursed under his breath.

Umbra reached back, grasped Waistcoat by the outline of his head, and yanked. Waistcoat slid out with such force that he flapped like a spring-loaded shade.

The guards converged, arms reaching.

Thinking quickly, Umbra held Waistcoat up to catch one of the guards, who stumbled out of existence. With a flip of his wrist, Umbra hurled Waistcoat out behind the remaining guard. The first crystal man tripped out of Waistcoat on top of the second. They clashed, fell to the ground, and shattered. Their parts jittered, trying to reassemble themselves.

Umbra set Waistcoat down and gestured him inward. Waistcoat gladly slipped between the double doors, and his comrades followed.

Within, they found the great hall as they had remembered it: a ceiling in black hammer beams, two blazing chandeliers made from wagon wheels, music from fife and fiddle, and talk from a hundred mouths. While outside folk fled the coming terrors, within people hailed those terrors with mugs of ale, pipes of tobacco, flipping cards, and flipping tongues. At round tables crowded the best and brightest of Sanctum.

One nearby niche hosted none other than the city's ruler, Governor Mother Zagorka, its chief historian, Elionoway, and its winch-runner and defender, General Stonebrow.

The three unmen edged nearer, listening.

"—not a certainty," the elf was saying, his bone pipe bobbing in his lips. "There is no equivalent word in our tongue, but 'witness' is the nearest match I can devise. We are spared, or perhaps held captive, to witness something."

"I've already got an eyeful," Zagorka said with a laugh, and she threw back the dregs of her ale. "Words becoming flesh, creatures that live in lava, soldiers you can see right through . . . Too much for these old eyes."

Elionoway smiled slyly. "In fact, they aren't using the same word for you as for the rest of us. They are calling you 'mother' instead of 'witness.' "

"I've been called that before."

The giant centaur, who stood in a sunken dining room in order to be on the same level with the others, shook his massive head. "They've driven out citizens but let in strangers like me. Folk of Krosan, Topos, Aphetto . . . Why?"

"Because what happens next will affect all those nations. We're meant to witness some great event and, I suppose, go into the world to tell the news," Elionoway explained. He blew smoke that spiraled upward like a snake.

Zagorka snorted, holding up her tankard for another draught. "Let's get on with it. Let me see whatever glory they have in store and get a little sleep."

The elf arched an eyebrow. "Not yet. They're waiting for the company of witnesses to be complete. Someone is missing."

"Oh, no, we're not," Waistcoat chimed in.

"Shut up!" said Sash.

A huge hand lashed out, grabbing all three of the shadows and clenching them together like paper. General Stonebrow lifted the three figures before his face and stared at them, no more than gray shades on the air. "What is this?"

"Nothing!" Waistcoat averred, his voice muffled by the fist. "Nobody."

Zagorka stood, her old eyes bugging. "You're somebody. I recognize your voice."

Umbra said, "You probably remember us as roaches. We've been dismembered since then, and we're just shadows now."

The crone goggled. "You're ghosts of roaches?"

"Sure," replied Waistcoat.

Stonebrow looked ill, but he didn't loosen his grip. "Elionoway, do the prophecies talk about . . . roach ghosts?"

Elionoway wore a delighted smile. "No. They're not in anything I've read or heard. No ghosts or roaches or living nobodies. You're not supposed to be here." His grin only deepened. "Something tells me that's good."

The great double doors of the Gilded Mage swung open. In stepped the two crimson guards. The fracture lines in their bodies gleamed where they had fused together.

Laughter died and conversation too. Everything in the room stilled except the languid gray ribbons of smoke from pipes.

One of the guards spoke. Its voice sputtered and popped. Only one creature there knew what it said.

" 'Mother, come tend mother,' " Elionoway translated quietly, though his voice carried through the packed room. "I know that doesn't seem to make sense, Zagorka, but, literally, that's what they are saying. 'Mother, come tend mother.' "

"No, it makes perfect sense. Look between them." Zagorka pointed toward the guards. "There she is."

Standing there in black silks was a very weary Phage.

SACRIFICES

Careful," said Zagorka, holding back the stairway door. Past her shuffled three living shadows. They carried a pregnant woman whose very touch was death. Things had gotten strange, indeed. "Straight up the stairs. Don't put her in the bed or on the rug. Lay her on the hearth."

"We know," Sash said. "We're her roaches."

"Yeah." Zagorka swung the door closed behind them and slid the bolt. She peered out the knothole, glad to see that none of the Glyphs had followed.

Up the stairs she ambled and entered her apartments. The unmen laid Phage on the stone hearth. She hadn't awakened since collapsing at the Gilded Mage, and she shivered terribly. Beyond her, the fire had fallen to embers.

Zagorka went to the fuel niche and pulled out kindling and logs. She stooped over Phage, arranged the wood, and blew the fire to new life. "I think I've still got some water. We'll need it warm to wash her." Zagorka lifted a pitcher and poured the last liquid from it into a kettle. She hung the pot on an angle iron and pivoted it over the flame.

"You'd better let us wash her," Umbra said, "unless you want to rot."

Zagorka looked at them suspiciously.

"We're nothing, Zagorka. We couldn't take advantage of her even if we wanted to," Umbra said. "Do you have any silk?"

The old woman averted her eyes. "I have one scarf."

"That'll work for a rag to wash her, but we'll need more to make a bed. She can't sleep on stone. If you could find a silk sheet, we could make a hammock, or we could make a bed of sand that we would cover with silk—something soft."

"Right," Zagorka said. She untied a scarf that hung from her bed-frame and laid it on the hearth but didn't move toward the door.

Umbra spread his hands. "Trust us. We promise. She'll be fine. Go get what we need, and we'll clean her and settle her in."

What could Zagorka do? Already, she was in surreal territory. Did she trust the death mother to the roaches with no bodies, or did she send them out among the living words to pillage empty houses for silk. Nothing made sense anymore. "Clean her up. I'll be back."

Zagorka headed down the stairs. It was a nightmare knit together by unseen hands. What could she do but lay down her life among the threads?

* * * * *

The door closed.

Umbra hissed, "Waistcoat, go throw the bolt. We don't want any-body stumbling in on us." As the pudgy shadow pattered off toward the stairs, Umbra and Sash stepped up to stand before Phage. She was deeply asleep. "This will be easier than we thought. It will take just two of us."

"Just two," Sash echoed.

They stared at her abdomen, flat despite the baby gestating within. It moved, and what might have been a head or a heel dis-tended her skin.

"One of us will bend down and slide her feet through—her legs, her hips, and on up until everything but her neck and head is inside. Then the other one will go the other way, from head down. When we meet, we just have to slide in opposite directions, and it will be done. We'll be halfway to being real."

"Yeah."

Waistcoat came chuffing up the stairs. "So, have you done it?"

Sash glanced at him. "Have *we* done it?"

"I barred the door. I thought you two were going to finish her off," Waistcoat said.

"You don't get out of it that easily," Sash said. "You're the obvious choice since you're the fattest one, and it'll be easiest to slide her into you."

"But I barred the door."

"Both of you are going to do this," Umbra said.

"Since when do you get out of it?" Sash asked.

"Our master died because you two abandoned him. I was left standing there. I've done nothing wrong. You two are the traitors; you might as well also be—"

"Murderers! That's what you were going to say," Sash snarled. "Since when has this turned into murder? This is an assassination— a political maneuver, not murder."

"Whatever," Umbra said. "You two have to do it."

"Look, this whole plan is ridiculous!" Sash said. "We're not killing two people. We're killing three. That baby is ready to be born. If we choose to do this, we steal these three lives. Where do you think the First is going to get bodies for us? He'll steal them from someone else. That'll be six lives, and will it stop there? We'll be slaves to the First, and what will he make us do? Kill more. That's all. This is no way to become real."

"What he said," Waistcoat replied.

Umbra was trembling. He knelt down beside the hearth, holding himself up with his hands. "I'm glad you agree. I couldn't do it either."

Waistcoat's said quietly, "You know what I think? I think when we were her friends, we kind of lived through her. That's a way to have a body, live through your friends."

"That's what's called empathy," Sash said.

Umbra reached above the fire and drew out a steaming pot of water. He lifted the silk scarf and dipped it in the kettle. "I wish I knew how hot this was."

"Too hot," Sash advised as he pulled back Phage's clothes. "Let it cool in your hand before you use it. Oh, look at that wound, and the sand packed there. We've got to clean that out."

Waistcoat said, "I'll wait at the door. Zagorka should be back soon."

"I hope she found a silk sheet," Umbra said. "Nobody should have to sleep on stone." He looked up at Sash. "Nobody with a body, anyway."

* * * * *

For a whole month, Phage had rested, but never once did the birth pangs begin. Her belly still didn't swell, but the creature within it convulsed constantly. Phage was weak and trembly. The unmen tended her by night and Zagorka by day, and Stonebrow kept them provisioned. They had an odd little family there, sheltering each other while outside their walls, the world grew more perilous. Glyphs patrolled the streets, their numbers growing as the escarpment spit them forth. Aside from the Glyphs, no one except the witnesses, the two mothers, and the three unmen remained. They all waited in nervous contentment, knowing that everything was about to change, and drastically.

A knock came at the upstairs shutter in Zagorka's room. It could be only Stonebrow. Zagorka was cooking and hadn't heard. Umbra set down the book he had been reading, rose from a rocker of twisted wood, and crept quietly past Phage on her sand bed. Sash glanced up from the corner and followed. The two unmen entered the bedroom where the window was and pushed back the shutters. Wood moved aside to reveal a giant simian face.

Stonebrow blinked at the apparently empty room. "So, who's there?"

"I am—Umbra. Sash is here too. Phage is sleeping, and Zagorka's cooking. Waistcoat slipped out."

"Slipped out?"

"There's a crack in the wall, and he slipped out. He's in back, trying to get in."

"Get him," Stonebrow said. "The Glyphs are summoning all the witnesses."

"We're not witnesses," Sash said.

Stonebrow nodded. "I know, but I think you should come. Whatever they have planned, it would be helpful to have some invisible operatives."

"Right," Sash said, and headed out the bedroom and down the stairs.

"What do you think they have planned?" Umbra asked.

Stonebrow shook his head. "Elionoway says this is the big moment." He glanced up the street. "Don't tell Zagorka or Phage, or they'd try to come. They're safer here." The centaur's mouth drew into a grim line. "You'll probably want to say good-bye."

Umbra nodded pensively. "We will."

"Everyone's gathering at the high, holy place," Stonebrow said, "Glyphs and the rest of us. Nothing will be the same after today." The centaur stepped back to gesture toward the brow of the hill.

Umbra craned his head to look. For the first time since folk had arrived in Sanctum, the cliff face was smooth, devoid of even a single petraglyph.

"They're all here. The war they foretell is at hand."

* * * * *

Most of the witnesses arrived via the lift, but the unmen could not very easily climb onto a crowded conveyor in broad daylight. Instead, they marched the switchback footpaths that led to the top. Occasionally, Glyphs crossed their trail, climbing effortlessly up sheer cliffs and onto the top of the bluff.

"It's a good day not to have a body," Sash decided. "No sweat."

"No panting. No side aches," added Waistcoat.

"Let's be quiet now. Here's the top."

They strode up over the final rise and stared out on a multitude.

The mountaintop seemed to groan under the weight of all those creatures. Outside the ring of monoliths stood a crowd of witnesses—three hundred folk deemed "pure." In their midst gathered every last Glyph—ten thousand of them. A gurgling noise came from their throats, lifted in song. In their weird hands, they held ancient instruments—rasps carved from shank bones, rattles fashioned from bleached skulls, drums of skin on hoops of rib. With these instruments they set up a rhythm like the pounding of an eager heart. To the bare cadence of it, they added their voices and the slow, turning dance of legs and arms.

"They want us to watch them dance?" Waistcoat wondered.

Sash pointed to the edge of the throng, where Stonebrow stood beside Elionoway. "If anybody knows what's happening, it's him."

In silent accord, the three unmen crossed the crackling slope of red sandstone to reach the elf and centaur. As they neared, the rhythm of the drums gradually quickened, and the timbre of voices became more strident.

Umbra tapped Elionoway on the shoulder. "What is this?"

Elionoway had long since learned not to startle when an invisible man touched him. "A prayer," he answered. "They're praying that all will return to what it once was. The drum is the heartbeat of the world. It's an old world, and its heart beats slowly. By increasing its speed, the Glyphs are turning back time to when the world was young."

Beside him, Stonebrow said, "We thought Sanctum was a ruin. Really, it was a seed."

"Yes," Elionoway said. "And somehow by settling here we not only caused the seed to germinate, but also nourished the nation that grew up from it. Whether we like it or not, we're the reason these creatures have returned."

The drums doubled their pace, and the voices trebled their pitch. The monoliths shook, not from the sound but from growth. Each of the great curved stones enlarged. It mounded up soil around it and grew like a stalk inward. As the columns met in the center, what had been an open ring of rock became a cage. They broadened still until their top sections fused into a dome. The song only intensified, reverberating from the stone vault to blast heavenward and roll in avenues out among the witnesses.

"Their temple!" Elionoway shouted above the roar. "It's now as it once was, just like their shrine. They are returning Sanctum to its former glory!"

"The rumble's coming from the city too," Sash said.

"I'll be right back!" Umbra said. He dashed for the trail head and peered down. His whole figure went limp, and he stared a while before waving the others over.

Waistcoat and Sash ran toward him while Stonebrow and Elionoway backed slowly away from the monoliths. Other witnesses retreated too, and they all joined Umbra at the trail head.

Just over the ridge, the city stretched in boxy splendor, a maze in stone. The pounding beat shook the buildings. Short walls grew, adding new courses until they were tall. Open-topped silos yearned upward, roofs forming slate by slate. Buildings shucked their wooden roofs and piled story upon story. Empty sconces grew statues. Footings bloomed with lanterns. It was as if the music made cobble and tile, wood and beam precipitate out of the air and accrete into new configurations—or very old ones.

This was no natural city but an otherworldly metropolis. It was founded on true stone, yes, but its upper stories were the smooth stuff of divinity. Every street gleamed like gold. Every building curved like ivory. The city ached for the skies.

As the witnesses watched, the first rooftop jutted above the cliff. Another followed, crimson-tiled and many-chimneyed. A third with an ironwork crown and a fourth with red gables . . . suddenly, hundreds of buildings soared above the escarpment.

"It's not just Sanctum," Elionoway said, excitement and dread in his voice. "Look there, on the south side of the escarpment."

More rooftops rose like teeth beneath the sky. No one from Sanctum had even suspected that another city had been there, but it wasn't another city. It was part of the same city, a part leveled in some ancient, world-rending war.

Elionoway gasped. "Now I understand. The northern buildings survived only because they were sheltered from the leveling blast. The whole summit had been the city, in front and behind, everywhere!" He fell to his knees. "They're bringing it back."

The song was almost deafening now, rolling from the domed temple and reverberating among the magnificent buildings.

Stonebrow stared in awe at the incredible transformation. "I feel privileged to witness these great things."

The tone of the song changed, from strenuous notes to a flowing melody, rich through all registers.

"What are they singing now?" asked the centaur.

"Praise," Elionoway said. "It is a song of praise for what the numen has wrought:

"O, Averru, behold your city
returned to you from out of stone.
The field is set and battle looms.
Your people wait to wage your war.
We offer up these sacrifices;
kill them first, and start the war."

"What sacrifices?" Umbra asked.

Elionoway had turned white, and his eyes reflected the gleaming towers. "It's an ambivalent word. In this context, it means sacrifices. In other contexts, it means . . . witnesses."

The song changed again, devolving from a paean to a battle cry. From each broad archway of the domed temple, Glyphs rushed. Their instruments were gone, and their hands had transformed into swords.

The witnesses stood frozen in disbelief.

A red-bladed hand fell and cut a man in half. The Glyph trampled him and struck a woman that stood beyond. Dozens more died in the next moments. Folk turned to run. They fled in panic, some right off the cliff. Others bolted for the winch wheel or the trail head, hoping to escape through the maze of stone.

Stonebrow prepared to defend their escape. "You, go, Elionoway. You can do no good here."

The elf didn't argue. He nodded gravely to his comrades. "I hope to see you again."

"We're going with you!" Waistcoat shouted.

"No, we're not," shot Umbra. "We're going to make ourselves into three more escapes."

"What are you talking about?" Sash said.

"Just follow me." Spreading his arms, Umbra ran toward the battle. He rush straight at the witnesses, striking them head-on so that they fell through him and into safety.

Laughing, Waistcoat and Sash followed, their arms outstretched. By ones and two and threes, they swallowed up the running folk. Whenever a Glyph barreled toward them, the unmen merely turned on an edge and let him rattle past.

Stonebrow smiled as witness after witness blinked out of being. His smile only deepened when the first Glyph reached him. He swung his axe, and the ruby man shattered like a glass statue. Its beautiful fragments swarmed through the air, hot and jagged, and crashed to scatter across the stone.

At last, he was fighting as mortals fight. He reared, huge above the field, and his spinning hooves shattered two more Glyphs. Stonebrow was indeed a witness, but he would not be a sacrifice. By his strong arm, many would not be sacrificed this day.

CHAPTER 24

DEPARTURES

Phage rolled over on her sand bed and sniffed. There was a strange smell in the air, something like lightning. A sound came with it. Thunder? Phage sat up. The apartment was warm, indolent with afternoon, and the walls occasionally creaked. A low fire burned at the hearth, and Zagorka busied herself in the side room. Outside, though, came that mounting roar.

A sudden hot wind poured through the shudders, rattling them. Sheets lifted from the bed. Paper flew off the table and out the back window.

Phage stood—hard work at ten months pregnant. The stone floor felt cool under her bare feet, but everything else was hot. "What's happening?"

Movement came in the side room, and Zagorka appeared in the doorway. She held a half-knitted baby sweater. "What?"

The floor bucked beneath them, flexing like a muscle. It threw both women backward. Phage landed on the sand bed, and the babe angrily kicked. Zagorka tumbled into the side room. Before either woman could rise, the walls began to twist and grow. The ceiling rose, and the stones stretched like skin. Phage's bed shifted, particles of sand transforming into hunks of gravel. She rolled off the bed and gripped the floor, but the stones there enlarged as well.

"Zagorka!" Phage cried.

The old woman shouted, "I'm coming!"

Through the warping doorway, Phage glimpsed the old woman crawling toward her. The posts of the door riled like snakes, and the lintel shrank. With a deep boom, the two sides came together and fused, shutting Zagorka away. The seam where the door had been rushed up the soaring wall, as if Zagorka and the room that held her headed skyward. Even as Phage watched it go, she felt the tremendous vertigo of a rapid descent. One woman headed for the heavens, and the other for the depths.

Phage could only cling to the floor.

Three walls and the ceiling melted away. Furnishings tumbled into a trembling street. Suddenly Phage was outside, and all around her, Sanctum grew. Buildings shot up like blades of grass—rapid and curved, reaching for the sun. The floor merged with the street, and Phage held on.

What else could she do? She could not even comprehend what was happening.

Around her, a platoon of Glyphs gathered. They formed a watchful circle, and one of them spoke in the common tongue. "It is time that you leave, Mother."

Phage glanced up at the enormous tower where Zagorka was trapped. It jutted above the cliff. "What's happening?"

The Glyph stared with queer eyes, and its voice sounded almost compassionate. "Our city is reborn. Our mother has brought it into being. She has given a new body to Averru. This is what the world mothers do; they give birth to the numen."

"Your mother?" Phage echoed, slowly standing.

"Yes. Zagorka is our mother. She brought this city into being, and this city will be the body of Averru. He has waited for twenty thousand years to return, and she has given him a body."

Phage's eyes narrowed as she peered at the tower that held her friend. "Zagorka," she said, unbelieving. "Your mother . . . ?"

"Yes, and you are a world mother, but not our mother. Your child will be Kuberr, and you must go now to his lands to bear him."

Phage could only shake her head in disbelief.

"There is one more world mother, who has already brought her numen child into being. She is Akroma. She appeared in dream and vision to Ixidor and transformed him, inspired him to give her substance, and delivered him unto death that he might return as a true numen. She even raised a priesthood and an army for him. These were the last things written in Averru's great spell, written in us. There are more things, but you must not know them yet." The crimson creature paused reverently. "Now you must go. Return to the coliseum and give birth to the creature you bear."

Phage looked down at herself—barefoot and weak with child, garbed only in a silken nightgown. "You would send me like this to the coliseum?"

The face of the Glyph was implacable. "Yes, the child and the terrors of bearing him are yours." With that, the crimson creatures parted, and they gestured Phage along the road.

Glancing one last time at the tower where Zagorka was imprisoned, Phage set off. Her feet knew the way. The street would lead to a path, and the path to the swamp, and the swamp to the coliseum, and the coliseum to Virot. If that long trail did not kill Phage, surely the man at the end of it would.

* * * * *

A motley band straggled eastward along the Corian Escarpment. These hundred souls were the only witnesses who had survived the metamorphosis of Sanctum. Most had literally stumbled into salvation. One moment, they had been running atop the escarpment, fleeing bloodthirsty Glyphs. The next, they had crashed into one strange quiet room or another, scrambled up against a wall, and watched more folk fall through that same hole in the air. Wherever they had landed, it was better than where they had been. All waited within the unmen as they slipped out of the city.

Thus, Umbra, Sash, and Waistcoat had each saved almost thirty souls.

Others had escaped on their own. Stonebrow had fought his way to safety. Chester the mule had kicked out an escape, shattering walls and the red men who patrolled them. Elionoway and a number of elves had escaped due to quick feet.

Reaching a wide plateau, Elionoway called a halt. The weary group shuffled to a stop. Most dropped in their tracks and sat, panting. For a time the setting sun warmed their dusty backs, but soon a great shadow rose from the distant west—a shadow cast by the city of Averru.

It was a red monstrosity on the escarpment, a rampant cactus with thousands of arms and billions of barbs. In every crevice, Glyphs swarmed like army ants.

Elionoway shivered and wished for warmer clothes—for any clothes but those on his back.

Stonebrow stood beside him, the only creature tall enough to see the sun. In moments, his face too went dark.

"We'll camp here tonight, but we can't stay here long," Elionoway said. "No water, no shelter, no food. In the morning, we'll have to choose our path."

"I can't go with you," Stonebrow rumbled. "I've chosen a different way." His massive hand strayed to the axe at his waist. "I made pretty good use of this thing back there, but there's someone who can wield it better."

Elionoway took a deep breath and let it out slowly. "We'll be sorry to do without you."

"You should head away from the war," said another voice, as if the air itself spoke.

Elionoway smiled. "Are all three of you here, Umbra?"

"Yes," said the shadow man, "and we think you should head to Eroshia. We've been there—far east and well ruled."

The elf nodded. "It would be only a temporary refuge. The war will surely reach that place too." He glanced back at Sanctum, demonic beneath the red heavens. "It sounds like you'll not be going with us."

Umbra replied quietly. "We're like Stonebrow. We have to go our own way. We need bodies, and we can't get bodies until we appear before Akroma. She may kill us, but it wouldn't be so terrible since we've never really lived. Or she may give us life, true life."

"She may do both," Elionoway cautioned. "She may give you real bodies just so that she can kill you."

"It's time to find out."

There seemed nothing left to say. The elf, the giant centaur, and the three unmen gazed at the city that had been home to them all. At last, Elionoway spoke. "I only wish we had gotten Zagorka out."

Stonebrow hung his head. "If she died, she died fighting."

Waistcoat added, "Aw, I bet she's in there giving them hell."

Lifting an imaginary stein, Elionoway said, "Here's to Zagorka. Give 'em hell."

* * * * *

With legs of steel, Akroma stood on the Nightmare Lands—the staging ground for her army. Tent camps checkered the world from horizon to horizon, and bivouacs made fiery constellations beneath the darkening sky. These were Akroma's three legions.

The first had come from the hand of the creator—crab men and putty people as infantry, jaguars and their riders as cavalry, and aerial jellyfish and barracudas for airborne. All these would be coordinated through an intelligence network of disciples. The second legion comprised the thousands of converts that Akroma had made from every nation—humans, elves, dwarfs, avens, mantis folk, goblins, centaurs, and horsemen. The third legion had come from allies north and south, nations with old grudges and new fears that centered on the Cabal.

War was inevitable now. The First had made it so. His machinations had forced Akroma to assemble this war machine, and now that it was assembled, it must be used.

Though the rest of the sky deepened into night, the west did not fade. Within its feverish hue, a single blue star trembled. It grew brighter, larger, and Akroma realized a disciple sped toward her. She lifted her brow to receive the thing. It struck her between the eyes, penetrating through flesh and bone and into her mind.

A demonic city grew from the very rocks. It reached endless towers up to gouge out the sky. Red devils cavorted in the streets, chasing down the populace and piercing them with terrible hands.

Stonebrow fought these monsters with the axe he had stolen from Akroma.

Zagorka raged against them from the height of her prison tower.

But one person was honored by them: Phage. Red devils stood in a circle around her, and she wore the silk robes of a priestess. The city grew to every side, and folk fled and died, but Phage spoke calmly to these things, and they called her Mother.

Somehow, she had brought an evil army to take Sanctum. She had conquered the buffer city between the Cabal and Topos, and her demons hungered to march.

Horrified, Akroma witnessed the wicked transformation of Sanctum.

What if she had not assembled this army? What would have become of Topos with a nation of demons at its border? Instead, she was ready. A month more for reconnaissance and planning, and she would march against those monsters.

"Thank you," she whispered, letting the disciple float from between her lips. It hovered, waiting for her next wish. "Go, gather all the disciples and send them to this new city—Averru, is it called?—to learn its layout, defenses, strengths, and weaknesses. Learn all we must to make a siege."

The spark darted away.

Akroma watched it go, a strange sense of peace filling her. She had been bent on war, and now war was bent on her. She had been right all along.

"I must see it with my own eyes."

Akroma stroked her wings, flattening nearby tents. While mortals struggled beneath collapsed canvas, the immortal Akroma took to the air. A second surge lifted her steel legs off the ground. Beat by beat, she climbed into the sky.

* * * * *

Something was wrong in the north.

The fans didn't notice, too busy watching the coliseum floor, where a family feud had turned deadly.

The First noticed, though. The red glow so disturbed him that he wandered from his luxury box. Hand and mind servants scrambled to keep up, and black-robed bodyguards flanked the master of the coliseum.

The First ignored them all. He strode through the corridors toward the northern rim. There, he would see for himself what was wrong.

Perhaps the assassins had done their work and Phage was dead—or Akroma. It didn't matter which. Perhaps Phage had gone into labor, and the monstrosity ate her alive. An entertaining idea but implausible.

The First reached the northern rim of the coliseum and stared out above the dark swamps. Will-o'-the-wisps appeared here and there, illuminating curtains of moss or the recticula of dead trees. The north sky glowed a swollen red hue. What would cause such a strange light?

There was one obvious answer: War.

Akroma had been gearing up for it. She had converted folk across the continent and gathered them in Topos. Spies told of three legions: one made entirely of converts, another of allies, and a third of monsters. Such reports were alarming, of course, but the First had raised six undead legions and had them waiting just beneath the brown waters of the swamp. It wasn't the size of Akroma's army that frightened him but their motives. Akroma's troops were fanatics—determined and implacable. There would be war because Akroma wanted war.

A dark figure floated in the sky. It was small and slender like a stab wound. The line pulsed once, and again, growing wider. It was black and glossy, configured in plumes, with a sharp and crooked beak. The bird soared toward the top of the coliseum, its eyes glowing orange.

The First only waited.

With scrabbling talons, the huge crow landed. It pranced along the rim, riffled its wings, and stared at the First. The bird's voice was a grating shriek, a sound so horrid that it cleared the top three rows in the stands.

Sanctum sprouts. It grows like corn. Up from the rock. Down from the rock. All around the rock. It glitters. The critters in it glitter like blood.

The First nodded gravely. Even a crow would not make up so outlandish a lie. With a screech that equaled the bird's, the First replied, *Who does this?*

The huge crow cocked its head, blinking quickly. Its talons scraped the stone. *A woman-bird. White she was. Spotted back. Glittery legs. She flew above and looked down.*

Akroma. The First had expected as much. She had somehow harnessed the creative power of Ixidor and had used it to take over Sanctum. It was hers now, a great city full of blood-red creatures. *What of our folk? What of the games? Do any of our hosts or hawkers remain?*

Stone circle gone. A temple there.

That damned angel. In the seat of Cabal power, she had built a temple to Ixidor. Perhaps, though, this terrible news might hold one bright spot. *What of Phage? Did she survive?*

The crow bobbed its head and squawked. *Wounded. Weary. On her way! On her way!*

Here? She's coming here? the First asked.

Aye! Aye! the crow replied. As if sensing its master's foul mood, the bird leaped backward off the bulwark. Its wings spread and caught the air. Cawing madly, the bird flew away.

The news did not anger the First, though. It made him glad. Phage, pregnant and wounded, was on her way back into his arms. He would welcome her. He would kill her.

CHAPTER 25

THE WAY OF SUFFERING

*P*hage staggered along a suspension bridge above a steaming swamp. Boards blackened under her feet. She dared not stand too long in one place, lest she drop into crocodile waters.

Still, she paused to catch her breath. If only she could steady herself on the bristly rail, but it too would rot. . . . All across her flat abdomen, muscles tightened. False labor, it was called, though it didn't feel false. Her wound had healed into a tender red mound, but it burned with each contraction. Closing her eyes, she rode out the agony.

Pain and peril were the price of birth, and Phage was paying dearly. Giving birth to a human baby would have been trauma enough, but her child was a numen—one of three great powers. He would be an ancient child, a future child, and his birth would turn back the world clock twenty thousand years.

The contraction eased, but the aches throughout the rest of her body rose to consciousness. Her feet felt like bags of bone—loose and disjointed. Her hips crackled as she walked, and spasms clutched her back. She wanted to soak in a hot bath until the child simply floated out of her, but first she had this long wooden road to walk.

Setting her teeth, Phage continued down the swaying bridge. She reached its low point, a dozen feet above the waters, and began to climb toward the far bank. There, a tower anchored the bridge, and in that tower would be Cabal guards. They would help her, provision her. . . .

The tower, made of dressed logs, looked like a giant tree trunk. It extended just above the cypress grove that filled the island. Narrow windows and X-shaped arrow loops would give everyone a good view of the struggling woman.

Phage counted her paces—a hundred and seventy-three—until she stepped onto packed ground. Slowly, she approached the garrison door. It was made of rough wood, and through its cracks Phage glimpsed a guard. She knocked.

"You are cleared to pass," came his gruff voice. "Continue along."

Phage took a deep breath. "I am Phage. I need your assistance."

"I am sorry. Our orders are explicit. We are to remain in our tower and not emerge for any reason. We are to pass all those who approach, providing neither hindrance nor help."

Weariness poured through her. "Who gave these orders?"

"They came from the very top."

Virot. Coward that he was, he would not attack as long as Phage might die on the trail. She could defeat him only by surviving to give birth. To survive, though, she needed food and water.

"A crust of bread?"

"We cannot," the guard said.

"Water, then?"

The guard replied with a coarse laugh. "It's a swamp. Help yourself."

Phage circled the tower. If they were charged to stay inside, they would have to toss their refuse toward the woods. Soon Phage found the spot, where gnawed bones and hunks of stale bread lay near the acrid offal of slops buckets. The queen of the coliseum, the mother of a numen, knelt in the filth to find what food she could.

The men in the tower laughed.

Phage didn't care. Soon, she would give birth to the past and the future, and these hecklers would be heading to war.

* * * * *

Stonebrow marched through Krosan, hardly recognizing it. His nostrils flared, drawing in the scent of rot. Kamahl had shut down the forest's rampant growth, yes, but he had also ended all other growth. Now Krosan was decaying.

Kamahl had become just like his sister—corrupting.

It was a grim thought. Stonebrow wondered if his mission were doomed. Would Kamahl even take up his axe? If he did, would he use if for good or evil?

Snorting the stench from his nostrils, the great centaur climbed a fetid pile of dead boughs. The tangle was spongy, encrusted with fungi. One hoof cracked through a hollow log, and Stonebrow struggled to break free. He set his other three feet and yanked. The hoof came loose, pill bugs showering from it. Stonebrow shook his leg clean and bounded higher.

Once, this thicket had borne ten-foot-long spikes to guard the Gorgon Mount. Now it was a ring of mush. The heart of Krosan was dying.

A sudden twinge gripped Stonebrow. What if Kamahl too had died? Who then would bear the axe to do what must be done?

As Stonebrow scrambled over the rounded edge of the thicket, his heart stopped.

There sat Kamahl, as gray as a corpse.

* * * * *

Phage panted, crawling from the shelter of a great willow. It had wept over her all night, its tendrils catching the warm rain that fell on the swamp and pouring it, drop by drop, on the ground. Dawn thrust its rosy fingers among the leaves. Phage climbed to her feet. Mud clung to her knees, and rotten leaves were pasted to her skin. She staggered toward the main trail across the island.

This journey had been a battle. Perhaps a month had lapsed while the wounded and pregnant woman staggered from the Corian Escarpment to the coliseum. All the while, she met no resistance and received no aid. Eating refuse and drinking swamp water, she had become emaciated. The baby fed off her muscles and bones, and its weight was terrific. Even so, it did not show. By the time this ingrown thing was born, it might possibly be heavier than she . . . if ever it was born. This was Phage's eleventh month.

Still, she owed her life to the babe. He had saved her from countless deaths, and until he was born, she would be invincible.

Oh, but the pain. Virot had much to answer for. He would, of course, pretend he did not know of her plight, and he would have a thousand complicit guards in his lie. Virot would feign deep concern for his beloved and child, perhaps execute a few guards to demonstrate his anger. Phage would let him act. This had been a slow murder, and she knew it, but to escape the hands of any murderer, a victim had to wait for her moment.

Phage came out from among the trees and found the trail. She followed it to the island's edge and the next bridge. There would be no more sleeping under willows, no more eating rubbish. The coliseum loomed on the horizon.

Smiling grimly, Phage headed for the bridgehead. So intent was she on the coliseum that she did not see a bough that had fallen during last night's storm. Phage sprawled full out. Her hands slapped the first board of the bridge, and she came down right atop the baby.

The agony . . . she had been in constant pain since leaving Topos, but nothing as excruciating as this. It felt as though she had ruptured her belly, broken her back, and killed the baby, all at once. She lay there, unable even to scream.

Vision narrowed. Thought closed down. It would be a blessing to die now, if only to end the screaming pain. Mercifully, she went black.

* * * * *

The giant centaur's pulse pounded as he clambered down the rotten embankment. Hooves threw hunks of wood in the air then clods of mud as he rushed to the prominence where Kamahl sat.

Though the man sat upright—legs crossed before him and elbows resting on his knees—there was no sign of life. Kamahl's skin was gray and broken, crossed with veins that looked like ivy vines. His hair jutted from his head in ropy dreadlocks, and his clothes hung on him in rags. The leather of his armor had rotted away. The metal plates lay on the ground, with little wells of dirty water in them. Despite his apparent demise, his eyes remained open and staring.

Stonebrow thanked the forest spirits that the birds had left those eyes alone. It was all he had to be thankful for.

The centaur fell to his knees, shaking the ground, and bowed his head.

"Why, Kamahl?" the centaur asked, head bowed. "Why did you simply sit down and die? Your battles aren't over. A greater war is coming. It's not just Phage against Akroma this time. Older powers control them: numena. They've carved up Otaria. Half the folk rally behind the duelists of the Cabal and the other half rally behind the tragic Vision of Ixidor. Only Eroshia and Krosan remain free, but not forever. . . ."

The centaur's lament trailed away. He drew the axe from his waist. "I brought this to you. It's a god's weapon, not made for me, but for you." With a truculent snort, he said, "Take it!" Stonebrow rammed the halberd into Kamahl's belly, but the man didn't move. "Damn it, Kamahl! You know what to do! That's why you came here and fell asleep and prayed for death. You know you have to kill them— your sister and Akroma, both. Only that will stop the war and break the spell." He shoved the hilt again. "Take it!"

Still, Kamahl seemed only a gray and rotten stump.

Roaring, Stonebrow grasped Kamahl's right arm and pried it up from the covetous ground. Tendrils snapped, but his hand gripped the earth like a gnarled root. With a great heave, Stonebrow yanked it free. Dirt showered across him, and humus clung to the white sucker roots that emerged from his fingers. Stonebrow pressed the hilt of Soul Reaper into Kamahl's hand and forced those woody digits to close over the grip.

"TAKE IT!"

The hand tightened around the weapon, forged for it and it alone. Motes of power dormant in the hilt emerged to encircle Kamahl's knuckles. His skin was bleached and pruny after long contact with wet ground, but the sinews beneath were still strong.

Stonebrow lurched back, coming off of his knees and staring in amazement.

A line of vitality moved from Soul Reaper up Kamahl's arm. It flung away the barklike scales that had encased his flesh and revitalized the thews beneath. His elbow flexed, biceps bulged, shoulder crackled as the axe rose. . . . Color and motion crept across his collarbones and up his neck, enlivening even that weary face. Kamahl's eyes sparked, and they swung around to stare up at Stonebrow.

The once-dead man spoke: "Kill her . . ."

Stonebrow returned his fierce gaze. "It's the only way, and you're the only one who can."

Kamahl dropped his voice to a dread whisper. " I know." Those two words spoke volumes. Kamahl had retreated to this place of bliss because bliss was ignorance, and ignorance could save him from the truth: He had to kill Phage. "I know."

At last, the wave of life reached every extremity, and Kamahl rose. The roots that had pierced his skin in hundreds of places dragged excruciatingly out of their sheaths of flesh. Kamahl shivered to his feet, pulling free of white umbilici. All the while, he held his axe and held Stonebrow's eyes.

The giant centaur again went to his knees, not in frustration, but in obeisance. Under his breath, he whispered a prayer: "Behold, the man."

Bleeding into the dirt that once had eaten him, Kamahl said, "I will do it. I will kill her. I will kill them both, but only if you take me to them."

* * * * *

She awoke to the uneven rumble of wheels beneath her, wheels on packed ground. It was a wagon. A board squeaked near her head, and a horse whickered. She lay on her back, which was cold and numb, and her fingers felt the edges of a marble slab.

A funeral procession?

Phage struggled to open her eyes. At first, her eyelids wouldn't respond. When at last they opened a sliver, the midday sky jabbed into them. She winced in pain.

The movement drew the attention of someone walking beside the wagon.

"Oh, you're waking up," said Virot Maglan. She felt the sting of his hand coming to rest on her arm. "I'm so relieved."

She could not respond, the breath too shallow in her lungs.

"When travelers sent word that you had collapsed nearby, I came immediately to carry you home. I flogged the guards in the tower. Imagine refusing you aid! I've ordered one man in every tower killed this night. Their idiocy almost slew you."

He spoke for the benefit of other ears around the wagon. That was why she was still alive. Virot was putting on a public show of his sympathy, prelude to his public grief.

"Do you hear me, Darling?" Virot asked tenderly.

Turning her head toward him, she slitted one eye. His stony face stared down at her, eyes sparking with what some folk might have thought was affection. Phage knew it to be greed. She nodded shallowly.

"Good! I'm praying for our child. How it could have survived that fall!" She must have startled, for he said, "Oh, don't fear. I've called the best chirugeon in the pits. He says you won't even have to endure labor. He'll cut the child out of you and sew you up just as you had been before."

A shadow drew its cold veil over Phage. The wagon had entered one of the arched corridors of the coliseum. At last, she could open her eyes. Groin vaults passed overhead, and a retinue of hand servants, mind servants, Cabal guards, and inner circle members paced solemnly alongside the wagon. Their eyes were grave. Among them walked the First, his gaze fixed on the distant doorway.

"Where . . ." Phage began, though her voice was scratchy in her throat. "Where are we going?"

"After coming so near to defeat, I wanted you to see this: our greatest *victory*."

Phage caught her breath and smelled the unmistakable odor of death. "Our greatest victory . . . ?" The coliseum was utterly silent. "Where is everyone?"

"Oh, they're within, waiting for us," Virot replied. "You see, war is coming. Akroma has taken over Sanctum and twisted it into a hive of giant wasps. We have to be ready. I've been amassing an army of undead, dredging them up from the swamps, but I needed more, and needed them immediately. A hundred thousand—a capacity crowd."

"You didn't . . ." Phage gasped. "You couldn't . . ."

His face was pallid beneath the dark vaults. "All the world is choosing sides. Akroma has taken half of Otaria, stealing their souls. I'm taking the other half, stealing their bodies. The very fact that these hundred thousand had come to my coliseum in this time of war tells that they already belonged to me. Now, they will be my army."

The wagon rolled beneath the final arch and out under that knife-bright sky.

Phage winced and shielded her eyes. At the periphery of her vision, she saw the silent stands, filled to capacity with bodies. Every last person had fallen over, slumping in his or her seat. Not a single creature stirred.

"How?" Phage croaked, feeling suddenly ill. She had killed many in her lifetime, true, but always they had been foes, or rebels. Never had she simply slain innocents wholesale. "How?"

"A simple contact poison on all the entrance tickets. A single touch kills."

The smell of death was pungent—not just meat turning sour but the reek of offal and urine. "What about raising them? When will you return them to life?"

"You see how much I care for you?" the First said gently. "I was in the midst of mass murder when I heard of your collapse. I abandoned my new army to come get you. I'll see you through your surgery before I come back to raise these."

A frisson of terror moved over Phage. If Virot was capable of this . . . what would he do to her and her child?

The wagon rolled from the coliseum into yet another corridor, and Phage closed her eyes and wept.

* * * * *

Braids sat in the luxury box of the First. She had been here when all these spectators died—a hundred thousand slumping as if in worship. Truly her master was great, to kill so many with such ease. Of course, they would rise again and show him to be greater still.

First, though, there was the matter of Phage and her baby. Braids would go in the garb of a midwife. Her hair was still short, her face still drawn. Phage would not know her. Braids would stand there while the First killed his lover and his child. Perhaps he would even raise them too, so that they might do him worship.

Braids could only weep at the greatness of her master.

CHAPTER 26

DELIVERANCE

*P*hage lay in silken bonds—soft enslavement, but enslavement all the same. By the way her wrists and legs were tied to the table, it seemed she had committed some terrible crime, but her only crime was being eleven months pregnant with an ingrown creature that was killing her.

Her head rolled on the silk as she swallowed the bitter wine that Virot poured down her throat. It was supposed to soothe her, ease the agony of the knife, but it welled in her mouth like blood. Most of the stuff went down, but one sanguine line spilled from her lips and soured on her cheek. Phage grabbed Virot's hand. It was the hand of her intended murderer, and simply to touch it stung horribly, but just now it was better than being alone.

Hand and mind servants surrounded the table, midwives and nursemaids, but none dared touch her. Beyond them the chirugeon sharpened blades, calibrated retractors, folded cloths, poured water, and readied spirits and needle and silk thread. With them, he would touch her. Beyond him were only the black walls and black ceiling of Virot's private chambers.

Virot had said, "Here, in my own suite, you will give birth to our child. I want it all to happen here." It all. The deliverance of mother and child, and the murder of them both.

He spoke again now, his voice clearing away the echoes. "How do you feel, my love? Is the wine in your veins?"

"It is."

Virot glanced up at the chirugeon, and they exchanged a quiet nod. The First squeezed Phage's hand. "What else can we do for you?"

Phage could only shake her head, her hair twisting on the silk.

The hand servants parted, stepping aside to allow the chirugeon through. He was a thin man and small. His head was the shape, texture, and color of a prune. Avid eyes perched above a crooked nose and a tooth-crammed mouth. He had rolled his sleeves back to the shoulder and wore chain mail gloves covered in silk. One hand held a long knife with a sharpened inner curve. The other drew the silk from her belly. His eyes widened as he studied her flat stomach, visibly rolling with the child's struggle. Her skin was pellucid, and the red wound—struck and healed and reopened and rehealed numerous times—jagged like lightning above the baby. He would cut her there. Spirits splashed across her skin.

Phage shivered as the stuff evaporated. "It's about to happen, isn't it? He's about to cut me."

"Yes," Virot said. He tightened his grip. "I won't let you go."

Yes, Phage thought. I know you won't.

The knife descended slowly toward skin that trembled with cold. Its hooked tip came to rest. With gentle pressure, it cut into her, and blood oozed from the small wound.

Phage closed her eyes and clenched her teeth. Her hand clutched Virot's. The pain of that contact helped distract her.

With a slow and steady motion, the chirugeon dragged the knife along the scar tissue. Its hooked end dug beneath skin and muscle and lifted them into the razor curve of the blade, severing them. Blood flowed freely now, spoiling as it crossed her stomach. The flesh pulled aside, thrust out by the bulk of the god-foetus so long contained. Now it swelled to its true, grotesque size.

Phage wept. She could feel the knife cutting, the retractors ratcheting to pull her open, the warm pool of her own soured blood beneath her. Pain piled on pain. Even so, she opened her eyes and stared intently into the face of the First. "Virot. Why . . . why are we doing this?"

A vicious grin split his face. "You are eleven months pregnant."

"No . . . not that. Why are we . . . trying to . . . kill each other?"

His face reddened around the eyes. He glanced at the midwives and nursemaids, as if forbidding them to remember what they just heard. "You are delirious."

"No. . . . You have been planning . . . my death. You fear . . . I've been planning yours. . . . Why are we doing this?"

"Hold still, now," Virot said, smoothing back her hair. "He's cutting into your womb. We'll soon see our son."

"Don't kill him . . ." Phage pleaded, clinging to his hand. "Don't kill me. . . ."

Virot wrung his hand free and stepped back from her. "It's almost over. No more foolish talk." Though he spoke to Phage, his eyes were on the hooked blade as it came to rest atop the red, muscular bag that held the child.

The hooked tip sank through, and amniotic fluid emerged. The blade dragged across the muscle, gathering and cutting it with small popping sounds.

Phage was glad for her silk bindings. If not for them, she would have bucked her way off the table and killed herself and her child. As it was, she squirmed, teeth clenched and lips holding her scream.

The knife lifted away from her, and the chirugeon inserted more retractors. Steel delved down into the watery darkness and cranked, opening the wound. As he worked, the chirugeon said, "In a moment, you'll see your child, heir to the coliseum and all the Cabal." The man slid a pair of gleaming forceps into the severed uterus, and after a moment of probing, grasped the child's head.

"Quickly now!" Virot said. "Pull it out!"

* * * * *

"Pull it out, you idiot!" Sash growled at Waistcoat, who walked before him down the trail.

Waistcoat had slung a thick stick over his shoulder and accidentally jabbed it through Sash's head. "Huh?" he asked, turning around.

The stick dragged Sash sideways as if he were a coat on a hook and laid him out over a nearby boulder, which vanished inside him.

Umbra could only watch this idiocy and wish he had a forehead to smack.

Sash scrambled up angrily, the boulder remaining within. "Give me that thing!" he growled, ripping the stick out of his own head. "What do you need a stick for anyway?"

"Fine! It's your stick, Mr. Stick!" snapped Waistcoat.

Sash tossed the branch aside. "Shut up, or I'll shut you up. Umbra and I'll jump through you, and you'll close forever!"

"Right! Like he'd jump through me instead of you," Waistcoat shot back. "Maybe *we'll* shut *you* up."

"Nobody'll shut anybody up," Umbra hissed. "Now shut up and get behind that rock!" Sound carried strangely here in the Corian badlands.

Yes, a month after leaving the other Sanctum refugees, they were still in the badlands—dawdling. Though they had set their faces toward Topos, intent on confronting Akroma, they hadn't set their feet. They waited for Akroma, knowing her army would approach soon. In part, they hoped to find some reason to flee, avoiding what might be a death sentence. The wait had only made them grumpy. No answers had come. Aside from a boulder and an old harpsichord, they felt emptier than ever.

Sash shook his head and hitched a thumb toward Umbra, who crouched nearby. "Listen to the ingrate. What's his risk? He returns the two traitors, and Akroma gives him the keys to the castle. We, on the other hand, end up dead."

"Nobody's going to end up dead," Umbra insisted. "Now, please be quiet."

Waistcoat chimed in. "Who's going to hear us?"

"They are," replied Umbra, pointing toward the horizon.

There, awash in the heat-shimmer of the wastes, marched the vast army of Akroma. The infantry and cavalry seemed only a gray blur, but above them drifted aerial jellyfish and flashing schools of flying barracuda. Aven troops were there too, darting skyward and spreading out to soar on close-range reconnaissance. In wider loops circled disciples, tiny blue stars that saw and heard and reported to Akroma.

"What does it matter?" Sash asked. "We want to meet her."

Umbra nodded. "On our own terms."

"What are our terms?"

Umbra replied, "The road cuts through the badlands a league south of here. We move among the stones, mere shadows, and wait until she passes, then we step out beside her."

Sash peered over a boulder. "You think we can reach the road before they do? They're a league away and marching double-time."

"Then we'll have to go triple time," Umbra replied. "Stay to the shadows, and try not to kick up any dust."

"Or any boulders," Waistcoat sneered. He darted away like a hare before a hound.

Sash lit out after his prey.

Umbra watched them go. They might as well have a bit of fun—the last they might ever have. He glanced one final time at the scouts that spread in placid rings across the sky, then he too charged after his comrades.

One benefit of having no true mass was that the unmen could run as fast as their legs could carry them. They never grew winded. Waistcoat scuttled from rock to rock, and hot on his trail skittered Sash. With efficient strides, Umbra closed the distance to the other two. His hand lashed out, catching Sash on the shoulder.

"You're 'it,' " he said and ran on.

"Why, you!" Sash growled, turning to charge after Umbra.

"I want in! I want in!" Waistcoat said excitedly. He pattered after his friends.

On toes that jabbed like daggers, Sash rushed up to Umbra. He smacked the shadow man's side and tore away.

"Argh!" Umbra snarled. He paused to glimpse the faint dust trail left by Sash and vaulted after him.

Waistcoat struggled on stumpy legs, unable to keep pace. He wanted to shout "Wait up!" but didn't dare, with Akroma's scouts nearby. Instead, he made his strides bigger, with larger bounds from foot to foot. His leaps doubled and tripled. The ground raced past so fast beneath his feet that he could hardly touch down. Next leap, and he sailed up into the air. . . .

He was flying! Well, why not? He was weightless, with only wind resistance to buffet him—a living kite.

Waistcoat held out his stubby arms and legs and soared smoothly. His feet trailed above the rocks where his comrades ran, and he overtook them.

Umbra was closing in on Sash when a faint gray shadow passed over him. He looked up. "What are you doing?"

"Flying!"

"Since when can we fly?"

"Since now."

Umbra ran beneath the drifting figure. He flung himself from his toes, higher, farther. He spread his arms and let air from Topos pour out of him, driving him upward. One foot shoved off a stone before him, and he was airborne. Umbra flew up beside Waistcoat, and side by side they soared.

Below them, Sash ran with long bounds, flapping his arms. In moments, he too lifted off. The last of the unmen drifted up beside his friends, and they all shared a suppressed laugh.

In a voice that was not much more than wind, Umbra said, "Imagine that. All along, we could fly."

"I wonder what else there is," Sash said. "What else we've never known to try."

"I still want a body," Waistcoat put in.

Sash glanced toward him. "Waistcoat, we're flying. You can't do that with a body."

"Yeah, but everything else . . ."

Sash pointed sidelong toward the army on the horizon. "You're willing to die to get one?"

"Yeah."

"Dying is ceasing to exist," Sash said. "It's nothingness. The story is over for you, and there's nothing ever again. That's what dying is."

Waistcoat looked at Umbra, soaring beside him. "Is that what you think? You think souls don't go on?"

"I don't know what I think—"

"We don't have souls," Sash interrupted. "For us, dead is dead."

Waistcoat moaned quietly, the wind curling about the edges of his outline.

"Let's just fly on," Sash said. "Sure, we're no better than ghosts, but once we're dead, we'll be nothing."

Umbra cocked his head. "Well, it's up to you two. We could float right on by that road. It's a pleasant thought. There's about to be a terrible war, not a good time to have a body. Flying is fun, but is it what we want?"

The other two unmen were silent for a time.

Waistcoat at last said, "I want a body."

The wind whistled through Sash in a long sigh. "I do too."

"Enough to risk death?"

Quietly, but in unison, Sash and Waistcoat said, "Yes."

"Even though we could live forever as shadows?"

"Yes."

Umbra floated on, considering. "I agree."

All three began to sink toward the road, letting the air pour through their beings. Their first flight—their last flight—was ending as smoothly as it had begun.

Aven shadows swooped suddenly upon them. Talons grasped their heads. One bird man seized Sash and Waistcoat, and the other clutched Umbra. Though a moment before, they had flown with sweet ease, now they rattled.

The aven scouts squawked and banked toward Akroma's army.

Sash, Waistcoat, and Umbra struggled but could not escape. They had agreed to appear before Akroma, but they hadn't wanted to come this way.

In the claws of raptors, they descended.

*   *   *   *   *

The First stared at the deep incision, muscle folded back in what seemed an enormous mouth, and he thought how grotesque life was. This bloody slit before him concealed his doom. No natural child could have developed there without showing. The thing in her, if it even *was* his offspring, would be some sort of monster.

It shouldn't have gone this far. The poisoned wine should have killed mother and baby both by now. The First had planned to blame the chirugeon. He even had a noose waiting in a side room, convenient for the despondent man to use to atone for his failure, but, no, Phage still lived, and the thing in her still kicked.

It made no matter. The First always had backup plans. When the monstrosity was pulled forth and all the witnesses saw it for the deformed beast that it was, the First would draw his dagger, denounce the thing as an abomination, decry Phage as a harlot who slept with beasts, and stab babe and mother in one savage motion.

The First set his teeth on edge and watched. His disgust was slowly turning to excitement. Any moment now, he would strike.

The chirugeon leaned forward. With hands inside chain mail gloves inside silk, he pulled the forceps. The head of the creature pivoted in the incision, but suction kept it inside. The chirugeon used steady pressure, and a purple, bald skull crowned through the opening. With another yank, the baby's head emerged.

The face was dark and clenched in a scowl, and the forceps had elongated the head. Sticky white material clung to the baby's skin amid blood and placental fluid. The head was rumpled and ugly, but it was human.

The First's breath caught. A normal child? His hand sweated on the pommel of his dagger. Perhaps its body would be the hideous part.

Easing pressure on the forceps, the chirugeon snatched up a pig's bladder to suck the mucous plugs from the infant's nose. It began to squeal, a hoarse cry like that of a terrified pig. The chirugeon set his knee on the edge of the table and pulled again. The babe slid upward, its body sloughing the bag of waters that had held it for nearly a year. Narrow shoulders, rubbery little arms, a purple belly, a penis and scrotum, and crunched-up legs. The umbilicus trailed like a kinked wire.

"A boy!" the chirugeon pronounced gladly.

The First couldn't say anything. His mind spun. How could this child be normal? It *was* a monstrosity, even if it gave no outward sign. In agony, the First muttered, "Kuberr! Oh, Kuberr!"

"That's what his name will be," Phage said. "Kuberr!"

The First gaped. With a sudden, terrible chill, he realized that this babe was his very god, born in the flesh. Kuberr and Phage had conspired against him, and Virot had been duped all along. He had feared that Phage might kill him, but now she had brought into being something even more power, more certain to do the job.

"Would you like to cut the cord?" the chirugeon asked.

Steadying himself against the table, the First drew his dagger. It glinted brutally, its blade long enough to pierce child and mother—god and Phage. A black poison frosted the blood-groove of the knife. The First lifted the blade for its horrible task. He might have to kill all the witnesses, the chirugeon, and anyone in his regime loyal to

Phage—another thousand deaths would merely mean another battalion of undead. With one ferocious blow, it would all be done. The First muttered, "Guide my hand," and struck.

It was the wrong prayer. The newborn god heard and did so. The First's hand followed a groove in the air that brought it inexorably down, between mother and child, and sliced the umbilical cord.

Panting in relief, the chirugeon held the baby toward the First. "Would you like to hold your son?"

The First reached desperately toward the child. "Give him to me."

The chirugeon's face darkened, and he stepped back, actually defying the First. He swung the babe into the hands of a midwife and said, "Let's get him cleaned up, get all the blood off."

The First's eyes flared in fury, but Phage grasped his hand.

"Silly. You can't touch him. That would be murder."

"No harm done," the First growled, then to the chirugeon, he said, "Sew her up. She must survive. When you are done, step into the side room. I will be waiting there to reward you for your hard work." He walked away, heading into the room.

The little chirugeon lifted the bottle of spirits, took two drinks, and sprinkled more across the open wound. He then selected a long, curved needle of steel and a thick cord of silk and began to stitch.

* * * * *

Dressed as a midwife, Braids took the child in her hands—the squalling, beautiful child—and she bore him away to clean him. "He won't kill you tonight. I will keep you safe, little Kuberr."

CHAPTER 27

EXECUTION

The First held his child in a steel trap. Braids had invented the "Father Couch" to allow little Kuberr to sit on his father's lap without dying. She had welded a breastplate to tuille and cuisse then covered all in down and silk. A pair of gauntlets let him touch his son, and a mask with leather lips allowed the First to kiss him.

Just now, he didn't wish to.

. . . and you must march your army by the end of the week. Put first in their ranks the oldest of the undead—many who lay in their watery graves even when last I walked the world. Among them are lieutenants and commanders of mine. When they enter the ancient city, they will return to their glory, and the war that abandoned them twenty thousand years ago will be joined anew. . . .

Kuberr did not speak with infant lips, of course. Like any babe, he only drooled and spit up and screamed. He spoke with his eyes— golden eyes, as if the coins placed there in death had somehow transmuted into the organs of sight. Those eyes were full of greed, and with greed they spoke:

. . . Averru is already there, for it is his city, grown from the heart of the escarpment. He is the games-man and his game board is the metropolis that bears his name, and his game is war. He draws us— me and Lowallyn—to make endless war in his city, for this is his

pleasure, but the war will not be endless. This time I will win. I will be the first among brothers. . . .

Behind his mask, the First listened. He wished this child had never been born, wished its eyes had never opened. The First glanced to his royal retinue, which acted as though this metal-flanged fatherhood was typical and wholesome.

. . . this body of mine is getting hungry. Go, make the preparations as I have told you and let me feed and rest. Return in an hour to report what you have done. . . .

The First lifted one gauntleted hand, patted the babe, and drew the swaddling clothes up so that they obscured the child's eyes. Lifting the boy in metal fingers, the First stood and let the Father Couch clatter to the floor.

A nursemaid approached nervously, bowed to the floor, and took the child. She withdrew to feed him.

The First cast aside the metal mask. It bounced twice, leather lips kissing the floor. He strode out of his audience hall, a flurry of servants rushing to him. The gray-stoned hallway beyond was utterly vacant. His boots boomed like mallets on the floor.

Virot's head pounded its own rhythm. Nothing had gone to plan. Somehow Phage had survived the virulent poison. While the First gave endless audience to his infant god, Phage recuperated in her private quarters. She had locked the doors and posted her own guards and remained within. Soon, she would be back to her full strength, and she would kill her lover.

No. It stopped today. Perhaps Virot could not kill the infant god, but Phage was no longer protected by him either. At least he could be rid of her.

The First gestured to his mind servants, and they leaned in to listen while he strode onward. "Gather a ram team—gigantipithici with knuckle implants. Tell them to smash down her door and kill her guards."

"When?" one of the mind servants asked.

"Now. Immediately. I want the door down and the guards slain before I get there. Don't let her escape."

Nodding, four attendants dashed away.

The First would not slow for them. Let it be a test. If they failed, he would smash the door down and kill the guards before he slew her. He descended, leaving the lofty upper reaches of the coliseum and entering darker passages. A small smile touched his face. Even if she did escape her apartments, she would not escape the coliseum, and he would hunt her like big game.

Down ten more spirals and into tighter halls he went before he heard the boom of a battering ram. Primate hoots followed in rhythm, and another boom. The grunts intensified. With the third strike, the obsidian doors shattered and cascaded to the floor. Then came wild, roaring howls. Shouts of warning turned to screams of desperation. Bones broke, and flesh tore.

The First rounded the final corner and saw the shattered doors and the dead guards, ape hair floating in the air. Phage was still within.

The First marched over the rubble and drew a short sword from his belt. He stepped over one body, then another, shoved between the gigantipithici, and strode on into Phage's private chambers. Her door was closed and, no doubt, bolted. He kicked. Metal snapped, and the door crashed inward.

She was there beside her bed of iron, crouched, with empty hands. Oh, foolish girl, that she would rest without a weapon.

The First swung his sword in a chopping blow. She dodged, but too late.

The sword cut into her shoulder and stopped only on her collarbone.

Instead of retreating, though, she rushed him. The sword grated through the wound, cutting deeper, but on she came. Her beautiful face rushed up toward his, as if to kiss him, but instead she struck her forehead against his and flung him to the ground.

Phage ran over him.

Growling, the First tried to ram the sword into her, but it only cut down her front. The laceration was shallow, the sort of thing she could heal in an hour. She leaped away, plunging through a cloud of hand servants.

"Seize her!" the First shouted.

They did, twenty hands grasping the woman. For a mere moment, they held her. Their flesh turned to mush and their bones tumbled like twigs. The hand servants shrieked, rot rising up their arms. They staggered back, and Phage ran from between them.

"Idiots!" roared the First as he scrambled to his feet. He rushed out through the carnage, past his dying servants, and nearly slipped on a trail of gray blood left by Phage. The spoiled stuff jagged away down the corridor. She would be easy enough to find. It would be hunting, just as he had hoped.

A mind servant rushed breathlessly up to the scene, took it in without shock or dismay, and awaited his next order.

The First said simply. "Seal all exits. Anyone who sees Phage must pursue and trap her but leave the kill to me. Summon Braids. She knows Phage better than anyone. She'll help me put an end to this."

Nodding, the mind servant rushed off to do his master's bidding. The First meanwhile strode along that gray line, hunting the mother of his child.

* * * * *

There was no escaping those talons; like vises, they gripped the unmen's heads. Kicking and wriggling managed only to dislodge a boulder and a much-abused harpsichord. The former hit the ground with a dull thud, but the latter gave a strange and lovely cry. Then it was only snapping strings and splinters.

With deep sympathy, Waistcoat watched the death of the instrument. "I feel suddenly empty."

This percussive death had a profound effect also on the army. Every creature turned to look, some pointing toward the avens, others gaping at the half-sunk boulder and the pile of ivory keys. None could have made out the shadows that twisted beneath the bird-men—none but Akroma.

Whistling once, Akroma brought that great leviathan of war to a halt. The thunder of forty thousand feet died to silence. Troops stood at attention, and Akroma's personal retinue of putty people seemed statues around her. In their midst, the angel-beast turned and watched as the three errant unmen descended out of the sky.

"Let me do the talking," Umbra said.

The other two were too terrified to utter a word.

With a final few wing flaps, the avens swept down before Akroma and dropped their captives. All three tried to leap aside, but the angel was too quick.

Akroma's hands flashed out and latched onto the creatures. They had thought the talons of the avens were powerful, but these hands were as strong as stone. With Sash and Waistcoat in one hand and Umbra in the other, Akroma glared, a cruel smile on her face. "At last, you have returned." She looked triumphant, blue disciples coming and going on her brow and lips.

"I found them, Mistress," Umbra said, his voice muffled by her fingers. "They were in far Eroshia. May I introduce Sash and Waistcoat?"

"Introduce?" she hissed. "Introduce? You bring me two traitors, and you wish to *introduce* them?"

"I'm getting outta here!" Waistcoat muttered, scrabbling for escape.

Akroma shook the two traitors, and they wobbled like rippling water. "What have you to say for yourselves?"

"We don't want to die!" Waistcoat said.

"We want to live!" added Sash.

Akroma snarled, "In search of life, you condemned your creator to death! Because of you, he languishes in the belly of a death-wurm, and here you are. Free. Flying—"

"But not alive," Sash put in. "Don't you see what we are? We are reflections of the creator. We are his shadows, aspects of him. If we wish for life, it is a wish born first in Ixidor. If we hope to gain bodies, we do so that we might more perfectly reflect his image."

The rage in Akroma's face melted, and she blinked. Her eyes traced their outlines, and something like recognition came into her gaze.

Umbra ventured, "That's how I found them, on the quest to become truly alive—creatures worthy of their master's image. We've been through countless misadventures since then—in high halls and low pits, in barns and bedrooms—but none of it brought us to life. We've made mistakes. We've wandered from the Vision of Ixidor, but now we're coming back. Life comes only through him, and that's what we need—life."

Akroma listened. She glanced back and forth from one hand to the other, considering the creatures that dangled there. "You wish for bodies, for true life instead of this . . . false semblance."

"Yes," they chorused.

Umbra clasped his hands. "Please, Akroma, don't wipe away these three vibrant images of Ixidor. Grant us bodies, and we'll serve you and him to the end of our days."

The angel's visage had gone cold and stiff. She whistled yet again, nodding toward the two nearest putty people. "Come here."

Gray and amorphous, the humanoids shuffled up to stand beside her. They were identical, with pasty flesh and soulless eyes, and they spoke not a word.

"You'll do," she said.

From her lips tumbled two disciples. The blue sparks flitted across the emptiness and impacted Waistcoat and Sash. Tiny motes of light affixed themselves to the planes of their portals and slowly spread like ink through water. In a mere moment, Sash and Waistcoat had blue heads. In another, the azure color had overtaken their shoulders and arms and bodies. It scintillated through them until their very outlines blazed.

Akroma nodded. "You want bodies. I will give them to you." She held up Waistcoat and Sash like a pair of blue suits and draped them across the putty people.

Energy congealed with matter.

The two unmen were gone, as were the putty people. In their place stood two Ixidors. One was tall and lean, with a high brow and a sarcastic turn of the lip. The other was short and stout, with a low brow and a ready smile. Unlike their master, though, these reflections each had two arms. They gasped and breathed and were unmistakably alive.

The unmen fell to their knees in thanksgiving, and Sash poured out a flood of praise, "Oh, Akroma! Thank you! Thank you for this gift of bodies, of life! You have done us such a service, and we will serve you and Ixidor all our days."

"Yes," Akroma replied. "Yes, you will."

Umbra spoke up. "What about me? I didn't betray you. You've given them bodies, but what about me?"

She released Umbra, setting him on his own feet. "Yes, you have been faithful, my shadow man, and you are not my captive. As you served our creator, you will serve me—a living escape route to Locus if ever I need one."

"But, I want a body too," Umbra said. "Why do they get rewarded, and I get punished?"

Akroma shook her head slowly, staring at Sash and Waistcoat. "These bodies are not a reward." She reached to her back and drew a steel lance, forged to look like her lightning lance. It trembled in her hand, eager for the backs of the newly created creatures.

Sash and Waistcoat looked up to see the thing descend on them. It jagged down, inescapable.

The lance flashed against the outline of a shadowy man hanging in midair. Umbra had hurled himself like a blanket atop his friends. He settled down over them. Sash and Waistcoat passed through him and tumbled into an empty room in Locus. The moment their bodies had cleared the portal, Umbra slammed closed forever.

Two likenesses of Ixidor rolled beside each other and came to a stop, looking back and shouting. It was too late.

The third likeness would never be again.

* * * * *

Braids trotted behind the First as he loped wolflike down the coliseum corridor. Phage had come this way. She was losing a lot of blood, and the First eagerly followed its trail. He'd cornered her three times, stabbed her, and let her run again. This would be the last time. The man's red-tipped sword flashed as he ran. He was closing in, pulling away from Braids.

She had to struggle to keep up. An image came to her mind of a manic blonde leaping like a mountain goat . . . running over the heads of her foes . . . riding a deathwurm . . . She had been unafraid then. . . .

That woman was gone. Nothing remained of her but scars. Her heart had been cut out, and her blood was pumped by fear alone.

"Ha!" the First barked as he rounded a corner.

Phage was there, crouched beneath a stairwell. The floor under her was slick, and she panted like a trapped animal.

The First crooked a finger and smiled at his quarry. "Come on out. This'll be the last time. I'll make it quick."

Braids came up behind him and stopped. She stared at Phage but saw herself: *She crouched in her cell and wiped away the puddle of her devotion.*

"Don't make me come in there," the First said, "or it'll be slow and painful."

"Why, Virot?"

"Don't call me that! I hate when you call me that!"

"Why? Why must you kill me?"

He spat the words as though they were dirt on his tongue. "Because I am the First, and I will be the Last."

He is so great, my master, Braids thought, and she felt her gorge rise. He is the First, and he will be the Last. *The room had paintings over the windows and horrors swarming in the darkness beyond the glass.*

"So, come out, and let's be done," the First said wearily.

Phage shifted beneath the stairs.

"That's my girl. There we go."

Braids shuffled across the slick floor, homage sticking to her feet.

Phage emerged. She straightened as if to show the four wounds she had suffered. Her hands spread to either side, and she waited for the blow.

The blade rose, red and ready. "Good-bye, beloved child."

He is so great.

Braids vomited, not bile, but a creature—a vile monster from that squirming darkness. She had broken the windows of her soul and let the monsters stream in. One of them, a leprous troll with an enormous mouth, squeezed out through her lips. It oozed into being and roared.

The First spun toward it, elbow raised to strike.

The troll's mouth closed around his upper body. Peglike teeth bit and met in the man's midsection. The troll trembled, stunned by the shocking touch, and spit out the man's torso. The First fell in two pieces on the floor.

Braids drew a deep breath, and the troll sucked back into her mouth and was gone. She smiled, a bit of troll stuck between her teeth. Braids was back. At long last, her mind was her own again. Though it swam with demons, they were *her* demons.

Phage went to her knees. "He's dead. The First of the Cabal is dead."

"Yes," said Braids. She clucked. "He could've had me. I would've been good for him, but there's no accounting for taste."

Phage bowed lower. "Braids, you saved me. . . ."

"None of that," Braids said. "No more worshiping. We've got a kid to tend. We've got a war to win." Striding between the halves of Virot Maglan, Braids giggled. "He was the First and the Last. Now he just needs a Middle."

Despite her wounds and her terror, Phage laughed.

CHAPTER 28

ON THE EVE OF WAR

Akroma's lance buried its head in the sand. She yanked it out. "Those idiots!"

Putty people blinked stupidly at the spot where the three unmen had been. Even the avens who had captured them were perplexed by the disappearance.

Only Akroma understood. She had glimpsed Umbra's outline as he threw himself atop the other two. He had saved them at the cost of his own life. Why? Umbra was meant to save a god, not lowly, sniveling, worthless mud men. It was absurd.

Akroma whistled. "March!" The army, like a great caterpillar, set off.

Something niggled about this strange sacrifice. As much as she wished to dismiss it as meaningless, in fact it felt meaningful. Perhaps Umbra had transcended his creation, becoming something more than Ixidor had intended. Was it so terrible a thing to transcend?

Akroma set her jaw and marched. Yes. Transcendence was rebellion. Ixidor had created all in perfection, and any deviation was evil. He had created Akroma to protect him and his lands, to fight, and that was just what she was doing.

"Onward! To the escarpment!"

* * * * *

A gritty layer of sand covered the floor. The stones were cold, dank . . . and hard.

Waistcoat sat up. He poked tenderly at his bashed nose. "Ow! Is my nose supposed to be this soft?"

Sash rubbed a bruised temple and an abraded elbow. "These bodies are softer than roach bodies. No exoskeletons. A little disconcerting. As to your nose, I don't think you've broken it. Human noses get out of joint."

"Least we're alive." Waistcoat glanced through the dead air toward the spot where Umbra had been. "He ain't. He sacrificed himself for us."

"It's more than that. All along we've been trying to find out what it means to be truly alive. We thought the secret lay in the flesh," Sash said, pinching his leg. "Umbra didn't have flesh, but he knew the secret. Being human is more than having a body. It's having a soul." He shook his head. "If there's a place that souls go after death, Umbra is there."

"Are my eyes supposed to be leaking?" Waistcoat asked.

"Tears. Yes. Mine are too."

"So, what do we do now?"

Sash shrugged. He liked the motion so well that he shrugged again. "We've got human bodies. Now we just need to find human souls."

Waistcoat shook his head despondently. "All right. We'll go join the war."

"Don't be an idiot! War is useless. Umbra sacrificed himself so we could live. It would be insane for us to simply die."

"I'm so glad to hear you say that," Waistcoat said, rising. "So, where to?"

Sash brushed the grit from his hand. "First, we get out of here. Then, Eroshia."

"Eroshia! I love that town," Waistcoat said. "But how do we explain the fact that we look the same?"

Sash extended his arms grandly. "We're brothers. It's as simple as that."

"Thanks, brother."

"Don't thank me," Sash said. "Thank Umbra."

The two ne'er-do-wells stood there a moment, their heads bowed toward the spot where their third brother had vanished. In time, they turned and headed toward the door. Waistcoat opened it, and Sash motioned him through. Out into the corridor they went, heading through the empty palace of Locus.

They were ready to take on the world, these newborn twins, and like all newborns, they were unabashedly naked.

* * * * *

Despite her many wounds, knitting slowly together, Phage knelt in the royal audience chamber of the coliseum. To either side waited the attendants of Kuberr, nursemaids all. Ahead stood Braids. She wore a cockeyed grin and pushed one hip forward, on which she balanced the young god, Kuberr.

Only a few days old, the babe could already hold his head up. His lips were no longer rumpled and wet, his body no longer limp. He had eyes as bright as gold, and with them he spoke:

I knew he must die, Mother, and I am glad of it. You are wiser in counsel, more tender in care, more ferocious in battle. Yours is a heavy burden, but you can bear it.

The Mothers of the numena gather for war. You must lead my armies. You will begin the battle for me, as every mother begins every battle for her son. I am yet too weak to wage it, but I will grow quickly—a day for every death. Slay a legion, and I will be a man. Then I will join you in the war and take over our armies. All of Otaria will fall to me, and I will rule.

Phage bowed her head. "It will be as you wish, my son. I'll stop the tide of Topos and kill as many as I must to bring you of age. Then the world will be yours."

Leave me, then. I hunger. Give me to the first girl; her milk is the best. They will care for me while you are gone. Gather your undead army and march to the City of Averru and there make war.

Phage bowed once more and stood, withdrawing. Her wounds had stopped bleeding, and she was solid again.

Braids frowned and unceremoniously handed off the babe to a nursemaid. She charged after Phage. "Where are you going?"

"Didn't you hear?" Phage asked.

"Hear what?"

"I'm heading for Sanctum."

"Oh, great. I'll go too," Braids said.

"No. A war is coming, and I can't have Kuberr in the middle of it. Stay and tend my son. Your arms won't corrupt him. Keep him safe."

"All right. Whatever," Braids said, waving her away. "There's probably something fun to do with a baby."

Phage smiled, wishing she could clap her friend on the back. "I'm glad to have you back."

* * * * *

Stonebrow stomped to stillness, his hooves crushing the last blades of grass before Krosan gave way to desert. "There, Kamahl. That's what I told you about."

Kamahl craned to peer past the centaur's shoulder. "*That* is Sanctum?"

On the rim of the world, a huge red canker had formed. Sanctum had swollen and festered until its every building was a thousand feet tall. The city straddled the escarpment, and it pulsed feverishly, red creatures glinting like drops of blood.

Kamahl looked back to his meager army—elf, mantis, and centaur. The crimson glow of the distant city covered their faces like war paint.

"Take a look, everyone. We're headed into that," Kamahl said. He took a breath, and his armor rattled dully. He had jury-rigged the metal to hang across his withered frame, though the scale mail wouldn't deflect blows. Its main effect was cosmetic, allowing Kamahl to seem the man he once was. That illusion alone had allowed the druid and his general to gather a small army.

"That's not a city," said an elf archer nearby. "It's a hedgehog! Are you sure we need to go there?"

Kamahl nodded.

"Why?" the elf asked wearily.

"Because my sister will be there, and the powers that made that place want to take over everything—desert, swamp, and forest," Kamahl replied. "If we don't fight them there, we'll be fighting them in Krosan." Kamahl averted his eyes from the distant city. Soul Reaper cast a bright wedge of light across his face, and he seemed for a moment his former, warlike self. "General, lead on."

With a snort, Stonebrow marched. The rest of the army fell in behind him, ready for the desert trek and the world battle.

* * * * *

Zagorka lived in delirium. How long had she been trapped inside this strangely twisted tower? How many times had she felt her way along the walls, finding doors but no escape, finding stairs that led down into the same room she had left? How long had she gone without water or thirst, food or hunger? She was a captive of space and time, and, strangest of all, of love.

These walls, this tower, these creatures loved her.

"Why?" Every question soared out into the emptiness to strike stone and echo back an answer.

*Outside their home, young Averru found a shoulder of red sand-
stone and attacked it with spike and maul. Ten strokes, and a fissure
cracked wide. Narrow slabs of rock broke free and clattered to the
ground. He bent over them, his face intent, and selected the right
pieces from the pile. Filling his shirt belly with them, he ran to a mud
patch. Averru rammed the slabs of stone into the mud, forming walls.
He placed more stones, making the walls turn and snake. Averru ran
out of stones and rushed back to his quarry. He snatched up maul
and spike, set them, and began to pound.*

Zagorka stood behind him, watching. "What are you doing?"

*Averru whirled, startled, and nearly struck his mother with the
maul. He grinned. "Making a maze."*

Zagorka smiled. "A maze for what? Mice?"

*"Ants," Averru said, filling the belly of his shirt again. "They
have to have a place to fight."*

"Is that so?"

*"The mud-patch is halfway between the red ant nest and the
black ant nest. They'll fight over who gets the maze."*

*Zagorka hitched her head at the boy's innocence. "I'm not sure
either nest will care."*

*"Oh, yes, they will," Averru said. "I've killed a bird. It'll be in
the center of the maze. They'll fight to get to it and fight over eating
it and fight over hauling it back to their nests."*

*"You know a lot about ants," Zagorka said. "You know how
they think."*

*Averru shrugged. "Same way as people. Once you know what
they want, you can get them to do anything."*

The vision fled, as all the others had, and it left Zagorka in a half-
lit chamber. She had begun to understand.

Sanctum was not a city but a maze—a place founded for war.
Its soaring towers and wide walls were designed for epic battle. The
last time armies met and fought in this maze, most of the escarpment had been leveled. Only a few buildings had remained in the

lee of the cliff. Zagorka and her friends had found them and, ignoring a sign that clearly read, "Battlefield of the Numena," had made it their sanctuary.

The settlement grew and grew. Averru drew them. He needed bait to bring warriors to his maze. The people of Sanctum were that bait. They had flown into the desert to seek safety and had found a likely spot and laid down, but Averru slew them, and now their carcasses were drawing warriors.

"Why do you keep me here? Why don't you kill me as you killed the others?"

Young Averru stood above his finished maze. A dead bird lay atop an altar at its center. The maze swarmed with ants—red and black, their bodies gleaming like little jewels. Averru smiled proudly and took Zagorka's hand. "Look what I made!"

Zagorka shook her head. "But I am not your mother."

Old Averru lay on a litter beside the waters. He was dying, and his city already had been destroyed. Still, a proud smile filled his lips. Attendants waved feathered fans above him, keeping him cool. Averru shoved the fans aside and stared up toward the brow of the escarpment. There, the carvers worked feverishly, transcribing the final runes of his spell.

"Tell them to work faster. They must be done before I die," Averru said. A messenger boy rushed toward the cliff above. The old man muttered, "War is life, and stories of war are immortality." He read the words written large above him and nodded his approval. "When they are read again, I will live again."

Zagorka understood. The Glyphs were the words of a great spell. When those words came to life, they made a new body for the god—the city itself. It was his body, and war was his life.

Now would be only war upon war until all was destroyed.

* * * * *

Morning dawned bright and fair above the red City of Averru. It was a huge ruby. Thousands of lofty towers formed the facets of its sides, and the domed temple at its height was its perfect face. That metropolitan jewel drew the armies of a whole continent. They converged to take it.

Akroma's army rose from their badlands camp. They were rested and ready for the fury of the day.

Scouts told that the undead legions of the Cabal were halting that morning, still half a night's march away. They were creatures of darkness, and they could not bear the blazing sun. Phage and her defenders would not arrive in time to hold their monstrous city.

Akroma and her legions were creatures of light. For them, there was time for breakfast, polishing armor, securing supply lines, and speaking of glory.

Akroma leaped atop a boulder. Behind her loomed the strange red city they had come to capture. Before her spread the legions she had brought to take it. Aerial jellyfish and aven contingents cast their shadows down around her. All the troops waited to hear the words of their mistress.

"This war is not new. It began with the Vision of Ixidor. He glimpsed truth and beauty—he alone in all the world. Ixidor showed the Vision to me and to his disciples, and we have shown it to you. The Vision transforms the world, destroying lies and ugliness.

"You were converted by an inward battle, but an outward battle begins today to convert the rest of Otaria. Where there are lying tongues, we will cut them out. Where there are eyes that gaze on ugliness, we will blind them. We will take this city today, and from it we will launch a campaign to take all of Otaria—all the world."

A fervid roar boiled up from the legions. Crab men clacked their mouth parts and putty people gave a ululating cry. The elves and humans and dwarves began a chant of "Ix-i-dor . . . Ix-i-dor . . . Ix-i-dor."

J. Robert King

Over their shouts, she called out, "On the other side of the World Wall marches an army of evil—undead reinforcements to help Phage hold her demon city. Her troops will arrive too late."

Another roar erupted, fists punching into the sky.

Akroma also lifted her hand. "Leave behind your tents, your provisions, your old lives. Beginning today, all is new. This dawn is the dawn of Vision for all the world. Onward, now, my people, to the palaces of Averru!"

A third shout rose, borne upward by more than fists. The whole army surged toward Akroma.

She turned and leaped out on the early wind. Her white wings suspended steel legs above the ground. Over the hilltop she went, with her screaming hordes behind.

* * * * *

Phage strode at the head of her massive army. They hadn't rested and didn't need to. Every morning, under the watchful eyes of Akroma's spies, Phage had dutifully sent her undead to ground. This morning had been no exception, but once the spies were gone, bearing their messages to Akroma, Phage ordered the full army forward.

Zombies, revenants, liches, ghouls, skeletons, all marched behind their mistress toward the southern slopes of the Corian Escarpment. She had a hundred and fifty thousand. They would reach the city by midmorning and destroy the measly contingent of Glyphs there. By midafternoon, they would rule its heights.

In the north, Akroma would arrive to find her foe on the high ground. Then, the true battle would begin.

Phage stared toward the heights. Soon, she and her nation of dead men would stand there. They would make war to free Otaria from the white witch and her dead god, Ixidor.

CHAPTER 29

SACKING THE CITY

Akroma stared down at her troops, beautifully deployed across the valley side.

Crab men took the vanguard, a terrifying wall of carapace that advanced to stand along the river. They clustered thickest at the ford, across from the great stone arch that had predicted this war. Behind them, putty people formed tight-packed ranks. Once the crab men had broken through and engaged, these clay folk would swarm among the defenders of Sanctum, take on their appearances, and slay them where they fought. Next, jaguar cavalry, centaurs, and allied horsemen would charge to take the center street and hold it. Behind them waited human, dwarf, and elf infantry, the slaying power of Akroma's army. A thousand priests of Ixidor mingled among them, chanting prayers that filled the air with glorious visions. They would lead the believers house to house and tower to tower, killing those who refused to see the Vision of Ixidor.

The time was done for tolerance. Truth and beauty could be denied no longer.

Glyphs in their thousands waited on the far shore, rubious hands held before them like broad blades. What did they know of war? They could not hope to turn this tide in the open, and yet they stood there, leaving the rest of the city sparsely guarded. How could they have known how to fight an aerial war, they who had never flown?

Akroma spread her wings, white and grand on the hillside—a signal.

A huge shadow passed over the sun.

The red creatures looked up and pointed, their mute faces raised.

From behind the hill rose an enormous jellyfish, the size of a cloud. Its body gleamed gray-blue in the sky, and its tentacles hung in noxious bunches beneath. The thing did not descend into the valley but rose, soaring toward the height of the city. A second siphonophor appeared, larger than the first, and a third and fourth. Now ten, now twenty. Amid the translucent monsters schooled flying barracudas. Above them all, aven troops and griffons charged the air. Here was the true vanguard. They would take the undefended heights of the city and sweep down toward the land troops.

In confusion, the Glyphs stared at the aerial assault, but none moved to engage.

With glee on her lips, Akroma bellowed, "Charge!" Her wings grabbed the air, and she soared down to be among the charging van.

Crab men pelted across the stony ford, their gangly legs flinging up sprays of water. Great claws snapped eagerly and hundreds of carapaced bodies rushed the stone arch. Glyphs retreated at the fury of their advance. A wide circle opened before the crab men, and they ambled in to fill it.

Gliding over the arch, Akroma came down in their midst. These Glyphs were clever, drawing them through a bottleneck and spreading them thin across a circular line. "Form up before attacking!"

The crab men fell into orderly ranks, with a column at the rear to replenish them as they marched to attack.

Akroma lifted her arm to give the command, but it died in her throat.

To a man, the Glyphs had knelt and laid their hands and faces upon the ground.

Perhaps Cabal troops might attack kneeling folk, but Akroma would not. She lowered her hand and stared. There was something beautiful in this gesture. What could have inspired them to bow like this? What except a glimpse of the Vision? In blue-white illusions, the glories of Ixidor danced above the valley.

Still, Akroma would not be drawn into a trap. "Do you surrender to us?"

One Glyph rose, taller than the rest. It spoke with a voice like lava. "Our city is yours. We welcome you. We will not oppose you as you enter and climb to the height to claim it."

Among the crab men, Akroma strode, her steel legs jabbing into the ground. "You give up allegiance to Phage so easily?"

"Phage is not here. You are."

Akroma was pleased at how soft these foes were, but as easily as they had turned on Phage they would turn on her as well. "How many of there are you?"

"We are ten thousand," the Glyph said. "We were ten thousand words and now are ten thousand souls."

"We will take a hundred of you, one for every hundred, and hold you hostage against your promise. The hundred will die instantly if ever there is sign of treachery," Akroma said.

The tall Glyph advanced. "I will be the first of your hundred. When written on the wall, I was the word Primus. I will gather ninety-nine others, words such as Submit and Surrender. We will be your hostages."

Akroma nodded. To the captain of the crab men, she said, "Take charge of these hundred. I myself will lead the advance to the heights." She looked toward the pinnacle of Sanctum and saw that her aerial troops were already setting down to securing the holy place. It was all too easy.

Akroma whistled to her troops, and the jaguar cavalry, centaurs, and allied horsemen charged across the ford. They joined their winged mistress in the midst of her army. Akroma led them up the open farm road, toward the city proper.

On the other side of this escarpment, half a day's march away, Phage and her scabrous reinforcements would be sleeping. Come nightfall, they would roll out of bed and realize their city was already conquered.

* * * * *

Phage ran at the forefront of her army. They galloped and shambled in her wake.

She had no need to marshal her forces: She had a hundred and fifty thousand troops, enough to overwhelm both the Glyphs and the armies of Akroma. Her warriors had no fear of death, and they could fight even after dismemberment. Tireless and rabid, they had advanced at a run since dawn.

Many of her troops had been human or elf in their former lives, but many more were gladiators from every species. Elephant revenants charged among aven ghouls and goblin zombies. The skeleton of a giant ground sloth clawed its way up the foothills of the Corian Escarpment. A flock of banshees wove keening among the troops. En masse, they tore toward the southern gate of the city.

The doors stood wide, as if to trap forward troops, and a small army of Glyphs filled the gateway courtyard.

Phage could only laugh. Her forces could bury those defenders in a mound of bodies and take the city anyway. She lifted her fist into the sky and cried. "For Kuberr!"

A hundred and fifty thousand jaws took up the sound—some without benefit of lips or throat or brain. That inarticulate roar bore them into the city.

Phage charged first through the gap, a pair of undead wolves loping on either side of her. Next came the skeleton of a giant serpent, its ribs like the white legs of a great centipede. These were the fastest of the beasts, though Phage had made sure to keep the brown mass of ghouls close behind, just as Kuberr had instructed. The ancient dead had lain in tannic waters for twenty thousand years. Their skin creaked like leather as they poured through the gate.

The Glyphs didn't have a chance. They didn't take one. They were bowed, knees and foreheads on the ground.

Astonished, Phage halted, but the tide of undead behind her was unstoppable.

They rushed through the gates and clambered over the bowing army. Rotten flesh smacked on glassy bodies, and bony fingers clawed them. Putrid mouths gnawed on hands and arms and heads— to no avail.

Wherever gray flesh touched red, the colors of death bled away and the colors of life returned. Where a gangrenous limb contacted a Glyph, health and wholeness came into the limb. Sockets nibbled clean by little fishes grew new eyes. Jawbones grew gums around their teeth and lips around their gums. The ghouls were returning to life. Even their uniforms stitched together from the paltry threads that remained, from the links of chain mail imbedded in old wounds. Tabards grew—purple and black, with the insignia of a grasping hand. Epaulets formed, with a black armband below. These were the assassin squad of Kuberr.

Minds filled empty skulls, and thoughts filled empty minds. One by one, the assassins climbed off the bent backs of the Glyphs, only to have more undead clamber on. In visible waves, the monsters transformed, a hundred every second, a legion every minute.

Phage could only stagger back out of the way and watch. Here was the will of Kuberr, manifest undeniably. Truly her son was a god.

A rumbling voice came from behind her. "We welcome you, Mother." She spun about to see a Glyph looming there, its blade hands spread. "You are not our mother, but you are the mother of our brother, Kuberr. These are our nephews and nieces, and they are welcome."

"I've come not for welcome but for war," Phage said. "Kuberr grows with each death, so I've come to slay."

"As it should be," the creature said simply. "Your foe has taken the northern gate and climbs even now toward the high, holy place. Take these assassin-children and meet her there and let war break forth!"

Phage stared at the enormous red towers above her, bent as if under the weight of the sky. She couldn't even see the height of the escarpment, but all she had to do was climb.

"Form up!" Phage cried, hooking her arm in a broad wave. She marched, and two hundred assassins fell in behind her, matching her stride.

The road ahead was lined with Glyphs. Most knelt, but others watched avidly from the windows in their endlessly tall towers. Bubbling groans of excitement came from their mouths, and some stomped their feet in time to the march. It was as though a festive parade passed by. The Glyphs cheered the coming war.

Phage ignored them. She did this for her son, her master. For twenty thousand years, this battle had remained undone. Today, it would be joined again, and soon, it would be finished.

"For Kuberr!" she cried, and her voice rang among the ruby canyons.

* * * * *

"For Ixidor!" Akroma shouted. The red towers all around echoed her call. Glyphs took it up, but their garbling voices seemed to cheer a different name.

Ahead, Glyphs draped crystal necklaces on the marching troops. Whenever a warrior received one, he stood straighter and marched with greater determination. A Glyph offered Akroma a crystal chain, and she took it in her hand. The central stone was uncannily warm, and magic moved within. Ahead, another Glyph handed out more necklaces.

Akroma called to him, "What are these for?"

The crimson creature said, "Fate and fortune, fortune and fate. You must have both to be complete."

Akroma marched past. Nearly all of her troops—whether elf, human, dwarf, aven, or other—wore the crystals. Every last one seemed empowered, ready for war. Akroma tentatively slipped the chain around her neck and felt a surge of power. Something had taken hold of her, some*one* whose arm had reached across twenty thousand years to touch her. The presence was like Akroma—an angel who had lain with a beast and birthed a numen: Lowallyn, lord of waters.

He had been born out of the highest and the lowest, the worst and the best. In him was the seed of beauty, for he created streams in the wilderness, lush places out of desolation, and majestic dominion from ignominious defeat. In him also was the seed of truth, and it was the opposite of beauty. The truth was ugly and beauty was a lie. The world as it should be was not the world as it was. Most folk abandoned the ugly truth to live the beautiful lie or abandoned the beautiful lie to live the ugly truth. Lowallyn abandoned neither but held them both in his mind, and therein lay his madness.

Opposites. Terrible and tremendous, they had made him—the angel and the beast, the beauty and the truth. They had unmade him, and all the while, his angel mother could only watch his demise.

In midstride, still marching, Akroma emerged from her reverie. She was much higher now. How long had she walked in that dreaming state? The crystal necklace had done it. She reached up to pull it off, but it was gone. On all those around, the glass beads were gone. It was as if they had melted into the flesh of their wearers.

Fury surged through her. She was stronger now, possessed of some new power—or possessed by it.

She fought for her son. She fought for Lowallyn, lord of waters. He would be reborn when Ixidor rose from death.

"For Lowallyn!" she cried, thinking of him within the belly of the deathwurm. "For Lowallyn!"

"For Lowallyn!" the Glyphs cried.

Strange—how *strange!*—to be suddenly so strong and wise, as if she had been alive for twenty thousand years but only now remembered it. She had lived that long, and she hadn't: Which thought was true, and which was beautiful?

Steel legs brought her to the summit of the city. The red towers curved all around, but on that bald pate of stone, only the dome of the temple stood.

She had brought him there and named him Lowallyn, and on that same day they had brought the other two, born at the right time, bound together in consecration, destined to rule.

Akroma marched across the hilltop, her feet grating on sandstone. Her army flowed behind her like a giant cape. It spread, enveloping the northern half of the mountain. Eager to reach the temple, Akroma ran. Her wings flashed, and she took to the air. The dome widened below. Akroma slid down out of silken skies to light on top of it. Beauty and truth were irreconcilable, she knew, and so she expected the very ugliness she found.

Phage stood there. She had her hands on her hips and a crooked smile on her lips. She bore no visible weapon except her very flesh, within fighting silks. A black corset cinched up her stomach, and she looked ready to kill. Behind her, an army of ancient assassins and undead monsters spread across the southern side of the mountaintop.

Steel spikes shrieked on the dome as Akroma shifted. There was a moment of indecision. She had done all this before, but did that mean she should do it the same way or do the opposite?

Base and ignoble, grotesque and horrid, Phage was true.

Lofty and regal, elegant and magnificent, Akroma was false.

The ugly truth faced down the beautiful lie.

Akroma reached over her shoulder, grasped her steel lance, and hurled it.

The jagged bolt flew above Phage, who had dropped flat to the stone. It bounded off the dome to impale an assassin.

Phage grabbed Akroma's metal forelegs, yanked herself upright, and wrapped her arms around the angel-beast's waist. Searing rot spread beneath her touch, melting the jaguar pelt.

Clasping her hands, Akroma smashed the woman's face and send her skidding across the temple dome.

"For Lowallyn!" roared Akroma, scrambling after her foe.

"For Lowallyn!" the army of Topos shouted as they surged in a great curve to the west of the dome.

"For Kuberr!" Phage countered.

"For Kuberr!" her troops cried, and they swept eastward around the dome.

While their leaders fought, the two armies curved after each other like serpents wrestling, tooth to tail.

Akroma rose on her wings and hurled herself at Phage, steel spikes beneath her.

Phage dived under the woman and rolled. She was not quite quick enough. One steel leg stabbed down to pin her thigh. Pain flared through her. Phage flipped over, grabbed Akroma's jaguar tail, and bit through it. The thing came off in her mouth, a squirmy snake, and she hurled it away to her troops.

Screaming, Akroma whirled.

Phage scrambled away from the impaling leg. She circled behind the angel and clambered up her back. Grabbing the wing nubs, Phage sent rot through them. "First the tail, then the wings, then the eyes, then the Vision," she hissed.

Akroma shuddered in rage but could not shake her nemesis loose.

Phage enjoyed the moment. She had waited twenty thousand years for this.

CHAPTER 30

WAR

Stonebrow plunged into the Deepwash River, and water rushed up to his shoulders and hips. On his back sat Kamahl, clutching his mane, and the elves and Nantuko behind him held on for dear life. The other centaurs swam alongside, trailing white foam across the deep flood. Crossing at the ford would have been less perilous, but the troops of Topos already held the main gate. As was his wont, Stonebrow had found his own way.

He and the other centaurs swam to the rocky bank and clambered out. Curtains of water poured off their flanks. Most of the squadron slid down Stonebrow's side, though Kamahl remained seated there.

"Can you make it up those foothills, General?"

"Yes." He nodded to the other centaurs. "These can too. Within the hour, we'll be in the city proper."

"Or improper," Kamahl said darkly, staring ahead.

Every building had grown like a stalk, and the city as a whole seemed a great red artichoke. Its lower streets were largely abandoned, though toward its top, Sanctum swarmed. Red Glyphs and blue-robed priests, warriors in steel and creatures in fur—it would be a grand melee, a slaughterhouse.

Kamahl had not come to fight but to end the fighting. Soul Reaper would do the trick. "Take us up, General."

Stonebrow leaped, climbing the boulder-strewn hillside. Behind him, a contingent of Krosan elves shook water off their longbows and ran to keep up. "Who are we supposed to shoot?" one of them asked.

"Only those who attack us," Kamahl replied. "We can't battle all of these folk. We must drive for the height of the battle, for the center."

"What's in the center?"

"Not what but who," Kamahl said. "Phage and Akroma are there. If they die, the war ends. I'll make sure that they die."

The elf only shook his head.

Stonebrow growled at the creature's insolence. "What is it?"

"Only that you young races have never fought a war like this before."

"A war like what? There's little difference between guerilla wars in the forest and those in the city," Stonebrow said.

"Not guerilla wars," the elf replied, keeping his bowstring taut as he climbed toward the city streets. "You've never fought a war of the gods."

Kamahl shook his head. "There you would be wrong."

* * * * *

Akroma roared, bucking to flip the clinging parasite from her back.

Phage struggled to hold on to the angel's wing, but the skin under her hands shredded and slipped loose. She hurtled over Akroma's head and crashed down on the great dome. Scuttling like a crab, Phage tried to get away.

Akroma lunged. Her steel spikes scratched along the limestone. One foreleg gouged Phage's calf, and another impaled her opposite thigh. Phage was pinned, and Akroma loomed up over her.

There was something supremely satisfying in this fight. All ambiguity was gone. This was good versus evil. No one could doubt whose forces represented life and whose represented death.

The unholy monster of death lay beneath her, ready to die.

Akroma drove her hind leg into Phage's other calf, and struck a new wound on the woman's side. Phage twisted in agony, and

Akroma avidly watched her. This might have seemed cruel, except that Phage was cruelty incarnate.

"I can do anything I want to you," Akroma said. "I am good, and you are evil. Is it wrong to torture Torment? Is it wrong to kill Death?"

Hissing, Phage clawed at her own side, gored by the steel leg. Her fingernails dug in, scratching away skin and rolling it in her nail beds. "You're the same as me, Akroma, but you don't realize you are evil."

Akroma's eyes widened. "You are a plague, and I am the cure!"

Phage hurled her hand up, though she couldn't reach Akroma. She didn't need to. She flung the skin from beneath her nail beds into Akroma's face. Yet-living flesh struck the angel's eyes and mouth and sucked into her nose. Rot began.

Akroma flinched back, sputtering to get the skin off her tongue, struggling to bat it out of her eyes and blow it from her nose. Never before had Phage's death-touch struck such tender flesh. Tears filled her eyes, and two black spots floated in her vision. She spat the skin loose, but her tongue felt numb and tasted rank. Part of her septum had collapsed.

Phage fled back, leaving ashen lines in her wake. She didn't even bleed as others did, blood spoiling as soon as it touched her skin. Her wounds were deep and true, four in the legs and one in the side. Phage walked spastically, her chest heaving with the effort. Still, with every step, she grew stronger. Soon, she would be whole again and would return to kill the angel.

Akroma wouldn't wait. She strode across the limestone dome, pursuing her prey. Her own powerful magic worked to heal the spots on her eyes and the dead place on her tongue. They merely provided more incentive for the kill.

* * * * *

Stonebrow gazed up the steep street to see a mass of Glyphs standing shoulder to shoulder. "Here's our reception."

"No," said Kamahl, still riding on his back. "They're facing up the hill, away from us."

Beyond, the true battle raged. Humans, elves, and dwarfs fought beside crab men and putty people and priests. All filled the street, cudgels and fists flying and bodies falling. Glyphs stood like spectators watching a game.

Stonebrow snorted. "How do we get past them?"

"You forded the Deepwash. We'll do the same here," Kamahl said. He gestured to the troops around Stonebrow. "Climb back up."

Stonebrow wrapped his massive hand around the nearest elf and hoisted him into position. "All of you, get up here—everybody who can't charge over those creatures."

A mantis-man ambled up his shaggy haunch and clung to his mantle of fur. Two more followed, and the elves all gave shrugs of resignation. The other centaurs clomped up to stand beside the general.

"It won't be easy," Kamahl cautioned them, still sitting foremost on Stonebrow's great shoulders. "They're strong, and once we flatten the back ranks, they might lash out at us."

The centaurs wore grim expressions, but they nodded all the same.

As the final elf scrambled up to cling in the lee of the giant centaur's back, Stonebrow said, "We charge on three. One . . . two . . . three!"

The centaurs leaped simultaneously, but Stonebrow leaped thrice as far as the others. He closed on the crimson line.

Shaken by the hoof beats, Glyphs started to turn. They seemed loath to take their eyes off the fight and only slowly came around to see their doom.

Stonebrow vaulted. Enormous hooves came down on the back rank of beasts. They toppled and shattered into a multitude of rubies. Stonebrow hurtled over them, his chest smashing three more of the creatures aside. Momentum carried him farther up the hill, the other centaurs bounding over the glassy piles.

Already, the pieces realigned. The Glyphs would be whole again soon.

On Stonebrow charged, with his smaller kin behind him. The last Glyphs shattered beneath his hooves, and Stonebrow bounded into battle. He slowed to a canter, letting warriors in the plaza beyond glimpse his bulk and crowd out of the way.

"Should we drop down yet?" an elf asked Kamahl.

"Wait till someone swings a sword at us. Don't attack until we are attacked," Kamahl responded.

"Where are we headed?"

Kamahl nodded toward the great dome ahead, where two women fought—an angel and a devil. "There."

* * * * *

Phage limped more than she needed to, stumbled as if her wounds were worse than they were. It was an old trick of predators, making themselves seem prey. It was working like a charm.

Akroma approached, her wings spread. Behind her tens of thousands of creatures filled the plaza. Faces shone momentarily in their struggles before darkening in death. Blades rose and fell, dragging streamers of blood in their paths. Priests chanted songs that sent beautiful blue visions whirling above the battle.

There was nothing beautiful about war. Even Phage of the coliseum, who had arranged for hundreds to die in mass melees, could not stomach the deaths of these thousands. It was simply a mass manifestation of the battle between these two women.

Phage circled to the side, setting up her attack. "There is no good or evil. There is only survival. In the end, you are as much a murderer as I."

Akroma's spike legs were trembling, and her muscles gathered to leap. "I *will* murder *you*." She bounded toward Phage, spikes raised.

Phage had invited the attack. She hurled herself into the air to meet Akroma. Chest to chest, angel to demon, they came together. Phage wrapped her arms around Akroma's neck and her legs around the woman's waist. All but silk and steel rotted away from them, and where flesh touched flesh, white smoke rolled out.

Akroma pummeled Phage's back and head, but each blow dented her fists as if they were warm wax. She tried to peel the woman away, but corruption melted her fingers. Even falling to her side did not jar the woman loose.

Phage clung like a child to her mother and whispered desperately, "We are opposites but the same—blinding light and blinding darkness. . . ."

Smoking, the angel-beast shoved herself upright and stood. She leaped into the air and stroked her wings, carrying her assailant skyward. Off the temple dome she rose—twice her height then thrice. She dived, wings folded.

Phage let go, trying to escape, but Akroma held her. Breast to breast, they fell from the sky.

"We *are not* the same," hissed Akroma, "because I will win."

They hit. Red bloomed in Phage's eyes, and blood poured from her nose. Her whole body went numb. She could not move her arms or legs could not breathe.

Akroma staggered away, the rotted outline of Phage across her midsection. In places, muscle was laid bare, and elsewhere, organs. The angel-beast clenched her eyes and teeth, summoning healing magic.

Phage lay and waited for her own dark sorceries to mend her. The last time she had been so wounded was on the birthing table—suffering to bring a god into the world.

The Mothers of the numena gather for war. You must lead my armies. You will begin the battle for me, as every mother begins every battle for her son. I am yet too weak to wage it, but I will grow quickly—a day for every death. Slay a legion, and I will be a man. Then will I join you in the war and take over our armies. Then all of Otaria will fall to me, and I will rule.

"How many have we killed, my son?" she wondered. "How old are you now?"

Feeling returned to Phage's feet and hands. She moved them gently, not wanting to draw the eye of her foe. She could breathe again, and whatever had broken in her back was fused. She sat up. She stood.

Akroma turned, scowling. Where once rot had covered her, now there was great body-scar. No organs or sinews showed through, though the skin was tough and wrinkled. The angel-beast advanced.

How many times must we die, my son?

* * * * *

Baby Kuberr was wailing.

Braids knew nothing about babies. She could sleep right through the screams of the damned, but a wailing baby was torture. She had tried walking him, feeding him, entertaining him—had even checked his clothes for baby droppings. Still, the wailing continued.

"What's your problem?"

The baby lay, tightly swaddled, on the First's throne. "My legs! My legs!" it cried. It wasn't supposed to talk. It was supposed to be an infant. "My arms!"

"What about them?" Braids asked.

"Unwrap them!"

Blinking, Braids bent and pulled the corner of the swaddling out of the tight fold where she had stuffed it. There came a *pop*, as if the fabric had been stretched as tight as a bowstring. The edges of the cloth fell away, and long, strong legs unfolded—the legs of a three-year-old and a body to match. Fabric welts covered his skin where the swaddling had cut off blood flow. The boy extended his legs and arms and flopped off the throne. He sat in a heap, his limbs trembling.

"You've grown!"

Kuberr smiled at her, golden eyes slivering. "I'm not a baby. I'm a big boy." As if to prove it, he gathered his legs beneath him and stood. Already, he was half Braids's height. "Bigger and bigger! Bigger and bigger!"

* * * * *

Zagorka clung to the windowsill and stared down at the terrible battle. Her tower curved directly above the domed temple where Phage and Akroma fought. The army of Topos filled half the city, and the army of the Cabal filled the other, but these were not modern armies. These warriors had fought before—twenty thousand years ago—and these women too, and their sons.

She saw her son.

King Averru sat upon a throne that stared out over a thousand miles. To one side, where the mountains fell into the inland sea, he could see the realm of his brother-king, Lowallyn. To the other side, where the mountains dropped away to immense everglades, there ruled King Kuberr. These three were the numena. They had been mere sorcerers but through great magic became kings and through great kingship became gods. They headed the three great dynasties that ruled Otaria and all the world. Indeed, they had named Dominaria, for the world was their dominion.

King Averru lifted his hand and stared into the ruby ring on his finger. It was a scale from the great Primeval Rhammidarigaaz. The ring held no true power, but it reminded Averru of the origins of his might.

When a mere sorcerer in the service of King Themeus, Averru had battled and imprisoned the ancient dragon Rhammidarigaaz. King Themeus gained all the lands of the Primeval, but Averru gained all the spell lore. The king sent the rest of his sorcerers to hunt down the other four dragon gods, and thus Lowallyn had gained the power of water magic and Kuberr the power of death magic. Averru was jealous of their power, and jealous that no others would become numena. Two brothers in magic were enough, and the three numena banded together. When the final two Primevals were trapped, the numena were waiting, and they attacked and slew the other sorcerers. They then turned on their king. Themeus, who enslaved dragonkind and freed humanity, was himself slain.

The ruby ring remained pristine, but Averru's hand had grown old and feeble. Even sorcery could not stoke the fires of life eternally. Averru had worked a great spell that would incarnate him in a new, immortal body, but for the spell to work, he needed a war.

Rising from his throne, Averru strode to the glass windows and peered down. All around him, his glorious city spread. Red towers rose a thousand feet from the foothills to the heights of the mountain. His magic had shaped this glorious metropolis. It was perfect, a maze made for war.

He remembered such a maze of rock and mud, remembered his mother's eyes. She had been dead a thousand years. She had been his physical mother, but his spiritual mother was Magic. She had given birth to him once and would again.

Averru would bring his brothers here. He would incite a war that none of them would survive. In time, though, they would return, born of their Mother Magic. Averru would rise from rocks and war, Lowallyn from waters and art, and Kuberr from swamps and greed. They would rise again to rule the world.

Zagorka sat back from the windowsill. At last, she understood.

She had given physical form to Averru by bringing his city back to life. Phage had given physical form to Kuberr by conceiving and bearing a child. Akroma had given physical form to Lowallyn by possessing the body of Ixidor. These three women were the physical mothers of the numena. Their spiritual mother, though, was Magic herself. Magic had cast a great spell—this war—to bring her three sons back to life.

The tyrants of old would divide up the world.

Zagorka had to stop them, but how? She had tried every possible escape and had been foiled. There was one impossible escape. . . .

Zagorka set her foot on the windowsill, leaned through, and launched herself out.

The window slammed closed behind her, too late.

Zagorka plunged among reaching towers, above the plaza that
thronged with killers, down toward the great dome where Phage and
Akroma battled. She had lived too long anyway—a near century in
this life, and twenty centuries before. It was time to die and in dying
to end this terror.

Zagorka fell with eyes wide open, fell straight toward the mothers of tyrants.

* * * * *

Stonebrow stomped through the melee, Kamahl and a contingent
of warriors crowding his back. The giant centaur seemed a galleon
sailing through a sea of armies. No one attacked him. His size alone
sent them scurrying back. Who did he fight for? If Stonebrow would
kill someone, they would know his allegiance, but for now he
marched a jagging path through war.

Kamahl sat erect, his eyes trained on the dome ahead of them and
his axe ready in powerful hands.

Stonebrow quickened from a canter to a trot, and the centaurs
behind him had to gallop to keep up. An avenue opened to the stony
dome at the center of the plaza. Its slope was steep enough that no
small creature could easily climb, and Stonebrow himself couldn't
reach the top unless he leaped at full speed.

"Centaurs, stay below," Kamahl bellowed over his shoulder. "The
rest of you, hold on!"

Stonebrow galloped. Hooves crashed across stones littered with
dead. The plaza shook with his charge, rattling a few arrows loose
from the armies. They arced harmlessly above his craning mane. He
launched himself into the air.

Stonebrow flew, as massive and weightless as a leaping whale.
He soared above the steep curve of the dome and landed with hooves
on the upper slope.

"Off!" shouted Kamahl.

J. Robert King

The elves and mantis-folk had little choice but to obey, tossed off by the impact. They tumbled to the dome, got up, and ran out along the temple perimeter.

Kamahl clung on, though, and he dug his heels into the giant centaur's sides. Stonebrow plunged onward. Just before him, at the flat pinnacle of the dome, fought Phage and Akroma. They wrestled like primordial forces, oblivious to their approach.

"Halt!" Kamahl commanded, and Stonebrow skidded to a stop.

Kamahl hurled himself up over the centaur's shoulder. He flew through the air and landed just behind the brawl. Soul Reaper rose, its gems glinting beneath the sky. Kamahl swung his axe in a sidearm arc and cried, "Forgive me, Sister!"

The black blade sang as it chopped into Phage's back, sliced muscle and bone, lung and heart, and emerged through her breast. She was gone in an instant, as if vapor. The axe hadn't slowed a whit, but seemed almost faster now, as if impelled by the soul it had drunk. It cleft through Akroma's chest, dismantled her vitals, severed her spine, and exited just between her wings with more force still. It struck a third body and halved it.

A third body!

The axe ripped from Kamahl's hand and spun around its whirling head. The three souls had become a vortex that lifted the blade above the dome.

Kamahl crashed down on one side of the dome. Stonebrow staggered back on the other side.

The bodies of the three women—Akroma, Phage, and Zagorka— poured their souls upward in a bright cyclone. The last wispy tails of spirit whirled into the axe.

A crack as bright as lightning opened in the blade. The axe trembled with a sound like thunder. Suddenly, its head exploded, and the power within it erupted like the birth of a star.

Kamahl's eyes slammed shut, and his hand clamped across his face. Even through eyelids and muscle and bone, the light was blinding. A gale struck him, the hammer of a god, and flung him out beyond the temple, beyond Averru. He would land and perhaps die. That was all he knew, but it was sufficient. Kamahl had done what he must do, and now it was time to die.

As he flew, Kamahl could only think, Forgive me, Jeska.

* * * * *

Stonebrow also was rocked by the blast. A huge sound split his eardrums. He heard the explosion in his breastbone and skull, and he flew above the battlefield.

Stonebrow opened his eyes. The shockwave flung him and all the rest of the armies. The air churned with bodies. All of them rode together in that storm of light and noise—the armies of Topos and the Cabal, the Glyphs and the creatures of Krosan. Priests of Ixidor tumbled amid their beautiful visions. The wave carried them to the edges of the plateau and hurled them against the buildings.

Some smashed through windows. Others struck towers and tumbled to the ground.

Stonebrow hit a wall and caved it, crashing through into the room beyond. He bounced against an inner wall and landed at last. He lay there. The tower might fall on him, but it didn't matter. He had at least one broken leg and two ruined ears. They were small prices to pay. Even his life would be a small price to pay to stop a war.

CHAPTER 31

MOTHER MAGIC

What do you think is in these waters?" asked Waistcoat, dog-paddling furiously across the gray lake.

"Nothing bad," Sash replied. He spurted water between his teeth and glanced at Topos, towering whitely behind them. "Nobody left in the palace . . . nobody left in the moat. . . . Akroma's taken every nasty to war."

Waistcoat shook his head and delighted to hear water droplets flying from his stringy hair. He had hair! "No, I mean germs—little beasties."

"Oh, you coward!"

"We've got bodies now," Waistcoat said. As if to demonstrate, he released a large and strange-smelling bubble behind him. "We have to think about things like that."

Sash's face lit with an odd light, and his eyebrows curled querulously.

Waistcoat stared at him. "Ain't it great to have expressions?"

Sash's jaw dropped, and he didn't seem to notice a gray wave pouring into his mouth. He gagged and blurted, "What the blazes!"

"What?"

"The blazes!"

"What? The blazes?"

"The blazes! The blazes!" Sash gabbled. He grabbed his comrade's arm and swung him around through the water, a motion that made them both submerge. When they came up, they saw that the western sky glared. It was as if the sun had given up its distant orbit and descended to vacation on Otaria.

"The blazes!" Waistcoat said. "What's wrong with the sun?"

"That's not the sun," Sash replied. He jutted a finger above the water to indicate a pale circle in the west. "That's the sun. What that is . . ."

"Don't look at it!" Waistcoat said, shielding his eyes and dipping under the flood. He surfaced facing the other way. "It'll burn out your rectums."

"You mean retinas, idiot," Sash replied, "and I can't help looking at it. It's beautiful." He swam toward the light.

Waistcoat stroked after him. "Where're you going?"

"I'm going to see what that light is. Doesn't it do something to you?"

"You mean, other than burn my rect—"

"I mean pull on your soul. Don't you feel it? Meaning. Beauty. Power. Transcendence. How can we see that light and turn away?"

"Well, if I just paddle this-a-way."

"Just look at it a moment!" Sash said, dragging his friend around again. "Look."

Waistcoat did. How could anyone see that light and turn away? "All right, then," he said, stroking toward the light. "Let's go see what's happened."

"Not what," Sash said, his face lit with certainty, "but Whom!"

* * * * *

Elionoway stood in the midst of his refugee band. They had not reached Eroshia, not by a hundred miles, and now it looked as if they never would.

The whole company, a hundred souls saved from the ravages of the Glyphs, stared longingly toward the city they had fled. They couldn't see it, but they could see its light. It beamed beneath a jealous sun. There was a strange quality to that light, like harmonies in music. Red and gold, blue and orange, purple, green, gray—the waves overlaid each other to form white. Like grand chords shifting tonic to submediant, mediant to subdominant, dominant to tonic, the cords of light moved and chanted and sang. They spoke to the refugees.

"We must go back."

"I've never seen such beauty."

"Why are we lost in this wilderness while Someone visits our home?"

Elionoway tore his eyes from that glow. Yes, it was beautiful—exceedingly—but it was also lethal. Somehow he knew it. He crossed the grassy hill and shook his comrades, as if to awaken them from a dream. "We can't go back now! We're heading east, toward Eroshia."

"No! No!"

"Not east!"

"How can we head east? The light's in the west."

"Death is in the west," Elionoway said. "Don't you remember what happened to us, to our friends? We can't go back."

"But *She* is there! How can we turn our backs on *Her?*"

Elionoway's heart sank; he too felt Her presence. Still, he had not led these footsore refugees across hundreds of leagues of wasteland only to have them run off now. "She? You mean Akroma? You mean Phage? You want to go back to see them?"

"No. Not them. Her."

"She doesn't want us to turn away."

"She calls everyone to Her light."

"No!" Elionoway insisted, slapping the man who had said it. "We will not turn away from Her, but neither will we travel back into death." A desperate lie entered his head, and he grasped it. "She wants us to create a new Sanctum on this spot. That's what She is saying to us. Look—see the river there? These hills? They will be easily fortified; and the plains there: We can plant and grow and live until She comes to us."

"We can make Her a home," a woman said quietly.

"Yes. Yes! She wants us to make Her a home. She will come to us and reward us. She will dwell with us forever."

"How do you know what She wants?" someone asked, still gazing westward.

Elionoway snarled, "How did I know about the Glyphs? How did I know about the numena? I'm an elf. I just know."

No one had an answer for that.

Elionoway went person to person, pulling off packs, massaging shoulders, speaking soothingly even as his own heart flailed like a landed fish. He wanted to see Her too. He wanted to return, even unto death, but he was an elf, and he just knew.

* * * * *

Kuberr wore only a silken robe left by his dead father. He was growing too fast to wear anything else. Black-haired, pale-skinned, and golden-eyed, he seemed perhaps nine, with all the precocious energy of that age. In a voice yet untouched by puberty, he called out, "Watch, Aunt Braids! This'll be the biggest one ever."

He ran from the doors of the audience hall toward the throne where his father had presided. With a running leap, he vaulted over the seat and onto a pile of pillows. Hysterical laughter followed as the young prince rolled, half-naked, among the cushions.

Braids had never seen a more demonic creature. He jabbered incessantly, willfully destroyed everything of value that he encountered, would not sit, would not listen, alternately begged for praise and ignored blame, sassed, shouted, pissed, ranted, laughed, scolded, sulked . . . Worst of all, he couldn't be put in a cage, sent into combat, or simply eaten by trolls.

"Was that the biggest vault ever, or what?" Kuberr enthused, coming around the throne and retying his robe. He grew visibly as he walked, taller, stronger. His voice deepened as well. "Soon I'll be a grown-up, then you'll see how high I can jump. I'll jump to the sky and tear down the sun."

Smiling a dagger smile, Braids said, "I would love to see you try."

"Oh, you will," Kuberr replied, winking at her. "Mother is here."

Braids scowled. "Phage? How could she—"

"No, not her, stupid. My real mother. Not *here*, as in, 'in this room,' but *here*, as in, 'in the world.' She's here."

"What are you talking about?"

As he walked back to the doors, Kuberr hitched his head toward the north and said. "You'll see. Now, watch this one. This'll be the biggest one ever."

* * * * *

Kamahl awoke at the base of a sand dune. He couldn't remember how he had gotten here, mantled in bruises and scratches, clothes ripped to rags. A glance up a nearby dune showed the roll marks of his elbows and knees, and at the top, a long, deep skid. What had he been doing at the top of a dune, and how had he rolled down?

All Kamahl could remember was killing his sister.

He sat up, coughing dust. His lips were cracked and bleeding, and the dunes oscillated around him. He lay back down.

A new light glowed in half of the sky. It was beautiful, and he wanted it.

Kamahl rolled to his belly and crawled up the trammeled dune. He wriggled like a worm until he reached the top and looked out. All around was a sea of sand in mesmerizing waves, but straight ahead beamed that glorious light.

She had come. He knew Her and She knew him. He had wished for Her without realizing it, and She yearned for him to come and serve.

Kamahl stood, from worm to man. On naked feet, on raw nerves and vessels, he shuffled toward the light. Suddenly it didn't matter how he had arrived here. All that mattered was that he would walk this whole barren desert to join her.

* * * * *

The boot box had been a joke of Ixidor's. He had made a grand entry, though he never would let anyone enter, and he had made an infinite boot box, though it would never hold a single shoe. It had been a perfect joke for Ixidor, and a perfect hiding place for his deathwurm.

But even a deathwurm did not wish to miss an epiphany.

She had come. The one Being who ruled death had come.

The box shook. Its stony lid blasted away, and its edges cracked and shattered. Hunks of marble skidded across the floor. Something huge and black like a titan's fist smashed its way up into the light.

The deathwurm's head filled most of the grand entry. It pivoted this way and that, and small nostrils pulsed as it sniffed the air. The thing's stupid little eyes blinked inside rubbery folds of flesh.

How sweet the air was, how right the song, like the cry of a wounded creature as it calls for death. She was beautiful. There were shades of Akroma, of Nivea, in Her, but She was much more. She did not draw the deathwurm as a victim does, but as a victor.

With a roar of delight, the enormous black creature wriggled farther into the entry hall. It rammed its head through a great bank of windows. Wedges of glass fell to slice its thick hide, some imbedding. The wurm didn't care. The air outside the palace was full of the glorious scent and the livid song. It would go to her. It would seek her out and bow before her.

Coil after fetid coil lurched from the broken box. Squealing in delight, the league-long deathwurm slid across the outer yard of Locus Palace and headed for the lake below. It headed for its mistress.

* * * * *

Where Stonebrow lay in his broken tower, he saw Her, as everyone saw Her.

Out of the blazing light, a figure took shape. She was huge—bigger than Stonebrow, though She hung in the air like a hummingbird. Her face was radiant, with wise and ancient eyes. She was slender and strong, and She hovered above the wanting throng. The three mothers had joined. They who gave bodies to the numena now gave their own bodies to the true Mother of them all.

Stonebrow knew who She was. Still, She told them.

"Behold, Otaria. Behold, Dominaria," she said, and her voice was like a choir, manifold and magnificent. "I am Karoma. I am magic."

Tales of Dominaria

LEGIONS
Onslaught Cycle, Book II
J. Robert King

In the blood and sand of the arena,
two foes clash in a titanic battle.

January 2003

EMPEROR'S FIST
Magic Legends Cycle Two, Book II
Scott McGough

War looms above the Edemi Islands, casting the deep
and dread shadow of the Emperor's Fist.

March 2003

SCOURGE
Onslaught Cycle, Book III
J. Robert King

From the fiery battles of the Cabal, a new god has arisen,
one whose presence drives her worshipers to madness.

May 2003

THE MONSTERS OF MAGIC
An anthology edited by J. Robert King

From Dominaria to Phyrexia, monsters fill the multiverse,
and tales of the most popular ones fill these pages.

August 2003

CHAMPION'S TRIAL
Magic Legends Cycle Two, Book III
Scott McGough

To restore his honor, the onetime champion of Madara must
battle his own corrupt empire and the monster on the throne.

November 2003

Legend of the
Five Rings

The Four Winds Saga

Only one can claim the Throne of Rokugan.

WIND OF JUSTICE
Third Scroll
Rich Wulf

Naseru, the most cold-hearted and scheming of the royal heirs, will
stop at nothing to sit upon the Throne of Rokugan. But when dark
forces in the City of Night threaten his beloved Empire, Naseru
must learn to wield the most unlikely weapon of all — justice.

June 2003

WIND OF TRUTH
Fourth Scroll
Ree Soesbee

Sezaru, one of the most powerful wielders of magic in all Rokugan,
has never desired his father's throne, but destiny calls to the son
of Toturi. Here, in the final volume of the Four Winds Saga,
all will be decided.

December 2003

Now available:

THE STEEL THRONE
Prelude
Edward Bolme

WIND OF HONOR
First Scroll
Ree Soesbee

WIND OF WAR
Second Scroll
Jess Lebow

FORGOTTEN REALMS

The foremost tales of the FORGOTTEN REALMS, brought together in these two great collections!

LEGACY OF THE DROW COLLECTOR'S EDITION
R.A. Salvatore

Here are the four books that solidified both the reputation of *New York Times* best-selling author R.A. Salvatore as a master of fantasy, and his greatest creation Drizzt as one of the genre's most beloved characters. Spanning the depths of the Underdark and the sweeping vistas of Icewind Dale, Legacy of the Drow is epic fantasy at its best.

January 2003

THE BEST OF THE REALMS
A FORGOTTEN REALMS anthology

Chosen from the pages of nine FORGOTTEN REALMS anthologies by readers like you, *The Best of the Realms* collects your favorite stories from the past decade. *New York Times* best-selling author R.A. Salvatore leads off the collection with an all-new story that will surely be among the best of the Realms!

November 2003

The Hunter's Blades Trilogy

***New York Times* best-selling author
R.A. SALVATORE**
takes fans behind enemy lines in this
new trilogy about one of the most popular
fantasy characters ever created.

THE LONE DROW
Book II

Chaos reigns in the Spine of the World. The city of Mirabar
braces for invasion from without and civil war within. An orc king
tests the limits of his power. And *The Lone Drow* fights
for his life as this epic trilogy continues.

October 2003

Now available in paperback!

THE THOUSAND ORCS
Book I

A horde of savage orcs, led by a mysterious cabal of power-hungry
warlords, floods across the North. When Drizzt Do'Urden and
his companions are caught in the bloody tide, the dark elf ranger
finds himself standing alone against *The Thousand Orcs*.

July 2003